Th

'A tasty, tense … oy and
Kate Atkinson with a bit of *Mad Men* thrown in. Fabulous'
Liz Hyder

'A homage to hard-boiled American crime fiction,
but told with a distinctive female sensibility'
Clare Chambers, author of *Small Pleasures*

'An atmospheric tale of repression and style at the
heart of the American Dream'
Stylist

…utifully crafted, claustrophobic and compelling,
…esper's skilfully woven suburban noir is as delicious
as a long drink on a hot day'
Stacey Halls

…per mixes a gripping plot with pithy views on class, sex and
race'
Sunday Times

'Loved this taut slice of classic noir'
C.J. Tudor

…eathtakingly stylish, hypnotic and masterfully gripping.
…paints the most beautiful portrait of 1950s suburbia,
…each page scratches away at the sunny gloss to reveal
the darkness beneath. Outstanding'
Chris Whitaker

…autifully written and brilliantly observed, as well as
being a page-turning mystery. The 1950s come alive
with issues that resonate today'
Simon Lelic

'A remarkably assured debut'
Guardian

'A triumph'
Evening Standard

'A tense, gripping exploration of the darkness beneath the sunny exterior of 1950s suburbia'
Zoë Somerville, author of *The Night of the Flood*

'A stunning debut'
Amanda Reynolds, author of *Close to Me*

'The perfect marriage of contemporary domestic noir and old-style Hollywood noir'
Laure Van Rensburg, author of *The Downfall*

'A perfect read . . . The desire for change rises from the pages like heat off a sidewalk'
Mary Paulson-Ellis, author of *The Other Mrs Walker*

'As well as being a sharp examination of privilege and oppression, it's also completely gripping'
Amanda Mason, author of *The Wayward Girls*

'Not just a beguiling murder mystery but [it] also has important things to say about race, gender and class'
Araminta Hall

'An atmospheric chiller'
Independent

'Evocative, stylish and gripping, *The Long, Long Afternoon* exposes the dark underbelly of 1950s suburban America in a thriller that is pure class'
Deborah O'Connor, author of *The Dangerous Kind*

'Beguiling and evocative'
Sunday Express

'It's a perfect period piece that manages to bring new light to the world we live in today'
Stephanie Butland, author of *Lost for Words*

'Lose yourself in the twisted thrills of a 1950s marriage'
Glamour Magazine

'A clever and absorbing debut by Inga Vesper, who bricks Joyce up in her perfect house, then smashes it to pieces with aplomb'
The Times

The Long, Long Afternoon

Inga Vesper is a journalist and editor. She moved to the UK from Germany to work as a carer, before the urge to write and explore brought her to journalism. As a reporter, she covered the coroner's court and was able to observe how family, neighbours and police react to a suspicious death. Inga has worked in Syria and Tanzania, but now lives in Glasgow, because there's no better way to find a good story than eavesdropping on the chatter in a Scottish cafe on a rainy day.

The Long, Long Afternoon

INGA VESPER

MANILLA
PRESS

First published in the UK in 2021
This paperback edition published in 2021 by
MANILLA PRESS
An imprint of Bonnier Books UK
4th Floor, Victoria House, Bloomsbury Square,
London, England, WC1B 4DA
Owned by Bonnier Books
Sveavägen 56, Stockholm, Sweden

A CIP catalogue record for this book is
available from the British Library.

ISBN: 978–1–83877–228–4

Also available as an ebook and an audiobook

1 3 5 7 9 10 8 6 4 2

Typeset by Palimpsest Book Production Ltd, Falkirk, Stirlingshire
Printed and bound in Great Britain by Clays Ltd, Elcograf S.p.A.

Manilla Press is an imprint of Bonnier Books UK
www.bonnierbooks.co.uk

To Birgit, for all the books

Chapter One

Joyce

Yesterday, I kissed my husband for the last time.

Of course, he does not know this. Not yet. In fact, I have a hard time believing it myself. But when I woke up this morning, I knew that it was true.

I am standing on the terrace, trying to discern my future. Right now, it seems to consist entirely of the morning air. Cool and still, but with the promise of heat.

This is as far as my future can be told.

For the next five minutes, I shall stand out here and drink my coffee and admire the colors of the garden in the first light of the day.

Oh, how many colors there are. The May-green lawn. The patio's salmon tiles. The white wall that surrounds the house. The crimson geraniums in their terracotta pot. The sky, hazy at the fringes, as my head is fogged with fatigue. The pool's blue is so deep and vivid I want to fall in and go under, and dissolve like aspirin.

I wish to paint this moment. To fix it on paper before

it slips away. But I gave away my materials long ago. Instead, I clasp my hands around the coffee mug and imprint the scene on my memory. A morning like this will never come again.

The geraniums need water. But they will have to be patient. Ruby won't arrive until the afternoon, and I am on the last day of my period. Frank does not like it when I water the flowers during menstruation. The female miasma will make them wilt, he says. Best let the help do it.

I agree with him, of course. I never point out that he also says Negroes have no talent for raising anything, which is why they don't have window boxes and their babies often die.

These are dark thoughts. They engulf the universe of my brain and swallow up the light. A Mellaril would snuff them out, but I don't think I'll need it. Not yet. There is hope in the morning hours, just as there is desperation in the afternoon, which stretches like gum and yet contracts into nothing, once it is filled with laundry and dusting and dinner and the children running around, always at risk of falling into the pool.

Where will I be tomorrow morning?

My heart begins to pound in my ears. For the first time in my life, I do not know. And for the first time in many years, I long for the afternoon.

I want to paint. I could pick up some supplies at the mall today, after I see the doctor. It would give me something to do while the children are down for their nap. Something to bridge the gummy hours, when the minutes crawl past like slugs. Afternoon, when the heat wilts the geraniums and my mind crumbles into dust.

My stomach thrums with half-remembered pains. The menstruation, of course. But something else as well. Dark thoughts. Galaxies of blood.

How far does my female miasma reach? I imagine it as a halo, framing me like a saint. But my halo is dark red, not light, and I am not a saint, but a sinner.

Gently, I set my coffee down on one of the pool chairs and pick up the watering can. The touch of the metal makes my palms tingle. My first revolution of the day. There is a little water left at the bottom. I sneak up to the flowers, one arm extended. But then a bawl from inside the house catches me out, followed by lazy, half-interested crying.

Lily is awake.

I freeze. I should head up and see to my daughter. My whole body yearns to stifle her wailing with a hug. But Frank showed me a clipping from the paper, where a Professor Summers said that instant response may spoil the child.

And something in me heartily agrees. I want a moment longer with the pool. I want to care for the geraniums before I care for my child. Does that make me a bad mother? Does it make me worse than I already am?

I ignore the crying, pour a sad trickle of water onto the

flowers and pick up my coffee. I shall finish it out here, alone with the pool and the sky mirroring its perfect color. Blue, so blue. False and True.

Me and You.

Chapter Two

Ruby

The bus jerks into motion, crawls ten yards along Southern Boulevard and grinds to a halt. Ruby stifles a sigh. It's hot. It was hot yesterday and it will be hot tomorrow, so what gives? That's what Momma would have said. *What gives, girl? It's hot, you deal with it. The Lord ain't changing the weather for your sorry ass.*

Speaking of which, her butt is so sweaty it sticks to the plastic seat. She arches her spine and pulls her skirt down. Too late. The cotton fabric is already crumpled. Mrs Ingram will have a fit.

Damn this job.

Today is a day for shorts, sandals and loose hair. Instead, her head is burning up under her little cap, and her feet are marinating in her sneakers. She almost longs for the clumsy white slippers the wives of Sunnylakes insist on, so they can trace every single molecule of dirt on the carpet back to the perpetrator.

A lost-looking white lady is sitting near the front, as far

away from Ruby as possible, with a big hat and a bag clutched tightly to her chest. She's not turning around, so it'll be OK to slip the sneakers off for a minute.

The sweet relief is accompanied by a whiff of cheese.

She checks her watch, a gift from Joseph. It's past noon. Oh, Lord, she's already been on this bus for more than an hour and she's meant to be at Mrs Ingram's at 1 p.m. and Mrs Haney's at five.

Finally, the bus crests the smog line and descends into Sunnylakes. The trees here are still small and do nothing to shield the road from the heat. The houses fly past her, one identical to the other, each surrounded by a pretty lawn and a pretty fence, the walls adorned with fake stone fronts. Pa says that stone fronts cost more, so all the men in Sunnylakes ordered them when they built these houses with their hard-earned dollars. Make mine stone, sir. Make it look like a fortress to protect my property against the Commies and the Japs and the Negroes.

Ruby chuckles. *Well, too late for that. I'm already in your house, mister.*

She disembarks at the corner of Pine Tree Avenue and Roseview Drive, and walks up Mrs Ingram's driveway, past the plastic parakeet Mrs Ingram has stuck into her lawn by way of sophisticated home decoration. At the pink front door, she digs the key out from under a flowerpot and sticks it into the lock. Every time she does this, her innards start to curl. The key is too easy to find. One of these days someone's gonna break in here and clear the place out. And then Mrs Ingram will know who to blame.

Inside, the house looks as if it's already been ransacked. Mrs Ingram works – a rare thing for a white woman – and doesn't have time to tidy, as she loves to proclaim.

Ruby puts on the slippers, and wipes and cleans and mops. The street is quiet. Just once a car drives past and she tenses for the inevitable arrival of Mrs Ingram. But it's not until just after 4 p.m. that the front door clicks open and the mistress of the house returns. Mrs Ingram passes by the toilet, where Ruby is elbow-deep down the U-bend, and makes a face like she's spotted a pile of dog poop on her carpet.

'Still in the bathroom? You're slow today.'

You're running late yourself. Ruby keeps her eyes on the sponge dunking in and out of the water. 'Good afternoon, Mrs Ingram. Sorry, my bus was stuck in traffic.'

'The bus goes along the highway. It's never stuck.'

Ruby bites her lip. 'Yes, ma'am.'

'Don't let it happen again.'

'No, ma'am.'

Mrs Ingram sniffs the air. 'And what is this? I smell an odor. Haven't you got a shower at home?'

No, ma'am, I wash at a fire hydrant in the street, 'coz I'm from South Central, and this is how we play.

'Sorry, ma'am.'

*

Normally, white folk try to forget as best as they can that the help is in their house. But today, once she's changed and freshened up, Mrs Ingram is after Ruby like she's expecting a photographer from *Better Homes and Gardens*. Bad day at the office, Ruby guesses, or perhaps she's just bored. Mrs Ingram runs fingers along surfaces, picks at invisible dust bunnies and tests the wetness of the cloth with which Ruby is rubbing down the sinks.

The best thing is to make a game of it by playing double meaning. Mrs Ingram is particularly good for that. She's got no husband and wears lots of bright-red lipstick and tight sweaters that bring out her cone-shaped breasts.

'Am I rubbing it OK, Mrs Ingram?' Ruby asks. 'Want me to make it wetter, Mrs Ingram? Would you like me to plunge faster?'

The women of Sunnylakes never wise up. Most of them are so uptight it's hard to imagine anyone here having sex. Mrs Ingram gives a thin smile, paces her crisp, clean house, powders her crisp, clean face and snorts and hisses and complains.

The next time Ruby checks her watch, it's almost 5 p.m. Fortunately, Joyce Haney never counts the minutes. She's always chasing after the kids, so she's got no time to go chasing after the help. Sometimes, she cracks open a soda and shows Ruby her sewing. They talk about patterns and family and the kids. Joyce pays for that time as if it were work.

At quarter past five, she tidies away the cleaning things

and pulls the front door shut. As soon as she is on the driveway, she catches the curtain twitch. Mrs Ingram is watching.

The afternoon light slides golden blades between the trees. Ruby stretches her knees and swings her arms. The worst is over now. Only two more hours, and she'll be on her way home with three dollars in her pocket.

The roar of an engine cuts the stillness of the street. A fancy car thunders out of the Haney driveway, turns the corner and speeds away toward President Avenue. It's a Crestliner, silver and black, with a green rear fender. Mrs Haney must have had visitors.

The Haney house sits a little back from the main road, because the property slopes down to the lake. The trees here are older and darker, and Ruby never likes to walk between them in the winter, when the night lurks between the branches. Behind the house, the trees have been cut away to clear the view toward the lake. But Mr Haney has built a big wooden fence, so there is no lake to see from the house, only tidy white boards that he paints once a year in spring.

Ruby stops. Joyce's car is parked up in the driveway. The front door is closed, the flowers planted on either side wilting in the sun.

Something feels wrong. Her stomach tingles with it.

She listens. The windows are open to let in the breeze, but nothing is moving behind the curtains. No pots clatter, no children scream, no radio babbles from the living room window.

A movement catches the corner of her eye. Ruby spins around and spots a flicker of color dancing among the trees. The breeze catches her skirt and sends a shiver up her spine. She balls her fists and wills her breath to stay calm.

'Hello? Who's there?'

A child's head pokes around a tree trunk. Blonde hair bristles over eyes that are large and blue and very wet. Joyce's daughter. Barbara.

Ruby kneels down. The pine needles are soft under her legs. She stretches out her arms. 'Barbara, come here. What are you doing out?'

'I'm waiting.'

'Waiting for who, baby?'

'Joanie's mom.'

It takes Ruby a moment to remember. Joanie's mom is Mrs Kettering, the family one house over. Barbara and Joanie are best friends.

'Come here,' Ruby says. 'Time to go inside.'

'I promised to wait.'

'Well, Joanie's mom didn't come, so you should go in.'

'I don't want to.'

'But it's nearly dinnertime.'

'No.'

Something about the girl's eyes makes Ruby's hands tremble. Barbara peers toward the house as if it contains a bogeyman or a dragon.

'Barbara, where is your mommy?'

'She told me to wait.'

'Shall we go see her?'

Barbara lowers her eyes. 'They made a mess, Whoobie.'

'Well, I'm here to clean it up. Now, come on, baby.'

Barbara detaches herself from the tree and takes Ruby's hand. Together they walk toward the house. Barbara's hand is hot. Her little nails dig into Ruby's palm.

Ruby rings the doorbell. No answer. But inside the house, Lily begins to cry.

'Mrs Haney?' Ruby shouts. 'Joyce.'

She rings again. The tingle in her stomach crawls into her chest. The way that baby's crying. Hoarse and hopeless, as if she thinks no one's ever going to come.

She gropes for the spare key under the porcelain eagle by the door and opens the lock. The hallway is tidy and there are fresh flowers on the sideboard. The Haney's house has a mezzanine, a term she had to look up after her first day. It means the bedrooms are halfway up some stairs, as is the big bathroom.

From the nursery comes the sound of Lily's crying.

The lavender carpet swallows Ruby's footsteps. She takes the stairs two at a time and bounds toward the nursery door. She flings it open. Lily is sitting in her bed, her eyes streaked with tears, her face red and tired. The room stinks. The girl's diaper is soggy. Something has run out of it and stained her playsuits.

Ruby lifts Lily up and unbuttons her clothes, but she

screams even louder and starts kicking. The diaper comes off in a wave of stink. Ruby flings it to the side and wipes Lily down with a cloth. She is just fastening a fresh diaper when Barbara enters and sits down on the floor. Her lips are trembling, and her eyes are full of tears.

'Barbara-baby, what's up?' Ruby tries to prop the screaming Lily up on her feet, but Lily punches her in the chest. 'Where's your mommy?'

'They're not here,' Barbara says. 'They made a mess.'

Ruby frowns and tries to think. Maybe Joyce had an emergency. Maybe a friend called her away. Maybe she forgot the pork chops for dinner. But her car is still in the driveway, so where—

She'd better leave. Something's wrong, but it ain't her problem. Plus, if Mr Haney comes back and finds his kids alone with the help, he's gonna have a coronary.

'Listen, Barbara,' she says. 'I'm going to call Mrs Kettering and ask her to come over. She can take care of you until Mommy's back, OK?'

Barbara does not answer.

'You're going to come downstairs with me, baby?'

Barbara shakes her head.

'OK, then.'

Ruby hoists Lily onto her hip. It feels weird being in the house alone, and now she's sure she *is* alone. In the hall, she picks up the phone and flips through the little address book with the golden corners until she reaches K.

Later, she can't remember Barbara slipping past her. But

all of a sudden, the girl appears in the kitchen door, her chin bobbing, terror in her eyes. She stretches out a soiled hand.

'Whoobie,' she says. 'I can't clean it up.'

'Don't worry, baby.' Ruby shifts Lily from one hip to the other and receives a kick in the guts for her troubles. 'I'll deal with it.'

Then she sees Barbara's hands and the floor tips over, sending her into free fall. The child's palms are caked in red.

Blood.

She yanks Barbara out of the way and throws open the kitchen door.

There is blood on the floor. Blood and paper towels and a crumpled cloth soaked in crimson. The sun beams through the curtains and paints the ghosts of daisies on the tiles. Blood on them, too, smeared and sticky, dreadful as the devil's tongue.

Ruby clenches Lily to her chest and screams as loud as she can.

Chapter Three

Mick

Mick mops beads of sweat from his brow with his sleeve. *Serves you right, Detective Blanke, fresh from the Big Apple, so excited about getting the corner office.* The southwest corner office. The chief must think it's a big tickle to give the hottest room to the new guy. When he received the keys and carried them proudly to his door, some of the boys had been snickering. That should have set his alarm bells ringing.

At ten in the morning, the place is already stifling. He sticks a finger into his collar to loosen it; it comes out wet. With heatstroke looming, he opens both windows and the door. But open doors let in strays, and soon enough Chief Murphy pops his head around the frame.

'Already at work, Blanke? It's only ten past ten. What about your beauty sleep?'

'Aw, Murphy. You need it more than me.' Mick grins. 'I work late, sir. I'm putting in the small hours.'

'Small as in few, right? Well, today's your unlucky day. Case for you down in the 'burbs. Missing woman, possible home invasion. Blood trail and all that jazz. Here are the files. Get your ass down there to check it out. Sergeant Hodge is waiting for you. G'day.'

Mick takes what Murphy calls the 'files', three flimsy sheets of typewriting, with a couple of notes scribbled in the margins. He puts his feet up on the desk, one of these modern ones made from wood laminate. Its legs are splayed like those of an East Tremont hooker. Swanky, better than his beat-up office in Brooklyn, which he misses more than he cares to admit. With his back to the window to escape the sun, he begins to read.

Police called to 47 Roseview Drive at 5.30 p.m. by a neighbor. First patrol car arrived to find the neighbor, the help and two children waiting at the scene. The help said that the children were alone in the house when she arrived. She discovered blood smears in the kitchen. The wife was missing, and still is. The husband is away at a conference in Palmdale. The children were placed with the neighbor and the help arrested.

Arrested?

He reads the woman's statement. She arrived at 5.15 p.m., went upstairs to find the younger girl and change her diaper, then came back down and found blood in the kitchen. She alerted the neighbor and waited until two officers arrived. The officers promptly arrested her.

Why?

He looks at her information. Ruby Wright, aged twenty-two, of 1467 Trebeck Row, South Central. Negro.

Ah. That's why.

'Chief.' He shuts the door behind him and strides down the hallway. 'Chief. The boys made an arrest on this?'

'Just as a precaution. Until we've checked out her story.'

'She's a witness. Not a suspect.'

'Yeah. But she might be involved. First on the scene, always suspicious.'

'I want to speak to her.'

'Don't you need to get down to the crime scene first?' Murphy pulls a fold of belly fat from his pants. 'Come on, Blanke, move it. Do some detecting, Mr Detective.'

'All right, Murphy. Don't flip your wig.'

Mick knows when he's lost a battle. The chief doesn't like him, and for good reason, too. He is a favor placement. The boss in Brooklyn pulled a few strings, and all of a sudden Santa Monica Police Department needed its own detective. Now he is stationed in California's most boring town. Where the sunshine makes him woozy every time he steps outside, and the worst crime committed until now was when someone stole little Timmy's brand-new Schwinn.

He gets lost twice in Sunnylakes. Curse the names of these streets. Hillview Crescent, Berrywood Road, Grand Park Street, Meadow Hills. The main joint is called, kid-you-not, President Avenue. Maybe Mr Eisenhower opened the damned place personally. It looks like something from an election poster. The tidy houses, the flags, the mailboxes glinting in the sun. The streets are so neat you could eat your dinner off them, but of course nobody would, because everyone here has a dining table and china plates mail-ordered from Wards.

On Roseview Drive, there is not a rose in sight. Number 47 is at the end, flanked by a pink house close by and a bigger, two-story home just about visible through the trees. Cars are parked up along the road, and people are milling about by the larger house in the distance. Must be the first search party.

Mick pulls up in front of the driveway beside a red Chevrolet Bel Air. When he gets out, the curtains move in the pink house. He's being watched. Which is interesting. In this quiet place, there is no way a stranger could drive up to a house and steal away its occupant without the neighbors noticing.

The door to number 47 has been taped off, but the tape is ripped. A loose end is hanging across the front steps. Mick looks around, feeling slightly furtive, and steps into the house.

It's . . . modern. The linoleum in the hallway has a purple square pattern and the lamps are made from chrome. He finds a family photograph displayed prominently on the sideboard. Joyce Haney, with the children on her lap. The little one is a baby still, the older has her hair in pigtails and smiles like she's in a Sunbeam Bread ad. Frank Haney, loving husband and proud father, stands behind them, his arms wrapped around his family in a way that is both protective and possessive. He has blond hair, blue eyes and a square jaw that screams former high school football quarterback. A face like a fire alarm, Mick thinks – you just want to smash it in.

Joyce's beauty is as much the result of careful pruning as it is natural. Brown, perfectly set hair, thin lips brightened with lipstick, brownish eyes, not very large, with the dreamy look of a movie star. It doesn't suit her, he thinks, that put-on look and the tender, tired smile. Somehow, she strikes him as a woman who cracks a good joke.

The kitchen is the only thing in this house that's out of whack. Brutally so. Mick stands in the doorway and takes his time memorizing the scene. There is blood on the floor. It runs from the sink toward the door in one long spatter. A half-unraveled roll of paper towels is lying in a corner, and in the middle of the blood puddle is a blue piece of cloth. The blood has congealed into a dirty brown. There are pieces of crumpled tissue where someone tried to wipe up the mess near the door.

He checks the bloodstain. During his former life in Brooklyn, he encountered the results of gang stabbings and Italian revenge torture and the crazy Japanese grandpa who plunged a knife into his abdomen and then disemboweled himself. Compared to that, there isn't a lot of blood here. But its presence in this suburban kitchen, with flowers on the windowsill and a child's drawing taped to the refrigerator, with tins for sugar, coffee and oatmeal lined up on the counter – now, that's eerie.

Upstairs there isn't much to see. A tidy master bedroom, the king-sized bed perfectly made and covered with a frilly spread. A lavender vanity sits in one corner, arrayed with cosmetics. A quick rifle through the drawers produces lots of underwear, all neat, nothing kinky. The husband lords over a harem of dress shirts folded away in the closet. His suits are ironed with pleats. Nothing's disturbed, and it doesn't look like anyone's packed anything, either.

The children's room is messier. The older girl's bed is made but the bedding in the crib is piled up at one end. There's a brown stain on the changing table and a soiled diaper lies on the floor, sulking in its stench. The bathroom and guest room are unremarkable.

On the terrace, Sergeant Hodge is sitting in a striped lawn chair overlooking a pool and the most meticulously manicured lawn Mick has ever seen. Hodge is holding a bottle of soda and looking like a man at one with his world.

Mick sneaks up to him. He slaps the sergeant on the shoulder, so hard he nearly spills his drink. 'Hope you brought your own Coke, Hodge.'

''Course, Detective.' Hodge scrambles from the chair. 'Wouldn't help myself from the refrigerator. Just putting my feet up. Damn hot to be standing around.'

Mick resists the temptation to sit down himself. The sun flares from the tiles marching around the pool. Not a single weed dares to rear its head through the cracks. A pot of geraniums on the terrace is the only nod to exuberance.

'Apparently the husband likes to garden,' Hodge volunteers.

Mick scoffs. 'Husband is neurotic, most likely.'

'Beg your pardon, sir?'

'Nothing.'

'So, what's your theory, Detective?'

Mick grins. 'Don't got none, yet.'

'But aren't you . . . ?'

'Keeping an open mind. It's too early to jump to conclusions.'

'All right.' Hodge nods as if he's understood, which he very clearly hasn't.

'So, what's the situation?' Mick asks. 'I mean, I got the files this morning, but I want to hear it from you.'

'First officer on the scene was Murray. He saw the blood and called headquarters. They're just a misdemeanor division in Sunnylakes. You know, drunk driving, domestics, and all that.'

'This wasn't a domestic?'

'Well, the husband wasn't home. He left on Sunday night for Palmdale. The wife was seen by witnesses throughout the morning. She went to the mall around 9 a.m. and left the older girl with the neighbor, Mrs Nancy Ingram. She came back at 11 a.m. and picked up her daughter, all in good spirits. Mrs Ingram had a chat with her before she went to work, they talked about lunch. Nothing unusual. Then . . . who knows?'

'The older girl was discovered outside?'

'By the help, yes. She was meant to be here at 5 p.m., but was running late. She's a Negro, you see? She found the girl, took her inside and changed the younger kid. When she came into the kitchen, she saw the blood.'

'So, you arrested her.'

Hodge shrugs. 'Sounded like a fishy story to me.'

'In what way?'

'She went to change the baby without checking if her boss was home.'

'Maybe it was normal for Mrs Haney to leave the kids with the help. Did you question her?'

'She was . . . agitated.'

'Did you try to calm her down?' Mick can taste something sour in his mouth. He can just imagine the scene. The blood, the screaming children, Sergeant Hodge yelling. *Agitated.* Hell, he'd be rattling his cage like a rabid monkey.

Hodge shrugs. 'You should have been here, sir. The baby was wearing only a diaper. She was kicking the help and screaming. Tells you something, doesn't it?'

Mick raises one eyebrow. 'It does?'

'The help was yelling at the older girl to stop touching the mess in the kitchen. You see, the little dear was trying to clean up her mommy's blood. Then the neighbor, that Ingram lady, came over and slapped her, and—'

'The neighbor hit the little girl?'

'No, the help. Just slapped her. We—'

'Didn't you close off the house?' Mick groans. 'Didn't you remove the witnesses from the scene? Who else was here? How many people have been stomping through this place?'

'Well, not many.' Sergeant Hodge holds up his fingers to count. 'There was me and officers Murray, Stanwitz and Anderson, and the help and the kids and Mrs Ingram. That's about it, really. Oh, and the milkman.'

'The milkman?'

'Showed up just before 6 p.m., sir. Said he'd forgotten the butter.'

'Christ in a cardigan.'

'But then we put some tape up. No one got in today. And them folks outside, they're planning to search the neighborhood. They're not here to gawp.'

Mick rubs the bridge of his nose and waits until he's calmed down enough to level his voice. There's no point in lecturing. It's too late.

'Evidence recovery and the photographer are coming this afternoon,' Hodge offers. 'We searched the surrounding properties and the lakeshore. No body. The car's still here, so she hasn't left in that.'

'Have you heard from the husband?'

'We had a little difficulty getting hold of him. He didn't return to his hotel until late last night. He's on his way back and should be here this afternoon to pick up the kids from Nancy Ingram.'

'Is there no other family? Grandparents, uncles and such?'

'The husband's folks live in Philadelphia. And the wife's . . . well, we're waiting for him to confirm who they are.'

'So, you've got no leads.'

'Not really.' Sergeant Hodge looks like a puppy when the treat bag's empty. 'We'll have more when we find the body.'

'We don't know she's dead, Sergeant.'

'Sure. But think about it: she's a mother. No mother in her right mind would abandon her kids.'

Mick decides he's going to leave it there. He follows Hodge's gaze toward the fence, and they stare at it for a moment, as if there's a chance that Joyce Haney will peep over it any moment now and wave a dainty, gloved hand. *Hello, boys, I'm back.*

Hodge pulls his shoulders up toward his ears, then lets them fall. 'Imagine putting up a fence like that. It's like they didn't want to look out.'

'Or perhaps they didn't want anyone to look in.'

'Sir?'

'Keep an open mind, Hodge.' Mick lifts his hat. 'Never good to make assumptions.'

Back in the kitchen, he opens a couple of cupboards, but finds nothing out of the ordinary. There is a shopping list taped to the refrigerator, written in practiced, slender handwriting: *eggs, mayonnaise, corn flakes, rice, cocoa, Spry*. The refrigerator is nearly empty.

He steps carefully over the blood, and his eyes catch on the blue cloth. A patch of white fabric is stitched onto one end. It has little rodeo cowboys on it, jumping over fences and falling off their horses. He pulls and the cloth, stuck to the floor with blood, comes away reluctantly. He lets go; no need to further mess up the scene.

It's not a cloth, it's a baby's sleepsuit. Soft blue fabric, tiny white feet, a bright collar and stomach patch with more cowboys, now stained brown. Mick tries to remember Sandy and Prissie when they were that size, but his memory is a haze filled with milk smell and sleeplessness and fingers so tiny he was scared to crush them in his hand.

He peels open the label. Yep, this sleepsuit is for a newborn.

Chapter Four

Mick

Nancy Ingram has been expecting a visit from the police. You can always tell with women. The hasty attempt to tidy the lounge, the lipstick, troweled on like insulation paste . . .

Now Detective Michael Blanke is sitting in a brand-new easy chair. Drinking a soda from a yellow-tinged glass with ice cubes clinking at the rim. Staring into Mrs Ingram's blue-green eyes, framed by lashes in which tiny mascara drops have curdled into chunks.

She bends her upper body across the coffee table, a move that makes her yellow sweater stretch across her breasts. Mick instinctively leans back and swirls his soda as if it were a whiskey, which he really damn well wishes it was.

'I'm sorry, I had no time to make things more presentable,' Mrs Ingram says with a darling flourish of her hand. 'But I've been looking after the kids. Barbara had three nightmares last night. And I've just rushed over to speak to Laura Kettering across the road while the girls were watching TV. No one has heard from Joyce. Did you see all these people? They want to start a search and . . .' She swallows. 'I might take the children out later. Or perhaps not. It might scare them. Oh, God, I don't know what to do.'

Mick takes the chance to get a word in edgeways. 'Have you been in contact with Frank Haney?'

'He's driving down from Palmdale right now. The poor man is beside himself. Have you found out anything? Has she called?'

'I assure you, our team is on the case. Meanwhile, can I ask you a few questions?'

'It's horrendous,' says Mrs Ingram by way of an answer. 'I don't know what to think. That kitchen . . .'

She looks tired underneath the makeup, and she hasn't yet asked for any salacious details or impressed her theory on him. She is worried for her friend, deeply worried, while trying to keep up the pretense for the girls. One of them is sitting outside on the terrace, forcing her doll to mop up an imaginary kitchen floor.

'Did you notice anything unusual when you last saw Mrs Haney?'

'No, not at all. She was dressed for town and had just returned from the mall. She left Barbara with me for a couple of hours.'

'Was that a normal thing for her to do?'

'Oh, yes. I adore her children.' A little tremble quivers

on her lip. She's got none of her own. 'I didn't mind at all. I don't start work until just before noon. And it's much easier for Joyce to do the shopping with just one.'

'Did anything strike you as odd about Mrs Haney's behavior when she returned?'

'She was a little rushed off her feet. She had a big bag of shopping with her and Lily clinging to her hand. We didn't talk long. She asked if Barbara had been good, and I said yes, and she said she had to make lunch so I let her go . . .' Mrs Ingram looks at her soda as if it were a crystal ball. 'Oh, God. I don't even want to think of what might have happened . . . All that blood.'

'It must have given you a fright.'

'I had just come back from work and was fixing my face. I heard Lily screaming. She would not stop, so after a while I went outside. The door was open, Ruby was on the lawn, screeching like a harpy, and I just . . .' She hesitates. 'I knew right away something had happened to Joyce. Call it a woman's intuition.'

Tears are peeping through Mrs Ingram's mascara. Mick feels compelled to quell them. 'Blood always looks worse than it is. It's hard to take a guess, but it looks like Mrs Haney was injured, hopefully not killed.'

'Could she have been abducted?'

'That's one option. She could have hurt herself and gone to get help. We have an officer phoning around the hospitals right at this moment.'

'She should have called me. Or Laura.'

'Laura Kettering? Is she a good friend of Joyce's?'

Mrs Ingram pouts a little. 'She is a great neighbor, but . . . very involved with her household. Her husband is a movie executive and works like a mule. She has three small kids – there's not much time for socializing. Her and Joyce are close, but not as close as Joyce and me.'

Mick shifts his butt and the easy chair emits a squeak. 'Why did you slap Ruby Wright?'

A hint of disgust flits across Mrs Ingram's carefully powdered face. 'Because she was hysterical. And she couldn't control those kids. Barbara was putting her fingers in the blood. And Lily . . . my God, dirty and naked like a street child. I just had to take control of the situation.'

'Miss Wright cleans for you?'

'Ruby has been my help for about two years.'

'How often does she come in?'

'Monday, Wednesday and Friday from 1 p.m. to 4.30 p.m.'

Mick can't help but look around the bungalow. What's there to clean for more than ten hours a week? 'After she's finished here, she goes to the Haneys' place?'

'When Joyce and Frank moved here, they asked me if I knew someone to help around the house and I recommended Ruby. Joyce is very house-proud, and with the two kids . . .' Mrs Ingram smiles politely. 'I am, unfortunately, not able to stay at home entirely, otherwise the household wouldn't be a problem. But since my husband died . . . I work at the Sunnylakes estate office when they need someone to do viewings.'

Mick takes another sip. The dark yellow glass makes the soda look like a particularly well-fermented urine sample. 'Can you tell me about the Haney marriage?'

'Oh, Frank is a wonderful man. Very caring and devoted to his wife. They are a happy couple. I . . .' She blinks a few times, fast. 'I don't even want to imagine . . .'

Mick puts down the soda and rises. There isn't more to glean here. 'Thanks,' he says. 'Please call us if you remember anything else of importance.'

Outside, a big, black Pontiac has boxed him in. He curses and shimmies his car back and forth until he manages to wiggle free. Through the trees he can see an array of dresses and hats. Joyce Haney's friends, searching for the lost lamb of Sunnylakes.

This gives him an idea. He leaves the car half-in, half-out and saunters over to what he assumes is the Kettering house. Halfway there, a woman emerges from the trees and cuts in front of him. She is stuffing a folded-up piece of paper into her bag. When she sees him, she freezes.

'Who are you?'

He lifts his hat. 'Detective Michael Blanke, Santa Monica PD. And you?'

'Don't see what business that is of yours.'

Oh, you bet there's plenty of business here. He scans her messy hair, the well-worn flats, the turquoise jacket engaged in a lethal clash with her purple skirt. She is youngish, but misery is scrawled all over her face.

'Have you just come from the house?' he asks.

'I'm here to help with the search.'

'You're a neighbor?'

She flinches. 'No.'

'A friend of the family then? What was the paper you were just putting away?'

'Flyers. To find her.'

'May I—'

'Deena, there you are.'

He spins around. One of the women has detached herself from the herd. She is wearing a bright green dress, white gloves and a grave expression.

'We've been waiting for you,' she says to the woman named Deena. 'The first search party has already left. You could catch up or wait with Laura. She'll stay here, just in case.'

'Laura Kettering?' Mick asks.

It is only then she graces him with a look. 'Yes, sir. Are you from the police?'

'Detective Michael Blanke, ma'am. And you are?'

'How wonderful.' Her smile is sad. 'Please, come on over. We are ever so worried. I am Genevieve Crane and this,' she gestures at the sullen woman, who looks away, 'is Deena Klintz.'

'A friend of Joyce's?'

'We all are,' she says. 'I run the Sunnylakes Women's Improvement Committee. You must be here to speak to Laura. I'll introduce you.'

Laura Kettering, movie executive wife and mistress of a two-story mock-antebellum villa, is small, mousy and red-eyed. Mrs Crane mentions that Mick is from the police and causes the floodgates to open anew.

'It's all so terrible,' Mrs Kettering sobs. 'And in our neighborhood. It's simply terrible.'

'It is,' Mick says. 'But we'll get to the bottom of it. Did you notice anything unusual yesterday?'

'No. I was in the house with the kids.'

'You didn't get a call to pick up . . .' He scans his mind. 'Barbara?'

'That's what is so terrible. Joyce would always call ahead. If I had known . . .' She shudders and lowers her voice. 'Do you think she has been . . . violated?'

'Let's not paint the darkest picture yet,' says Mrs Crane, but a shadow crosses her face nonetheless. 'Laura, just answer the detective's questions.'

'What can you tell me about the Haney marriage?'

Mrs Kettering looks at him blankly. 'What do you mean?'

'Is it happy? Has Joyce ever confided in you with any problems?'

'As far as I can tell,' says Mrs Crane, 'Joyce Haney is happily married.'

'Apart from the usual stuff,' says Mrs Kettering.

Three small hairs begin to rise at the back of Mick's neck. 'The what?'

'Oh, nothing,' Mrs Crane says quickly. 'Frank works hard

and Joyce struggled a little after Lily's birth. A bit of the baby blues. She got some great medication and picked herself up soon enough. They've always been a happy couple.'

'And the kids,' says Mrs Kettering. 'Adorable. Always so nicely turned out. Joyce has a real gift for color. Have you seen what she's done with the lounge? It's simply—'

'Did you know Joyce before she moved here?'

'No.'

'And does she ever talk about her past?'

Mrs Kettering looks at Mrs Crane, who answers for her. 'Not much. She grew up in Philadelphia with stepparents, as far as I know. Her own parents died when she was young. She met Frank while she was working as a secretary. They married and had Barbara, and relocated here two years ago when Frank got a promotion. They had had enough of the rain.'

'You must have been glad to get such nice neighbors,' Mick says to Laura Kettering.

'Oh, yes. I've been feeling much safer knowing there's trustworthy people nearby.' Her voice drops. 'Now, of course—'

'I wouldn't worry too much.'

'Indeed,' says Mrs Crane and sends him an earnest glance. 'I am sure the detective and his men will do their best to find Joyce.'

Mick tips his hat and casts his glance around for Deena Klintz, but she has disappeared. He marches back through the trees, jumps into his Buick and burns his hands on the steering wheel.

At the office, he pulls off his jacket and flings his hat into a corner. His shirt is wet under the arms and a ring of moisture has blossomed around his neck like a goddamn watery garrote. He puts his feet up on the table, just because he can, and spends a few minutes with his eyes closed, trying to think about nothing.

Joyce Haney. Up and vanished. Why the blood? Had she fought someone off? A burglar? Or had she slipped and banged her head? Tottered out into the bright sunshine and down the street without anyone noticing? And why had she sent her daughter to wait outside?

The sleepsuit. Something is off about the whole arrangement. He's missed a clue and it's nagging at the back of his head. He cannot put his finger on it. It makes him desperate enough to pick up the phone and call his wife.

Fran answers promptly. 'Hellooo, Blanke residence.'

Because she cannot see him, he rolls his eyes. 'Shouldn't that be Mick's kingdom? Or Pretentious Palace?'

'What's eating you?'

He groans. 'Why are you answering the phone like we're the Rockefellers?'

'What do you want me to say? Rest home for disgraced detectives?'

That stings. It really does. But he has no chance to

think of a response, because Fran's already working those jaws.

'I am really busy, honey,' she says. 'Prissie's cheerleading on Saturday and Sandy's still not sure if she can make it because of the afternoon traffic. But she might bring Brad. I'm planning an extendable dinner that night. What do you think, chicken or lamb?'

'Whatever. I—'

'Well, what do you fancy?'

'I don't know.' Mick pinches the bridge of his nose. 'It's only Tuesday.'

'Still, you've got to know what you like, don't you? You like chicken.'

'Fran.' He clutches the receiver until the plastic creaks. 'Stop talking about chicken. I'm at work.'

'So am I, honey.'

Mick closes his eyes again and takes a deep, deep breath. These are the moments when he regrets not smoking. A nasty, long, tarry draft would come in handy right now.

'You don't work,' he says.

'Is that so? Housework is work – the clue is in the name. Or do you think I cook your dinners for fun?'

Right after they moved to Santa Monica, Fran discovered the local Women's Improvement Committee. She's been going religiously, and her life has very much improved. His own, on the other hand . . .

'Listen,' he says. 'When Sandy and Priscilla were little, how long did they wear newborn sleepsuits?'

'Usually only for about a few hours, before they had a mishap.'

'Fran. You know what I mean. How old were they when they stopped fitting into them?'

'About four months.'

'Not older?'

'No. Especially Sandy. She had long legs. She was running holes into them with her toenails.'

'And these sleepsuits, did they get dirty?'

'Mick.' There's indignation in her voice. 'You weren't the most hands-on father, but even you have to remember—'

'I mean, did they wash out white?'

'What kind of material?'

'Huh?'

'What kind of material is that sleepsuit you found?'

Mick grins. Fran is a sharp cookie. 'Soft stuff,' he says. 'Not woven. Like a towel, but without the little loop-things.'

'Flannel. And what is it you actually want to know?'

'Can you tell from looking at a sleepsuit whether it's new or whether it has gone through some, well, babies?'

'You can't wash flannel too hot, otherwise it'd shrink. If it's a well-used one I'd expect at least some discoloration.'

Aha. So the sleepsuit was new. The little white feet were spotless.

'Unless it's Sanforized flannel,' Fran continues.

'What?'

'Sanforized. You know.'

'I don't know.'

'When it gets put through a machine by scientists. Then you can wash it at all temperatures and it stays perfectly white.'

'Great.'

'So, anyway, chicken, or—'

'Later, Fran.'

He hangs up. Back to square one.

No. Not quite. There's one more person he urgently needs to talk to.

He grabs his notepad and goes to the kitchen, where he finds the two least chipped mugs and makes coffee with lots of milk and sugar. He measures the water carefully and lets it brew up just a little bit stronger than usual. Because ahead of him lies what may turn out to be the trickiest task of the day. A conversation with Ruby Wright.

Chapter Five

Ruby

The cops show up in the afternoon and take her to another cell. Ruby shakes all the way. She can't stop it. The shakes rattle her knees and ring hollow in her stomach. She's vomited out all its contents during a night spent crying and praying and fearing every sound.

The new cell has a table and three chairs, instead of the metal bed and unflushable toilet that have been her only company for the long hours. The cops plop her down on a chair and take the handcuffs off. Then they leave. One of them remains in front of the door; she can see his peaked cap and closely cropped hair through the mesh window.

Another shake crawls down her spine. She fights the panic, tries to press it small like an empty milk carton. It doesn't help much. Many a woman like her has gone into a cell like this and never come out, or never the same.

There are footsteps in the corridor, followed by a muted conversation. Ruby folds her hands in her lap and prays, fast and hard. *Lord, deliver me from evil. Lord, send me back to my family tonight. Lord, let me leave this place alive. Please, Lord, please.*

The door spits a man into the room. He's dressed a little tweedy, but his eyes are blue and piercing, the kind of eyes she's learned to fear. He puts two mugs of coffee next to the tape recorder on the table and grabs himself a chair.

'Good afternoon, Miss Wright,' he says. 'I'm Detective Mick Blanke, Santa Monica PD. Thought I'd bring you some coffee.'

He pushes one of the mugs across the table. Ruby fixes her eyes on it so she doesn't have to look at his face. He helps himself to the other mug and takes a sip. Then he flicks on the recorder.

'This is an interview in the case of Joyce Haney. It's Tuesday, August 25, 1959, time is 5 p.m., and present in the room are Detective Michael Blanke and Miss Ruby Wright, resident of Trebeck Row, LA. Now, Miss Wright, would you please run me through the events of yesterday afternoon?'

Ruby holds on to the seat of her chair as if it were a life raft. She cannot talk. Her throat is all clogged up with sour stuff. She can only think of one thing. Any word that comes out of her mouth is gonna go on that recorder, and that will play in court and put her away for the rest of her natural life. Or worse.

'Miss Wright,' the detective tries again. 'This is a serious situation. You've been arrested at the scene of a violent crime. If you cooperate, I'll make sure you get to leave here within the hour.'

That's what they would say, of course. *Spill the beans, little girl. Trust the big white daddy to make it all right.*

Oh, no, she won't fall for that. On her momma's soul, she won't.

Her stomach gurgles. The detective looks up. 'Hungry again?'

Again? They pushed a sandwich through her door this morning. When she opened it, the cheese on it was moldy and covered with the telltale glisten of spit. She didn't touch it, but then one of the officers had yelled at her to eat. *Eat it, you ungrateful nigger.* So she had broken it up and dropped it down the toilet and concealed the sodden crumbs with the last two scraps of toilet paper.

The detective sighs. 'Just a moment.'

He switches the recorder off, leaves the room and comes back two minutes later with a bottle of Coke and a lunch box with a Chevy on the front. The Coke is still capped. He hands it to her and disentangles a bottle opener from his key ring.

She inspects the bottle for any signs of tampering, finds none and cracks it open. The bubbles make her stomach churn, but she drinks in long drafts.

When she's polished off the bottle, she catches the detective's look. There is anger clouding behind his forehead. But he doesn't seem to be angry at her.

'Now,' he says, 'I'm not going to switch the tape back

on just yet. That way, we can have a chat before anything goes down on the record.'

Ruby sits still.

'Look, this arrest . . . it shouldn't have happened. I'll try and get you out, but you've got to help me. You were the first on the scene. Your impressions are incredibly valuable to our investigation. I know we haven't had the best start, but . . .' He shrugs.

Ruby sits and waits while the sugar rush clears her head.

'Is there anything else you want?' the detective asks.

Yeah, call my pa to tell him I'm all right. Buy me a bus ticket. Get me my purse and my things, you pig. Let me wash.

The detective stifles another sigh. 'Look, I'm treating you as a witness. You don't have to say anything, but it would really help me if you did. I can call you a lawyer, if that would make you feel better.'

Tears crawl into her eyes. She bites them down with all her might. Ain't no use crying in here. Not in front of him.

He looks alarmed. 'You have been informed that you have the right to a lawyer, yes?'

No, she hasn't. And anyway, what gives? She's got the right to a diamond tiara, but, sure as hell, there ain't none forthcoming.

The detective mutters something that sounds like a curse. Then he leans back. 'Listen, I'm worried about Mrs Haney. Doesn't make sense what's happened, does it?'

'What's happened to her, then?'

She could kick herself. She didn't want to say anything. The tape recorder is still off, though. Not that it would matter much. If they decide to blame something on her, they will find a way.

'We haven't found a body, if that's what you mean.' He gauges her reaction. 'We know that Mrs Haney went out shopping in the morning, then returned to her home to make lunch and put Lily down for a nap. After that it's all a mystery, until you showed up.'

Ruby's insides clench, and it's not just from hunger. Joyce. What on Earth has happened to her?

'So, let me see. When you finished at Mrs Ingram's, you were running slightly later than usual, right?'

Seems he knows everything already. Which makes things easier. She ain't gonna say nothing.

The detective waits a while. 'I'm hungry,' he says suddenly. 'Let's see.'

He opens his lunch box. It contains a sandwich, an apple and a banana. He pushes the box to the middle of the table.

'My wife made this. It's good. Bacon and salad. You can have half.'

Ruby stares at the food. Her stomach, the old traitor, emits another loud gurgle.

She slowly reaches out and takes a sandwich half. The detective takes the other one and bites into it. She waits until he's swallowed, then she starts eating hers.

It's good. The bread is soaked with bacon grease, but

the salad is still crisp, despite the heat. She grins inwardly at the sight of the fruit, though. The detective doesn't look like a man who likes his fruit.

They eat in silence. When she's finished, he offers her the fruits for dessert and she chooses the apple. She has to think of the poisoned apple from Snow White, but that's a fairy tale. Ain't much you can put inside an apple without opening it up, and this one's without a blemish.

Once lunch is over, the detective glances toward the door. 'OK,' he says. 'How about now?'

She checks the tape recorder. It's still off. 'I had to work a little later than usual at Mrs Ingram's house.'

'What time did you leave?'

'Around quarter past five. I went up the driveway to Mrs Haney's house. I saw Barbara among the trees.'

The detective looks satisfied. In fact, a little light of excitement has begun to burn in his eyes. 'Why was the girl outside?'

'She was waiting for Mrs Kettering to pick her up. The neighbors help each other out with childcare.'

'But Laura Kettering didn't show. Why?'

Ruby shrugs. Hell knows why. She probably found out that Joyce had gotten the last Saturday hair appointment and that was her way of taking sweet revenge.

'So, you picked up Barbara?'

'We went into the house. I heard Lily crying, so I checked on her and saw that she was all wet.'

'And you didn't look for Mrs Haney?'

Her insides contract. She's gotta be careful now. He'll twist her words and spit them right back at her.

'I was very concerned for the well-being of the children and wanted to call Mrs Kettering to come help. I sensed something . . . untoward as soon as I entered the house.' There, how did that sound? Untoward. Good, meaningless word.

The detective looks happier. 'And then you saw the blood?'

'In the kitchen.' She clenches her fists. It's not a nice memory. 'I didn't wait around to get an eyeful of that. I beat feet and ran right into Mrs Ingram.'

'You didn't search the house?'

'I had two little kids with me, sir. We stayed outside till the police came. I was scared there might be someone in the house. And I didn't want Barbara to . . . to walk all over it. She'd already put her hands in it.'

'OK.' The detective peels the banana. 'And that's all?'

'Well,' she says, as innocently as she can. 'You know the rest.'

He takes a bite. In the quiet room, Ruby can hear the sound of his teeth coming down on the soft, yellow flesh.

'Sergeant Hodge told me that Mrs Ingram slapped you. That true?'

'He gave her sh— He told her off for being in the house. She got angry and . . .' Ruby casts her eyes down and lowers her voice. 'It was a nightmare in that house.'

'I understand,' he says slowly. 'For what it's worth, I think you stayed quite level-headed.'

She peers up into his face. His blue eyes are sharp and impatient.

'Anything else you've seen or heard?' he asks between bites. 'Anything out of whack?'

'Nothing, sir.'

'Mrs Haney – what is she like?'

'Always happy and friendly.'

'A good boss?'

'Yeah.' *And a good friend. But I'd never say that. Not to anyone. Especially not you.*

'And in the weeks leading up to yesterday, did you notice anything unusual about her behavior? What was she like?'

'Normal. She talked on the phone, she played with the kids, she got them dressed up all nice and tidy, she put dinner on. Nothing else.'

'What about Mr Haney?'

'I don't see him. He doesn't like the help in the house when he gets back from work. So I always leave before he arrives.'

'Hm.' The detective finishes his banana and folds the peel back into the lunch box. 'I've got to admit, this totally beats me.'

Ruby doesn't answer. What's she supposed to say?

'I mean,' the detective continues, 'we've not found a body and there wasn't that much blood. She might still be alive. Could be an abduction or a robber, but the house wasn't otherwise disturbed. Could be a crazy guy, but even crazy guys are normally not that stupid. Who'd kidnap a housewife in broad daylight?'

Come to South Central, Ruby thinks, and you might get an idea.

'Anyhoo, the kids would have heard if there'd been a struggle. And the neighbors would have noticed a strange car.'

In Ruby's mind a memory rises, fast and fleeting. A Crestliner, silver-black like shadow, burning rubber down the road. She pushes the image away. There's no point getting the detective all hot and bothered about something that might not even matter.

'All right.' The detective sighs. 'I need something on the record. Can you repeat all that on tape?'

Twenty minutes later, the Lord has worked a miracle. Ruby is at the bus stop, her purse around her shoulder and two bus tokens in her hand. It happened so quickly she barely had time to figure it out. Detective Blanke took her to the front desk and shouted a lot. He grabbed some papers and signed them. Then he gave Ruby a paper to sign, stating she'd received all her belongings. She never had time to check, but now, waiting for the 168 to Compton, she's digging through her purse and everything's still there, even the dollar bills from Mrs Ingram.

The sun is burning the flagstones. They throw the heat right back against her legs. Santa Monica smells of asphalt and gasoline, and the palm trees are swaying in the breeze. The sky is blue and wide and open and she is under it and free. It's only just starting to sink in. She's made it. She's gonna go home.

It occurs to her that she didn't even say thank you. Right away, she can hear Momma's voice, from farther away than the human mind can fathom. *You don't got nobody to thank for nothing, girl. You done good all by yourself.*

The bus turns the corner with a silver flash. She is crying when she stamps her token. The driver is white, but he sends her a worried smile. 'You all right, honey?'

'I'm fine.' She smiles back. 'Don't worry, sir. Everything's cooking.'

She takes a seat at the back and turns around to watch the police station recede from her life. Chances are she's out of a job; Mrs Ingram won't want her back after that slap. But it could've been worse. Hell, it could've been so much worse.

She clutches her purse. Inside it, slipped into the tiny pouch that holds her keys and wallet, is a dog-eared calling card. The detective pressed it into her hand just before she left the station. 'Call me if you can think of anything else,' he said.

She won't. But she'll keep the card. You never know.

Chapter Six

Mick

The Seafront View Motel is probably the biggest scam this side of Brentwood. There's no seafront in sight, and neither is there a view, unless you consider the delectable sight of the Interstate 10 a visual highlight.

Frank Haney waits in apartment number 7, which boasts two double beds and a tiny coffee machine on a tray balanced precariously on the dresser. To Mick's surprise, Nancy Ingram is there, sitting in the room's only armchair, and she has brought the children. Haney is cradling the younger girl on his lap. She has burrowed her head into his chest and is sucking her thumb. The older one is sitting on the bed, her legs drawn up and her eyes fixed on the television, which is running with the sound off.

Mick looks for a place to sit and, awkwardly, settles himself on the spare bed. He takes out his notepad and draws a little snake on a blank page. Haney turns around, his face smudged with worry.

'Any news about my wife, Detective?'

'We're doing all we can. If we find her, you'll be the first to know.'

'There must be an explanation for all this. Dear Lord, if she's injured . . . if she's . . .' He gulps and buries his chin in his daughter's hair.

Mick glances at the older girl, Barbara, her tiny face whitened by the TV's glow. 'For now, we're working on the basis that your wife is . . . doing OK. She may have sustained an injury, but I would not be unduly worried.'

'Not worried?' Frank Haney squeezes the child on his lap. 'Then where is she? I heard there was blood on the floor. What the goddamn hell has happened to her?'

Mrs Ingram gets up from her chair and, with an apologetic smile, takes Barbara's hand and leads her outside. Barbara follows willingly, looking at no one.

'Sorry,' says Haney. 'I'm just . . . this is terrible. Who would do such a thing?'

'What do you think?'

Haney stares at him. His eyebrows dip from fear into anger. 'You tell me, Detective.'

'Let's start with your wife's past.' Mick puts on his old buddy face. 'She was born in Philadelphia?'

'On September 2, 1930.'

'And her parents?'

'Oh, so you found out already.'

'Found out what, Mr Haney?'

'About the fire.'

Mick hasn't a clue, but he sure as hell won't let on. 'I'd like to hear the story from you.'

'Joyce's parents died in a fire when she was twelve. She was the only one saved from the burning apartment. Apparently, her mother . . .' Haney looks sideways and swallows. 'She wasn't very well in the head. Joyce never liked to talk about it. She loved her parents, but the circumstances were . . . Well, I think she had a better life with the Delawneys. They took her in after the fire, gave her a new . . . a better home.'

'Joyce was close to her stepparents?'

'Devoted. We visited Bill and Florence every other weekend when we lived in Philly.'

'Then the move down here must have been hard for her.'

'Yes, but she wanted to get away from the bad weather and the dirty air. For the children, you know? We were planning to drive back east for a visit next year, when Lily's old enough to stand the long ride. We . . .' He breaks off. Tears shimmer in his eyes. 'I haven't called the Delawneys yet,' he whispers. 'Should I?'

'Perhaps not today,' Mick says. 'We're checking all the hospitals and there's a huge search effort going on.'

'Yes,' says Haney. 'All the ladies from Joyce's committee.'

'There you go. Most missing person cases get solved in twenty-four hours.'

'It's *been* twenty-four hours.'

Mick ignores that. 'What else can you tell me about your wife's past?'

'She was good in school, very clever. Went to college and graduated with honors.'

'What was her degree?'

'Art history. Then she went to work for Griffin Corps as secretary for the head of PR, who happened to be my boss. We ran into each other almost daily. I asked her out for lunch and the rest, as they say, is history.'

He gives Mick a wan smile. His daughter stirs in his arms. She hiccups, then begins to cry softly.

'Any difficulties in your marriage?' Mick asks. 'I'm sorry, but it's a question I have to ask, just in case your wife left . . . voluntarily.'

'Bogus.' Haney begins to sway from side to side as the little girl's crying intensifies. 'We are very happy. Joyce is a devoted mother, and a great wife. I mean, we grind each other's gears just like any other married couple, but never—'

'About what?'

'Oh, come on.' Haney glances at Mick's wedding ring. 'You're married. Household allowance, decorating, child-care. That sort of thing. Nothing serious. We want the same from life, Joyce and I. We love each other. We . . . Dammit. Enough.'

He rises and yanks the door open. Mrs Ingram appears as if she's been waiting by the window. She plucks Lily from his arms and coos.

'Thank you, Nancy.' Haney looks out into the dusk settling over the motel's parking lot. 'Where's Barbara?'

'Playing.' Mrs Ingram points to a rickety swing set near the reception building, on which the little girl sits unmoving.

Haney closes the door and wipes his face. 'I'm sorry, Detective Blanke. It's . . . I am so worried about Joyce.'

'Of course,' Mick says, and he believes him. Haney looks distressed, and angry, too. He is talking about his wife in present tense and hasn't once slipped up.

Haney grows impatient with the silence. 'I don't understand what all these questions are about. You should be out there, catching that gangster.'

'You believe it's an abduction?'

'Jesus Christ. What if she surprised a burglar and he killed her to make sure she wouldn't run to the police?'

'We'll have to ask you to check if anything's been stolen, and whether any of her clothes are missing. Any jewelry, personal items, photographs—'

'How the hell should I know?'

'You don't know your wife's closet?'

'You should see it. Stuffed to the brim.' Haney sighs. 'OK. I'll take a look.'

'Another thing. Your older daughter was sent outside that afternoon. I was wondering—'

'What about that?'

'Your wife might have had a visitor.'

'Goddammit, what are you implying?'

Mick keeps the buddy smile going for all its worth. 'Mr Haney, please. It's something we have to ask. Routine question, you understand?'

'Well, if she's got time to hang out with a fella, she's a bloody miracle worker. She has two kids and the housework and the shopping to do. And, before you ask, I'm not one to play around. I come home at 7 p.m., come hell or high water. I spend every weekend with my family. Unless she was stowing a man in the dryer, my wife had no time for flings.'

'Did your wife go out much?'

'Just to the mall or to take the children for check-ups. Oh, and the Women's Improvement Committee. You may have heard of it.' He rolls his eyes to signal the brotherhood of men.

'I have,' Mick says. 'My wife goes every week. To the Santa Monica one.'

'Ah, well, then you know what I'm talking about. Joyce only went when she could get childcare.'

'I understand Mrs Ingram was looking after the children on the morning your wife disappeared?'

'She's a treasure. She's been helping us a lot.'

Mick nods and pretends to take notes. From outside comes the sound of Lily wailing, followed by the desperately cheerful encouragements from Mrs Ingram. 'Things are OK, baby. Honey, listen, it's OK. Come on, little bean, come on, honey, it's OK.'

'Mr Haney,' Mick says. 'Were you planning to have more children?'

And there it is. A sharp glance, quick and nasty, like a shot from the hip. Gone in a split second, but its echo rings in the room.

'Not quite yet,' Haney says. 'But maybe once Lily is a little older. The house is big enough and . . . well, of course I would have liked a boy.'

Mick nods, and this time he makes a note in earnest.

He's not going to get more out of the man, not tonight. Try again in a few days, when the shock has had time to settle. Or, he prays, when Joyce Haney has shown up in a hospital or been rescued from the apartment of some nutcase, a former boyfriend, perhaps, or a drugstore attendant who has taken a twisted fancy to her. Joyce Haney, shocked and shaken, but alive. She'll have nightmares for a few months, maybe grow scared of the dark. But she'll be back to hug her kids and iron the pleats in her husband's pants and buy everything that's on the shopping list taped to the refrigerator.

Haney interrupts that particular train of thought. 'When can I return to my house?'

'Once we're done with it. End of the day tomorrow, I hope.'

'The children are upset.'

'Yes, I understand.'

'They need their home. And their mother.'

Mick nods and gets up. 'We are working as hard as we can. Meanwhile, if you can think of anything that could help us – any acquaintances from your wife's past, anything she said or did that would hint at—'

Haney steps close to him. 'My wife is a lovely, happy, delightful creature,' he says, and his voice is dull with fear.

'There's no one in her life, past or present, who'd wish her any harm.'

'Of course,' says Mick. *Of course that's the case, Frankie-boy. Until it isn't.*

Back in his car, he flips to the notes he's taken. He's written down only one sentence.

I would have liked a boy.

There it is. The past tense. As if that option is forever eliminated. Crumpled and squashed, like a certain blue sleepsuit that now lies in an evidence box in the Santa Monica PD's filing room.

The only thing that could make this day worse is running into Chief Murphy, and of course this happens with the same galactic inevitability with which the Giants lose to the Colts.

'Blanke, what a delight to find you here.' Murphy detaches himself from the coffee machine and grins like a raptor. 'Hodge told me about your, shall we say, cursory investigation of the house.'

'Evidence recovery is in today and tomorrow, right?'

''Course. And let's hope *they* do their job properly.'

An icy silence ensues. Mick wonders whether he should be the first one to break it, just to vent the steam that's boiling in his veins. But he leaves it. He's dealt with enough Irish mobsters to know that, sometimes, silence is way more infuriating than insults.

'Anyway.' Murphy grunts. 'Give me an update before I go home. What's the husband been up to?'

'Away at a conference.'

'None of the neighbors seen anything?'

'Nope. Nancy Ingram, the closest neighbor, was out. The other folks, the Ketterings, can't really see the property. Too many trees. Besides, the Haneys put a big white fence all around their little haven. I spoke to Mrs Kettering. Seems the Haneys kept to themselves.'

Murphy folds his arms and blows up his cheeks. 'You shouldn't have let that Negro girl go. She's our prime suspect.'

'Right. And she's never going to talk to a cop if she's cooped up in a cell.'

'Well, now she's back in that rat's nest of South Central, and her folks are surely going to give her an earful. I got a cousin who used to work the beat on Cooper and Twenty-Second. Goddamn life-threatening job, that was. I'm warning you – they don't like the police.'

What a surprise, Mick thinks, but he doesn't say it out loud. He puts on his hat and prepares to make like a tree. But Murphy isn't finished.

'You know,' he says, 'when they told me you were coming, I knew straight away we'd be in trouble.'

'Chief?'

'Thing is, you and your methods don't really fit in here. This is Santa Monica. We're a civilized people. No one's going to deliver their grandma up for cash or rat someone out to get a plea bargain. You're out of your depth. I'm giving you until Friday. If Joyce Haney hasn't shown up, dead or alive, you're off the case. We don't need you fucking things up down here like you did in New York.'

An image flashes through Mick's mind. Beverly Gallagher, her pale skin, sulking lips and large brown eyes. Eyes a man could get lost in, and many of them did, and it never ended well.

He wipes the memory from his head and grins. 'Don't worry, Chief,' he says sweetly. 'There's only two kinds of fucking I intend to do tonight. The first involves the words "off home". The second . . . well, depends on my wife's disposition.'

With a tip of his hat, he heads off into the evening heat.

Chapter Seven

Joyce

Nancy agrees to take Barbara for the morning while I head to the mall to see the doctor. Nancy is an utter treasure. It must be difficult for her, having lost a husband so early, without any children of her own. She turned thirty last year, and there is no new marriage on the horizon.

I wave goodbye and put Lily onto the back seat. It's a slug on the small roads, which are always clogged. But once we hit the highway, we fly. Sunnylakes recedes and vanishes. There's only us, the blue skies and the freeway bridge, still under construction, a giant arm reaching out into nothing. I will not be here when it touches the other side. Happiness explodes in me like fireworks. I'll swoop over this bridge and into the blue yonder, full of wonder.

Jimmy and I used to park up under a half-constructed bridge like this when they were building the Walt Whitman Bridge. Just for a laugh, I decide to tell Lily about it.

'Bunny,' I say, 'do you know that the first time Mommy

drove a car it was with Jimmy? I thought I couldn't do it, but he said you just have to push the pedal down and steer in the right direction. I laughed so much my belly hurt.'

I press my hand to my guts. My belly is hurting now. Still hurting.

Jimmy. Everything blurs and bulges in my memory. All the ups and downs. The highs and lows, ebbs and flows. Lily smiles and I giggle like a schoolgirl. Frank hates it when I rhyme my words. But Genevieve Crane says that there is a poet in every woman. 'You cannot help becoming a poet,' she says. 'There is so much that women cannot say straight out.'

My moods are getting out of whack again. When I'm like this, I am prone to taking risks. The doctor says I need to learn to settle myself. I dig a Miltown from my purse and swallow it down. Lily stops smiling.

The exuberance drains from my head like dishwater, leaving only stainless steel, beautifully blank. The sunlight dims and my skin turns to stone. Nothing can come inside me now. And what's inside cannot escape.

When we enter the mall, people stare. I am wearing my yellow dress and Lily is in a little pinafore number with cherry hair clips. She looks absolutely adorable. Even the doctor says so. Genevieve Crane was right, he is so understanding. He takes me into a private room, sends out the nurse and gives me what I crave.

Afterward, I clutch the plain little packets. Lily and I walk around the mall. I should not go to Reubens, but I cannot help take a look at the storefront. It draws me like a magnet.

Unfortunately, Mrs Reubens is at the front, stocking shelves. I walk right past and enter the store next door. A young girl immediately runs over to assist me, and because I feel embarrassed and the memories are pulling at me, I buy a blue sleepsuit. The girl packs it up and glances at my stomach, which is smooth and cinched, thanks to Appetrol and discipline. It responds to her stare with a cramp. But no emotion follows. Nothing at all.

We leave and pass Reubens again. Lily and I look with abandon. I am glad I didn't bring Barbara. She is all her father, always demanding, never satisfied. She would tear at my skirt and grab at things she wants, and throw a tantrum when she doesn't get them.

Lily, however, is still malleable. She oscillates between babyhood and childhood, between her mother and her father, between amazement and dashed hope. She looks at everything, but merely because everything is wonderful to her. I want to reward her for that wonder. She needs to know that she should never stop being amazed.

So I go in.

When did I stop being amazed? When did I stop painting? Why should I have to stop at all?

These questions prey on my mind as we choose the crayons, and suddenly I have the answer in my hand. Watercolors. Lemon yellow, cadmium blue, rose madder.

A pocket-sized rainbow. More joy than a pill packet could ever give.

I should not paint. Frank does not like it, even though Genevieve Crane says I have amazing talent. It's a bad example to the kids, a mother who indulges, when there are meal plans to be made and carpets to vacuum and flowers to be arranged.

Lily tugs at my skirt while I pay and shoulder the heavy bag. She starts crying, but I cannot carry her, too. I drag her along to the car, walking so fast her little legs almost cannot keep up.

Chapter Eight

Ruby

Under the sheets the world is warm and peaceful. Joseph's skin smells of cinnamon and soap and something that is impossible to name. It's him alone.

Ruby shifts her head just a little bit. She loves it when her cheek brushes his collarbone, loves how he responds, half asleep, by tightening his embrace. Then his arms relax again as he drifts away. His chest rises and falls, carrying her body in constant ebb and swell.

The sun burns through the curtains, which are cut from an old bed sheet and tacked against the frame. The room is stuffy with sleep. She does not want this moment to end. Soon enough, Mimi will start a row and Pa will holler for his breakfast. She runs her hand along Joseph's arm. There is so little time in this world for just the two of them.

Someone starts shouting in the street. There's a smash of glass and a scream. Joseph shoots up from the bed, rips the curtains aside and yells: 'Get the fuck out of our neighborhood!'

Ruby wraps herself in the sheet and joins him at the window. Too late. All she sees are three shapes running, turning the corner. Across the alleyway, one window has been smashed in of the ancient Ford that Mr Roan keeps parked up in front of his house.

Stupid thieves – there sure ain't nothing to steal in there. But maybe they didn't mean to steal. Maybe they just wanted to break something up.

'This . . . This . . .' Joseph grasps for words as he pulls on his underwear. 'I hate seeing this. Boys reduced to theft. Robbing a brother. And for what?'

'There was nothing there to rob,' Ruby says. 'It's just Mr Roan's Ford.'

'Smashing and stealing, instead of working and doing right by themselves. It makes me sick.'

'They didn't take nothing, I don't think.'

'. . . shackled to a life of crime and property, which begets more crime. Shackled, Ruby, that's the right word for it.'

'Yeah, they should get a job.'

Joseph spins around. 'There are no jobs. That's the whole problem. They won't hire blacks. No jobs for us.'

'I have a job. And so do you. Old Man Toby hires only blacks.'

Joseph scoffs. 'Yeah, 'coz we're cheap and Old Man Toby is a cheap-ass bastard.'

'He's nice enough. He drove Momma to hospital in his tow truck. Remember?'

'And he charged you three dollars.' Joseph's words muffle momentarily as he disappears into his shirt. '. . . That's why we gotta keep up the fight. Slavery is over, they say, segregation is dying. But you get an ambulance for your mother? You see mixed schools? You see Black boys with ties and careers, going steady to their office? Huh? You see that?'

He's right. You don't see that.

'And now stealing. In front of our own house.'

Ruby's heart warms up. *Our* house, he says. Like it's where he lives now.

But he mistakes her expression. 'Why are you smiling? That funny to you?'

'It's not funny. The plight of the Black man—'

'The plight of the Black man creates the prosperity of the whites,' Joseph continues. Once he gets started, he can go on for some 'n more. 'The terror of being Black . . .' He pauses and seems to remember what happened yesterday. He swoops his arms around her and presses her against his chest. 'Well, you know what I'm talking about.'

Ruby closes her eyes. *That's better. Don't talk for a bit. Just feel me. Feel how I'm still alive.*

'Rubeeeh.' Mimi's voice can carve through brick. 'Ruby, lemme in there now.'

'Whaaa?' Ruby shouts into Joseph's chest. 'We're sleeping.'

'You ain't sleeping. You're talking.'

Joseph rolls his eyes. Ruby plants an apologetic kiss on his lips.

'My sister wants to get dressed,' she says, and grabs a clean pair of underwear and her towel. 'You get outta here and give the girl some space.'

In the kitchen, Pa has started breakfast. There's a pan of eggs sizzling on the stove and coffee bubbling in the kettle. Ruby waves good morning and slips into the shower, whacks two roaches with her towel and stuffs the plughole with tissues. Don't need more roaches looking at her privates while she's trying to get clean. The patter of droplets on her shower cap soothes her nerves. The sound of normal.

Afterward, she sits down in the kitchen and grabs yesterday's *LA Times*, as always folded to the sports section. Dizzy's blowing a tune on the radio and Pa's pouring coffee. She starts to read, and the words of Mrs Cannon, her former teacher, bubble up in her mind. *A body has to read. The more you read, the more you know.* She's made it a habit to sift through the rest of the paper while Pa is on the sports, and she's starting to pick up quite a bit.

But just as she's halfway through an interview with the new senator from Hawaii, Joseph comes in and starts chatting with Pa.

Ruby puts the paper down and eyes her men. Pa is polite; he has resigned himself to the fact that his little girl is a woman now. And him and Joseph, they always got lots to talk about.

'Civil rights are no good if they're happening just on paper,' Joseph proclaims. 'We need a revolution in this country, a real change.'

'But how're you gonna get that without a fight?' asks Pa. 'And you don't wanna start a fight. I've seen it before. They be down here in minutes, guns blazing. Firing at anything that moves. I've seen it, boy. That's not the way to go. So, what are they talking about in your committee?'

'Peaceful marches. Like the Indian guy – whats'name.'

'Mahatma Gandhi,' says Ruby.

'Like him. March for our rights. And stop working. Go on strike. Show them what we're worth.'

'You just said nobody's working, anyway.'

Joseph ignores her. 'That's the way to go. The Black Man's Advancement Committee got another meeting tonight. Leroy's chairing. We gotta get our voices heard.'

Ruby looks up. 'Can I come?'

'Don't you have to work for the Funnylakes folk?'

She shakes her head. Not after what happened on Monday night. Mrs Ingram left a message via Mrs Estrada to say that Ruby's employment was terminated. So she might as well fill her evening.

'I'd like to hear what they're saying.'

Joseph gives her an uncertain smile. 'Ruby. It's the Black *Man's* Advancement Committee. To advance the lives of men like me and your father. You should stay home, be with your family.'

My life needs advancing, too, Ruby wants to say. But it just sounds too corny. So she goes down another route. 'Leroy's sister goes,' she says. 'Don't she?'

Joseph looks right past her. 'Not really. Not often. Why? You jealous?'

Jealous of someone as tall and glamorous as Tamona? The Lord knows how, but Tamona's in good money, even though she's not working. The other day, Ruby saw her at the nail parlor, with her hair all kinked around her head like a halo. Natural-looking. Crazy.

She wants to make a snappy reply, but Joseph has already turned back to Pa. 'You coming?'

'I'm too old for this, boy.' Pa smiles weakly. 'I seen it all come and go. We moved out here to escape the lynching, but it didn't get better. Then we went to war and it didn't get better. Now segregation is going. But it ain't better. We still separated, black and white. Separate homes, separate jobs, separate lives. And it's always gonna be like that.'

For some reason, Joyce pops into Ruby's mind. She'd sit her down at the kitchen table and ask questions. *You should get some books on teaching, get a head start on college. You can do it, Ruby, you'll see. Don't ever let things hold you back.* Joyce never once mocked her aspirations.

'You know,' she begins, 'Mrs Haney, she's—'

'She's exactly what I'm talking about.' Joseph wiggles his head. 'Have you seen this?'

He snatches the paper from her and flips it to the front page. There's Joyce's face. Underneath, it says: *Sunnylakes*

Mystery – Housewife vanishes in broad daylight. Ruby reaches for the paper, but Joseph holds on to it.

'Listen.' He reads out loud. 'Seventeen policemen searched the lake and waterfront, while another dozen undertook house-to-house searches. Neighbors combed the area all afternoon, but found no trace of the missing woman. "We're doing all we can," says Detective Michael Blanke, who leads the investigation. "We're still hoping to bring Joyce home to her children and her husband, alive and well."'

'So?' Ruby says.

'They'd never make such trouble over a Black woman vanishing. You think Mrs Estrada from upstairs disappears, the police are gonna send thirty people to search for her? They won't send no one, and you know it.'

'That's not Mrs Haney's fault.'

'And what happened to you yesterday?' Joseph shakes his head. 'I'm telling you, you stay away from the white folk. They may seem nice, your prim little housewives, but all you are to them is cheap service.'

Anger rushes into Ruby's chest, red-hot and searing. She jumps up, spilling her coffee over the table.

'Money's money,' she shouts. 'I'm doing my best. Don't you ever say I'm cheap.'

'But what they pay you is peanuts to them. The society we live in puts you in the—'

'I said. Don't. You. Ever.' She takes a breath, her heart pumping. 'Say. That. Again.'

She yanks open the kitchen door, then remembers to not slam it, because it has a habit of coming off its hinges. That somewhat interrupts her flounce. Then she walks straight into Mimi, who is standing in the hallway, her hands on her hips.

'Phone call for you,' she says.

Ruby comes to a dead stop. Mrs Estrada is filling the front door. She is wearing a huge quilted duster with faded flowers and a yellow bow around the throat, which makes her look like a gigantic birthday present. But her expression is more a portent of a funeral than a party.

'Always on my line,' she says. 'Always I'm gonna have to come down the stairs to get you. Or your sister. Or your pa. Always it's on me. My phone is not a—'

'Yes, Mrs Estrada.'

Ruby fishes a nickel from Pa's jacket and squeezes past Mrs Estrada into the hallway. She realizes only halfway up the stairs that she's still in her towel. Mrs Estrada, of course, notices it, too.

'Ten ay-ehm, girl, and you're not even dressed. And who's talking with your papi? You got a man staying over? If your mother knew. She's not dead a year and you're already giving it up to—'

'No, Mrs Estrada. No men. I just took a shower.' Only half a lie.

Mrs Estrada lords over the building's only telephone and makes most of her money with other people's phone calls. Her telephone sits on a table in a little alcove. Now it is unhooked, the receiver lying next to the Mexican bowl where you put your nickel.

Ruby picks up the receiver. 'Yes, Ruby Wright?'

'Hello, Frank Haney here.'

Ruby's heart skips. What could he possibly want? He's got no business calling. The police let her go.

'I found your number in Joyce's address book,' he says. 'When do you normally come in?'

'Monday, Wednesday and Friday,' Ruby says. Her voice is not quite stable. 'At 5 p.m.'

'Oh.' Mr Haney sounds annoyed. 'Make it earlier today. The police are finished in the house and, well . . .' He makes a sound like the squeak of a puppy. 'It's very messy. The kitchen . . . I don't want the children to see. I'll pay you overtime.'

Ruby inhales. 'How much?'

'Two dollars an hour. That should be enough, I think.'

His words thunk the air out of Ruby's chest. Two dollars. That's . . . That's like . . . Mrs Ingram only pays her sixty cents.

'You still there?' says Mr Haney. 'Look, I understand your reticence. For today, I'll give you a ten dollar bonus. It's a . . . disagreeable job.'

Ruby digs her hands into the knot of towel above her chest. College just jumped a little bit closer. 'Yes, Mr Haney. That's all right. I'll jump on the bus right now.'

'Make it quick.' He hangs up without saying goodbye.

Mrs Estrada gives Ruby a look that's pure curiosity, varnished with a layer of contempt. 'Who that?'

'A man.' Suddenly, Ruby feels like being fresh. 'He wants me.'

'You gonna go see him? Shame on you, girl. What would your mother—'

'Don't worry, Mrs Estrada.' At the door, she turns around and juts out her hip. 'I'm getting paid. Hourly rate, you know?'

Back in her room, there's a problem. Her uniform is still soaking in a bowl of suds. And she's got only the one. Plus, she doesn't want to be alone in the house with Mr Haney in a skirt. So, she picks a blouse that makes her look like a church girl and some dark pants. Flat shoes round it off, but she cannot resist putting her plastic butterfly clasp in her hair. Two dollars an hour and ten dollars extra today. Come Saturday, she'll be halfway to college.

When she emerges, Joseph raises his eyebrows at the sight of her. 'Where are you going?'

'To work,' she says, trying her best to sound nonchalant. 'Can I have the newspaper, for the bus?'

'Work where? That Funnylakes lady said she doesn't want you no more.'

She stuffs the front page of the *LA Times* into her purse. 'Got another job. Or, more like, got my hours extended.'

'At the Haney place?'

'Yeah.'

'Just you wait.' With two steps he's by her side and grasps her arm. 'Are you crazy to go back there? You barely got away with it last time.'

'Got away with what? I've done nothing.'

'Yeah, but they don't care about that.'

'You gotta let me go,' she says with emphasis. 'I got work to do.'

'Ruby, you're crazy.'

'I'm not crazy. I need money. He's paying more than anyone.'

'I swear, if you're going—'

'Then what? Joseph, I got plans, too.' She arches her back to face him. 'I got money to earn. I got to pay for my teacher training. College starts in autumn. I need five hundred dollars. You see them falling from a tree?'

'Then do sewing. Or piecework. Stuff you can do from home.'

'No.' Something's pushing in her chest. She can't quite describe it, but she needs to be on the bus now, and Joseph's hand off her arm.

'Joseph,' she says. 'You stay out of my business. I want to be working. In a real job. You said us folks are still shackled – well, don't you go shackling me as well.'

That, of course, shuts him up.

Chapter Nine

Ruby

By the time the bus arrives, Ruby is regretting her words. Joseph means right by her. Hell, some men send their girls to white folks and take all the money they bring home. Some pimp them out at the truck stop or in the side streets off the Harbor Freeway. Some men laugh at the way the white bosses feel up their sisters and joke over the bruises the white wives inflict when the feeling-up gets too obvious. Joseph would never do that. He cares.

To take her mind off it all, she unfolds the paper and begins to read. The police have no leads on what happened to Joyce. There's an appeal for anyone who might have seen her to contact Santa Monica PD, who'll pay a handsome reward for information that helps solve the case.

Fortunately, the article doesn't mention Ruby's arrest. She wonders if she has Detective Blanke to thank for that. Or maybe the police didn't want to admit they had locked up a Negro and then let her go.

On Roseview Drive, there is no wind between the trees

and the air is white with perspiration. Joyce's car is still parked in front of number 47, and Mr Haney's black Chrysler is in the garage. Ruby hears a child scream and glances toward Mrs Ingram's house. Nothing's moving behind the curtains or in the yard, but the child's wail is unmistakable. Lily, crying for her mother.

Her heart suddenly heavy, she walks up the drive and knocks on the door. Mr Haney opens it. His hair is disheveled and his eyes jumpy. He looks right past her face and ushers her in quickly, his lips crimped as if he's worried the neighbors might see.

'The sooner you can get it done, the better,' he says. 'Nancy has the kids, but she's been taking care of them for a while and I don't want to impose any longer.' He waves toward the kitchen door, which is closed. 'In there. Don't open any drawers and stay out of the bedroom. Let me know when you're done. I'll be watering the lawn.'

He fumbles with his cuff links, tiny black circles with a white line around them, like the wheels on his car. Once he's rolled up his sleeves, he goes into the living room, takes the phone off its little table by the couch and sets it down on the floor as near to the garden doors as possible.

When Ruby walks into the kitchen, her hands are clammy. The sight isn't nearly as bad as it was before. The blood has darkened, and now looks more messy than frightening. But still . . . Joyce would hate it; she loved her kitchen sparkling clean.

Well. Time to sort it out for her return.

She ties an old tea towel around her waist as a makeshift apron. There are five aprons in the cupboard, all nicely starched and with jolly polka-dot patterns. Joyce would always give her one, but somehow she senses that Mr Haney would go ape if she simply helped herself.

The blood is hard and sticky. Two days of summer heat have left it caked to the tiles like nail polish. It requires a soak, and then a lot of scrubbing. Ruby gets some on her fingers. There are gloves on the sink but, again, they're probably not hers to use. Every time she wrings out the cloth, the water in the bucket goes more red. The scent of King Pine and something else, something alive and fetid, fills the air. She wipes her hands on the tea towel, leaving a pink mark, and opens the back door.

Outside, the air is trembling with heat. The pot of geraniums taking pride of place on the terrace is looking quite the worse for wear. The flowers are hanging their heads. A few petals have already turned brown.

A pang echoes through Ruby's heart. These flowers are Joyce's pride and joy. She waters and prunes them every day, and she's told Ruby on more than one occasion how much she loves them, that they must always be taken care of. It would be a shame if Joyce came back and found them dead.

Ruby tips the bloody water into the sink, fills the bucket and empties it gently over the flowers. The water shimmers like a veil. A wave of warmth rushes through her body, and for a moment she feels a presence, benevolent and grateful.

What gives? She sets down the bucket and looks around. She is alone, as expected. And yet it's there, *she's* there. Momma believed in spirits and, right now, Ruby believes in them, too. Joyce is watching. And she is thankful for the water.

A breeze strikes up and the feeling vanishes. Ruby flinches. She's getting all worked up over this.

Back in the kitchen, she gets to work on the cupboards, which have a good deal of splatter on them. There is paper towel sticking to it, too. More paper towels sit on the counter, next to a brown beer bottle. Blue Ribbon brand.

The more she stares at it, the weirder it looks. It sits prominently in the sunlight, capless and empty. There are traces of dust along the neck and across its belly. The label looks like someone's worried at it quite a bit.

Joyce doesn't drink beer. Mr Haney does, probably, but she's never seen beer in the house, unless there's been a barbecue. And if he'd drunk this in the last few nights before Joyce went missing, she would have thrown the bottle out by now.

Slowly, she stretches out her hand and picks it up. The powdery dust picks out faint splotches. It's been fingerprinted by the police.

Her neck tingles and for a moment she feels sickness spreading in her stomach. This is a crime scene. Joyce is gone, and the Lord may keep her safe.

She stares at the fingerprints for a moment, before catching a movement from the window. It's Mr Haney with the garden hose. Some little voice in the depth of her mind pipes up, warning that he better not spot her going over things that ought not to be her concern.

She grabs the trash can and throws the bottle inside. It disappears with a muffled thunk. She kneels back down and scrubs at the blood again, turning it into a waterfall that rushes over the kitchen tiles and pools around her knees.

Outside, Mr Haney switches off the water and starts talking to Nancy Ingram, who has just appeared. She is clearly angry. Their voices are growing louder. Ruby stops wiping and listens.

'All day,' Mrs Ingram says. 'And last night, too. Lily . . . I don't know what's wrong with that kid. She doesn't settle.'

'The house is not ready,' Mr Haney says firmly; he sounds as if he wants to scream. 'Not now, Nancy. Not yet.'

Lily's cries rise up and Mr Haney makes shushing noises.

'Yes, now,' says Mrs Ingram. 'Frank, I need to go to work. I can't stand it any longer.'

'How do you think I feel?'

That seems to soothe her. The voices grow quiet again. Ruby commences to wipe the same spot over and over. But there is nothing else to hear.

A movement draws her attention. She turns around and

nearly flips. The kitchen door opens slowly and a tiny face peers around the door frame.

It's Barbara. Her eyes are red and tired, her hair stands up like a mop. The lace on her left shoe is untied and her dress is crinkled as if she's slept in it.

'Whoobie,' she whispers.

Ruby drops the cloth into the pink water and opens her arms. Barbara stumbles into her embrace. Ruby pats her back and strokes her hair and mutters soothing nonsense. Barbara does not make a sound. She is so floppy that Ruby eventually holds her at arm's length and looks into her eyes.

'You OK, Barbie-baby?'

Barbara averts her face. Her gaze roves over the kitchen floor and up to the window. 'Is Mommy back?'

'No, not yet. You need to be patient.'

'I wanted to help clean up.' Barbara's lips begin to tremble. 'I wanted to be good. I promised I'd be good.'

'You're being very good, baby.'

It's too late. Big, crystal tears form on Barbara's eyelids and roll down her cheeks. 'I wanted to clean,' she squeaks. 'I wanted to help. They made such a mess. I wanted to make it nice again for Mommy.'

'But you see? I already made it nice,' Ruby replies, but then she considers.

She opens the Cocoa Puffs and sprinkles a few on the floor just out of Barbara's sight. Then she takes a clean cloth, rinses it under the faucet and hands it to the girl.

'Look over there. I forgot that bit. You can clean it for me.'

A little smile emerges beneath Barbara's tears. Ruby gets the kiddie apron that hangs in the cupboard and places it around Barbara's waist. The girl gets to work, silent and scrupulous, as if she also has a boss who'll run a gloved finger across the surfaces to check.

When they're done, Ruby gives Barbara a glass of water, which she downs eagerly. Some of it spills over her dress, which needs changing anyway. So she takes Barbara's hand and walks her up to the nursery.

Just at that moment, Mrs Ingram comes out of the lounge, her fiery red lips pressed into a line. She stops dead when she sees Ruby. 'Frank,' she shouts. 'Come here.'

Mr Haney steps into the hallway. He has Lily on his arm and there is sweat running down his temples. 'What are you doing?' He frowns. 'I'm not paying for playtime.'

'Just getting Barbara a fresh dress.'

Mrs Ingram clicks her tongue. '*She* is still working here? Are you mad?'

'Someone needed to clean up the . . . the kitchen.'

'My God, Frank. Don't even remind me. I can't bear it.'

Mrs Ingram lets out a little moan and lifts her hand to her face. Mr Haney shifts Lily to his other hip and pats Mrs Ingram's shoulder. But his own voice is shivering. 'Nancy, it's all right. She'll be back, you'll see.'

Mrs Ingram nods. 'I need a drink, Frank. Shall we have a drink? Ruby can take the children, just for a bit, right?'

Mr Haney frowns a little but then hands Lily over to Ruby. 'Just put her down . . . I don't like to leave the phone, in case they ring.'

'Sure thing, sir.' Ruby does the math in her head. She can stretch bedtime to at least half an hour. *It's your money, mister.*

In the nursery, she settles Lily in her bed. The girl is still crying, quiet but inconsolable, with occasional little hiccups. Ruby remembers how eagerly Barbara drank her water. Thirst. That's what it is.

She fills up a bottle and snatches a few cookies from the kitchen. Lily downs her water with her little cheeks pumping. Barbara devours three cookies, then curls up on the floor and falls asleep. Lily doesn't want to eat, but soon closes her eyes as well.

Suddenly, all is quiet.

Well, not quite. Voices are drifting from the living room. But the nursery is up on the mezzanine, too far away to hear.

Ruby lifts Barbara into her bed, arms herself with Barbara's dress and goes into the bathroom, which is right at the top of the mezzanine stairs. The sink is by the door, so she can stand in the doorway and put her head out and pretend to wash the dress.

Mrs Ingram is sitting on the sofa, her back facing Ruby, while Mr Haney is pacing up and down the lounge, doing a prayer dance around the telephone. He's holding a glass with something amber in it.

'Do you . . . do you think she found out?' he says.

Mrs Ingram takes a puff from her cigarette. 'Not from me,' she replies. 'No, Frank. I don't think so. How would she know?'

'She might have seen something, or overheard . . . Hell, Nancy, maybe we made a mistake.'

'Are you regretting it?' Mrs Ingram's voice is cracked, as if she's trying to hold something down with great force. 'Are you saying you're regretting everything?'

'Nancy. My wife is missing. Joyce is . . . This is not the time.'

'I'm sorry, Frank. I miss her, too. I—' Mrs Ingram exhales. 'Did you hear from the detective?'

'He asked me whether Joyce was seeing someone. Whether she . . . Oh, I am such a damned fool.'

'You're not, Frank.' Mrs Ingram gets up and lays a hand on Mr Haney's arm. 'She wouldn't. She couldn't. I know that better than anyone. She loves only her children.'

'And me,' Mr Haney says. 'Joyce loves me.'

Mrs Ingram lets her hand drop from his arm. In the ensuing silence, Ruby turns up the water faucets and makes a good splash with the dress. Then she goes to the kitchen and drops it into the laundry basket.

When she returns to the hallway, Mrs Ingram is gone. Mr Haney is standing by the garden doors. The bright sunlight looks all wrong on his face, which is drawn and pale. He has turned into a ghost, and the telephone is the bell that's gonna summon him to heaven, or to hell.

'The children are sleeping,' Ruby says and adds for good measure: 'Lily was thirsty.'

He looks up, as if waking from a dream. 'Took you long enough.'

Without further ado, he fishes a ten dollar bill and a couple of bucks from his wallet and holds them out. His hands are strong and big, broad-palmed like a farmer's.

'Same time tomorrow,' he says. 'I just . . . there's so much to do. I might have to head into the office, and the laundry needs doing. Nan— Mrs Ingram will do some shopping. When you're done, you can feed the kids and put them down.'

There is a little twang of warning in Ruby's belly. She ignores it and says: 'Of course, Mr Haney.'

The phone rings. Mr Haney all but somersaults toward it and picks it up. He waves her out, and she shuts the door behind her.

While Ruby waits for the bus, she checks her nails. There are traces of brown stuck in the grooves of her skin. She rubs them against her blouse, but the blood won't come out that easily.

Chapter Ten

Mick

'And when, goddammit, were you going to let me know?'

Mick slams his coffee mug on the table. It makes an ominous bang and a zigzag line appears around the handle. Coffee slops out and pools on his desk. He is seeing red, literally. Bubbles of it are dancing in front of his eyes. They blot out the moronic face of Sergeant Hodge, who is standing there, cap in hand, chewing on his words. Standing, because a senior officer of the force can't even get a second chair in this godforsaken backwoods shithole of a station.

'Didn't seem important, sir.' Hodge crumples his cap to his chest. 'On account that we found nothing.'

Mick closes his eyes until the red spots fade and he's reasonably certain he's not going to keel right over with a coronary. He spent the whole morning running around the mall, only to find out that Hodge and Simmons had already done interviews there without result.

'It was her last damn trip to the outside world, man.

She must have talked to someone. Paid at the grocery store till. Had some boy carry her bags. How can she walk around that place with her cute little ankle-biter dressed like a show doll and no one notices?'

'Dunno, sir,' says Hodge.

'And now I've wasted half a day.'

'Sorry, sir.'

Mick picks up the mug and slams it down again just to hear the satisfying crack of the handle breaking off. Hodge makes use of the moment to beat feet. On his way out, he bumps into Jackie, the secretary, who is waving a pile of papers. She takes in the state of Mick's office, of the man himself and the broken mug. Her face pinches.

'Detective, the call-ins.'

'Thanks, Jackie.'

'And might you keep it down? I can hardly hear the phone.'

'They've been ringing, then?'

'About three dozen callers.'

'That's a lot. Any good ones?'

She looks up and there's a flicker of surprise in her eyes. Seems her opinion doesn't get asked much around here.

'Two or three, I'd say.' She smiles. 'Also a UFO crank, three unemployed bounty hunters and a long-lost sister.'

'Thank you.'

She lingers a moment, half-hopeful. 'Anything else?'

Mick thinks about throwing her a bone, but he is in no

mood. 'Get me a second chair,' he snaps. 'And close that door.'

He flings the mug into the trash where it cracks apart entirely. Business thus taken care of, he spreads the call-ins out on his desk.

He warned Murphy that this would happen, but the chief was adamant that there should be a reward for information, and it should get advertised in the press. The mayor, keen on maintaining Sunnylakes's image as the ultimate idyll, has pegged it at one thousand dollars. Now, three dozen nutcases have burned up the lines, all sure that they've solved a riddle that's dumbfounding a professional detective. Three dozen more problems fanned out on his desk, slowly soaking up the coffee stain.

Seems like everyone who went to Paradise Plaza Mall yesterday has some kind of theory. She's been zoomed away by aliens, dragged into a van by 'Soviet-looking' foreigners, carried off by two big Negroes. A few callers are a little more sedate: 'Saw a woman with toddler struggling to park her car, offered help, was rebuked'. 'A neat-looking woman sat by the fountain and fed a child some strawberries, which are out of season, thought it strange, please call if reward'. 'Woman in question bought painting materials – would recognize'. 'Woman, possibly victim, looking slatternly, seen at Clarkson's inquiring about marital aid. Might have gone off with lover.'

Mick sighs. He'd talked to every goddamn shelf-stacker in the grocery store until the manager asked him to leave and come back after hours. But what's the point of that? It was as if Joyce hadn't been there at all.

And then he realizes. The refrigerator was empty, the shopping list still tacked up on its door. Joyce Haney had, in fact, not gone grocery shopping at all, but had been looking for something else.

Maybe . . .

Blood rushes to his head. He shuffles the papers, then finds the one he is looking for. *Painting materials – would recognize.*

He grabs the phone, dragging his tie through the coffee stain, and misdials only twice before he gets a connection. The phone is picked up by a matronly-sounding woman. 'Reubens Arts and Crafts, how can I help?'

Paradise Plaza Mall is dowsed in twinkly music, a mirage in the dust-strewn nowhere between Sunnylakes and what's been built so far of the Santa Monica Freeway. Inside, walkways crisscross the space at every level. In the foyer of this air-conditioned splendor stands a metal sculpture depicting some sort of fan or garden rake or inter-dimensional force field. Modern. Everything here is modern.

Mick resists the urge to kick a little boy who is leaning over a chrome pool shaped like a honeycomb. Behind the pool sits the information bubble – that's the best description for the plastic barnacle growing out of the floor. The bubble is manned by a guy in a green suit.

'Reubens Arts and Crafts,' Mick says. 'Where can I find them?'

'Section B,' the man responds.

'All right, and where's that?'

'This is section D.'

Mick rests both his palms on the bubble. 'And how, my good sir, is a body to get from section D to section B?'

'Please keep your hands off the glass, sir. Section B is on the second floor. Up the stairs, past the partition and into the red zone.'

'The red zone? I thought they weren't big on consumerism over there.'

'Pardon me?'

Mick bows. 'You've been extremely not helpful, thank you.'

The man gives him a pained smile. 'Have a wonderful day, sir.'

Mick heads upstairs and onward until the carpet changes to brick-red. On the other side of a walkway he discovers Reubens Arts and Crafts.

The store is flanked by an underwear retailer displaying discrete bathrobes and children's petticoats, and a radio store crammed with gleaming steel and beige plastic. In contrast, Reubens' store front is a jumble of colors and materials. Yellow knitting wool in a green box. A set of inkwells next to a rainbow of crayons. An antique frame with a neat little watercolor, leaning against a basket of twine that only women would know the use for.

On entering, Mick's neck muscles tense. It's the same feeling he gets when he's forced to attend Prissie's high school plays or pick Fran up from her committee. He's in foreign territory, trespassing in an alien world.

A lady approaching her autumn years sits behind the counter. She licks her finger and flicks a page in an exhibition catalog, then looks up and pulls her eyebrows into quizzical union. Keen to maintain a veneer of professionalism, Mick picks up a ball of wool, looks at it and puts it back. But it's too late. The woman knows he's an impostor.

'Can I help you, sir?' she asks.

He flashes his ID. 'Mrs Reubens? I'm Detective Blanke, Santa Monica PD. We spoke earlier?'

'Oh, yes.' Mrs Reubens closes the catalog and puts it aside. 'I'd be only too glad to help. But if someone enters the store, please pretend you're a customer. I wouldn't want . . .'

She leaves it unsaid, and something about that makes her instantly sympathetic. She's not out to get a lick of fame. She really wants to help.

'You knew Mrs Haney?' Mick asks.

'Not exactly.' Mrs Reubens adjusts her glasses. 'She frequents my store. Not a regular. But she would come in every . . . oh, three to four months, perhaps. A few times a year.'

'Doesn't sound like often enough to remember her.'

'Well, sir, it's a funny business. She would browse for a

long time. She'd look at all our inks and paints and paper stock. She'd open a box of crayons, run her fingers along the weighted paper, really take her time. But she never bought anything.'

'Never?'

'Not even an eraser, sir. And when I asked if she needed help or if she was looking for anything specific, she'd just decline politely and move to another area of the store. At first I suspected her of . . . well, of being long-fingered.'

'You thought she was stealing?'

'Maybe.' Mrs Reubens looks to the side. 'I don't mean to talk ill of my customers, but the folks in Sunnylakes are . . . there's a lot of theft. More than we used to get in the city center.'

'You had a store elsewhere before?'

'In Clifton. But business there was on the downturn ever since the freeway cut us off from Brentwood. When they built the mall, I knew it was sink or swim. I relocated.'

'I see.'

'Anyway. Mrs Haney came in on Monday, and bought a set of watercolors, several reams of paper, a sable brush, coal pencils, a putty eraser, whitening and a box of children's crayons.'

Mick takes out his notebook. Now there's something to digest. 'But you said she never bought anything before.'

'That's why it was so remarkable.'

'You talked to her?'

'Not much. She seemed . . . elsewhere with her thoughts. I didn't want to frighten her away.'

'Did she use store credit?'

'Oh, no, she paid for everything in cash. But I remembered her face and outfit. She had her little girl with her. I put all her items into a big bag, and added the small bag she was already carrying. I asked her if she had a significant project planned. She said yes and I said I hoped she would enjoy it, or something along those lines. And she said, "Oh, I will not enjoy it. No one enjoys purgatory".'

'That sounds odd.'

'It did. She left in a hurry.'

'You said she already had a bag. What was in it? Groceries?'

'No, it was too small for that.' Mrs Reubens cocks her head. 'It was a brown paper bag. Not branded. But when I picked it up, it rattled. And there were bottles inside. Pill bottles, I should say.'

'You didn't ask her about it?'

'Of course not.'

Mick opens his notebook and writes 'Pills' on a blank page. Then he draws a lot of little circles around the word. Watercolors. Paper. Coal pencils. And crayons for the kids.

'What was she wearing?' he asks Mrs Reubens.

'A yellow dress and matching hat,' comes the answer, fast like a gunshot. 'The dress had a bow around the waist. She was also wearing gloves. Very neat, I thought.'

'What do you mean?'

'Well, I had the impression that she was dressed for an occasion. Maybe something to do with the Women's Improvement Committee.' Mrs Reubens points at the catalog. 'The first time Mrs Haney came here, it was with the leader of the committee, Mrs Crane. She shops here frequently and organizes art classes and trips to the city . . .' She holds up the catalog. 'Amblioni is exhibiting in LA at the moment. I thought maybe Joyce Haney had signed up.'

'So, she might have been on her way to an art class?'

Mrs Reubens hesitates. 'Well, if she was, she wasn't looking forward to it.'

'I don't understand.'

'Her eyes were . . . stirred, somehow. I can't quite put my finger on it.'

'Scared? Angry?'

'No, not like that. She was all smiles and friendliness. But it seemed to me that the dress was a show. That underneath it she . . .'

Mick waits.

'She was coming undone,' Mrs Reubens says. 'Her eyes were dazed. You know, when the letter came that my brother, God rest his soul, had died in Korea, my mother had the same expression. Desperate and fearless, because there was nothing left to fear. She . . . Joyce Haney looked as if Fate had already brought down its hatchet and she was just waiting for her limbs to fall off.'

Mick wants to reply, but he is interrupted by the twinkle of chimes. A lady with a little dog on a leash and a sour expression enters the store. She is carrying a bag from which poke several balls of baby-pink wool.

Mrs Reubens puts on a professional smile and waves. 'Hello, Mrs Smith. Was the color not right after all?'

'Thank you,' says Mick. 'You've really helped me.' And looking at Mrs Smith's curious expression, he adds loudly: 'You've helped me immensely. I cannot wait to tell my wife about your incredible store.'

Outside, he examines the store window again. There are more colors here than he ever knew existed. Their names sound like magic spells – viridian green, phthalo blue, alizarin crimson. By comparison, the handful of items displayed by the underwear store look cheap and sterile under the fluorescent lights.

He takes a closer look – and freezes. In the window, sprawled out over a plastic cube, is a blue sleepsuit with little white feet and tiny cowboys falling off their horses.

He rushes into the store and is immediately surrounded by several young women in gingham dresses, who are wearing too much hair spray and don't know anything about anything. Finally, a matron appears and confirms that several sleepsuits were sold on Monday, and yes, one of them to a lady in yellow. The sleepsuit is a popular item, she says, and no, they don't keep a record of customers.

He eventually finds the mall's exit and steps out into the dusty afternoon. The freeway is a silver river. Traffic has narrowed to a trickle around the huge construction site on the road to Sunnylakes, where they're building the flyover bridge to connect the burbs to LA proper. Mick gets into his Buick and inches his way back toward Santa Monica.

So, Joyce Haney had picked up some pills. For what? Pain? Periods? A cold? He's going to have to find her doctor and have a long and serious talk with him. Because he has a nasty little suspicion. What if she went to have something else seen to? A little problem best taken care of while the dear husband is out of town? Something illegal, something the doctor needed to do in the privacy of her own house, in the afternoon?

What if that something went awfully, terribly wrong?

And another thing pesters him. Where are those art materials? Certainly not at 47 Roseview Drive. The search of the house turned up nothing. And he doesn't recall any watercolor paintings on the wall. What happened on Monday that made Joyce Haney crave an artistic outlet, just hours before she disappeared?

One thing is for sure. When he's done with the doctor, he will have to pay a little visit to the Sunnylakes Women's Improvement Committee.

Chapter Eleven

Mick

The mall doctor, a Dr Morton, proves a total dud. Mick calls from his office and finds out that the pills were for indigestion. Yes, several bottles, because Mrs Haney is a busy housewife and does not have much time to drive around. How she found him? He was recommended, by a Mrs Genevieve Crane.

Mick gets Sergeant Hodge on the job to check Dr Morton's alibi for Monday afternoon. He wipes his forehead with his shirtsleeve, takes one look at the paperwork in front of him, opens the door and shouts in the general direction of the front desk, 'Jackie, get me some details on the Sunnylakes Women's Improvement Committee. And chase the boys on the switchboard for the Haney family's phone records.'

'On it, Mr Blanke,' comes the swift reply.

The heat clogs his brain. He shimmies open the window to about a hand-width. It won't budge any further. A breeze enters the room, shy like a prom girl, and just as unobtrusive.

To while away some time, he flicks through the crime scene photographs of 47 Roseview Drive, which were delivered this morning, along with a complete inventory of the house. They confirm what he already knows. There is no sign of any art materials, nor any mention of pill bottles. There were pills in the medicine cabinet: acetaminophen, Appetrol lunch substitutes, Miltown, children's aspirin and cough syrup. Nothing for indigestion.

He mulls over his theory. It will be very difficult to prove, but it fits the picture. Dr Morton, trusted doctor of the Sunnylakes ladies, might be providing illegal abortions. And Mick, unfortunately, has been to more than one Brooklyn tenement, staring at what happens when abortions go wrong. It would explain the blood and the paper towel, and perhaps even the sleepsuit.

So, here's how it goes down. Joyce Haney goes to Dr Morton, asks for an abortion and obtains some pill bottles, maybe painkillers to prepare for the operation. She then patronizes Reubens Arts and Crafts and buys all the trappings for an aspiring watercolor artist. And when she exits the store, she passes the underwear store, sees the blue sleepsuit and buys that, too. Why? Well, who knows. Hormones, maternal hysteria, grief. Something like that. In the afternoon, Dr Morton comes to the house to perform the operation, while the younger girl is asleep. The older one is sent outside. But it goes wrong. Joyce is injured. Or dies.

He sets the photographs out again. Even in black and

white, the kitchen looks sunlit and picture-perfect. Except for the blood. And the beer bottle on the counter.

A beer bottle? He spools back to his first visit to the place and his mind comes up blank. How could he possibly have missed it? And whose beer would it be? Haney's, perhaps, or maybe Dr Morton had to steady his nerves before . . .

Jackie pokes her head into the office and hands him a note. 'Got her address.'

'What? Whose?'

'The head of the Sunnylakes Women's Improvement Committee, Genevieve Crane. Lives in Portland Road.'

He nods and waves her away. It's just past 4 p.m. Still an hour or so of visiting time left. But first, he dials the Haney's number.

Frank Haney picks up after the first ring. 'Hello? Yes, hello? Haney here.'

His voice is breathy. It gives Mick a tingle in his spine. It's been three days and no news from his wife.

'It's Detective Blanke,' he says. 'Just calling you with an update. To be honest, it's still tricky. We've had some reports from the public. Your wife was sighted at the mall.'

There's a pause. 'I know that, I spoke to your sergeant. You got nothing. Three days, and you've got nothing. You're useless.'

Whatever sympathy Mick felt drains away in an instant. 'I did speak to a Mrs Reubens this afternoon. She owns Reubens Arts and Crafts, and she said your wife was in her store on Monday morning.'

The silence on the other end of the line is just a second or so too long. 'So?'

'She bought watercolors, paper, brushes, erasers and so on. But we didn't find any of that in the house. Have you seen any art supplies floating about?'

'Nope.' Haney's voice is very even.

'Does your wife like to paint?'

'She used to. When we met. She gave it up when we had the kids. Maybe . . . she could have bought the paints for a friend.'

'Which friend?'

'Oh, I don't know.' Haney's voice grows impatient. 'Someone from the women's committee. They very much enjoy art, as far as I know. There was a girl there who was friends with Joyce and didn't have much money. Joyce sometimes helped her out with rides and such. Diane or something. I can't remember her name.'

'Thanks, we will look into it.' He thinks of the skittish woman he met on his first visit to Sunnylakes. He'd bet his right arm it's Deena.

'You better. I'm running ragged here. I want my wife back. If you don't find her by the end of the week, I'll file a complaint for negligence.'

'Sure, Mr Haney.' *Have a wonderful day, sir.*

But Frank Haney has already slammed down the phone.

Mick doesn't even get time to wipe his forehead before the phone rings again. He picks up and grunts.

A woman's voice responds. 'This is Florence Delawney.'

It takes him a moment to connect the dots. 'Joyce Haney's mother?'

'Stepmother.' The voice is curt and cutting. 'Have you any news about our daughter?'

'Nothing yet, I'm afraid,' Mick answers. He pulls the phone across his desk and tries to lean away from the sunshine. 'Thanks for returning my call. I'm Detective Blanke, I'm working on the case.'

'I really don't see how we can help you.'

'Well, let's start at the beginning. How old was Joyce when she came into your family?'

'Twelve. She was a ward of the state. She had lost her parents. Bill and I decided we should do the Christian thing.'

'You knew her family?'

'Dear Lord, no. No, we do not associate . . . We were looking to take in a child from a disadvantaged background, but we had no prior knowledge of the family circumstances. If we did, we might have . . .'

An ominous pause ensues. Mick uses it to reach for his soda and takes a deep draft. 'Joyce's parents died in a fire?'

'Yes.'

'And was Joyce deeply affected by that?'

'A little. Her mother was the one who started the fire. As far as I know, her mental health was . . . degraded. She tried to abscond with Joyce several times. Taking her daughter out of school, going to bars alone, letting the household go to rot . . . Joyce's father tried to get her institutionalized. Of course, we knew nothing about the mother's problems at the time. It only came out during confessionals we held with Joyce.'

'Confessionals?'

'Prayer, meditation. Reading the word of God. To make her better.'

'Why?'

'Mr Blanke.' Florence Delawney clears her throat with a cough so sharp it pangs in Mick's ear. 'Joyce had terrible nightmares. It was the devil meddling with her brain. We decided that the word of Christ would be the best remedy. But we were never deceived. That child held a lot of secrets, and secrets are a sin.'

'What was she like in school?'

'Oh, clever enough. We quickly took her out of the sciences and put her into domestics. She insisted on going to college but, thank the Lord, then she met Frank.'

'You appreciate Frank as a son-in-law?'

'He made her a wife and mother. As Joyce was growing up . . . well, we got a little worried. With her history, she wasn't the most attractive match.'

'You think her mother's mental health could have scared away suitors?'

'That sort of thing runs in the family, doesn't it?' Mrs Delawney sighs. 'And now it has come out. That's what I always said to Bill, as soon as we learned the truth about Joyce's parents. Blood will out, I said. We better gird our loins with the word of the Lord.'

The image of Florence Delawney's loins flashes through Mick's head, followed by a quiver of revulsion. He decides it's time to take off the gloves.

'Was there anyone in Joyce's past who could have encouraged her to run off?' he asks. 'Or someone who might have something to do with her disappearance? A former boyfriend, perhaps, or a date?'

The pause on the other end of the receiver is telling. 'We would not approve of that,' says Mrs Delawney.

'Sure, but was there—'

'We run a respectful home. It was made very clear to Joyce that men would not be tolerated unless they proposed marriage.'

Mick translates this in his head. So there was a boy. A college flirtation, perhaps, or a neighborhood sweetheart.

He finishes the soda and sets the bottle aside. The sweetness of it has made him queasy. 'Thank you so much,' he says. 'You've definitely been really helpful. Have a wonderful day.'

Once she has hung up, he takes one look at his watch and decides to postpone the visit to Mrs Crane and her women's committee. His own little realm of domestic bliss is waiting.

When he gets to the Blanke residence, dinner isn't even started. Fran arrives a few minutes after him and patently ignores his growling stomach and his not-so-subtle hint that she could have left him something on a plate if she knew she was going to be late.

'If you're that hungry, Mick,' she says, 'you can make yourself some egg on toast.'

'I just got home.'

'So did I.'

'I'm investigating a disappearance.'

'Start investigating the stove. It's still making that weird noise when I turn the gas flame up high.'

'Why don't you give me a demonstration?'

She sighs. 'Again?'

'Yes. And put some spaghetti on while you're at it.'

'Mick!' Fran frowns. 'You're in a mood.'

'I'm hungry.'

Fran rolls her eyes and disappears into the kitchen. Mick follows, his stomach gurgling. He demonstratively flings open the refrigerator door and reaches for a glass of pickles. But Fran has eyes in the back of her head.

'Don't you dare touch those.'

'What? Why?'

'They're for Saturday.'

He puts the pickles back and cuts himself a few slices of cheese while Fran putters about with the pans. She prattles on about the Santa Monica Women's Improvement Committee meeting. Eventually, she has to breathe, and Mick moves in before she can continue.

'So,' he asks, 'what sort of stuff do you talk about with the ladies?'

'Oh, everything. The woman's role in the home, recipes, childcare, husbands . . .' She gives him a meaningful look.

'And health care?'

'What do you mean?'

'Like, birth and things. Pregnancy.'

Fran blushes. 'It's a bit past that for me.'

'But the younger women . . .'

'It comes up, yes. The question of when to have children. And, you know, how not to.'

Oh, yes. That's exactly what he's getting at. 'What's the general advice?'

'Mick.' Fran looks aghast. 'Why do you need to know about that?'

'Right . . .'

'Michael Blanke, I'll ask you again. What do you need to know about preventing a pregnancy?'

He clocks her anger just a little too late. 'Jeez, Fran. It's for a case I'm working on, dammit.'

'Mind your mouth.'

He sighs. 'Sorry, darling. It's been a long day.'

'Don't you "darling" me.' She nods. 'I know. It's the Haney woman. The case is bothering you.'

Mick takes the last bite of cheese and watches Fran pour frozen peas into a pot of water. 'You're right. I have to find the bad guy, but he's staying hidden.'

'Because the suburbs are not your world, Mick. You're out of your depth. This isn't the war, where every bad guy wears a swastika.'

'A rising sun,' he corrects, and allows himself to think that it was never that easy.

Fran opens a can of cannelloni and tips it into a pan. The cannelloni make a slurping noise as they fall, trailing sauce. Inside Mick's stomach, something flicks.

'Look,' Fran says, 'there's got to be something you can get your teeth into.'

'There isn't. My wife forgot to cook.'

'Maybe I can go undercover for you. I'm a housewife and mother. Do you think I'd blend in?'

Mick watches her scrape sauce from the can. Her hair's had a recent dye job and a summer of barbecues and potlucks has added a lovely little wriggle to her hips. He resists the urge to pinch it and wonders if, in a decade or so, Joyce Haney will start to go through that same transformation of middle age, her trim little figure expanded, her dreamy eyes enveloped by wrinkles. With Fran, the process seems natural, a marital act of solidarity to match his own receding hairline and achy knees. But for Joyce Haney, the image does not quite work. It's hard to imagine her growing old.

His guts contract. Maybe she never will.

While they eat, Fran launches into the details of Saturday's cheerleading dinner for Prissie and the art exhibition that she really *must* see, because *simply everyone* in the committee is going. Mick zones out when she starts to hint at the cost of the tickets. In his mind, he turns over her earlier words. He hates to admit it, but Fran is right.

He needs someone who understands the Sunnylakes folk and their secrets. Someone who can go undercover and be neither seen nor heard.

An idea creeps into his head. *Ruby Wright.*

It's mad. But then again, he's always had a penchant for unusual methods.

Chapter Twelve

Joyce

After Nancy drives off for work, I shoo the children up the driveway and struggle under the weight of the bag. What a face Frank would make if he knew. I haven't bought any of the things we need. No corn flakes, no rice, no steaks for dinner. Instead, I've spent my budget on colors. Wonderful, beautiful colors.

I stick the paints into the back of the closet where he cannot find them. A wave of guilt rushes through me. I should focus on my duties. No matter how hard I work, I never focus on my duties well enough. He will find the proof. A dusty shelf, a sticky juice puddle on the floor. A trashcan that smells of diapers.

In the kitchen, I check the children's work. Barbara is drawing dull little houses and stick figures and flowers. But Lily does not draw yet, Lily paints. She grabs the crayons tight in her fist and lets rip. Today she's chosen red and yellow and orange. Her jagged lines cross the page with such vigor they've extended onto the EZ-Wipe tablecloth, marking her domain.

I plant a kiss on her hair. Barbara looks up at me, expectantly. But Professor Summers says not to praise a child who hasn't done good, so I ignore her and start lunch.

They don't know how good they have it. I had no paints as a child. No kitchen table covered in EZ-Wipe. Rarely a lunch simmering on the stove. I spent my nights hiding in cupboards and under the stairs. I pestered Mommy for the scraps of cabbage and the rotten oranges she begged off the grocer's. I ran after her when she fled into the night. I sat with her in the corridors of the shelters that took us in and the waiting rooms of nurses who mended the worst. I prayed with her in the pews of churches, where everyone heard our plight and no one lifted a finger to help.

And, of course, I followed her, demurely and with my braids knotted tight as ropes, when we returned a few days later. When the money ran out or Daddy found us, dressed in his best suit, with roses in his hands and a softness in his voice. I nodded when he asked me if I wanted to come back and I learned that a man is never wrong for long.

I broke nights appeasing Daddy, stroking his hands, gently, carefully. Sometimes it worked. Then he would sleep and not throw Mommy about until her screams made the neighbors pound on the wall. He would snore, his head on the kitchen table, and I would sit by him and not dare move for fear of waking him, until my feet froze to ice.

Of all those nights, I remember one the most. I was

twelve and a bit. He did not sleep but neither did he fly into a rage. Instead, he told me he loved me.

I still don't know how Mommy found out. I never breathed a word, and never will. My daddy had told me he loved me. That was a treasure too beautiful to share and too painful to bear. Love, love, treasure trove. But Mommy knew anyway. Because something inside me broke, and she found the shards of it in my panties. And this time she did not run.

She should have. Daddy threw her against the kitchen counter and she slowly turned white. He kept kicking regardless. *Get up, get up. Get up, you stupid whore bitch cunt you're too dumb to fuck so how dare you question me dumbo bitch how dare you tell me what I can and cannot do with my own daughter—*

She never got up. Daddy threw a blanket over her and said, *It's you and me now, honey.* You and me. Lemon tree. We'll be happy as can be.

I should be upset by this, shouldn't I? I should find myself raging and crying. But I am calm as an ocean in the sun. Because it does not matter. Nothing matters today.

I pick up Lily's drawing. The colors dance across the page like flames.

I never told anyone the truth about my dad, and I never will. Mommy told everybody about her bruises. The district nurse and the police and the preacher.

And what good did it do her?

Chapter Thirteen

Ruby

All through Thursday morning, Barbara clings like a shadow. She follows Ruby around the house, stands in doorways and by tables, always silent, sometimes sucking her thumb. Ruby tries to involve her. She hands her a cloth for the baseboards and even squirts a little soap on the bathroom tiles so Barbara can help with the mopping. But she gets no response.

It's when she is crouching on the floor and wiping around the back of the toilet, where Mr Haney's pee dribbles and dust bunnies gather in unholy union, that Barbara sneaks in and simply leans against Ruby's back.

Ruby freezes. She turns around and curls her arms around the girl's body, swallows her right up. She runs a hand over that doll hair and pats the tiny shoulders. The bones of Barbara's spine are frail as a bird's.

But then Mr Haney's footsteps sound in the hallway. Ruby untangles Barbara's arms and resumes scrubbing. Barbara takes up position next to the sink and observes.

'Whoobie,' she says after a while, 'can you stay in my room?'

'I don't stay here, baby. I gotta go home.'

'But can't you stay tonight? I don't want to be alone.'

'You're not alone. You got Lily and Mr . . . your daddy.'

Barbara looks at the floor. 'I had a nightmare.'

'Poor baby. What was it?'

'I saw a bad thing.'

'It was just a dream, Barbie-baby. It . . .'

She hesitates. The way Barbara is looking down – it's not shyness or dejection. She's scared. The girl is damn scared.

Ruby throws the cloth into the bucket with a splash and kneels down by Barbara's side. 'Do you want to tell me?'

'I found Mommy's dress,' Barbara says.

'In the dream?'

'She got angry. She told me to get out. I woke up to go tell Daddy. But Daddy wasn't home.'

'And then what happened?'

'I dreamed I was driving with Mommy but then she fell down and got full of dirt.'

'It's not real,' Ruby says, but her stomach hums with queasiness. That's some messed up dream for a little girl.

Barbara follows her to the kitchen and watches from the doorway as Ruby wrings out the cloth and scrubs the bucket clean. She leans against the door frame, her thumb stuck deep in her mouth. But she doesn't come in.

*

When Ruby knocks at the open living room door to tell the boss she is done, she spots Mrs Ingram walking across the lawn. Mrs Ingram is bouncing Lily on her hip. The little girl is wearing a green sun dress speckled with daisy flowers.

A memory slams into Ruby's mind and plays back like a movie. Joyce made that dress from scraps left over after she sewed one for herself, the fabric way too wild to wear in Sunnylakes. She'd wrapped herself up in it like a Roman lady. *Look, Ruby, I'm a field of flowers!* It had been just two months after Momma's death. Momma would have loved that fabric, and Ruby, so tired and sore, burst into tears.

Joyce had dropped the fabric and given her a hug. Ruby had never been hugged by a white woman, but she didn't even have time to be surprised, because Joyce told her a secret so big it bonded them forever. *My mother was murdered, just like yours. She was killed by a man who thought she did not deserve to live. Don't make my mistake and be quiet about it. You tell the world what happened to your mom.*

Problem is, the world doesn't want to listen. Just thinking of it now drives tears into Ruby's throat. She swallows them down and breathes out slowly.

Lily shrieks with joy. Mrs Ingram laughs and gives her a kiss. Mr Haney looks up from the TV, which is playing on silent in the background, and gives them a brief, painful smile.

Then Lily points at the TV and says, 'Mommy'.

She's right. Joyce Haney's face is flickering across the screen.

Mrs Ingram puts Lily down and gasps. 'A thousand dollars. My, that's a tidy sum.' Then she turns around and spots Ruby. 'I see *she's* still coming in. Oh, well. If she's keeping time . . . That reminds me, I have to head off to the office.' She smiles at Frank. 'Can I have Ruby for an hour or so? I've got so much laundry.'

'Sure,' says Mr Haney.

Ruby flinches. Be nice to ask her, too. Maybe she ain't got the time to spare.

But no discussion of this ensues. Mrs Ingram walks back to her house. Ruby follows her the roundabout way, through the kitchen and the back door. Barbara, still lingering, watches her leave from underneath her eyelashes. Ruby bends down, so her face is level with the girl's.

'I'll be back soon, baby,' she says. 'Try not to dream.'

At Mrs Ingram's, plates of dried-up food sit on the dining table. Remnants of a long-devoured dinner seethe in the oven and the sideboard is covered with tumblers. Mrs Ingram makes an off-hand gesture at it all and smiles.

'Had a guest last night. Get that fixed up, will you?'

'Yes, Mrs Ingram.' Ruby clenches her fists. *You said just laundry, you lying bitch.*

It takes the best part of an hour to tidy everything up and wash the dishes. Mrs Ingram spends that time in the bathroom. She emerges with her lipstick redrawn and rouge spots high on her cheekbones.

'Take the sheets down as well, Ruby,' she says. 'They need changing.'

With all that makeup on, Mrs Ingram looks horrid. Those bright red lips and her smile so full of teeth, like a vampire. Ruby nods politely and makes her escape upstairs.

Mrs Ingram's bedroom smells as if it hasn't been aired in days. It's a sharp, cloying scent, hinting at sweaty work under sheets. Ruby pinches her nose and sighs. Cleaning up other people's private mess is always the worst part of the job. Mr Haney's piss spots and Mrs Ingram's tampons. And now her funny business.

The curtains are still drawn. Ruby pulls them open and jimmies the window up. The bed covers are all over the place and the pillows are pressed flat. Both of them. Two heads slept here last night.

Ain't none of her business, really. But what a difference there is between Mrs Ingram and Joyce Haney, who would still be slipping a dirty dish rag into the wash and scooping out the ashtray while Ruby was pressing the doorbell. Of course. Ruby always pretended not to notice, and Joyce pretended that she never lifted a finger at home. *Hello, Ruby, do come in. I am sorry the house is such a mess . . .*

She shakes out the blankets and picks up a stocking that is lying next to the bed. Tangled in the covers, she finds a cuff link, shaped like a tiny wheel with a white line running all around . . .

Her stomach rolls over and heat flushes across her face. It's Mr Haney's. She puts it under the stocking on the bedside table. Out of sight, out of mind. Ain't seen a thing.

Next, she tackles the sheets, which are dark purple and match the lavender carpet and curtains. When she pulls them off, she finds two little smears in the center.

Nausea rushes over her. Since she's got Joseph in her life, she knows where those smears come from. The thought of Mr Haney rolling around atop of Mrs Ingram, grunting and groaning . . . Oh, Lord, did Joyce ever know?

What if she found out? Frank and Nancy think she was oblivious, but . . .

A stab of fear pierces her heart. She drops the sheets and picks up the cuff link again. Yes, what if Joyce found out? What if she confronted her cheating husband? What if he got really, *really* angry and—

'Put that down.'

Ruby shrieks. Her muscles freeze up in terror. Slowly, she opens her hand. The cuff link drops to the floor.

Mrs Ingram is standing in the doorway. She is wearing a black blazer over a flesh-colored blouse, unbuttoned just far enough to show the canyon between her breasts. Her lips part in a strange smile. Ruby snaps for air. That's it. She's gonna get sucked dry by a vampire woman.

But Mrs Ingram merely asks, 'Are you done in here?'

'Nearly, ma'am.' Ruby exhales until her heartbeat stops pushing up her throat. 'Just getting the sheets.'

She picks up the pile of laundry and walks toward the door. Mrs Ingram steps aside. Her eyes fall onto the white smears and then lock with Ruby's.

The look in her eyes is . . . triumphant. She had sex last night, and she wants Ruby to know. Now she and Ruby share a secret, and that gives Mrs Ingram power. She drinks it right up through her parted vampire lips.

Ruby's heart starts to race like a pimp's Corvette. The carpet wobbles underneath her feet as she makes her way downstairs. It feels like walking over the crooked floorboards at Aunt Emmeline's house. She moves on autopilot into the kitchen, where she stuffs the sheets into the washing machine. Her hands pour in the suds and press the buttons, but her mind is a maelstrom of panic.

She doesn't know I know who she was with. She cannot possibly know that I recognized those cuff links. Dear Lord, make that she doesn't know. Dear Lord, who gave His only son, protect me from the sinners and hold Your hand over me, amen.

Eventually, her eyesight clears and she's able to breathe again, careful and controlled. When she walks back into the hall, Mrs Ingram is already by the door.

'Time to go. I haven't got all day.'

Ruby looks her square in the face. Like Momma said, you gotta tackle the devil head-on. But all she can see in Mrs Ingram's eyes is impatience, and that slight hint of toothache that so many white people get when they look at a Negro.

Outside, Mrs Ingram gets into her car and drives away. Ruby crosses the lawn back to the Haney house. The afternoon sun tickles her skin. She closes her eyes for a moment and lets the light dance on her eyelids. Her stomach feels just like it did when Joseph showed her how to drive in Old Man Toby's tow truck. That pulling sensation as you accelerate; exhilarating and scary.

A sigh escapes from her chest. It's over, and she's OK.

And then the realization hits her like a slap to the face, followed by a flush of red-hot anger: Mrs Ingram has forgotten her pay.

At number 47, Mr Haney is on the phone. His voice comes flying through the living room doors, which are flung wide open. He sounds agitated. Maybe it's about Joyce.

Ruby stands by the front door, not sure what to do. She's gotta get paid. But disturbing Mr Haney would not be a good idea. And if she just hangs around here for much longer, someone's gonna see her linger and call the police.

With a pang of anxiety, she slips around the house and onto the terrace. Barbara is sitting on one of the lawn chairs.

'You're not Mommy,' she says by way of hello.

'Your mommy's coming soon.' *Pray those words will be true.*

Ruby looks around the terrace. Mrs Haney's geraniums

are drooping their heads. They're getting too much sun out here. She gets the watering can and puts it under the kitchen faucet. When she walks back out onto the terrace, Mr Haney's voice has risen.

'Please, Mother,' he says. 'I can't manage. I've got to go to work again on Monday. The children don't have anyone to look after them.'

Don't let Mrs Ingram hear that. Ruby starts pouring water and listens.

'Yes, the help is coming in every day. You won't have to do cleaning. Just cook for them and keep the kids away from the pool. I'll talk to Mr Erskine, I'm sure I can leave the office early, considering the circumstance . . .'

Then he pauses. The person on the other line – presumably Grandma Haney – seems to argue quite a deal. Mr Haney makes noises like *hum* and *aha*, and finally interrupts her.

'No, you're being ridiculous.' His voice grows sharper. 'You don't need to bring the gun. Sunnylakes is as safe as heaven, and anyway, we've got one. Yes . . . yes, I know, but that's not . . . Honestly, that has nothing to do with it.'

Ruby heads into the kitchen and puts the can under the faucet again. The hiss of water drowns out the next part of the conversation. But when she steps back outside the voices are clear.

'Mother!' Mr Haney sounds aghast. 'Joyce is fine. Her birth mother's health has nothing to do with what's happened. No . . . that was a momentary lapse of judgment. I know . . . I know, and we've dealt with it.'

Ruby bites her lip. Whatever that momentary lapse of judgement was, Mr Haney does not sound happy about it.

'She is not mad,' he says, 'she's missing. Look, let's talk about it when you're down here. I'll pick you up.'

Ruby pours water over the geraniums until it runs out the bottom of the pot, flushing away the dead petals that lie scattered across the tiles. But Mr Haney says nothing else.

Joyce wouldn't like this. The dry petals look like old wrapping paper for a present long since discarded. Ruby plucks off the dead buds and sweeps the petals aside. When she is done, the geraniums are starting to lift their heads. With a little love, they might just come right up again.

Chapter Fourteen

Mick

Traffic on the Santa Monica Freeway has come to a dead stop. The sun is beating down on Mick's Buick, gently broiling its occupant. The police radio clipped to the dashboard promises heavy traffic all the way to the 'burbs.

Mick tugs at his collar, then pulls off his tie. He better cool off. Looking like a human spam-in-a-can is not going to go down well with the Sunnylakes Women's Improvement Committee. Neither will the half-hour he is already running late. If only that damned bridge was being built somewhere else, preferably on the other side of the planet.

At the next junction, most of the cars make a right turn toward the mall. The road clears and Mick floors the pedal. Air streams through the open windows and blasts the sweat off his forehead. A quick check of the map confirms what he already knows. Portland Avenue is not in Sunnylakes proper, but in the downtown area, a town formerly known as Speckleton.

Mrs Crane's house is a handsome thing with bay windows, dark green shutters and a weathervane perched on the gable. The driveway is occupied by a big, black Pontiac and several other cars are parked along the curbside. Mick leaves the Buick and saunters up to the place, bracing himself for the inevitable protestations of concern, subtle glances at his wedding ring and the heavy cloud of perfume. And secrets. Women always have secrets. He needs to find out what really goes on in this committee, and whether it might solve the puzzle of Joyce's disappearance.

Mrs Crane opens the door, greeting him with a polite smile. 'You are a little late, the debate has already started. Please, come right in.'

She takes him to a large lounge with a thru-way to the kitchen. Around half a dozen women are sitting on scattered chairs, listening attentively to the speaker. He recognizes Mrs Kettering, dressed in a peach number that makes her pale enough to fade, and the spent-looking girl with the bad hair. Deena Klintz.

The speaker is an older woman with a tight bun and a brown skirt suit. She stops as he enters and throws a glance at Mrs Crane. 'A visitor?'

'Please, Dr Steps, continue,' Mrs Crane says.

But it's too late. His appearance has unsettled the flock. Mrs Kettering clasps her hands. Two women with pillbox hats start whispering urgently. Deena shirks away like a weasel spotting a wolf.

'Very well,' Dr Steps says. She seems a little irritated.

'As I was just illuminating, the science of home economics follows the motto that living begins with leisure. The modern kitchen must reflect this, while fostering the values of our age: efficiency, cleanliness, propriety. Look here.' She unfolds a cardboard picture of a square kitchen with white counters all around, a large refrigerator, a freezer and a humongous six-ring gas stove, which squats in the corner, dull and dominant like a Chi-Nu tank.

'The gauze curtains prevent the eyes from being drawn to the street. Other distractions, such as the radio and telephone, have been firmly banned to the living room. White surfaces and floors will show the smallest speck of dirt, thereby encouraging constant vigilance against germs. But that's not all.' Dr Steps attempts a winning smile and comes last in the competition. 'By arranging the necessary appliances in the most effective manner, a housewife can save significant time. Tests in our laboratory found that, with the right set-up, the number of footsteps needed to prepare a chiffon cake can be reduced from one-hundred-and-seven to seventy-nine. Just imagine how this will save your pep and reduce wear on the slippers.'

Some of the women whisper in appreciating tones. Mrs Kettering is taking frantic notes, while Deena chews the crumbly lipstick off her lips. Mick glances at Mrs Crane, who is sitting very erect, her face unreadable.

Dr Steps turns toward him. 'Now, sir, what do you think? Isn't it incredible how the science of economics can be just as valuable in the home as in a business?'

Mick nods. The kitchen truly looks as efficient as the office of a Wall Street tax adviser. But then Joyce's kitchen flashes into his mind. Look closer, and you'll find a trail of blood on the tiles, padded walls bulging out and every single dinner plate smashed to pieces.

'It's almost frightening,' he says.

Evidently satisfied, Dr Steps takes measure of the room. 'Now, does anyone have questions?'

Mrs Kettering pipes up. 'What brand is that stove?'

Dr Steps opens her mouth to answer, but Genevieve Crane raises a hand and, as if Laura Kettering did not exist, says, 'Thank you so much for your efforts, Dr Steps. You said your motto is that living begins with leisure. Yet, I did not see much provision for leisure time in this set-up.'

'Well.' Dr Steps looks taken aback. 'Of course, the kitchen is not a space to relax. The efficiency savings we project can be utilized in other household areas. At the vanity table, for example. Or while engaging children in nurturing play.'

'Yet, historically, kitchens were the heart of the house,' Mrs Crane continues, a little smile on her lips. 'A space for the whole family. A source of nourishment and warmth, where women gathered to share their burden, be it physical or emotional. Does your efficient design provide at all for the kitchen's historic purpose?'

'Scientifically, this is an antiquated view,' says Dr Steps and folds the cardboard picture with a snap. 'The reason why so many women in our age are succumbing to depression is precisely because they have to endure old-fashioned kitchens with all the entailing inefficiency.'

'Is it not, perhaps, because these women are in the kitchen in the first place?'

There is a moment of the finest silence Mick has ever encountered. Eight women are holding their breath at once.

Mrs Crane sees Dr Steps out. The other women start talking in hushed whispers. Laura Kettering puts her notepad away, picks up a plate of chocolate donuts and walks over to him.

Wisely, Mick asks his first question before taking a bite. 'Tell me about your committee. What do you actually do?'

'All sorts of things. Classes in art and domestic science. Fairs and summer parties. We also have a book club, and once a month we run a debating afternoon.'

'Can you tell me about Joyce Haney?'

'Oh, what a sweet girl.' Mrs Kettering's eyes fill with tears. She puts the plate down and motions for the other women to help themselves. Deena Klintz is the only one who does. 'She is ever so clever. You should see her art. She's the best of all of us.'

'Did she work as an artist before she married?'

'Well, I am not the best person to fill you in on that. You should talk to Deena. Her and Joyce are such good friends, of course.' There is something in Mrs Kettering's voice that doesn't sit right. She lowers her voice. 'We all used to think of Deena as . . . well, from the wrong side of the tracks. But Mrs Crane says it does not matter where you're from, we're all sisters of the world.'

A thought flashes through Mick's mind. He should ask Mrs Kettering if Ruby Wright could attend the next committee meeting. That would be a nice little trial by fire for the Sunnylakes sisterhood.

'Joyce used to pick Deena up from Crankton, for our meetings,' Mrs Kettering continues. 'Deena has no car.'

'Then how did she get to the search on Tuesday?'

'I gave her a ride.' Mrs Crane has reappeared. 'Do you have any news about Joyce?'

'It's been five days,' Mick says carefully. 'It's possible that she has come to some harm.' He gauges her reaction and finds none. 'Do you ever discuss healthcare issues in your committee?'

'From time to time.'

'How about family planning?'

There is a hint of guardedness about her now. 'Of course, children are an important part of a woman's life. We talk about how to raise them, how to instill good manners. And, of course, the experience of pregnancy and birth.'

'What about preventing that experience?'

Mrs Kettering's eyes widen. But before she can say anything, Mrs Crane, her voice low and cool as steel, steps so close he can smell her perfume. 'Detective, would you care to join me in the kitchen? I think we're out of coffee.'

He wants to make some quip about whether her kitchen is efficient enough for the purpose, but the words get stuck in his throat.

The place is huge, with bright windows and an ancient, much-scuffed kitchen table. Polish earthenware with hand-painted flowers lines the counters. The shelves are cluttered with herb jars, cookbooks and tins of tea.

Mrs Crane takes a coffee pot from a shelf and all but slams it onto the counter. She fills the kettle with water.

'Why are you asking about such things?'

'Joyce Haney may have been pregnant. She may have had an abortion. She went to the mall and saw Dr Morton, on your recommendation, and walked away with a whole load of pills. Can you give me an explanation?'

'About a dozen.' Her voice is frosty. 'Monthly pains. Headaches. Bloating from the heat. The prospect of one long week alone, with the kids grinding on her nerves and the dust piling up.' She lowered her voice. 'Did you know all the women here are on drugs?'

Fortunately, Mick hasn't got his coffee yet, otherwise he might have spat it all over her dress. 'Drugs?'

'Medical drugs. Doesn't that strike you as odd? These women are perfectly taken care of. They have it all: the prettiest dresses, an endless supply of Diet Rite and the best countertop mixers money can buy. And yet they all suffer from terrible ailments. Anxiety, depression, panic attacks, hysteria . . .'

Mick wants to reply that this sounds like just about normal for most women, but he's wise enough to swallow it.

'And Joyce Haney?' he asks. 'She was on such medication?'

'Yes.' Mrs Crane shovels coffee powder into a filter and places it onto the pot. 'She told me her mother had suffered from bouts of mania, and she herself had a breakdown after Barbara's birth. The move to Sunnylakes happened, in part, to calm her nerves.'

'You don't think it did, though.'

'Detective.' Mrs Crane sighs. 'I am not sure how honest I should be with you.'

'Brutally honest, please.'

'Most of the women here marry out of college. They become homemakers and raise their children and go to church. And that's it. No one is interested in their wishes and dreams. No one cares about their talents and opinions.' The kettle whistles. She takes it off the hob and pours the water carefully. 'Trust me, no one ever asked Joyce Haney what she thought about the world. She didn't need a change of location, she needed a change of . . .' She stops, takes the coffee pot and walks back out into the living room. Her frown makes Mick wonder about Mr Crane. He imagines a little man with a moustache. A henpecked fellow banned from this kitchen, who drives a big black Pontiac that gives him the respect on the road he doesn't get at home.

Mick follows Mrs Crane, looking around for Deena Klintz, but cannot find her. He approaches Mrs Kettering instead, who is standing beside a woman wearing a hat the shape of a meatloaf, gracefully offering coffee refills.

'Have you seen Miss Klintz?'

'Oh, she left.' Mrs Kettering hands him a mug. 'Sugar?'

He accepts two spoons. 'Where has she gone?'

'To work,' says Mrs Kettering. 'At the Old Country Inn. She doesn't often stay for the discussions, especially not without Joyce . . .'

'Poor Deena,' says Mrs Meatloaf. 'Her and Joyce are so close. So alike, you know?'

'When did Joyce Haney join the committee?'

'The first time she showed up was shortly after the family moved here,' Mrs Kettering says. 'She came twice, or maybe three times, but then she got pregnant with dear, little Lily. Of course, that put a stop to things for a while . . . but then Mrs Crane paid her a visit. From then on, Joyce was a regular.' A flicker of anxiety crosses her face. 'I mean, she *is* a regular, Detective. I'm sorry.'

Ah, the dreaded past tense. *Interesting.*

'You believe she might be dead?'

Mrs Kettering shudders. 'What a terrible thing to say. I'd never . . . I don't know. But Deena mentioned something . . .'

His ears prick up. 'What?'

'Well, I am sure it's not important.' She glances at Mrs Meatloaf, and the sparkle in her eyes betrays her words. 'Deena said that Joyce had one too many slip-ups in the past.'

'In what way?'

'I wouldn't know. I'm not aware of any . . . slip-ups.'

'Wasn't there something with her mother?' says the other woman.

'I don't know.' Mrs Kettering's voice falls to a near whisper. 'All I know is that Joyce's mother had . . . episodes of sorts. But that's all. Deena likes to tell a tall tale to make herself look interesting.'

'Yes, sadly she does.' Mrs Meatloaf sighs. 'No wonder poor Nancy was not at all delighted when that friendship blossomed.'

'Nancy Ingram, you mean? She wasn't happy about Deena and Joyce?' Mick tries to mimic them, raising his eyebrows and throwing them an astonished glance. It works.

'Of course not,' Mrs Meatloaf says. 'A person like Deena is improper company, especially around children. Don't you agree, Laura?'

'Indeed,' says Mrs Kettering. 'Who knows what Deena might have picked up in that diner, if you know what I mean?'

They nod with purpose.

Mick takes a sip of coffee and burns his tongue. It tastes sweet and bland. Suddenly, he feels afloat without an anchor, surrounded by sharks in starched blouses. He wonders if this is what this place is like for Deena.

He puts down his mug. 'I should head off,' he says. 'Thank you for having me.'

'Of course.' Mrs Kettering smiles winsomely. 'I hope you learned something.'

He finds Mrs Crane again and says his goodbyes. She guides him to the door. In the hallway, another thought overtakes him.

'Can I see some of Joyce's paintings?'

'They are locked up at the art center. But I could bring some round after our next session.' She opens the door, then looks him right in the eye. 'I am worried about Joyce. Very worried.'

'I know. We're doing our best.'

'No, you don't understand.' She lowers her voice. 'I encouraged Joyce to open up. To speak her mind. She has so much talent. She could have been a great artist and I thought . . . I thought she ought to try.'

'So?'

'Maybe that was wrong. What if I . . .' She stops herself. 'Please, call again if I can help in any way.'

Mick wants to say something, but then one of the women calls out from the living room. Mrs Crane slips on her perfect smile and closes the door.

Chapter Fifteen

Mick

On the drive back, Mick is in a foul mood. He cannot pin any of these women down. That's not only an unfortunate figure of speech, but the ugly truth. Especially that Genevieve Crane. She's outfoxed him. He can sense it.

He steps on the gas. He's not going to let this happen again. He needs some answers, and fast.

The Old Country Inn is a diner-cum-bar-cum-shelter for the down-and-out. Mick parks the Buick and frets about whether it will melt into a puddle if his chat with Deena Klintz takes too long.

He need not have worried. As soon as Deena sets eyes on him, her whole body tenses in alarm. She looks different here. Tired and cowed. Her pink uniform doesn't do anything for her skin, and neither does the cheap auburn hair dye growing out at the roots. An imitation of Mrs Crane's color, he thinks, and files that information away for future reference.

'I wanted to catch up with you at the committee,' he

says. 'But you slipped away. Please, just give me ten minutes. I'm sure you want to help your friend.'

Deena gives him an uncertain stare. 'I'm busy, sir.'

Mick looks around. The diner is occupied by a bag lady and her cold coffee, and two old men sharing a plate of eggs and a newspaper.

'Maybe we can sit down for a formal interview after your shift.'

'I work late today.'

'How about tomorrow?' He lowers his voice. 'Miss Klintz, time is a factor here. Joyce Haney's been missing for five days. I understand you were friends?'

She shrugs, and there is such dejection in her eyes he almost feels sorry for her. What on Earth could make her change so much between Sunnylakes and this place? He came prepared for brash, cunning, spiky Deena.

The answer is provided by the kitchen door, which releases a man who wouldn't look out of place in an underpass gutter. He's wearing a greasy shirt and his left eye peers through a throbbing shiner.

'Whaddya want?' he grunts.

'I'm just talking to Miss Klintz here.' Mick rolls his shoulders back. 'I'm from the police.'

'I can see that. You get outta here, mister. Don't need no cops in my business.'

'But Miss Klintz—'

'She not talking to you. You not talking to him, baby, all right?'

Deena nods.

'That's right. Take Ol' Daddy Gene's advice and don't talk to no cops without a lawman present. See? We know our rights, mister.'

Mick could insist, of course. He can be persuasive. He made Jason Griggs give up O'Leary's gang even though they had threatened to blow up his mammy's pie stall. With her in it, of course. But he has a feeling that while good old threats might get him somewhere with this fellow, they won't endear him to Deena.

'When's a better time for you?' he asks her.

A shrug is the only answer he gets.

'She's smart.' Ol' Daddy Gene grins. 'She not gonna talk to a cop without no lawyer.'

Mick grins back, then turns to Deena again. 'Then how can I contact your lawyer?'

She stares at him, and her lower lip starts trembling.

'Look,' he says. 'Give me a ring later and tell me when is convenient.'

He hands her his card, sends a glowering look at the fellow named Gene and leaves the establishment.

The Buick has only stood in the parking lot for ten minutes, yet somehow it has turned into a portal to the fifth level of hell. Unearthly heat billows out when he opens the door. He opens both doors and waits, while sweat seeps through the brim of his hat.

The women are the problem. Mrs Ingram, Mrs Crane, Miss Klintz. Fran is right, he just cannot get with the

Sunnylakes folks. And that's bad. Time is running out for Joyce, if it hasn't done so already.

The answer to the problem is simple, and yet incredibly complicated. There is no guarantee Ruby will say yes. In fact, he's pretty sure she'll slam the door right into his face. But he's got no other chance. If the women are the problem, maybe a woman is the solution.

He starts the car and hits the freeway. But this time, he passes by Santa Monica and heads right into LA.

The Old Country Inn is a Hawaiian vacation compared to South Central. The mayor likes to call the place 'disadvantaged'. But Mick didn't expect the broken windows, the trash in the street, the stink of sewage and burned rubber.

He turns into Trebeck Row and stops in front of number 1467, the three-story box that is Ruby's home. A 49-cents store occupies the first floor, its windows stuffed with pink toilet paper, laundry detergent and cheap matchbox cars. On one side, the wall is blackened as if there has been a recent fire. Paint is peeling from the fire escape, which is missing several steps.

He parks next to an ancient Ford with broken windows. Three little boys in washed-out shirts watch him from the doorway of the house across the road. He nods. One by one, they pull their heads back into the darkness beyond.

The door to Ruby Wright's home has no names next to

the doorbell button. After some determined pressing, the doorbell emits a feeble scream. Across the road, the little boys are replaced by two men who watch him with their arms crossed, unsmiling.

Mick's throat constricts. He rings again and calls out, half-heartedly. A curtain twitches on the top floor and a woman glances down. She's wearing a pink duster and rollers in her hair. Her face is round and very sweaty.

'Excuse me, ma'am,' he shouts.

The woman ducks away. Mick rings a third time. Then he bangs on the door. 'Miss Wright. It's Det— Mr Blanke here. Please, open the door.'

Inside, there is shuffling and the hush of whispered voices. Finally, the door creaks open to a hand-width, revealing a middle-aged man in loafers and slacks. He gives Mick a steadfast stare, but apprehension emanates from him like tobacco smell.

'My daughter is not in,' he says, each word carefully enunciated.

'I need to speak to her urgently.' Mick digs out his badge and holds it up in his palm, so the rest of the street folk won't see. 'It's regarding the Haney case. When will she be back?'

'Not for a while,' says the man, glancing backwards, where the sound of a phone conversation is drifting down the stairs.

'Look,' Mick tries again. 'I need her help. If it's all right by you, I'll wait in your place.'

'I said she's not—'

A door on the upper landing is cracking open. The face peering out from behind it is familiar.

Mick grins. 'I'll wait as long as it takes,' he says.

The man makes as if to answer, but then Ruby emerges on the stairs and cuts him short.

'It's OK, Pa, better let him in.'

Ruby guides him into the kitchen. Here, a young man leans against the counter. He flashes Mick a look of deep-set anger. Ruby's older brother, perhaps. Or a sweetheart?

Mick inhales. He didn't expect a warm welcome, not after Ruby's arrest on Monday. But that young man's glance is burning. He'll have to tread carefully.

Which is a shame, because the place feels familiar, like the hundreds of tenement kitchens he visited in Brooklyn. The sink balances haphazardly on the pipes and the wiring of the gas stove is the stuff of nightmares. But the floor is swept clean and the coffee mugs lined up on the counter are brightly colored and unchipped.

The old gentleman sits down on a chair with arm rests. Ruby plops herself onto a white plastic chair, pushes aside an open book spread out on the table and folds her arms.

'What do you want?' says the young man.

Mick turns to Ruby and sets out the case in broad brush strokes. 'So, you see,' he says, finally, 'I'm at a dead end. I need your help. I thought you could give me some inside information on the Haney family. Any clues you come across, and—'

Ruby looks at her father, who flinches. There is a brief moment in which something unspoken passes between them.

'Nah,' Ruby says at last. 'If they find out, I'm gonna lose my job. Plus, what do you think Mr Haney is gonna do when he figures I've been snooping? I got arrested once over this. That's more than enough.'

'I wouldn't call it snooping.' Mick tries a smile. 'But you must know something about those folks. Something Joyce Haney said or did, or about her family, or—'

'I know nothing.'

Mick sighs and reaches for the secret weapon. 'There is a reward,' he says. 'A thousand dollars, for whoever provides the information that solves the case.'

A second goes by, in which Ruby, her father and the young man exchange hurried glances.

'I don't want your money,' Ruby says. 'What good's that to me if I'm in jail?'

'That wouldn't happen, everything will be confidential,' Mick replies. 'I promise that not a word will get out about anything you say to me, although you might have to sign a—'

'She ain't signing nothing,' says the young man.

'Joseph.' Ruby shoots him a flaming glance. 'I can talk for myself, you know?'

'I'm just saying, don't sign nothing.'

'And I ain't. You see a piece of paper in my hand? You know what?' She jumps up and, gently but firmly, ushers the men out of the room. 'Let me have a talk with the detective. Eye to eye.'

She closes the door and sits back down. Mick smiles, but Ruby's face remains unmoved. 'You saying that you're stuck with the case?'

'Well, I—'

'That's bad. Joyce deserves better. She's got two babies, too. I don't want to help you, but I'd sure want to help her.'

'I've got authority to protect vulnerable sources.'

'Even colored ones? Or you gonna tell me now how the law doesn't see color?'

Mick swallows. 'Well—'

''Coz you know, Detective, if you change your mind and you rat me out, then I'm juiced. And if you serve me up as your prime suspect, I'm gonna hang. Simple as. So, how am I gonna know you won't screw me right over?'

A ping echoes through Mick's stomach. He prides himself in being enlightened about the race issue. *You've got to meet their community with politeness and respect*, he's said before to colleagues from traffic and Fran's bowling club friends, *and eventually they will cooperate.*

But faced with Ruby's blazing eyes, this tidy theory crumbles into dust. 'Because I promise I won't scr— reveal your identity,' he says. 'I mean it. As an honest man.'

Ruby snorts. But then she cocks her head and gives him

a smile that could be classed as sweet, if it weren't for the knife-edge in her gaze. 'I don't want your promise. Let's make a business deal. I'm gonna give you information. But only as much as I think is worth it.'

'Sounds fair enough.'

'And if you don't deliver, mister, I'm going to call on my momma in heaven and she'll tell God all about it. And he'll be the judge, because he ain't seeing color either, and his law is more just than anything we have on Earth.'

'All right,' says Mick, and his stomach roils.

'Then here's your first purchase. When I found Barbara among the trees . . . well, we went into the house and I picked Lily up and changed her diaper.' A nervous flicker runs along her nose. 'Barbara came out of the kitchen. And she said, "They made a mess".'

'They?'

'That's what she said. So there must have been someone else in the house.'

'Did you ask her about it?'

'No. I . . . I saw the blood on her hands. I thought it was paint but then I spotted what was in the kitchen. All that blood . . . And it was all so weird-looking. I had that same feeling when I was cleaning it up yesterday. The sunshine and the beer bottle. It just didn't fit.'

Mick's thoughts flit back to the crime scene photos, the bottle of Blue Ribbon parked on the countertop. He still cannot remember seeing it there when he inspected the scene. Just goes to show, he's not getting any younger. He doodles a bottle into his notebook with great care.

Ruby watches him draw. Her face pinches. 'That's all I'll say.'

'Come on, Ruby. What else? What was the Haney's marriage like? What's the word in the neighborhood?'

'It's Miss Wright. And you think the neighbors talk to me? You gotta be . . .'

Something closes up in her face and Mick knows he's not going to get any more today. He reluctantly puts on his hat, which is still moist around the brim, and tucks his notebook away.

'It's a pleasure working with you,' he says.

Ruby eyes him carefully. 'One more thing.'

'Sure. What is it?'

'Sunnylakes is a snake pit. Those women like Mrs Ingram'll say anything for the money. You better make some good choices about who you listen to.'

Mick hesitates. 'Why are you calling out Mrs Ingram? She's Joyce's best friend.'

'Yeah, right,' Ruby replies.

Chapter Sixteen

Ruby

'Ruby, you're crazy.'

Joseph enters the bedroom just as the detective's car disappears around the corner. Ruby moves away from the window and steels herself. This is gonna be a tough one.

'What's your problem?' she says. 'I ain't doing nothing wrong.'

'You're getting mixed up in shit that's gonna come back and haunt your ass. That man can't be trusted. You want to get arrested again? You think they're gonna let you go next time?'

She crosses her arms. 'I'm not gonna incriminate myself.'

'No need for that, the cops will be perfectly happy to do that for you.'

Pa appears in the doorway. He looks worried. And yet there is a glint in his eye. 'Couldn't hurt to keep your eyes open,' he says. 'If there's a reward.'

'It's dangerous,' Joseph replies. 'And sorry, sir, but do you really think they're gonna pay a Negro some money?'

'I told you, I don't care about the money.' Ruby fidgets. Why does Pa have to get involved? This clearly ain't the ideal scenario for a fight. 'Joseph,' she says, 'let's get out of this place. I'm boiling. Let's get an ice cream.'

Outside, the sun is beating down so bad you could probably fry an egg on the hood of Mr Roan's Ford. Ruby crosses Brookes and Joseph follows, the anger between them leashing their bodies together. Arguments flit through Ruby's head like glowworms, winking out before she can catch them.

'I gotta do it for Joyce,' she says, when they reach Florendale. 'She's not a bad apple. If she's still alive, maybe the detective can find her. She's got kids, Joseph.'

'Your mother had kids. Think about what happened with her.'

'You don't know a thing.' She strides ahead. Her chest burns with anger, because the memory breaks open so many smoldering wounds. 'When Momma died, Joyce was the only one who listened. 'Coz her Momma was also murdered.'

Joseph stops dead. 'She told you that?'

Ruby shrugs. 'Guess there was no one else in Sunnylakes who wanted to hear a thing like that. I . . . we understood each other. We knew how bad it felt and—'

'She didn't. Mrs Fancyhouse with her Chevrolet. You shouldn't have said a thing.'

'I had to tell someone. You don't know what it was like. Pa wasn't talking to no one. Mimi cut her arms. I had to keep it together, like, it was all on me. But Joyce really listened. She was the only one who did. We boosted each other up. She told me about her mom and I told her about Momma, and she said I should save for college and do my mother proud.'

Joseph scoffs. 'Yeah, while she got to sit in her house by her pool, doing nothing all day. Because she had you laboring for her. Some sort of friendship that is. You should hear what Leroy has to say about your dependency. At my committee—'

'Did you know Joyce went to a committee, too?' Ruby interjects. 'But one for women. Where they learn how to do for themselves.'

'And a fat lot of good it did to her.'

'Joseph.'

'She ain't no model for you.'

They have reached the ice cream parlor. Ruby feels in her pocket for cash and finds a crisp five dollar bill from the money Mr Haney handed out this morning. Joseph's hand also flies to his pocket, but comes up empty. He bites his lip and gazes over Ruby's head.

'Don't really feel like something cold,' he says.

She knows what that means. She could treat him, of course. Take out those five dollars and say, *Hey, baby, it's on me today.* But somehow, that is not an option. So she answers: 'Yeah, me neither.'

They walk back. All the while, Ruby wracks her head about how to make him see. He's right, of course. Joyce's and her life were so far apart the gap could never be bridged. But they had stuff in common, too. Things they both wanted and couldn't get. Dreams that kept going unfulfilled.

'Imagine you let girls join in with your committee,' she says. 'Like the women in Sunnylakes. That would be a thing.'

'That would be crazy, Rubes.'

'But Tamona gets to go.'

'Tamona's Leroy's sister. And she ain't no model for you, either.'

'Maybe not, but where's my committee? You think you got it all fixed up, just repeating whatever Leroy says. But I ain't learning from no one what to do.' She balls her fists. 'I got to find my own way.'

'Your way is the wrong way.'

'And yours is better?' Ruby has started to holler, and she doesn't care if people are looking. 'You always wanna change things but what have you done to change? I'm just trying to get somewhere, so I don't end up like Momma, working away all her life and dying in the street like a dog.'

Joseph shakes his head. His eyes remain dark. They make Ruby feel like she's just tried to kill a house fire by dowsing it with gasoline.

'I want to stop being just the help,' she says, and her voice cracks on her lips. 'I wanna be someone.'

'Some what? You think you gonna be an aeronautics engineer, Miss Smartypants? You gonna be a congress-woman? You gonna be president?'

'I'm gonna be a teacher.' She folds her arms. 'A science teacher. Like Mrs Cannon.'

'That what the Haney lady told you?' He scoffs. 'Seems like she failed to mention that you'll be teaching a Black school with no funding. Educating kids for jobs they'll never get. She may have been sweet to you, Ruby, but that's not enough. That white woman never actually helped you. Not one bit.'

'Well, sadly, there ain't no Black man helping me, neither.'

As soon as the words slip out she wants to take them back. But she can't. Joseph's face hardens and something in his eyes, something incredibly vulnerable, flares up and winks out.

'Joseph,' she says. 'I didn't mean—'

'Do what you want.' His voice is dead-flat. 'But don't come crawling back to me when that detective slams your ass in jail and your lovely boss ties a noose for you to go up on a tree.'

And then he turns and walks away.

Ruby stands on the sidewalk, hot and heavy and ready to scream. *You can't say that. You bastard. You don't say something like that to me.*

But instead of speaking, she sits down on the sidewalk and cries until the sun starts to set and the street grows busy with shouting and strange faces.

*

The next day, Mr Haney pays her no attention. His mother is coming down, so he's pouring over the map to figure out his route to the airport, while snapping at the girls and wondering where to get fresh flowers in this god-awful heat.

Finally, he manhandles both girls into his car and drives away, leaving Ruby to finish up.

This is her chance to look around. While dusting the shelves in the spare bedroom, she lets her eyes wander from the black-and-white sofa bed to the pale blue carpet and the silver vase, curved like a rocket ship.

And she realizes, for the first time, how truly alien this house is. Everything inside it looks like a page in a catalog. It's hard to imagine that Joyce chose these things, that she went to a store and pointed at that vase and said, 'Yep, sir, that's the one.' It's like the house is trying to convince you of perfection from the outside in. An imitation of happiness.

Only, imitation is not the real thing. It strikes her then, the secret behind Joyce's smile and her desire to be friends. Joyce was not happy. She thinks too of the stains on Mrs Ingram's sheets. She wonders if that was the last thing she thought of, before someone left a pool of blood on her kitchen floor.

Ruby lifts a few pillows, gingerly opens a couple of drawers and even leafs through a book stamped with the Sunnylakes Library emblem. But she finds nothing of interest.

How do you do what a detective does? How do you

find the truth? She'll need to educate herself. A book might hold the answer. That's what her teacher Mrs Cannon used to say. *When you're stuck, find a book.*

She tidies up and leaves the house. On the sidewalk, she thinks it over. There is no library in South Central. The one in Watts is too small to have the kind of book she needs. But there is one person who can probably help. Mrs Cannon herself.

She walks down Makee Avenue and checks her nails. Which is silly. She's an adult now and no teacher has a right to ask her any dumb questions about keeping clean. Then again, she was in school longer than she's been out of it, and Mrs Cannon has a way of instilling things so that they never leave you.

The house she is looking for is a small bungalow with a well-kept lawn and an iron fence badly in need of a paint job. The windows have proper curtains, which are always drawn, turning the front room into a red-and-yellow tinted cave of wonders. She's only been inside a few times, but they were always magical hours.

She runs her fingers along the name written underneath the doorbell, Laureen Cannon, and cannot quite bring herself to ring. Perhaps she isn't even home. Maybe she's still at Parkland, marking papers.

But then she hears muffled footsteps, and the door is flung open by a small, round woman with gold-framed glasses and a stern top knot.

'Ruby Wright, if I am not mistaken. Now there's a surprise.'

'Mrs Cannon. I . . . How's . . .'

'You come inside, first. What can I get you?'

Ruby follows her through the hallway, past a floor-length mirror. Lucky-loo that she's wearing a Sunnylakes outfit today, drab and dour. Mrs Cannon does not approve of bright shorts and bangles, and she has a way of letting you know.

The living room is just like Ruby remembers it. Tidy and neat, with wooden furniture and bookcases on every wall. Books are piled up on a table beside the couch. More books stand on the windowsill. The room smells of paper and peach water.

Mrs Cannon goes to the kitchen and returns with two glasses of water. 'What are you reading?'

The question catches her off guard. 'I'm working now,' she says quickly. 'Ain't got much time for—'

'There's always time to read. So?'

'I read the papers and stuff. But actually, that's why I am here. I need a book.'

'Surely you're capable of filling out a form for a library card.'

'Yeah, but this is the sort of book you can't get in any library. It's about criminal stuff. Like, interview techniques . . . Mrs Cannon, can you keep a secret?'

Mrs Cannon nods. Ruby tells her about Joyce and the detective. Not everything, but enough to make her former teacher pinch her chin.

'And now you want to play at being in law enforcement?' There is a hint of scorn in Mrs Cannon's eyes. 'That's quite the . . . aspiration.'

'No.' Ruby takes a sip of water. 'Actually, I want to become a teacher.'

There is a moment of silence, with just the street noise filtering through the curtains. Then Mrs Cannon swallows. 'Really?'

'Yeah . . . because of you. You were a great teacher.'

'I'm flattered, but what does that have to do with your friend's disappearance?'

'Well, I thought you could help me, because you always helped us so much when you brought us in for detention.'

'It was supposed to be a punishment, Miss Wright.'

'Yeah, but honestly, like . . .' She dares a smile. 'It was really for our education, wasn't it? Like, to make us appreciate learning new things. Challenging ourselves. Looking stuff up and questioning everything and . . . My pa always says the world ain't changing. And my mom used to say it, too. But coming here changed my world. That's why I want to be a teacher.'

'To change the world?'

'Well . . . yeah.' And she won't even need a stupid committee to do it.

Mrs Cannon blinks twice. She takes her glasses off, then puts them on again. 'All right,' she says. 'How can I help you?'

'I need a book on investigative police techniques. You can get me one, can't you? I . . . I can pay.'

'What makes you think I have access to such books?'

'You know people at universities, right? Like, at Black colleges. Where they have all the books.'

'I'd rather you check the local library.' Mrs Cannon stares at her waterglass. 'I'm sure they can provide . . .' But then something happens behind her eyes. She flexes her hands and bites her lip as if to stifle a roar of anger.

'To hell with it,' she murmurs. 'Lord forgive me, here I am sounding like the goddamn board of education and all I'm doing is insulting your intelligence. But for the record, I think what you're doing is dangerous.'

'Not if I know how to ask the right questions. I need to help Joyce. I feel like I can find things out there that no one else can.'

'I see.'

Mrs Cannon hesitates, but just for a moment. Then she grabs a piece of paper and a pen. Ruby has to bite down her grin. She's won.

Mrs Cannon writes for a bit. 'I have a friend at Howard who can help. And perhaps Anthony at West Virginia State . . . I will get something sent to you.' She puts down the pen. 'And how far have you gotten with your plan of teaching?'

'Still saving up for college,' Ruby says, and the brightness of her voice catches in her throat.

'How's that going?'

'It's hard, kinda. My pa says it's not gonna happen.' It's out before she can stop herself.

But Mrs Cannon's face does not slip, and that's why she is so fantastic. 'You have to make it happen. I have faith in you, Ruby. That's why I used to invite you here. I have faith.' She rises and walks over to the bookcases. After a little bit of searching, she pulls one out and presses it into Ruby's hand.

'There, that's a start.'

Ruby stares at the title. *Critical Pedagogy – Teaching the Way from Disadvantage to Freedom.*

'You make good use of that,' Mrs Cannon says, and takes her glasses off to clean them.

Chapter Seventeen

Joyce

The girls are sleeping and I lean the door to, but not without taking one last look. Barbara has a twist in her mouth that makes her look like Lucille, my mother-in-law. If only Frank could see how very much his daughter takes after his family.

That was my first mistake. I had Barbara, a girl. Then I had another, but by the time Lily came around I had made so many more mistakes that both Frank and I had stopped counting.

I shut the door completely.

The paints in the closet are calling me. But the kitchen must come first. I obliterate all traces of lunch, scrub the surfaces and spray a little King Pine. By the time Ruby arrives I will be gone, and I don't want her to find a messy house. We have some laughs together, her and I, and we've cried together, too, over our mothers who were killed by men who saw them as trash. I told Ruby things I never told anyone. That she does not have to forgive, that she should be angry over the injustice of it all. That she is allowed to hate.

Ruby has been happy as of late. She's in love, and from what she's divulged he's a decent fellow who treats her nicely. Until a few weeks ago, I hated to see young girls in love. I wanted to strangle them. Which is, of course, entirely irrational, and rather disquieting.

Then Jimmy called.

After the fire, when I came to live with Mother and Father, everything was gray. The years blended together like LiteBake, and tasted just as bland. I was praying and cleaning and getting punished. Until I started college.

Jimmy wasn't exactly a student, but he was part of the student crowd. We started talking. Then we started kissing. Then we started driving, and soon we got to the back seat.

I did not want to, at first, but Jimmy kept insisting. He said that only frigid girls held back these days and how could he be sure I really loved him if I didn't let up? So I did.

And here I made another mistake. I liked it. I liked his kisses and the way he clasped me around the waist to get me in position and I wanted it when he pushed. I really, really did. And afterward, I wanted more. I went back to him and did not care about the Bible and Mother and a wedding ring.

Jimmy, I should add, also went back to me.

He abandoned me, too. Before I married, and during my marriage as well. But he always came back. No matter how far his jobs would take him from Philly, no matter how many girls surrounded him – bar girls and his friends' girls and army girls – he always came back to me.

Which reminds me, I must get myself ready. There are only a few hours left. I run to the bathroom and open the faucets. In the bedroom, I fling my clothes away. It makes me giggle. Naked as Eve, nothing left to grieve, all just make-believe.

The bathwater is hot but I submerge myself regardless. I want to feel heat on my skin, the heat of his breath, his body pressing onto mine, the forbidden fire that Mother tried to kill with prayer and the doctors quell with medication. But the fire still roars in me, and with the afternoon approaching, I cannot wait any longer. It wants to be fanned. My fingers dance across my breast already, each touch a spark of flame.

Oh, Frank, it was never like this with you. I felt guilty about that, for many, many years. But then you stayed away when you shouldn't have and the guilt died, along with everything else that ever was between us.

Mother called me a hussy and a whore but there were only ever two men in my life. Jimmy and Frank. Shimmy and crank. You dally, you choose, you win and you lose.

One last afternoon and everything will change. I run my hands along my thighs like Jimmy used to do. My head arches back for a kiss that will not come. My palm nestles between my legs, where secrets pulse in anticipation.

Genevieve is right. I don't need a man. I can break myself quite joyfully.

Chapter Eighteen

Mick

Mick slurps a soda and puts his feet on the desk. The answer feels so close, but . . . The sleepsuit, the women's committee, Joyce's sudden love of painting. There is a secret there that he is unable to see. He might have to get Mrs Crane to hand over all her records, the details of all art teachers that ever showed up at their meetings, the names of anyone who can shed light on what goes on in Sunnylakes. The doctors.

But to do this, he'd have to ask Murphy for permission. And just as he contemplates that particular avenue of pleasure, the chief's voice comes bellowing down the corridor.

Tentatively, Mick peers around his office door. Murphy is swinging a verbal branding iron at two officers, one of which is Hodge. Or, as they say down here, he's laying down the *laaarw*.

Mick takes pity. 'Hold the fire,' he says. 'Don't waste your bullets on the greenhorns.'

Murphy spins around. 'Blanke,' he yells. 'You are the biggest failure since the fucking Pusan Perimeter.'

'I have a theory that would explain—'

'We all have a goddamn theory, Blanke. Mine is that she was struck by ball lightning and instantly evaporated. What the hell were you doing, having tea with all the womenfolk?'

'I was questioning important witnesses, if you don't mind. I—'

'I swear, if you pull over here what you pulled in New York, you'll get more than a goddamned transfer. I'm not having my officers screw a civilian just to tie up a case.'

Hodge whistles through his teeth. 'That why you're out here?'

'First of all, I wasn't scr— It was all part of the plan to infiltrate O'Leary and his boys.' He's not sure why he feels the need to explain the thing with Beverly to these idiots, but something in Hodge's astonished look begs for correction. 'That girl was a means to an end. And I kept it professional, no matter what they might have told you.'

'They told me you overstepped your boundaries, Detective.'

Mick balls his fists behind his back until he's about to break his own knuckles. 'I wasn't found culpable,' he says.

'And yet they booted you all the way across the nation, as far away from that little minx as possible. How old was she, Blanke? Legal, I hope.'

'Twenty-four. And she . . . misread the situation.'

'Sounds like she wasn't the only one.' A mean smile creeps onto Murphy's face. 'Well, at least you know your way around the ladies. Let's hear your damn theory, then.'

Mick pauses for effect. 'Abortion,' he says.

Murphy's eyes bulge out like he's auditioning for a Haunted House. Then he composes himself, folds his arms and growls two words. 'You're kooky.'

'Think about it, Chief.' Mick smacks his lips. 'How about this? Joyce Haney falls pregnant, but she doesn't want the child. She waits until her husband goes away to a conference and schedules an appointment with Dr Morton at the mall. In the morning, she goes to the mall to get pain medication. The doctor makes a house call in the afternoon, when the street is quiet. The younger child is sleeping, so she sends her older daughter out to play with the neighbors. They perform the operation in the kitchen, where . . . where it's easiest to clean up. That would explain the blood.'

Murphy puts one finger to his chin and taps it. 'Where's Mrs Haney now?'

'She could have been injured. Picture this. The doctor realizes she is bleeding internally. So he puts her in his car and drives off. Maybe he wanted to take her to a private hospital, but if she died on the way . . . well, he got rid of the body.'

Murphy sways his head. 'You mentioned a sleepsuit.

Doesn't make sense to buy that if she was planning to scrape the little bastard out.'

'Sorry, Chief. I've got no explanation for that one.'

Hodge opens his mouth and utters with some difficulty: 'Female hy-steria?'

'Do me a favor,' says the chief. 'Don't mention your shitty theory to Frank Haney, not before you're certain.'

'Gotcha, Chief.'

Back in his office, Mick presses himself into the last remaining bit of shadow and thinks. Genevieve Crane was hinting that not all was well in the Haney household. Joyce had mental problems, and Frankie-boy seemed to take it hard. Maybe he buckled under the strain and—

Before he can finish the thought, Jackie pops her head in. 'A Mrs Crane called. She wants to see you about someone called Deena. Can you stop by her house?'

'I can,' Mick replies. 'In return, can you see if you can get some tickets for the Amblioni exhibition? It's for the case.'

Jackie nods. 'Will do. You going to fill out an expenses form for me?'

But Mick is already out of the door.

Genevieve Crane opens the door in her gloves and hat. She locks up behind her and directs him to the black Pontiac parked up in the driveway. As if it were the most natural thing in the world, she opens the driver's door, sits down and unlocks the passenger side.

'Please,' she says.

It takes a moment for the whole truth to dawn. This is not Mr Crane's car. It's hers. That is . . . incredible.

She turns the ignition with an elegant flick of her wrist. Mick sits down on the passenger seat and his eyes fall on her knees, how her legs muscle up as she pushes on the gas.

Mrs Crane graces him with a half-smile. 'Are you all right, Detective?'

He pulls himself together and looks straight ahead. Mrs Crane reverses elegantly and rolls into the street. They glide out of Portland Avenue and through old Speckleton toward the freeway. The Pontiac floats like a yacht under full sail.

'It's Deena's day off today,' Mrs Crane says, accelerating. 'She wants to talk to you, but she asked me to be there, too. She's not comfortable with law enforcement. But I suspect you get that a lot, don't you?'

He dodges the question. 'This Deena, she seems an unusual addition to your group. She's not very "Sunnylakes", is she?'

'There are two sides to this community, like there are two sides anywhere in America,' Mrs Crane replies. 'There is Sunnylakes as you know it. The spacious houses, the barbecues, the husbands who work and their wives in the home. Then there is the other side. People struggling to make a dime for breakfast. The side where marriage and home ownership are a far-off dream. I invited Deena to our committee because I felt it important that the other women understand that their world and all its privileges are not awarded to all of us.'

Mick shifts in his seat. Some kind of smart sociopolitical observation seems to be in order. But all he can say is 'I see', which is only one step up from going *huh?*

Mrs Crane, undeterred, flashes a driver swerving into her lane. 'Of course, not all of the women agree with that. But Joyce and Deena hit it off immediately. Then Nancy warmed to Deena as well and the three were quite inseparable.'

That is not quite what Mrs Kettering said, but he'll keep that to himself for now. 'Why do you think Joyce and Deena got on so well?'

'I always thought they had something in common. Some kind of kindred spirit, or shared experience.'

Two orphans from the wrong side of the tracks, Mick thinks. Two women thrown into a society where they don't belong. But at least Joyce got the chance to play pretend, with dresses and a car and two beautiful children.

They exit the freeway at Crankton. Mick has never been here before, and he soon wishes it had stayed that way. Crankton is half trailer-park, half run-down farmland. Plastic bags flutter in the dusty shrubs that line the road. Cans gleam in the ditch, and unpettable dogs peer warily, their kennels made from chicken wire and palettes. There's a smell in the air: fertilizer, spiced up with a hint of sewage.

They stop at a trailer that was likely once blue but has now faded to a moldy gray. Mrs Crane parks the Pontiac, turns off the ignition, and the car gives off a purr like a panther at rest. She leads the way up the porch and, since the doorbell is hanging from its wires, knocks against the wall.

'Deena, it's me. And Detective Blanke.'

Deena Klintz emerges behind the screen door, her pale face blurred by the mesh. She flips three latches and lets them in.

The door leads right into a living room, which also serves as dining room and closet. The furniture – a sofa, coat stand, TV set and folding table – is battered, but some attempt at neatness has been made. The same could be said for Deena, who has washed her hair and put on a new blouse that reveals a little too much of her blotchy bosoms. Her lipstick is the same color as Mrs Crane's, but thick and mealy.

Coffee and bottled soda are produced and Mick, uncertain about the state of the kitchen, opts for the latter.

'Now, Deena,' says Mrs Crane. 'Tell the detective everything.'

'It's about Joyce,' Deena says, as if that weren't obvious. 'There's something you might like to know.'

Mick sips his drink and waits for the revelation. But when it comes it makes him sit up so fast, he spills a little soda on his pants.

'Jimmy showed up,' Deena says.

'Who's Jimmy?' Mick wipes at the soda stain. 'And why the hell haven't you told us before?'

'She's telling you now,' says Genevieve Crane.

'I promised,' Deena says. She adds quietly, 'I swore not to tell, because of Frank. Jimmy is an old friend of Joyce's. From back when she lived in Philadelphia. They hadn't been in contact for years. He joined the army and went to Korea. But now he's back.'

'Five years after the war ended?' Mick raises an eyebrow. 'Joyce wa— is married with children. He must have been a very good friend indeed.'

Deena cringes. 'I swore on my soul . . .'

'Tell him,' says Mrs Crane. 'Tell the detective, for Joyce's sake.'

Mick digs his nails into his legs and smiles. *The detective will strangle you if you don't spill the beans right now.*

'Joyce said that Jimmy wanted to marry her,' Deena explains. 'You know, before he went off to Korea. But while he was away, Joyce met Frank.'

'And when did this Jimmy show up again?'

'About three weeks ago. He came to her house.'

'To her house?'

'One afternoon, when Frank was out. But Joyce sent him away.'

'Do you know why? Did they argue?'

'A little. Joyce said that it took him so long to track her down. He asked why she had abandoned him. She was . . . embarrassed. And obviously worried that Frank would find out. So, she told him to come here instead.'

'This man was here?'

Deena lowers her gaze and blushes. 'Just . . . briefly. Just so they could talk in peace. Joyce didn't stay long. She told him the truth. That she wanted to stay with Frank.'

'Do you think her marriage was happy?'

Deena looks at him as if she does not know what this means. Which, Mick reflects, is probably the case. His suspicions are confirmed by her answer.

'Frank never hit her,' she says. 'And he gave her money every month for the household. She never went without.'

And if that a happy marriage makes, one Mick Blanke would be constantly somersaulting with delight.

Mick clears his throat. 'And the full name of this Jimmy?'

'I don't know. He . . . he left also. I just wanted to tell you in case it helps to find Joyce. But that's all I know. I swear, Detective.'

Mick has a feeling that this isn't quite true. 'What happened? Did this Jimmy get angry when Joyce rejected him?'

'A bit. He said he'd give her some time to think it over.'

'Ah. I thought she'd already said no.'

'Some men don't necessarily accept such an answer outright,' says Mrs Crane.

Deena nods along. 'I heard there's a reward out,' she says. 'Nancy told me.'

'Word travels fast. It's a thousand dollars for whoever

provides the vital clues that solve Joyce's disappearance.'

'OK.' She cocks her head. 'I guess . . . I will let you know if I can remember anything else.'

Of course she will. Mick clicks his tongue and fixes her with his best cop stare. 'We don't pay unless the information works out. And there's a fine for false reports and wasting police time.'

'Sure.' She holds his gaze. 'I'm not gonna waste anyone's time, sir.'

He takes a description of Jimmy from Deena and does not return to her comments until much later, long after they've driven back to Sunnylakes and he's said goodbye to Mrs Crane.

By the time he's stuck in traffic near the half-finished bridge again, he has forgotten what he meant to figure out. He curses himself for being dippy as a school kid. Something wasn't said in that battered house. Something reached for air and was drowned again before he could catch it.

Chapter Nineteen

Ruby

The moment Ruby sets foot in the Haney house she knows she's not welcome anymore. Mrs Haney senior has arrived. She is a plump lady with blueish-white hair and a crimped expression that tightens as soon as she opens the door.

'You must be the help,' she says. 'Are you always this early?'

'Mr Haney asked me to come in the mornings, ma'am.'

'How very inconvenient. What's with the bag?'

Ruby lays her hand over her tiny purse. 'My money and my bus pass.'

'Leave that on the doorstep. I'm not having you walking around this house with a bag.'

'Yes, ma'am.'

'That outfit . . . you need a uniform with slippers. Our carpets are expensive. We'll have to halve your salary for today.'

'Yes, ma'am.'

'And don't touch anything belonging to the children.'

'Yes, ma'am.'

Mrs Haney senior stares at her like the mother of all dragons. Her bile-green dress and dead hair complete the impression. She's about to shoot flames from her mouth when Mr Haney appears. He has Lily on his arm, and his chin is covered in stubble.

'The garden is suffering,' he says. 'When you're done, go water the flowers. They're drying up. It's so—'

'I don't see why you need those geraniums, anyway,' says Mrs Haney senior. 'They're in the way. The children could stumble.'

'Mother, they belong to Joyce. She wouldn't—'

Ruby doesn't catch the rest because suddenly Barbara starts wailing and she uses the moment to slip away into the kitchen.

Once the floors are done, she escapes outside. She is just drawing water into the can when Mr Haney rounds the corner. His shirtsleeves are rolled up and his hands are dirty from plucking out weeds. His mouth is twitching. Bad news. He takes the watering can from Ruby's hands and pulls five bucks from his pocket, neatly folded in half.

'My mother thinks it's best that you go,' he says.

Well, that wasn't a long time coming.

He mops his forehead. 'She thinks she can manage

alone with the kids and the cleaning. But you can come back on Tuesday for the floors. At your former rate.'

'All right, Mr Haney.'

Just at that moment, Mrs Ingram makes an appearance. She is wearing a gardening apron and clam-digger pants that make her butt stand out. The perfect outfit to fish for a man like Mr Haney. She quickens her pace and takes the watering can from Mr Haney's hands.

'Oh, Frank,' she says. 'Don't worry about the flowers. Not now.'

'They're looking horrid,' Mr Haney replies. 'Especially the potted ones. I hate to see wilting flowers, but I just can't keep up . . . there is so much to think of. Mother thinks we should get rid of them. Oh, God. I should have—'

Mrs Ingram lays a hand on his arm. 'You have other things on your mind than flowers. Give them to me. I'll throw them out.'

Ruby presses her lips together. This ain't right. These flowers are Joyce's pride and joy. And now Mrs Ingram, with her tiny butt and her hair freshly plumped, is gonna dump them in the trash. As if she's already making space for her plastic parakeet.

'How about you give them to me?' The words are out before she can stop them. 'I . . . I could look after them.'

Mrs Ingram crumples her nose, but after a moment Mr Haney smiles. 'Yes, that's a great idea.'

'Really?' says Mrs Ingram. 'You're giving them to her?'

'Why not? Better than throwing them out.' Mr Haney lifts the pot with a groan. 'Just take these home and do your best. You can bring them back once Joyce returns.'

The pot is heavy, even though the soil inside is all dried out. Mr Haney and Mrs Ingram smile at Ruby, and she realizes with horror that they're expecting a thank you.

Five minutes later, she is wondering how a body can be so stupid. The pot is huge and heavy. Most of the geraniums inside have wilted. Scraps of brown decay fly into her face every time the wind picks up. Her arms begin to ache before she's past Mrs Ingram's house. And Roseview Drive stretches on and on.

At the bus stop, a glance at her watch reveals that she has twenty minutes to wait. The watch also reminds her of Joseph, and her inner scaffold comes crumbling down. He hasn't called. She doesn't know what to do. He's her first, after all. She's still figuring all this out. But she's real gone for him. Which makes the pain so much worse.

Then it occurs to her that she just got fired. Which means no more money. And without access to the Haney house she's not gonna help find Joyce, so she won't win the reward, either. There goes the dream of going to teachers' college. She's got no man, no money and no future. *What gives?*

The bus arrives. The pot gets wedged in the gangway and the driver shouts at her to move. A white man in a cowboy hat hisses *that* word and it stabs her to the bone. She sits down in the very last row, leans her forehead against the pot on her lap and cries all the way to Compton.

By the time she gets off the bus she is wrecked with tears and thirst. Enough with this. She should leave the damned pot right here on the sidewalk. Let someone else have mercy on those flowers.

But then what will happen if Joyce returns and wants them back? *Sorry, I left them on a ghetto street. They got drowned in hobo piss.*

If only Joseph were here. He's strong. He'd lift this pot, and Ruby herself, with ease.

At home, she is greeted by Mimi, who doesn't even notice the burden in her arms. 'Where's Momma's hatbox?' she shouts by way of greeting. 'It was under my bed. Why d'you always put stuff where no one can find it?'

'Why don't you tidy up our room sometime?' Ruby hollers back. 'Then you wouldn't have that problem.'

'If you didn't have boys round the house I wouldn't have to tidy.' Something vicious creeps into Mimi's eyes. Sister love and sister hate. 'Well, sounds like Joseph's beat it, so that's one problem solved.'

'Bitch.' Ruby puts down the pot and lashes out, but Mimi dodges into Pa's room, where Ruby last saw the hatbox on top of the closet, next to the broken guitar and the suitcase with Momma's church dresses.

Tears press at her eyes once more. The geraniums turn into splotches of red and brown. She picks up the pot and maneuvers it toward the kitchen. She'll put it up on the fire escape and hope for the best.

Pa, driven out of his room by Mimi's frantic searching, comes in just as she jimmies the window open. 'What the hell is that?'

'Gift from the boss,' Ruby murmurs and hauls the pot upwards. 'I'm just gonna—'

At that moment Mimi rushes into the kitchen, hatbox in hand. 'Here, Pa,' she shouts. 'Can I have—'

And she bumps right into Ruby's back.

The pot drops from her arms; she tries to grab it but it's too late. It hits the floor with a crack and breaks apart into three shards. Earth spills out, and flowers and petals and tangles of dried-up root.

'Idiot.' Ruby pushes Mimi into the hall. 'You stupid bitch. They gonna take that out of my pay.'

'You're clumsy as a cow,' Mimi retorts. 'Anyway, those were damn ugly.'

Pa grabs them both and pulls them apart. 'Girls, stop it. Mirabelle, get your ass to your room.'

'I'm going out with Pam and Ginnie.'

'No, you aren't. You're staying put till that room of yours is cleaned up. And Ruby, you take that shit out of my kitchen. We ain't got space.'

'But Mr Haney gave me—'

'I don't care. Throw it out and stop fighting with your sister.'

Ruby sobs. She doesn't want to, but she just can't stand it anymore. The yelling, the anger, the damn awful heat. And now that she's out of work, it's gonna be this way all day, every day.

She takes the trash can from under the sink and begins to pick up the shards. What was left of the geraniums is now flattened by the weight of earth. Their roots are entangled around a few white sticks, and when she pulls at them, they come apart. She picks them up and dumps them, then shovels the earth up with her hands. Underneath the roots is something else, something curved and white. Porcelain? An old, white planter?

She brushes the earth away and picks it up.

The world stops. Her breath sticks in her throat. A cocoon rises up around her, drowning out all sound. She can do nothing but stare at what is in her hands. So small and delicate and terrible.

Pa turns around. His jaw drops. He says something, but the words do not make it through. He reaches out and pulls her up. The tiny, white skull falls from her hands and onto the earth, to nestle once more among the roots where it has been sleeping all this time.

Next thing she knows, Joseph is there. He pulls her to his chest and everything goes dark. She finds her breath again.

It comes out in great heaves against the warmth of his shirt. Somewhere behind her, Pa is exclaiming, 'Oh, Lord. Oh, Lord.' Mimi is crying. Even Joseph shakes. He keeps repeating something. 'I told you there'd be trouble. I told you. I told you.'

Ruby stays motionless until he pushes her away. He darts over to the window and pulls the curtains shut, even though only Superman could possibly get a look in. Then he kneels down and pokes at the skull with a fork.

A baby skull. Ruby, now freed from her spell, cannot stop looking. It's so perfect. Round and white, with large eye sockets covered in dirt. She wants to clean them out so the little thing can see. Joseph prods at the earth and finds what looks like a hand with tiny finger bones. There are more bones nestling among the roots. The sticks. The sticks are bones. It's a whole baby. Buried under the plants.

Joyce's baby. Joyce had a baby and she never told no one. Except me. She told me to take care of it.

'Blanke,' Ruby says. 'We need to call Detective Blanke.'

Joseph looks up and anger bursts onto his face. 'I told you not to get involved.'

'And I told you I ain't involved. This is not my fault.'

'You brought this home.'

'Joyce always said I should look after them.' Ruby's voice goes brittle as paper. 'She told me to take care of—'

Joseph jumps up and grabs her shoulders. 'Ruby,

goddamn. What's going on? What did she tell you? What do you know?'

'I know nothing.' She pulls his hands off. 'Please. Let me call Detective Blanke.'

'No detective. We've got to get rid of that.'

'You can't.' Ruby looks at the little skull again. 'The detective needs to know. It's important. Please, let me call him.'

'The hell I will.' Joseph starts spooning earth and bones and wilted petals into the trash can with his bare hands. 'We're gonna dump this. Somewhere far away. Glendale, perhaps, or somewhere on Cross.'

'No.' Ruby throws herself against him. 'Leave it.'

'Ruby, you're hacked. Get off me.'

'No.' She punches Joseph's arm. 'It's a crime scene. Leave it.'

'Ruby.'

'Don't touch anything.'

Joseph drops the earth from his hands, scattering bone fragments. 'Do whatever. But I'm gonna cut out.' He throws a dark look at Pa and slinks out of the kitchen.

'Suit yourself!' Ruby shouts. 'Save your sorry ass and don't ever haul it back in here again.'

'Ruby, honey.' Pa's voice is very soft. 'Maybe he's right. We shouldn't—'

But Ruby cannot bear it no more. She grabs the change she got from her bus fare and darts out the door. No way she's gonna call from Mrs Estrada's phone. She runs down the street and on to Brookes, and keeps running and running until she finds a pay phone that isn't all smashed up. And all the way she is praying that the detective is in his office.

Chapter Twenty

Mick

Sometimes there is no way to sugarcoat things. There is a dead baby spilled out over the Wright family's kitchen floor. Mick makes sure to breathe slowly. He's seen skeletons before, and this is not the worst specimen. There was poor Giuliani in the acid barrel, with bits of flesh hanging from him like rags from a scarecrow. Or the remains of the prostitute who washed up on East River, with all the soft bits nicely chewed away and only her girdle and stockings holding her together.

But those were adults. Failed, nasty, dangerous adults, who maybe didn't deserve what they got, but did their share of bad things to folks who didn't deserve it, either. This one . . . this is different.

The baby peeps at him from hollow eyes, a little fairy head growing in the ground. Flower petals lie scattered over the skeleton. The geranium roots have grown through the ribcage, embracing it with an odd gentleness. The sight moves something deep inside him. *Little baby angel. Why were you hiding from us?*

Behind him, Ruby sniffles. 'What are we going to do?'

He gets up. Ruby is sitting slumped on a kitchen chair, terror written all over her face. Her sister lingers in the bedroom door. Old Mr Wright is pacing up and down the hall, muttering prayers under his breath.

Ruby looks up, and with a shot of embarrassment Mick realizes he's been staring. He clears his throat and considers touching Ruby's arm to stop her from shaking, but then decides to pour her a soda instead.

'Here,' he says. 'You need sugar, as my wife would say.'

She drinks in small sips. Tears brim in her eyes and Mick desperately searches for the right words, and finds nothing. 'Lay it on me, now,' he says. 'Tell me everything that happened today.'

Haltingly, Ruby explains. Mick listens until he's sure she has gotten it all out.

'So,' he says, 'Joyce told you to look after the geraniums? When?'

Ruby shifts in her chair. 'A few weeks ago. I was watering the pot. She came out and we were talking about how nicely they were coming on. She said this was her favorite treasure, and' – she stifles a sob – 'and if she was ever going away I should look after it.'

'She said she was going away?'

'Something like that.'

'And that didn't strike you as odd?'

'I thought she meant a vacation or something.' Ruby's eyes swivel toward the heap of earth. 'I swear I didn't know about . . . about this.'

Mick nods. 'Of course.'

'But they won't see it that way. They're gonna say I knew what was inside. They'll wonder why I asked to have it. And Mr Haney'll blame it all on me.'

Yes, that's a problem Mick's been thinking about. 'I'll figure something out,' he says. 'This won't come back to you.'

Old Mr Wright pokes his head in and mutters darkly: 'That's what Ruby said before. And now look at that mess.'

'Have you got a crate of sorts?'

Ruby thinks. 'We have a tray.'

'Can you spare it? You probably won't get it back.'

She pushes a chair up to the cupboard and produces a battered breakfast tray covered with flower-patterned oilcloth.

'That'll do.' Mick takes a pan lid from the dish rack by the sink and gingerly scoops up the baby's body. Then he brushes up as much earth from the trash as he can and adds the shards. Finally, he covers the tray with a dish cloth.

'What are you going to tell them?' Ruby asks.

'Oh, something or other. Can I use your phone?'

'We ain't got one.'

'Oh.'

'Why? Who're you gonna call?'

'The chief. He needs to get a medical examiner in.'

'Don't you have a radio?'

'Sure. But I don't want the whole station to hear.'

'And . . . and there won't be trouble?'

'I'm going to get yelled at a fair bit.' Mick grins. 'But don't worry about that, OK? Now, I'll take that thing away and you lay low for a few days and get some rest. Treat yourself to something.'

He immediately wishes he hadn't said that. But Ruby nods, the closed-up look creeping back into her eyes.

He means to say something more, but can't. There's a barrier in between them, built up over centuries. And try as he might, he cannot tear it down.

If Genevieve Crane is surprised to hear from him again barely two hours after he left her Pontiac, her voice does not betray it. In fact, she sounds a little amused.

'I need your help,' he says, 'but it could potentially lead to a bit of trouble.'

'I'm all ears,' comes the response.

'Some evidence in the Haney case has shown up, but I cannot reveal how exactly I got it. I need to keep someone out of the conversation. So, how would you feel about having taken a drive this morning, along President Avenue?'

'I think I might have quite enjoyed that.'

'Good. Now, during that drive you ran into Ruby Wright, didn't you?'

'I guess so, if only I could recall who she is.'

'Joyce Haney's cleaner. She was carrying a big pot of geraniums, wasn't she? Joyce's geraniums.'

'Oh, yes. I remember.'

'And since she was struggling with the heavy pot, you offered to take it for her. And that's how I came to spot it on your lawn after we went to see Deena. You asked me to carry it round to the garden for you. But clumsy me, I dropped it in your driveway.'

'Did you?'

'Yes, and you gave me an old breakfast tray to carry away the shards.'

Mrs Crane chuckles. 'That sounds very much like me. But tell me, Detective. What surprise have you found in the flowerpot?'

Mick clenches his hand around the receiver. 'I'd rather not say. Not yet.'

'Come on, I have to know. I've made it a habit not to lie for a man without good reason.'

'You're not lying. You're just helping me establish the truth.'

'The truth about what?' There is an edge in her voice now. 'What on Earth have you found?'

Now that the truth has stared up at him from a pile of earth, he is somehow reluctant to voice it. It's always been his theory that Joyce had a dark, little secret she concealed even from her loving husband. Especially from him.

'Well . . .' He squeezes his chin with his free hand. 'Remember how we talked about abortion?'

A little pause. 'Yes?'

'I have uncovered evidence that Joyce Haney might have had another child.'

'And you think she aborted it?'

He pictures the perfect little skull, the finger bones as delicate as lace, the ribcage, enmeshed in roots.

'I am not sure.'

'You think the child might be alive?'

'It is definitely not alive.'

'Oh,' Mrs Crane says, and then, more quietly, 'Oh, my.'

'Please. I will explain it all eventually. Right now I just need your assurance that if my boss freaks out you'll back me up. And in front of Mr Haney, too.'

'All right.'

'Thank you. Listen, I'll call you, and maybe then we can talk it over.'

'Sure,' she says. 'But, Detective, I must ask for a favor in return.'

Mick holds his breath. 'Yes?'

'I know why Joyce went to see Dr Morton. She needed more medication. The amount she was getting from her regular doctor . . . they just weren't enough. She was over-excited. Nervous. Exhilarated. Frank found it difficult to cope with her.'

'Did you recommend this doctor?'

Another pause. 'Yes. But . . . this is the favor I need from you. I will lie for you about the flowerpot, and you will ensure Dr Morton is not linked to me or my committee. He acts in the best medical interest and with utter professionalism. He is very understanding toward the women.'

Mick lets that sentence hang. But Mrs Crane is wise enough to say nothing more. For a few seconds, her breathing is the only sound on the line, calm and constant like the distant rush of waves.

'All right,' he says. 'You got yourself a deal.'

Two hours later, Mick watches Wilson, the medical examiner, bend over the tray of bones. He cannot help mention the abortion theory, which prompts Wilson to point out that this baby was 'carried to term'.

Mick eventually deciphers this to mean that it was fully grown, and that whoever carried it would not have been able to conceal the pregnancy. It's been dead for a while, which is sort of staring them in the face. But Wilson cannot estimate a cause of death or the age of the corpse. The only guess he deigns to make is that the child has probably been in the pot for at least three years, judging by the absence of flesh and the roots growing through the elfin ribcage.

Mick lets his mind wander. Three years. Just before the Haneys moved to Sunnylakes.

'We've got to get Frank Haney in,' he says to the bones. 'The man has some explaining to do.'

*

Murphy sends Hodge and Officer Souza to the house. One hour later, Haney, flanked by the two officers, is paraded through the station. He looks anything but happy.

'Was that really necessary?' is the first thing he says when he's made to sit down opposite Mick in the interview room. 'You're making me look like a criminal in front of the whole neighborhood.'

Mick leans across the table. 'That's what worries you? Don't you want to know what's new? Why you're here?'

'If you had found Joyce, you would have called me.'

'True. Well, here's the surprise. We found something else.'

Haney looks up, fear dancing in his eyes. Almost imperceptibly, he leans away from Mick.

'Your housekeeper,' Mick says. 'She took a pot of geraniums away today?'

'Yes. Why? Whatever she said, she's lying. We let her go, so she's probably trying to—'

'She said nothing. She gave the flowers to Mrs Crane, where I confiscated them. During transport, the pot was broken. Want to guess what was inside?'

'I don't know. And I'd appreciate it if you got to the point.'

'Well.' Mick balls his fists. 'We found skeletal remains.'

Haney snaps for air. His chest heaves up twice and his voice breaks. 'Joyce?'

'An infant. A newborn baby.'

Silence. Then a shudder runs through Frank Haney's body as if the man is bursting apart from the inside.

But Mick's not here for sympathy. 'Care to explain?'

'I don't know.' Haney gasps. 'I don't know. I . . . I can't imagine how it got there.'

Yes, you very well can, Mick thinks.

'Mr Haney, I ask you again. Do you know whose baby that is?'

'No.'

'It's Joyce's flowerpot. How long has it been in the possession of the family?'

'I really don't know. The flowers were her job. I only deal with the mowing and the trimming and the—'

'Mr Haney, did you move here with the pot or did you buy it in Sunnylakes?'

'I don't know. The movers—'

'I will call them for the inventory list. It's just more work for me.'

'I think we did bring it from Philadelphia.' Haney slumps. 'Yes, Joyce insisted we take it in the car. She loves geraniums and . . . Oh, God.'

'What?'

'I don't . . . I can't . . .' All of a sudden, tears well up in his eyes.

'How many children do you and Joyce have?'

'Two, Detective. Just two.'

'Judging by the decomposition, we estimate the child to have died at least three years ago. Just before you moved to Sunnylakes.'

'Yes . . . perhaps.'

'Mr Haney, is there anything you want to tell me?'

'I love my wife,' Frank Haney stammers. 'I love her. I never meant . . . Oh, God help me.'

'How did that baby end up in the flowerpot?'

'I don't know.'

'Was your wife pregnant before you moved to Sunnylakes?'

'There was no baby.'

'So, she was? What happened? Did she have an abortion? A very late one?'

'Never. She would never . . . There was no baby.'

He sobs and rocks as if he is being punched by an invisible heavyweight. He hunches over and slowly slides from the chair. On the floor, he curls up and cries into his fist.

Mick taps his fingers on the table, then switches off the tape recorder. He is not going to make sense of the man in this state. A night in the cells might calm him down. That would also give Mick time to talk to Joyce's parents again, and to Frank Haney's mother.

'Mr Haney, I'm placing you under arrest for your suspected involvement in the death of an infant.'

He grips Haney's arm. But Frank Haney doesn't move. He is still shaking uncontrollably.

'Mr Haney, please. Get up or I'll have to add resistance to your charge sheet.'

'Out on the terrace.' Haney's face is the color of a handkerchief at the end of a bad winter. 'All this time. And she was watering the flowers. Every day.'

In the end, the boys have to drag Frank Haney to his feet and guide him to his cell. At the door, he turns to Mick. His eyes are red-rimmed and glassy, and yet oddly intense. 'Was it . . .' He swallows. 'Was it a boy?'

Mick shrugs. 'Impossible to tell. There's only bones left.'

It is then that Frank Haney screams. He screams the whole station down. An animal cry, a howl that will still ring in Mick's ears hours later, when he's lying bed and cannot find sleep for the specter of a tiny rib cage entangled in the convolutions of his brain.

Chapter Twenty-One

Ruby

That night, after the detective has gone away with the tray, Mrs Lucille Haney senior calls. Everything she said that morning seems to be forgotten. Mr Haney, she says, had to go away suddenly, and Mrs Ingram can only take one child at a time, so she needs someone to mind Barbara while she goes about her business.

Ruby has nightmares all night. She wakes up while the sunlight is still milky, her stomach filled with stones. Ain't no good thing going back to that house. Not after everything that's happened. But staying away is no answer, either. So she puts on her uniform and makes for the bus.

In Sunnylakes, the mother of all dragons receives her in full empress mode. She is wearing a purple dress and purple pillbox hat with a little veil dangling over her hair. The hair itself is freshly waved and crimped. She has completed the outfit with black leather gloves, like the Nazis wear in Joseph's comic books.

Mrs Haney senior greets Ruby with a dog-poop stare that would win silver in the national championships. 'I must go to Santa Monica and meet my son,' she says. 'I may be a while. Do the kitchen floor, the nursery and the bathroom. If you need to wash your face, use the kitchen sink. And see to it that Barbara goes down for her nap.'

'Yes, ma'am. Where is Barbara?'

'In the garden, of course.'

Mrs Haney senior heads out without another word and locks the front door.

Barbara is playing on the terrace, a safe distance away from the pool. Ruby sits down on one of the pool chairs – a terrible violation – and shields her eyes from the twinkling water. In the hazy heat, she grows aware of a voice, whispering. Her mind jumps back to the presence she felt out here when she was watering the flowers. But it's just Barbara, talking in her play.

'Barbara-baby, you be a good girl,' Barbara tells herself. 'You wait in your room. Mommy's going to talk to him.'

Ruby inches a little closer. Barbara takes her baby doll and puts it behind a pool chair leg. Then she walks another doll, a long-legged plastic thing with vicious eyes and a stripy bathing suit, toward her knee. There, it meets up with a dog-eared paper boy whose head has been scribbled on violently with black pen. She lays both of them down and picks up the baby doll.

'Bye, Mommy,' she says. 'Don't get a boo-boo.'

Ruby thinks of the book that arrived yesterday in the

post, rerouted via Mrs Cannon. Dr Matt Futterer's *Interview Techniques for the Criminal Investigator.* It came with a card from a real professor who'd wished her luck in her studies. She hid the card under her mattress, next to her college savings, and stayed up reading till 2 a.m.

She kneels down beside Barbara and runs a hand along her back. 'What are you playing?' she asks.

'House.'

'And why is Mommy in one room and the baby in the other?'

'Because they don't want the baby.'

'Really? But mommies and daddies love their babies very much.'

'Mommy left the baby alone outside.'

Ruby thinks of the little skeleton and shivers. Barbara could not possibly know about that, could she?

Ruby picks up the paper boy and walks him over to the baby doll.

'Look, Daddy's coming back. He's saying: "Poor, little Barbara-baby. I'm coming back and I love you very much." Right?'

'That's not Daddy.'

Ruby halts. Dr Futterer says you ain't supposed to ask leading questions. Let the kids tell by themselves. So she tries to phrase it carefully. 'If you tell me his name, I'll play him.'

'Whoobie, can I have a soda?'

'Barbara, let's play our game.'

Barbara puts the dolls down. 'I'm thirsty.'

'Was this man here when . . . when Mommy went away? Did you see—'

'I want a soda.'

With a rustle of her petticoat, Barbara dashes into the house and flings open the refrigerator. By the time Ruby has collected the dolls, the girl has taken out a bottle and is struggling with the screw-top. Ruby takes the bottle from her hands, opens it and pours cherry soda into a cup.

'Sit at the table,' she says.

Barbara drinks with violent little sips. Ruby gets out the mop and bucket and runs the hot water. She waits until the bucket is half full, then sets it down and pours in the King Pine. Barbara watches her, slurping loudly, her little legs dangling.

'Barbara,' Ruby tries again. 'Do you remember last week, when I met you outside under the trees?'

Another slurp.

'Mommy told you to wait for Mrs Kettering, but she never came. Ain't that right? What was Mommy doing?'

'Where's Lily?'

'She's with Auntie Nancy. Listen, Barbara, what was—'

'I want Lily.'

'You can't go see Lily now. I asked you a question. Now you have to answer me. I—'

'I want my mommy.' Barbara throws her head back and slides off the chair. The cup tips over and unleashes a sickly pink flood over the table.

'Barbara.' Ruby jumps forward and takes the girl by the arm. 'Now look what you've done.'

'Mommy, Mommy. I want Lily. I want Daddy.'

'They're not here. You're being very bad. Be quiet now—'

'Mommiiiieeee.' Barbara twists in Ruby's grip. Ruby pulls her forward but Barbara is faster. She hurls herself back, slips and bangs her head against the corner of the chair.

It makes a hollow sound. Barbara's eyes grow wide. There's a moment of stunned silence. Time freezes, and Ruby's heart falls into empty space. Then Barbara opens her mouth and, thank the Lord Almighty, takes a big breath.

And then she screams. Shrill and loud. Loud enough to be heard till the end of the street, and if this doesn't send Mrs Ingram running, Ruby doesn't know what's what.

She grabs Barbara's head and presses it into her chest. 'It's OK, baby,' she murmurs. 'Barbie-baby. It's fine. You're good. It ain't gonna hurt for long.'

But Barbara writhes and kicks and hollers. Ruby pushes her away and holds her wrists with her hands. 'Stop it, Barbara. Enough. You gotta stop yelling right now.'

'Mooommiiiie!'

The noise is deafening. It's got to stop, or she's done for. She grasps Barbara's arms in one hand and smacks the little fingers. Once, twice. Harder. The third time, Barbara stops crying. She just stands and stares. Ruby sits back and exhales.

'There. Wait till I tell your daddy what a naughty—'

'So that's what goes on when the boss is away.'

Ruby spins around. A man is standing on the terrace. A white man, with black hair and a blue shirt. The grin on his face is utterly terrifying.

'Don't mind me,' he says, and steps into the kitchen.

Ruby jumps up. 'You can't come in, sir. It's . . . We . . .'

'The old bitch is out, right? Good. Don't worry, sweetheart. I'm a family friend.'

'No.' Ruby shoves Barbara behind her. 'You gotta leave.'

'Or what?'

'Or . . . I'll call the police.'

'Really? Funny, I was about to do the same. Don't like to see a nigger abuse a little girl.'

Ruby's insides grow ice-cold. She reaches out behind her back and puts her hand on Barbara's hair, where a bump is growing. Her brain is screaming to get away from this man. But her legs are stuck to the floor.

'I wasn't . . .' Her voice squeaks like a sorry-ass mouse. 'That's not true.'

'Honey, I saw what I saw.' The man walks past her and peers into the hallway. 'Say, Frankie-boy's out, huh?' He goes into the lounge and starts to open the cupboards. Two fingers on his right hand are short and stunted, as if he's had a bad accident with a sledgehammer. 'You know where Joyce keeps her paintings?'

Ruby shakes her head. 'I don't know who you are, but you're not welcome in this house.'

He turns around and grins. 'Oh, you don't know a thing.

I'm very welcome here. Friend of the family, so to speak. And I want to find Joyce as badly as her darling husband. So, think about this. I could tell Frankie what you've been doing to his lovely daughter. Or I could not. So, are you going to snitch, sweetheart? Because I think it'll be best if we say no more about it, huh? We'll pass like ships in the night.'

Ruby picks Barbara up from the floor. The girl hangs across her chest, limp as a towel, tiny fingers digging into her skin. She tries to think of a good reply, but all she can focus on, all her mind is willing to process, is panic racing through her veins. *Danger*, it screams. *Danger, danger, danger.*

The man chuckles. 'So, I guess we have a deal. Now, be a good girl and tell me where Joyce put her paintings. There's one that I want and I better get it before Frankie finds out.'

'I don't know. She ain't doing no painting.'

'Come on. You seriously never sniffed around this place?'

Ruby backs into the hallway. He pushes past her, up the mezzanine. He smells strongly of aftershave. His slacks are freshly pressed and his hair is slicked back and shiny. He's youngish, probably just hitting thirty. But there's something off about him, something rancid and used-up.

'Then who would know, sweetheart? Care to point me in the right direction?'

'I only clean,' Ruby says weakly. 'I dunno.'

'OK then. I think I know who to ask, anyway. Over the tracks and far away. Now, you sit tight.'

The man beelines for the bedroom. He's been here before, Ruby thinks. He knows what's where. His shirt bulges at the back where it conceals something stuck in his waistband. Ruby grasps Barbara with a new surge of horror. She's lived in South Central long enough to recognize the shape of a gun.

Her knees buckle and she's glad for the wall in her back. The man turns around. He takes one look at her face and smiles. He knows what she's seen.

'You know what, why don't you come into the bedroom, sweetheart?' he coos. 'Can't have a good look around with my back turned to you.'

Ruby shakes her head.

His smile slips. 'Come on, move. Do as you're told.'

Ruby tries to answer. *Go to hell, mister. You're bluffing. I ain't gonna get into that bedroom. Because once I get in, I'll never get out.*

But her mouth is dry as coal dust. She shifts Barbara in her arms and walks backwards. One step, and then another.

The man snarls. He strides toward her and grabs her arm with iron hands, the stunted fingers poking into her flesh. 'I said move, bitch.'

Barbara whimpers. It's a tiny noise, but it does the trick. Something inside Ruby snaps. *Hell, no, daddy-oh. You ain't getting us that easily.*

She twists under his grip and brings her knee up fast like they do in movies, right into his jewel box. She strikes true. The man lets go and stumbles backwards. He makes a sound like a dying donkey, but then steadies himself and lunges at her.

Ruby punches him. Her fist connects with skin and hair. It hurts. The pain comes as a surprise, shooting up her arm. But she's dealt more pain than she's received. The man recoils, groaning.

Enough. She turns around and runs, fast. Holding Barbara as tight as she can, she races through the kitchen, into the garden and sprints around the house.

As she reaches the driveway, something slams against the front door from inside. Of course. He doesn't know it's locked. Ruby runs toward Mrs Ingram's house, stumbling between the trees with Barbara clasped to her body. Fleetingly, she sees a car, silver-black. The car. *His* car.

She pounds against Mrs Ingram's door and screams: 'Open up, open. Please, Mrs Ingram. Open, please.'

It takes an eternity of pure horror, during which she waits for the inevitable shot to ring out and splinter her skull apart. But then the door flies open and she falls inside, almost into Mrs Ingram's arms.

'There's a man,' she stammers. 'A man. Joyce's killer. I saw his car, the silver one. He broke into the house.'

You gotta hand it to Mrs Ingram, she ain't wasting time. She slams the door shut, ushers them into the upstairs bedroom, flings open the closet and pulls out a gun.

Ruby shrieks at the sight of it but Mrs Ingram, lipstick shining like warpaint, grins. 'It's Frank's. He gave it to me yesterday, just in case the criminal came back to the neighborhood. Well, who would have thought he'd be right?'

And with that, she runs back downstairs.

Ruby sets Barbara down on the bed, where her little sister is sleeping. She has to pry away each of Barbara's fingers; they leave grooves in her skin as deep as South Sea tattoos. Then she tiptoes over to the window. The Haney house is just visible through the trees. She can see the bedroom window. But nothing stirs inside.

Barbara begins to cry. Ruby sits down on the bed and pulls her onto her lap. While she is rocking, she looks around the room. This time, there is no sign of gentleman company, thank the Lord.

Her eyes fall on the open closet. Mrs Ingram's clothes are a jumble of pink and turquoise and purple, and plenty cheap as well. But there, in a dry-cleaning bag and crisp as the morning, hangs a canary-yellow dress with a tapered skirt. It looks . . . familiar.

Ruby sets Barbara down next to her little sister and takes a look. The dress is not Mrs Ingram's style. But it's very beautiful.

At that moment, the door opens and Mrs Ingram sweeps in. 'I saw no one. He must have gone,' she says. 'Hey, what—'

Her eyes lock on Ruby, who is frozen stiff, one hand on the dress. A moment passes between them, distrust and anger, and, suddenly, surrender. A sad smile crosses Mrs Ingram's face.

'Lovely dress, isn't it?' She pulls it out and holds it up. 'I bought it for our exhibition on Sunday. We're doing a little display in the library with the committee. Joyce and I were . . .' Her voice breaks off. 'We were both going to make a day of it. Go to town, just us, and . . . Oh, it doesn't matter now.'

She puts the dress back and her face hardens. 'You get yourself home, now,' she says. 'I have to get ready. I'll tell Lucille what happened once she comes back.'

Chapter Twenty-Two

Mick

On Saturday morning, Mick is in the office, in an attempt to get away from Fran's incessant party preparations. He rings Dr Morton first thing. Their conversation is short but insightful. After hearing about Mick's conversation with Mrs Crane, he admits to prescribing a few things here and there to help the ladies of Sunnylakes through their day. His alibi checks out. Joyce Haney, Dr Morton says, came to him to deal with her mood swings.

'She had previously been diagnosed with low moods and lack of enthusiasm for marital relations,' he explains to Mick. 'I continued the medications she brought with her from Philadelphia.'

Apparently, these worked well, until about three weeks before her disappearance. All of a sudden her husband, dear Frankie the Magnificent, complained about anxiety and nervousness in his wife. So Dr Morton, always concerned about the marriages of Sunnylakes, topped up her usual subscriptions.

Mick draws a heart on his notepad. Three weeks. Just when her old steady showed up and churned the calm waters.

'I took it to be a periodic recurrence of the old problems,' Dr Morton says. 'It's quite common among homemakers. The stress of children and housework and husbands . . . you understand.'

'I do,' Mick says, and thinks of how he would feel if he were faced with another perfect day in Sunnylakes, locked up in a perfect kitchen, waiting for the perfect kids to go to bed so the perfect husband can pump another one inside you. Last night, he ripped out a Miltown ad from one of Fran's magazines and pinned it up on his wall. A pristine housewife at the end of a productive day, graciously receiving a peck on the cheek from the man of the house, while polishing the last of the dishes. *Since I take Miltown, our fights have turned to kisses.*

The names of Joyce Haney's medicines are trailing down the pages of his notebook. Mellaril, Butisol, Methedrine, Miltown-meprobamate. They sound like the names of jungle tribes. He reads them out in the voice of a TV narrator. 'The primitive Meprobamatians sustain their meager existence by hunting and spear-fishing, always battling for resources with the neighboring tribe of Butisol.'

A thought comes to him. What does this shit do to you when you're pregnant? When Fran was carrying Sandy, her hormones gave her emotional stability of a pre-school ballet dancer and lowered her intelligence to that of a plate of mash. Now, if you added some Thorizuma-whatever into the mix, what would—

A knock on the door rips him from his thoughts. He pulls his feet off the desk and dislodges a pile of papers, which flutters to the floor.

'Come in,' he shouts.

It's Jackie. 'Mrs Haney is here to see you.'

For one heart-stopping moment, Mick imagines a young woman with dark hair and a witty smile, dressed up in a yellow number, rosy lipstick perfectly drawn. *Well, hello, Detective. I hear you've been looking for me. Hop-a-skip, I'm back . . .*

The woman who enters his office shatters the illusion. She has silver-white hair and wears a purple dress tucked in a little too tight at the waist. Her expression is not unlike that of a boarding school mistress who has just discovered that one of her charges has been impregnated by the stable boy.

'Mrs Lucille Haney,' Mick says, a little too enthusiastically. 'Please, what can I do for you?'

'For a start, you can release my son. He's innocent.'

'Unfortunately I cannot do that until we have made further inquiries.'

'You have nothing against him.'

'Ma'am, I hate to remind you, but there is the not unimportant matter of a skeletal infant in your daughter-in-law's flowerpot.'

Lucille Haney scowls. 'Frank has nothing to do with that. It's Joyce's fault. Hers alone.'

That stops Mick in his tracks. 'You mean, you knew about this?'

'No.' She pales a little, and Mick can see that her body is bearing up by sheer will alone. All of a sudden, he feels a pang of sympathy. She has lost a daughter-in-law and may also lose a son, and all over a dead infant, which, if she was unaware, must have been a considerable shock.

'Please, Detective Blanke.' She clutches her purse. 'Let me talk to my son. There is something he needs to explain to you, and I think it would be easier for him if I was there.'

He scans his office, but the second chair he asked for has not materialized. So he simply shrugs and smiles. 'If there's anything you need to tell me, I'm all ears.'

'Well.' She clears her throat. 'I did know that Joyce was . . . in the family way, back in '56. After she had Barbara.'

'And you never wondered where the baby went?'

'The circumstances were . . . not favorable. There was marital trouble, you see, and . . .' She halts.

Mick unscrews a soda and watches her, patiently. He's got all the time in the world.

'How confidential is all this?' she asks at last.

Mick grins. 'Why?'

'Sometimes the police leak things to the press.'

'Correct. We're about as leaky as the SS Lurline after an encounter with a Jappo submarine. But I promise that I won't pass on anything you tell me, unless it's to secure a conviction. I won't even write it down.'

'And in return, you will do your best to find Joyce?'

There is an insinuation that he isn't already doing that. But Mick is not going to risk a good source over a bit of vinegar tongue. 'Her case is my top priority,' he says. 'My only priority.'

Mrs Haney senior sighs. 'Joyce wasn't exactly what we had hoped for. A little . . . far across the tracks, if you know what I mean. But Frank loved her and she was a sweet girl. It was a happy marriage – still is, I should add – but after Barbara's birth there were . . . problems.' She stares at her purse while her jaws are formulating the next part. 'It was lack of compliance on Joyce's side. I believe the medical term is frigidity.'

So Frank Haney wasn't getting none. That must have been a right pain in the old ass for Mr All-American Homeboy and his chiseled chin.

'The doctor prescribed medication to . . . increase her willingness to submit to conjugation.' Lucille Haney kneads her fingers. 'At first it didn't seem to work, but then Joyce fell pregnant. Unfortunately, it was a little too soon for her health. Her mental health. It . . . it was not a good time for them.'

The telephone breaks the spell. Mick picks up the receiver and slams it right down again.

'You mean Joyce didn't want the kid?' he says.

'I am not sure. She concealed the pregnancy from Frank. Banned him to the spare room for three months and wore only big sweaters and smocks. It was early summer when he discovered she was more than seven months in. They had a terrible row about it. She threw him out. Frank took Barbara and came to stay with me for a while. He feared it would mean the end of the marriage. I've never seen my boy so beaten down. But in the end . . .' She exhales and steels herself. 'In the end it solved itself. Six weeks or so after he came to stay with me, she called and said she had lost the child. Frank hurried back to her side. He looked after her, bought her new dresses and took her to the movies. He was very patient. Soon, they were quite in love again. But the sad thing was, of course, that there was no baby.'

'No baby,' Mick repeats. His fingers, curled around the bottle, are suddenly very cold.

Mrs Haney senior casts her eyes downward. A tinny sound emerges from her lungs. She cuts it short with a shrug and clicks open her purse. A handkerchief flutters to her eyes. After a lot of prim, little dabs she finds the strength to look at him again.

'It was hard for Frank, very hard. A terrible, terrible burden to bear. He felt guilty, and he grieved for a long time.'

'And how did she take it?'

'Sorry?'

'Joyce. How did she react?'

'Oh, with medication she soon became her lovely old self. The doctors said that she needed sunlight, so her and Frank decided to move. It was a good idea.

Sunnylakes is good against . . . against the dark clouds in the mind.'

Mrs Haney senior's eyes look right through him and for one moment Mick wonders what dark clouds linger in her mind. But she continues on before he can ask.

'Then Lily was born,' she says, 'and even though it was a disappointment that they had another girl, Frank was delighted. He said they'd try for a third.'

The phone rings again. Mick yanks the plug out of the wall. 'Go on,' he says.

'With Lily, Joyce had no problems. She was on Miltown throughout most of the pregnancy. It evened her moods quite splendidly.'

'Sounds like the perfect little family,' Mick says.

Mrs Haney senior frowns at him. 'Frank always assumed the baby's body had been taken away in the hospital and buried somewhere proper.'

'Only it wasn't.'

Her face is white and immobile. 'I guess not.'

They are silent. Mick contemplates his next move while Mrs Haney senior dabs at her eyes again. There is something in her posture, something concealed by layers and layers of primness, that suggests fear. But he is not sure what she is afraid of. Losing her son, perhaps, or maybe it's concern for Joyce. Or something else. Fear of the truth.

'You said she lost the baby in the summer?'

'In August '56.'

And exactly three years later, she disappears. Mick licks his lips. 'And you swear your son wanted this baby?'

Just the slightest hint of hesitation. 'Yes.'

Mick takes two steps toward her and lowers his voice. 'Mrs Haney, believe me, if he had anything to do with the death of this baby, we will find out. If you cooperate, on the other hand, we can help him. Call it a spontaneous act, if you will, brought on by the stress and the fear for his family. A judge would be very lenient toward that.'

Mrs Haney senior purses her lips. The old look is back in her eyes, harsh and cool and superior. 'He would have loved a son,' she says. 'Detective, Frank would never kill a child.'

Yes, Mick thinks. But neither did he bother to check whether it had lived or died.

He wastes half an hour or more collating witness statements and doodling in his notebook. He should really get home. Fran will be stuck choosing an outfit for Prissie's game. She'll need him there, so she can pick exactly the opposite of what he recommends. The game is at 2 p.m. He'll see Sandy, which will be nice, and Brad, which will require the exchange of sports analysis and manly quips. And then it will be two hours of excruciatingly boring college football, only lightened up by Prissie cavorting across the pitch like a Greek athlete on ketamines.

No, the afternoon's prospect holds no enticement. What

he really wants to do, he has to admit, is talk to Genevieve Crane. Maybe she'd take him out in her Pontiac again.

The specter of Fran forbids any further ruminations. The brokenness in her face after the thing with Beverly came out. He shudders. He'd explained the whole debacle a thousand times to his chief and the boys and the rep from the governor's office. But the hardest thing was going home afterward and explaining it to her.

Something in him wonders if he's running the risk of making a fool of himself again. There's not much similarity between Beverly Gallagher and Genevieve Crane, except for the auburn hair, but still . . . a woman in distress is a woman in need of a hero. He ought to be Fran's hero, of course, and he possibly still is, but with her being so damn capable and level-headed, his attempts at heroism tend to go somewhat unnoted.

He allows himself to wonder what it would be like to take a woman like Mrs Crane for lunch, once he's solved the case, in some place with books and salads and single malt whiskey. The evening sun would set her pearl earrings on fire, and they'd talk about the Democrats and the deployment in Vietnam and whether the Hawaiian statehood bill is really such a good idea.

His ruminations are violently brought to an end by Murphy, who barges through the door with a bang.

'Blanke,' he bellows. 'Why's your phone not working?'

'Because I unplugged it.'

'Why the fuck would you do that?'

'Why the fuck would I want to answer it right in the middle of questioning a witness?'

Murphy's belly heaves. 'Because we've got a dead woman.'

'Yep,' says Mick. 'And I'm trying to find out who—' His heart falls through the floor. 'She's dead? For sure?'

'She's been shot. A neighbor called the police. Hodge is waiting at the scene, so you better beat it, pronto.'

'Who called?' Mick jumps to his feet and grabs his notebook. 'Was it Mrs Ingram from Roseview Drive?'

'Dunno what the heck you're talking about. You're not going to Roseview Drive. This stiff is waiting for you in glorious Crankton. Hope your rabies shot is up to date.'

'So, it's not Joyce Haney?'

'Jesus, Blanke.' Murphy rolls his eyes. 'It's a Deena. Deena Klinke, or something. Get a move on before I screw some skates to your ass and push you down the hill myself.'

Chapter Twenty-Three

Mick

The heat isn't doing Deena Klintz any favors. Fortunately, Mick was smart enough to stop by the drugstore for a purse-sized tub of Vicks. He dabs a little under his nostrils and opens the door to the trailer.

All the windows are shut and the curtains are drawn. The place is suffused with the sweet, sickening smell of death, not unlike roses scattered over rancid meat. There are not as many flies as he expected, but there is a lot of blood.

Deena is lying on the floor right next to the couch. She is on her belly, but her skirt is down and seems undisturbed, which is a small comfort. Her hair has fallen over her face, obscuring the worst of the mess, but through the greasy threads he can clearly make out the entry wound on her temple. More hair and blood are splattered across the couch and the small table, along with little, yellow-gray clumps. Brain tissue. She's been shot right there on the couch. Likely she fell off it in her final convulsions.

He scans the rest of the place. On the table are soda

glasses, one half-full, the other empty. A plate covered in cookie crumbs stands between them, a half-empty box of Nabisco marshmallow sandwiches on the counter. There are dirty pans in the sink and laundry piled up in a corner. A half dozen beer bottles wait in two neat rows by the front door. Beer bottles. He makes a mental note to have them all fingerprinted. Another door, half-open, leads into the bedroom. The bed is ruffled and several sheets of paper have been spread out over it. Mick picks one up.

It's a painting of a windmill squatting on a hill, outlined by a greenish sun that cannot decide which way it should throw a shadow. It's an amateur work, just like the others on the pile. Mick flicks through inexpert still lifes, windows with flowerpots and bridges in the mist. Trite subjects for a trite hobby that probably did little to ease a trite and hard existence.

He unearths Deena's watercolors in a cupboard. They are cheap, like those Fran used to buy for the children's school projects. Here, phthalo blue has become navy, and cadmium lemon is simply yellow.

Engrossed in thought, he steps outside. The air of Crankton tastes like dust and motor oil, but it is sweet ambrosia to him. Hodge, who is standing guard by the door, watches him inhale. Mick expects a sneer, because he's just a Yankee wimp who can't take a bit of decomposition on the chin. But Hodge's face is that of a man whose mind is fully absorbed with the question of how much longer his stomach contents will stay down.

'Found anything, sir?' he asks.

'Nothing yet,' Mick replies. 'You said a neighbor discovered her?'

'A Mrs Ethel Bibberson. Said she nipped round this morning to borrow a cup of flour and called the police when no one answered and she noticed the smell.'

Mick looks toward Mrs Bibberson's trailer and remembers the beer bottles by Deena's door. Flour? Unlikely.

'Any witnesses to the crime?'

'None whatsoever. But Mrs Bibberson said there was a silver car parked up on this road yesterday afternoon. She heard the exhaust bang. Soon after, the car drove off.'

'She could have heard the shot. Did she recognize the car? Did she get the make and number?'

'Naw. She wasn't even sure it was someone gone to Deena's place.'

As if on cue, another silver car appears on the road; a dust cloud announces its progress long before the glint of metal is visible through the trees. It's Wilson, the medical examiner.

In the house, Wilson circles Deena like a vulture deciding where to take his first pick. He flips back her hair. The insides of Deena's head are visible, gray sponge flecked with reddish veins. Mick looks away, then feels bad about it. He composes himself and turns to Wilson in a manner he hopes is worthy of a Brooklyn cop.

'What's the deal?' he asks.

'What do you think?'

'Shot in the temple.'

'Well done, Detective.' Wilson roots about in Deena's head. 'Side shot,' he says. 'Split the skull right open. Quite nasty. Could have been a bad aim, someone who doesn't know how to handle a gun. But then again, could have been deliberate.'

Mick snorts. 'Anything I can't see for myself?'

'Doesn't look like there's been sexual violence, at least nothing recent. A couple of marks on her arm, but they are older. A week, perhaps.' Wilson scrutinizes the bruises. 'Someone manhandled her, that's for sure. You can see the thumb imprints here and here. But, like I said, I don't think it was the killer. I think the shot came as quite the surprise.'

'Why?'

'The angle. I won't be certain until after the autopsy, of course, but I think that whoever killed her must have been sitting right next to her on the couch. Check out those glasses. They had a nice little refresher and then – bam!'

Mick pinches his nose and tries to look as if he's thinking hard, but really he's just trying to get a good sniff of Vicks. 'Any defensive wounds?'

Wilson smiles. 'Nope.'

'She must have known the killer, then. But why on Earth would they sit down for a chat before he does the deed?'

'Perhaps her and her murderer got into a fight. Could have started quite friendly, and then somehow the little tea party turns bad.'

'I don't think so . . .' Mick forces himself to look at Deena, the whole sorry remainder of her, and something odd tugs at his belly. 'I've met her a few times alive. She wouldn't have opened the door to someone she was scared of. There would have been . . . She'd have fought back. But I don't see any sign of that. No broken glass, nothing flung.'

'Fair enough.' Wilson crumples his nose. 'You're the detective, sir. My job's just to look at the meat.'

'She's not . . . Ah, forget it.' He holds back. Never piss off the medical examiners. They know all your weakest points and how to get there fast with scalpels. 'I'm just saying it's weird. The killer must have come armed and ready. Why did he sit down first for a soda? Why bring cookies?'

Wilson shrugs. 'Sadism? Perhaps our man enjoyed coddling his victim in safety before whipping out the gun. Some of them like that sort of stuff. You make 'em feel secure, so their fear is all the sweeter when you finally turn the tables.'

Sure, Mick thinks. That's one explanation, but there's another reason to hang around for a chat. *To get information.*

The purring of another car jolts him from his thoughts. He looks through the window and spots Mrs Crane's Pontiac. From it emerges the lady herself, dressed in vivid green, with white gloves on her hands.

Mick leaves Wilson to his work and closes the door with such haste it slams. Mrs Crane turns around, and the look on her face startles him. Her mouth is a thin red gash and her eyes are glazed with worry.

He hurries toward her and blocks her view of the trailer with his shoulders. 'I'm sorry. This is not a good time.'

'Deena.' She tries to look past him. 'My God. What happened?'

'I am not able to divulge that right now. You go back home. I'll stop by in a couple of hours and—'

'How did she die?'

The question catches him off guard. Nothing's yet been issued to the press.

'Mrs Crane,' he says, 'I understand you must be very upset.'

'Who did it? What happened to her? Was it one of the bastards from that diner? Please, Detective. I want to know what happened.'

'And I want to know what you're doing here,' he says, with as much conviction as he can muster.

'I called your number and spoke to one of your boys at the station,' she says. 'I just found out that Deena took away Joyce's paintings. This fellow – Barnes was his name – told me that a woman called Deena Klintz had been murdered, and that you were at the scene.'

Curse those rookie cops. Mick heaves a sigh. 'Look, it really is quite upsetting. Not a good place for a lady. Why don't you—'

'Deena took Joyce's paintings. What do you think, Detective Blanke? Does that play a role?'

'This investigation is really just beginning. If you would—'

Tears well up in her eyes and drown the steel in them. She pulls a handkerchief from her purse and closes it with a decisive snap.

'The paintings,' she says. 'We met for class yesterday evening and Nancy mentioned that Deena and Joyce often compared their work.'

Mick flinches. 'There were some paintings spread out on her bed.'

'May I see them? I could tell which ones are Joyce's and which Deena's.'

Out of the question, Mick wants to say. But then the idea doesn't sound so bad. Maybe the paintings are important.

'I'll get them,' he says.

Wilson is just vacating the place. He scans the Pontiac and its driver, and throws Mick a demented grin. 'Nice ride, Detective.'

Mick ignores him and opens the door. He gathers the paintings on the bed into an untidy pile. When he turns around, Genevieve Crane is standing in the doorway.

'Don't come in here,' Mick says. But it's too late.

Mrs Crane steps into the lounge and looks around with a serene composure that is both admirable and frightening.

'Bastards,' she says, each syllable quiet and sharp as needle stabs. 'Bas-tards.'

'I'm sorry,' Mick says. 'But you have to get out.'

'I won't touch anything. Do you have any suspects?'

'Nothing so far. A witness saw a silver car on the property last night, but that's about it. Do you know if Deena had any enemies?'

Mrs Crane snorts. 'A dozen times a dozen.'

'Really? Who?'

She raises the corners of her mouth into a smile, but her eyes remain aglow with anger. 'If by enemies you mean people that were a danger to her . . . just talk to every trucker and every traveling salesman and every goddamn drunkard who traipsed through that diner and called her a frigid slut for not accepting his paws under her skirt.'

Mick stares at her, dumbfounded. 'This looks like a surprise job,' he says carefully. 'She didn't put up a fight. I mean, I don't think this was some date gone wrong, or an admirer who got a little too excited—'

Mrs Crane's eyes shoot right through his heart. 'The correct word for such admirers is rapists,' she says. 'And admiration plays little part in it. Quite the opposite, Detective.'

Mick swallows. 'What I mean is, it looks planned. As if the killer wanted to make her feel comfortable before . . .'

'Why?'

'Don't know yet.' Mick holds out the paintings. 'Here, what do you think?'

Mrs Crane takes them and flicks through clunky fruit bowls and blotched rivers. She hesitates for just a moment over the painting of a pink hat and dress hanging over a chair.

'Deena,' she murmurs, and a film of moisture pulls over her eyes. 'Poor, poor Deena.'

Then she holds up a painting of an orchid. Only it's not merely a painting. It is a vision of blue and purple blossoms. The leaves are swords of green, the petals are drawn with gentle brush strokes, each fade of color merely suggested, yet perfectly clear.

'Joyce,' Mrs Crane says. 'That's Joyce's talent. She had a gift like Amblioni. Has, I mean.'

Mick studies the painting carefully. He knows just as much about art as his dog knows about Danish philosophers, but he recognizes skill when he sees it. Joyce has captured the soul of an orchid. Languid and tender and bulbous.

Mrs Crane hands him the paintings. 'The others are Deena's. Strange, there ought to be more from Joyce. I'll check again at the art center.'

'Appreciate it,' Mick says. 'I'll let you know what we find out here.'

As he ushers her to the door, he casts a final glance toward Deena. With her head on her arm, you could almost pretend that she's just resting. But her thighs and hands have gone dark where they press against the floor. The medics will have a hell of a time flattening her on a gurney.

'Find him,' says Mrs Crane. 'Find that bastard.'

Mick nods. She looks at him a little longer, then turns on her heels and steps outside.

He follows her. He wants to say so many things. *Thank you for crying over Deena, because hell knows no one else will. Thank you for being tougher than me, for not looking away. Thank you for caring.*

But the moment passes and soon she drives off.

He exchanges a few more words with Hodge and goes to sit in his car until the medics arrive. He leaves the doors open and waits for coolness, which will never come. And then it hits him. Sandy and Prissie and Fran. The game. It's quarter past three. He's missed it.

Which means Fran won't speak to him for the rest of the weekend. Which, in turn, means it doesn't matter if he goes home now or stays out a little longer. And who could resist South Central on a Saturday night?

Chapter Twenty-Four

Joyce

I spend half an hour fixing my face and putting on the outfit I have chosen. I want to wear my daisy dress, but Frank says it makes me look girlish, and today is too important to be playful.

Inside my abdomen, something cramps. It's not the menstruation. When I came out of the bath, I found myself clean. This is something more archaic. My body has a memory of its own. These are the pains of childbirth, echoing deep inside me. A pain known by uncountable women since Eve was damned to give life to her sons in agony.

I listen at the door of the children's room. Lily is still sleeping. Barbara murmurs under her breath, putting her dolls through a fashion routine. I sneak into the bedroom and pull out the bag of painting materials, along with the sleepsuit I bought. I run my hands along the fabric.

I will give it to Jimmy. For our son, I will say. The one you never met, and perhaps for another one we are still to meet. If I should be so blessed.

My son. He would be three today. Last year, on his birthday, I numbed myself with my leftover Mornidine and lay on this bed in delirium, while Lily screamed and screamed. Eventually Nancy arrived, grabbed the children and took them God knows where. I don't remember Frank coming home, but I recall his face when he opened the bedroom door and looked at me. He did not say anything. But he thought that I deserved this. And I did. But even the longest purgatory must come to an end.

I have begun to sweat. The room spins. I can hear my own heartbeat. Panic surges through my body with each pulse. I deserve this. I must not—

I cannot stand the pain in my belly, so raw and yet so soothing. I hate it and yet I want it. A limb that hurts is still alive. What has stopped hurting is truly dead.

The Mellarils go down easy. I close my eyes and I see him. My beautiful, pearly boy. He was blue and red and white and purple. Black hair and yellow fingernails. All the colors of the rainbow. He squirmed. That is the worst of it. He squirmed and opened his eyes. He lived and then he died, I laughed and then I cried. He died, I died inside.

My abdomen cramps and I groan. Frank says I should forget. But I cannot. I will remember every little detail. His tiny fingers opened like geranium blossoms. The curve of his upper lip was fine and lofty, just like Jimmy's.

I will paint him. The thought electrifies my joints. I will capture him on paper. I will present him to the world. My beautiful rainbow boy.

When I rise, the room spins. I grab the paints. In the kitchen I fill several glasses with water. Lily's orange-red-yellow drawing on the refrigerator catches my eye and I think again about purgatory and whether it could be at all worse than the hellfire on the night my mother died.

First, it was just one match. I lit it while crouching on the kitchen floor, my insides still burning from Daddy's love. I did not think of anything. It simply made sense to light a match and take it to Daddy's coat and suits, and then another and another, until the flames danced so merrily.

I run out onto the terrace, unroll the paper and stick it to the terrace tiles with tape. Here among the geraniums I will paint him. So Jimmy will see what he would have looked like. So they all will see what a wonderful, beautiful boy I had.

I was so alone. Oh, Frank, you will never understand how terribly alone I was. I took the pills and the pills made me numb, so I laid down and laying down made me anxious, so I got up and took other pills and walked around in waves of pain. I missed Barbara. I missed you. And all the while my baby boy kicked inside me, wanting to come out and embrace the world.

After he was gone, silence. Silence from you and from Lucille. The same silence that surrounded my mother, the silence of the firemen and the lady from the welfare office. The silence that envelops the room when Deena shows up with a bruise or someone asks about Genevieve's husband. It's the silence of those who don't want to know.

You must have known, Frank. Oh, yes, you knew. But you never asked.

I did wrong. I broke our happy family. I could not bear your touch, Frank, but I welcomed another's, and that is my fault, and you have every right to be angry.

But it wasn't my boy's fault. Your silence killed him. There, I said it. I will paint it into the grain of this paper. Your silence killed him, and you, Jimmy, you killed him, too. My father and my husband and my lover, they all conspired against my boy and now he is dead and I—

Barbara is banging against the terrace door. I have locked it. I am not to be disturbed. Not this afternoon.

His face is perfect. He is the essence of our love. Jimmy and me, coffee and tea, river and sea.

It was not my fault. *It was not my fault alone.*

Chapter Twenty-Five

Ruby

This time round, the detective has the decency to phone ahead and announce his visit, rather than just rocking up at her house like a preacher. He says he'll meet her on Skid Row, which is good, because there's more white folk there, and it won't look so weird for them to talk. Mrs Estrada is listening to every word of their call from her living room, so all Ruby can answer is 'yes' and 'all right' and 'u-huh, let's do that'.

When she gets back home, her heart is hammering. Maybe the detective has solved the case. She still thinks about the baby all the time. Poor little thing.

She pushes the memory away and starts to rummage through her clothes. What do you wear when meeting a white man? Definitely not a dress. She ain't gonna risk it. Slacks, then, and a top. But nothing too bright. She doesn't want to look exotic, even though she loves her oranges and reds. Pa always says her and Momma shared the same appreciation of color.

She picks out a blue church blouse and her best pair of pants, which she folds up at the ankle so they look like they're cuffed. Then she swats her hair down with the hot comb, lathers Vaseline on her bangs and pulls her kinks into a ponytail.

Suddenly, there is a pressure at the back of her throat. She fights the tears and pushes them under. It's no good crying. She doesn't even know what she's crying over. Joseph, perhaps, or the letter from the lawyer saying the civil suit was dropped and there'd be no damages paid for Momma's death. The fading dream of college. The tiny baby in the flowerpot, an angel now in heaven. She folds her hands and prays. *Momma, if you find Joyce's baby up there, please tell that kid I pray for him in my heart of hearts. Tell that baby he's not alone.*

Mimi bursts into the room. 'What are you looking like rainy weather for?' she demands. Her eyes run over Ruby's outfit and a grin spreads on her face. 'Going to ask Joseph to take you back? Or is it a new fella?'

'None of your beeswax.' Ruby pushes past her sister and breezes into the living room.

Pa is staring out the window without seeing a thing. The dreaded letter that arrived this morning is still on the kitchen table. Mimi brought it in with a smile, but as soon as Ruby saw the crisp white paper and printed address she knew it was about Momma and it would not be good.

They'd spent their savings on a lawyer to sue over her death. Pa, still sluggish with grief, had told the city that there should be something for the girls. Hoping against hope, like you always do. And now . . .

Pa. The sight of him standing at the window gives Ruby a pang in the chest. He looked like that after Momma died. He just stood there, staring, for days on end.

She's gotta stay strong for him. Let him know it's all OK. She splashes some water over her hands and turns to him, smiling. 'Don't beat yourself up. We'll appeal.'

'We don't have money to appeal.'

'Mr Haney's paying me overtime. I'll scrape it together.'

'Ruby, you shouldn't . . .'

He doesn't finish the sentence. He can't. Ruby bites her tongue and forces a smile onto her face. 'I'm just heading out for a bit. Gonna go see the detective about some results.'

'Oh.' Pa frowns. 'Joseph coming with you?'

'Might run into him.'

'You back together?'

She shrugs and turns to leave. But then Pa walks up to her and puts his hands on her shoulders. She shrinks back. Since she's got a job and a man, he's stopped being affectionate. Now his hands press her into the floor with gentle weight.

'He's a good boy, that Joseph,' Pa says. 'But he gets too whirled up about things. They all do, those young men. And it ain't gonna lead to nothing good. You two should make up. He needs a girl like you. Someone who can keep him grounded. Someone to anchor him.'

Ruby tries to meet her father's eyes and fails. It's not

that Pa is not right – he is. But her heart is singing a different tune lately. One fueled by the Haney's dollars and the detective's calls and Dr Futterer's book.

'Yes, Pa,' she says, and swallows down the question that is burning on her tongue. *If I'm always gonna anchor him, when is it gonna be my time to fly?*

Pa squeezes her shoulders. 'Good luck with the detective. Don't say the wrong thing.'

'Pa, don't worry.'

His eyes go to the letter. 'It's just . . . take care.'

Ruby grasps his hands and pushes them off her shoulders. 'I'll be back before you know it.'

He gives her a queer look. 'You just remember your momma,' he says.

Ruby hits the street just as the sun hangs low enough to scrape the roofs. The neon signs have sprung on. The air is silver and smells of desert wind. Pa's words burn in her heart. *You just remember your momma.* Well, she's thinking about Momma every single day. And maybe Pa is right. When it comes to white folks, you cannot take anything for granted.

Skid Row's always teeming on a night like this. White people come here to drink in blues bars. Students and war veterans and those at the margins. Ruby settles on a bench in Pershing Square. It's a prettyish place during the day, with trees and a fountain. Often, there are pigeons sitting on the statue of a man on a horse. But now, at night, the square is full of shadows.

It's not too long until Detective Blanke arrives. He pulls up to the curb and slams the car door without locking it. Ruby smirks. *Could be that South Central is gonna teach you a lesson tonight, mister.*

'Thank you for coming,' he says and plonks himself down on the bench. 'I really need to talk to you.'

'Did you find out what happened?'

'How do you know?'

'Know what?'

'That Deena Klintz . . .' Realization dawns on his face. 'Oh, you mean what happened to the baby?'

'Why? What happened to Deena Whatshername? Isn't she the diner girl?'

'You know her?'

Ruby folds her arms. 'She came over to Joyce's once or twice after the women's committee. Her and Joyce, they'd have coffee on the terrace.' She hesitates. 'But it's not like I ever talked to her.'

'She was killed this afternoon.'

Her breath catches in her lungs. 'Because of Joyce?'

'I don't know. Hell, I've got no friggin' clue about this case. It's as if . . . it's so close, but I can't get into their heads. These people – Frank and Deena and Mrs Ingram and Mrs Crane. And Frank's mother.' He groans.

'The mother of all dragons.' It slips out before Ruby can stop herself. She holds her breath and digs her fingers into her thighs. *Mistake, girl. Big mistake.*

But the detective laughs. It sounds like his first laugh of the day. 'You can say that again. She knew Joyce was pregnant. And so did Frank. But they never wondered where the baby had gone.'

'Lord, how'd it get into . . . into the pot?'

The detective's eyes darken. It's not often you see white people unsure of what to say. He presses his lips together and shakes his head. 'Either they didn't know, or they didn't care,' he says.

Her throat starts to feel like she's swallowed chewing gum. 'They gonna trace it back to me?'

'No. I buddied up with someone. The story we're running with is that she saw you walking with the pot and took it from you to keep for Joyce.'

'Who is she?'

'Genevieve Crane. She heads the Sunnylakes Women's Improvement Committee.'

'The boss lady with the big car? Why's she gonna help me?'

'Because I asked her. Because she's a woman who can be trusted.'

Ruby says nothing more. That's what the detective thinks. But the detective doesn't know the women of Sunnylakes.

A couple come out of a bar and totter toward them. At the end of the square they start yelling. The man slaps the woman, hard, and shouts, 'You crazy whore!'

The detective spins around, but before he can jump up another man emerges from the bar and pulls the woman in, laughing.

The detective frowns. 'I think we should go somewhere else. This is . . . not a great place to talk about a case. Are you hungry?'

Ruby eyes him. She's hungry, yeah. Who isn't, at this time of night? But what's he planning?

'I know a diner about three blocks down,' he says. 'The Tropicana.'

'I can't go there.'

The detective looks confused. 'Why not?'

The answer is, just because. Because she ain't welcome there. Because the owner is gonna get out his shotgun. Because they'll put on the dog shit face and she's not gonna be able to eat one bite. They'll probably lace her burger with piss and strychnine.

The detective misunderstands. 'Come on,' he says and scoffs. 'This isn't Alabama.'

'And thank the Lord for that.' Anger rises in Ruby's stomach. Sometimes this detective is really, really dumb. 'You think it's fine just because there's no sign on the door telling me to stay out? You go talk to the man who runs the Tropicana. There's no need for a sign. I . . . I can't go there.'

He sighs and looks away, a little uncomfortable. She knows that look. Even Joyce had it, when things got too close to the truth.

She still doesn't trust the detective. But she has an idea. A little test, if you will. Let's see those liberal credentials in action.

'Listen,' she says. 'We're going to a different place. And I'm driving.'

'What?' He looks at her as if she's asked to move into his hobby room. 'But you don't—'

'I ain't going nowhere unless I'm going there myself.'

He considers this with a glance at his battered Buick. His chest heaves and sinks. 'Can you drive?'

Kinda. She's had a few gos at it with Joseph, in Old Man Toby's tow truck. You press down the clutch and crank in the gear and let the brakes come up.

'Yeah,' she says. 'Of course I can.'

She cannot. The Buick is different. The seat is too far from the steering wheel and the gears don't want to shift. She yanks the gear lever into drive and slowly lets one of the pedals come up. The engine purrs, then sputters. The car jolts and chokes with a snarl.

'Handbrake's still on,' the detective says hoarsely.

Ruby feels her face flush hot. 'It's a different model,' she murmurs. 'I'm just—'

'Try again now.' He releases the handbrake. 'Let the pedal come up halfway. Feel that resistance? Now you step on the gas, just a little, and don't forget to steer.'

The car rolls forward. He flips on the blinker for her and she floats into traffic. She remembers now. Use only one foot, push down the gas. Keep the steering wheel near the middle of the road.

It's beautiful. The car swims along Crotona, leisurely and smooth. Other cars stream ahead, a shoal of fishes in an ocean of night. Red ones and silver ones, and even a bus, lumbering along like a whale. She chokes the engine at a traffic light, but the detective takes great care to look relaxed about it.

'Clutch down, restart,' he says, and she pushes the pedal and turns the key.

The radio plugged into the dashboard crackles and spits out a stream of police talk. '1-4-1 over in the Hills. Sergeant Woods, repeat. Location check, unit seven.'

The detective switches it off.

They cruise out of South Central. She keeps waiting for him to say 'stop' or 'not like that' or 'what are you doing?', but he doesn't. He just turns on the stereo and hums along to Pat Boone. Ruby sets the blinker and pulls onto the Harbor Freeway. They fly along and she lets the car gather speed, faster and faster.

It's magic. Out here, the asphalt is smooth as velvet and the lights of LA blink in the distance. The world sweeps past, dark and wide and open. Streetlights flicker across the hood. Her heart soars. She forgets about the letter and Momma and the unfairness of it all. This is freedom. When she gets her money and an education, she'll go driving like this every night. Just by herself.

They coast along until the Central Flavor Late Nite

Diner comes into view. Ruby's been here once before, years ago, with Momma and Mimi. Mimi was little then, they'd been on the way back from the doctor and the bus broke down. The waitress gave Mimi a free pack of crayons and the Black chef came out and asked if Momma wanted her eggs cooked all through or with the yolks still runny.

When she exits the freeway, the car swerves left and the detective goes: 'Woahwoahwoah, slow down.' She breaks too hard, then slips off the pedal and the car makes an ugly jump. The detective winces. She steps on the gas and sweeps into the parking lot. The tires squeal, she pops the clutch and the engine chokes out with a rattle.

That's done it. He's gonna kick her out of the driving seat forever. Tears shoot into her eyes. She does not dare look at him.

'Sorry,' she whispers.

He exhales. 'The old girl can take it. Been through worse with my daughters.'

He has daughters. She didn't even know.

The diner is full of folks grabbing dinner after the movies or before hitting town. A waitress brings menus. It turns out they've put the prices up by half a dollar. Ruby takes her time choosing. She's got five bucks in her purse, but she doesn't want to spend her hard-earned money on waffles and burgers. So it's gonna be plain fries and a coke. Which is a shame, because the food here, as far as she remembers, is pretty good.

The detective looks up from his menu and raises one eyebrow, which makes him look like a news announcer. 'By the way, choose what you like.'

'Huh?'

'I'm saying, don't worry about the price.'

She smirks. 'It's on you?'

He puts the menu down with a grin. 'Even better, it's on the State of California.'

Chapter Twenty-Six

Ruby

The waitress brings two soda floats. The detective pushes one across to Ruby and clutches his own glass with both hands.

'I'll sum up where I am,' he begins. 'Stuck down the rabbit hole. First, there's the baby. Frank's mother said Joyce had a mental problem at the time of the pregnancy. It got so bad Frank moved out. He . . . they left her completely alone. And afterward, they never even asked what happened. The baby was gone, and that, it seems, was the end of that for the Haney clan.'

Ruby thinks of the geraniums and Joyce standing on the terrace, bathed in yellow sunlight, snipping at the crumpled buds. 'That's nasty,' she says.

'It doesn't make sense. Frank and Joyce just went back to normal. They moved down to California, had another baby and played happy house.'

Yeah, only there were stains on Mrs Ingram's bedsheets

and a crazy man who broke into the house. Happy family? So much for that.

The detective rubs his temples. 'Anyway, next thing you know, we find Deena Klintz rotting in her living room. She took some paintings Joyce had made. But the paintings have disappeared, apart from one. Did her killer take them away? No one has a clue. No one's coming forward with anything. I just don't get it. So, what do you think?'

Paintings, huh? Ruby suppresses a shiver. 'I think no one's gonna tell you the truth in that place.'

He looks up, annoyed. 'You sound like my boss. I'll get the hang of it, don't you worry. But . . . it's a different ballgame than Brooklyn. Those boxy houses. The gingham curtains. Women going to drawing classes. Driveways and pools and housewives waiting with drinks ready for the husbands when they come home . . .'

Ruby bites down a laugh. 'I know. Aprons with frilly bits and the same frilly bits on the bedroom curtains.'

'Sanforized flannel.' The detective snorts. 'Morning shopping at the mall. It's not my world.'

'You gotta rethink,' she says, and utters a quick thank-you prayer to Dr Futterer. 'Who's got a motive? Who's not what they seem to be? Everyone there's got something to hide.'

'That's crazy.' He picks up a spoon and starts pushing the ice cream in his float under the surface. Tiny bubbles of soda settle on the orb of cream, trailing veils toward the bottom of the glass.

Ruby bides her time and considers. 'Yes, they do. Joyce had a big secret. It was eating her up, and yet there was no one to talk to. The Sunnylakes folk, they live in dreamland. And they don't want anyone popping that bubble. They . . . play-pretend. You must have noticed.'

'Yeah . . .' He frowns. 'Kinda.'

'So you gotta stop expecting them to help you and start digging at the deep, dark secrets that they've got. Which brings me to another point. I need an insurance.'

'A what?'

'To make sure you won't blab to the Haneys or anyone. I . . . I'm saving up for something important and I need that job.'

The detective raises an eyebrow. 'What do you want?'

She puts on her sweetest smile. '*Your* darkest secret. Tell me something you don't want anyone to know.'

'What? Why?'

'So I can trust you. You gonna get some secrets from me. So first you give me a secret in return. Something that hurts.'

He flinches. His skin looks sallow in the lamplight. He's tired, Ruby thinks. Really tired. Like he's had a long and horrible week. But there is something else under his skin too. Something he's varnished over with male swagger and white confidence.

'I could tell you why I got transferred,' he says slowly. 'That good enough?'

'Nope. That's not a real secret. Your boss knows the

reason, and your colleagues, too, I guess. I want something better. Something you never told no one.'

He stares at her, and she's almost expecting him to get up and leave, but then he sighs.

'All right,' he says. 'Maybe . . . I've got something. I was drafted in '45 and deployed in the Pacific theater. I thought at least I'd get to shoot some Nazis but . . . well, our enemy was yellow, not blond. But when they shipped us to Mindanao, our allies were also yellow, so you couldn't really tell. Woodruff urged us to shoot whatever, shoot first and ask questions later. Didn't really matter to most of the boys . . .' He sighs. 'One of them was Billy Benson.'

Ruby scrutinizes him. The way his face has gone ashy . . . it's a true story, all right.

'On Leyte, the general put together a corps to hunt down the remaining Jappos hiding on the islands. Me and Billy went in hooting and shooting. We didn't expect there to be . . . you know . . .'

'I don't know.'

'People.' He swallows hard. 'It sounds stupid, but the Japs were wiped out already. We just assumed it'd be an empty island. But there were villages filled with locals, terrified fathers trying to protect . . .' He stops himself and closes his eyes for a moment. 'Billy was far ahead of me. He shot some young man. A teen. His chest just . . . exploded. Then this older guy, maybe his father, came running from the house with a knife. Billy raised his M1 to fire, and it jammed. So I raised mine. But I . . . I couldn't pull the trigger. I was frozen. I had two little girls at home. Prissie was not yet a year. I just kept thinking what would I do if some maniac shot one of them in the chest? Wouldn't I come running just the same?'

'What happened?'

'The old man stabbed Billy in the leg, but then Billy fixed his gun and killed him. Billy never saw me until I caught up with him and helped him remove the knife. It was a rusty, dirty blade and it went right through the big artery. We lost nineteen of the boys that day, and Billy two days later. Then they dropped the bombs and we got shipped home. I've never told anyone, not even Fran.'

'OK . . .' She's not sure what to say. 'I understand, though. I don't think I could kill anyone, ever.'

'Well, I always thought I could . . .' For a moment, he is far away. But then his attention returns to his soda float and he waves a hand impatiently. 'Now, your turn.'

She pushes her own float away. 'First of all, I think Barbara's seen something important. When we went inside and there was all this blood in the kitchen . . .' Ruby pauses; the detective leans forward. 'I saw her playing through that afternoon with dolls, and it seems there was a man at the house. She was playing it out with her dolls. And remember what she told me. *They* made a mess.'

'She saw her mom with someone. Who?'

'I'm trying to get it out of her, but it's hard.'

'Well, keep at it. But be careful. Kids don't remember things like we do. They—'

'I know. Don't ask leading questions, and all that.'

He grins. 'That's right.'

'Second riddle, and perhaps the answer to the first. A man broke into the house yesterday.'

'The Haney house?'

'Yep, while I was there alone. He was searching for Joyce's paintings.' The memory dries out her throat and she takes a spoon of ice cream.

'Her paintings? What for?'

'How should I know? I didn't bother asking. He had a gun.'

'My God, are you OK?'

'I was scared to jeebies. He said he'd been to see a friend of Joyce's and did I know where her paintings were. I said no, and then I grabbed Barbara and ran over to Mrs Ingram.' Something strikes her, then. 'How come you don't know? She said she'd call the police.'

'Don't think she did.' The detective frowned. 'Could be that the boys at the station forgot to tell me.'

'Or could be that she didn't believe me. She said she didn't see him, after all. Probably didn't want to bother for a Negro.'

Part of her expects him to say something, then, but he just clears his throat. *Figures.*

'Can you describe this man?'

'Black hair, a bit scruffy. Kinda hard to tell, maybe thirty years old? He was . . . It wasn't his first time there. He knew the house, and I think he knew Barbara. Oh, and he had two stunted fingers.'

'Jimmy.' For one moment, the detective looks spooked. 'He's Joyce's old flame. Did she ever mention him to you?'

'No.' She never breathed a word. Not even when they spoke about Joseph.

'Seems he's been shaking up the Haney's domestic bliss a fair bit,' the detective says. 'You said he was looking for paintings? When was this? Before noon?'

Ruby looks at him and then terror dawns. Deena died that afternoon. And that man . . . She clutches her drink. 'Oh, Lord in heaven. You think . . .'

'Perhaps.'

Unease gnaws at her belly. Deena is dead. Deena, with the bad teeth and the uncertain look in her eyes when she sat on Mrs Haney's couch.

Not that she liked Deena. White trash have a way about them. When they encounter Blacks, some see kinship, but others see a lower rung. They like it when someone's lot in life is even worse than theirs.

The waffles arrive. The detective gobbles down his food as if he's been starved. Ruby scans the mountain of goodness on her plate. There's bacon and eggs, with the yolks nice and solid, and syrup in a glass jar and cheddar slices with pickle. But her appetite has passed.

Well, actually, she *could* eat, just a little bit.

While the detective is munching away, she takes the chance to ask a few questions herself.

'How old are your daughters now?'

'Sandy's twenty-one and Priscilla is seventeen. Sandy's

at college, and Prissie is a cheerleader.' There's a spark of pride in his eyes as he says this, but then his face falls. 'Prissie had a big game today. My wife's been preparing for a week and I missed it. I was at Deena's investigation. Fran is going to fry my balls in . . . oh, sorry. Didn't mean to swear.'

'Don't worry, mister.' Ruby smiles. 'I had a momma with a mouth like God gave her. You should have heard her laying it on my pa.'

The detective smiles. 'What about Joyce and Frank?' he asks. 'Do you think Joyce ever put Frank in his place? Did they row?'

'Mr Haney's a creep.' Ruby rolls the word over her lips, enjoying the feel of it. 'He didn't like me being there. And the reason, I think, was because Mrs Haney did. He was jealous.'

'Jealous?'

She roots for an explanation. 'You know,' she begins, 'my momma, she always said there's two kinds of men. Some care about you and some care only about themselves. They will do for you, but they're just doing it to get you where they want you. Down low. Now, Mr Haney, he's that second kind of guy. He didn't care about Joyce, but he put her in a place where she couldn't escape. He wanted her to think about nothing but him and their perfect little world.'

The detective nods. 'You know, that's pretty astute.'

Ruby swallows her waffle. 'I haven't yet told you my third clue,' she says. 'But this one . . . it's just a suspicion.'

'Right now, I'll even follow up tarot card readings.'

'Mrs Ingram. I . . . I think she has a fling with Mr Haney.'

'Really? You sure?'

'She . . . well, my momma would have said she's an easy woman. And she likes people to know it. I saw cuff links like Mr Haney's in her bedroom. And stains. You know.'

Before her inner eye, the sheets rise from the washing machine, the telltale stains shining. And Mrs Ingram's look. Something about that makes her shiver. A predator look. A cat who got the mouse and now shows it off to the kittens.

'Hm.' The detective mops up sauce with the last piece of waffle. 'I'll bear it in mind.'

'What if Joyce found out?'

He pauses, his fork halfway to his chin. 'You think Frank would kill his wife to get with his sidepiece?'

'Maybe.'

'He could just divorce her. And he has an alibi for the day of Joyce's disappearance. We checked with his hotel. And don't forget Deena. She was killed on the same day we found the baby. Frank Haney was in custody.'

'Not until the evening.'

Ruby chews on the last piece of bacon. How is she gonna make him see? If the detective gets stuck, Joyce will never be found. And if she's dead, her killer will get away with it. She's got such a bad feeling about Mr Haney. There was the beer bottle, suggesting he'd been back. The fact that he gave Mrs Ingram a gun to look after, on that very same day Deena was shot.

'About that reward,' the detective says. 'If all this is true, you might win it.'

Her mind sweeps away. A thousand dollars. That's a mighty fine sum. She'd go to college and have spare for Mimi still. No more mopping and scrubbing and the stink of King Pine.

But the thought of coming into so much cash over the death of a mother just feels . . . wrong.

The detective seems to feel the need to hammer in the point. 'You could treat yourself. Go on vacation or something. You could do anything you want.'

'I want to go to college,' she says to the waffle.

'There you go. What do you want to do? Domestics?'

She shoots him a glance. 'Science.'

'That's . . . nice.'

'But with my own money. My momma always said it's no good coming into a windfall like that. It brings bad luck.'

He looks confused. 'Maybe you should have a word with your mother. This isn't some lottery. You're helping me out, after all. Hell, you're helping the whole PD.'

'Momma's dead.' She doesn't know why she tells him this, but it just slips out. 'She got hit by a truck last year.'

'Oh. Oh, that's . . . She had an accident?'

The bite of waffle swells up in Ruby's mouth. She swallows. 'That's what the city ruled.'

His eyes narrow. For a moment, he is a true detective. 'You think it wasn't?'

Of course it wasn't. The crosswalk was clearly marked. It was broad daylight. Momma wore her orange dress. She was carrying her bright green bag and walking slowly, because of her bad leg. Walking out into a street that was empty, the witnesses said, until the garbage truck hurled around the corner. The driver was on his way to the depot. End of his shift. The lawyer said his client didn't see Momma, didn't notice the thump her body made as it hit the fenders. That's why he drove right on. *Dennis Huffman is a family man, sir, a God-fearing, hardworking family man. A beacon in his community. You have to understand, sir, my client was just trying to get home in time for the football. The game meant very much to him.*

Which is the worst part. Because, by inference, Mrs Prudence Wright, her infectious laugh, her coarse hands and her collection of porcelain angels, meant nothing at all.

'I told Joyce about it.' It seems important all of a sudden. Important he understands. 'I told her what I thought and she believed me. They ruled it an accident, but the truth is it was deliberate. The guy got off with a warning. Joyce said that's just typical. No one ever wants to know the truth. Not when it's so damn bad.'

The detective looks at her for a long time. 'I'm sorry,' he says finally.

'That's what I meant with all the secrets. That's what you have to understand. The people in Sunnylakes, they only wanna be seeing the side of things they like. The other side, the dark stuff, that stays hidden. No one saw what happened to Joyce because no one wanted to see. Not even her. She was hiding the baby like you're hiding your own secret. It just gets pushed out of sight and out of mind. Until . . .'

She swallows. How do you even start explaining?

'Until it comes out, regardless.' The detective takes a bunch of dollar bills from his wallet and spreads them on the table. 'I think I get it.'

Ruby nods. He doesn't get it. Not really. But at least it's a start.

Chapter Twenty-Seven

Mick

Sunday morning stretches like chewing gum, endless, pink and sticky-sweet. Fran and the girls discuss going to church, then decide to leave it. They hit the chaises and Brad gets his running shoes out. Mick watches him disappear down the driveway and tries, with a faint flicker of hope, to recall the Santa Monica stats for hit-and-runs. That makes him feel guilty and, since the best way of dispelling guilt is work, he sneaks into the bedroom, rummages in his papers for Jackie's home number and makes the call.

If she is at all bothered to have her Sunday morning interrupted, she does not show it, and neither does she flinch at his question. 'Yes, I think the beer bottle was fingerprinted,' she says cheerfully. 'I can look it up right now.'

'You have the case files at home?'

'Murphy wanted me to make a copy for the LAPD, just in case they need to come in.'

'I see.' He swallows the sour taste from his mouth. 'Likes to be prepared, our Murphy, doesn't he?'

'I'm sure it won't be necessary. Ah, here it is. Size-wise it's probably a man's hand, but the fingerprints are unknown, meaning they do not match any member of the household.'

'So they weren't Frank Haney's.'

'No, but if you recall . . .' She pauses and changes tone. 'I mean, I am probably wrong, but there were some other men at the scene, weren't there? The milkman . . .'

'Goddammit, if we have to fingerprint every man who was in Sunnylakes that day I'm going to chop Hodge in half and feed him to the dolphins.'

'Perhaps not every man,' she says, and he can almost see her grin. 'The prints are quite unique. According to the notes, the ring finger and little finger are not present.'

'What does that mean?'

'Either our man drinks beer like a French dandy with the fingers splayed, or he's got two fingers missing.'

'Crap. I mean, thanks.' A shiver runs through him, and he cannot tell whether it's the excitement of the chase or anger at how he could have missed that damned bottle.

'One more thing, Detective.' Her voice is all sunshine now. 'The art exhibition organized by the Sunnylakes Women's Improvement Committee is opening today. I got a flyer in the mail.'

Mick's mind skips to the afternoon ahead, to be spent

making small talk with Brad and struggling to light the barbecue. Or perhaps . . .

Once Jackie's hung up, he fishes out a fresh shirt and starts rummaging for an artsy tie. Fran, of course, is not amused. 'You're leaving? On a Sunday? I thought the whole reason why we moved to California was so you could work more social hours.'

Mick helps himself to some lamb cutlets from yesterday's wrecked family dinner. 'The reason we moved to California was because I burned my fingers. Anyway, a murder's a murder.' He shrugs. 'There's no regular hours.'

'But this is Santa Monica.'

'Doesn't matter if it's Harlem East or the Vatican. If someone's dead, I've got to figure out whodunnit. Believe me, I would love to stay around and get to know Brad and—'

'What do you think of him?'

Mick swallows too fast. 'He seems nice enough . . .'

'Because, I really think we ought to talk about what this means for Sandy's future and . . .' Fran hugs herself. 'He's just not quite . . . I don't like him.'

'He's a dumbo.' Mick grins, relieved at the rush of honesty. 'I'm surprised he can string three sentences together. Don't worry, Sandy'll see through him soon enough.'

'You think?'

'I'm a detective, I'm always right.' He sprays on some eau de cologne and leans in to kiss her.

'What's all this?' Fran grabs his lapels, a sudden darkness in her eyes. 'You smell like you've got a woman waiting.'

He forces a smile. 'A whole suburb full of them.' Guilt washes over him. He thinks again of Beverly. He ought to stay, enjoy Sunday with the wife and kiddies. Hell, he's come too close to losing them once before.

But then again, there's two girls out there whose mother has vanished. He's got to do his job.

He gently releases Fran's fists. 'I'll make it up to you. Day out in LA, just you and me, baby.'

'Peace offer accepted.' She kisses him back. 'Just watch yourself around those women.'

Outside, he backs the Buick out of the driveway, cranks the window down and the radio up. His mind flicks to Ruby's revelation that Frank Haney and Nancy Ingram have a thing going. It sounds like something out of *Aunt Jenny's Real Life Stories* – the war widow and the single father, a hot summer's night, her eyes . . . what's the word they always use? Limpid. Her limpid eyes floating over quivering bosoms. That's Nancy Ingram, all right.

Except it's not that easy. Frank is a married man. Humping your wife's best friend is generally considered a big no-no. If Joyce found out about this . . . what would she have done? Would she have confronted them, or run?

*

Sunnylakes Library is adorned with red-white-and-blue ribbons and a banner that says: *The Art of the Home – the Sunnylakes Women's Improvement Committee Exhibits.*

Mick pays his 50 cents entrance fee to a teenage girl who is sweating in her best plaid dress. She hands him a ticket and a leaflet featuring Joyce's photo and a call for donations to fund a nation-wide TV appeal. He fishes another quarter from his pocket and drops it into the donations box.

The exhibition is in a function room above the library. It is filled with women of that age range when they start looking like their mothers. The women wear teal and beige day dresses with matching hats. There is an abundance of subtle lipstick and pearls. Only Genevieve Crane stands out. She has put on a small black number with bare shoulders. The neckline is plain, giving all the more prominence to her delicate collarbones and the giant, sparkling hummingbird brooch pinned to her chest.

Mick heads toward her, then hits an invisible wall and scoots off to a quiet corner. Dammit. It's hard to admit, but Ruby is right. He needs a different approach – the old confrontation won't work here. *Hello, I'm Detective Blanke. By the way, ladies, has any of you had an abortion? And who here owns a gun and really, really hated Deena Klintz?*

He swerves toward the paintings. Still lifes, Dutch landscapes, a laughably childish drawing of the Abraham Lincoln memorial. Seaside watercolors, where the beach bleeds into the ocean and the parasols look like drinks umbrellas.

But there is one that stands out. A painting of a pool. He recognizes it immediately. The white tiles running around the perimeter, the hint of a garden shed in the corner. The geraniums. Dozens and dozens of them. Petals everywhere, a sea of red. They dance before his eyes. He blinks and looks at the pool again, a perfect square of azure, sunlit and clear. As if you could leap right into it.

The feeling spooks him; in fact, the whole painting makes the hairs twirl in the back of his neck. The signature at the bottom, in easy, curly letters, confirms what he already knows. This is Joyce Haney's work.

'Quite something, isn't it?'

Mick spins around and finds Nancy Ingram, wearing a pink cocktail dress.

'It is, Mrs Ingram,' he replies. 'Joyce really has a remarkable talent.'

She nods earnestly. 'She even bested our teacher. Mrs Crane said she should talk to a couple of painters in LA about exhibiting in a . . .' She pauses and looks away. 'Have you found out anything new?'

'Still hoping to ask Mr Haney a few more questions.'

'Oh, yes. I spoke to Frank's mother last night. Lucille is very concerned. He's innocent, you know.'

Mick thinks about Frank Haney's mom and Ruby's description of her.

'He wasn't even here,' Mrs Ingram implores. 'He was in Palmdale when Joyce disappeared.'

'That's true. But we are investigating him in other matters. I cannot—'

'Detective Blanke, I actually wanted to talk to you about something.'

His mind cranks up a gear. The desperate look in her eyes. The way the tip of her tongue flicks over her fiery lips. Mrs Ingram has information. That's how it shows with women. That neediness. Men who want to spill the beans talk straight, but women grow sticky like caramel sauce.

'I might have some . . . evidence.' She peers over her shoulder, then leans in a little closer to him. He can smell perfume emanating from her peroxide hair, which, up close, looks stiff like a scarecrow's. 'I heard there is a reward. But you must promise not to breathe a word to Joyce or Frank. It is a matter of strictest confidence.'

'Promise.'

'Detective, you have heard about the man who broke into the Haney house on Friday? I called the station to report it. Well, I believe it was a certain Jimmy—'

'Jimmy the Boyfriend. Yes, we've got an officer trying to track him down.'

If Mrs Ingram is surprised that Mick is one step ahead, she doesn't show it. 'Well, I hope you find him soon. Because, you know, Jimmy and Deena . . .' She blushes. 'They slept together. She told me, just after Joyce went missing. She asked me never to speak to anyone about it. I crossed my heart and swore to die.' She laughs nervously, then chokes on it. 'But now Deena is dead and . . .'

Mick balls his fist in his pocket. This is where it all comes out. The clues align. In the library. With the lead pipe.

'Did Joyce know?'

'Of course not. Deena told me it happened after Joyce rejected Jimmy, a couple of weeks before she disappeared. Joyce drove off, Deena offered Jimmy a drink, one thing led to another . . . Deena was devastated over it. I mean, Joyce and her were such good friends.'

'Why did she do it, then?'

'Well.' There is just a little hint of self-satisfaction in Nancy Ingram's voice. 'Deena always had the hots for men.'

Mick's mind flicks to what Ruby told him last night about Mrs Ingram herself. *Careful now, Nancy. You're not so ice-cold either.*

'Why do you think Jimmy broke into the house?'

Mrs Ingram presses her lips together and squints, the very picture of a woman trying to think hard. 'I don't know. Is it true that a murderer always returns to the scene of the crime?'

'We don't know if Joyce is dead. I hope—'

'Because I think I saw his car on Monday. I . . .' She flinches. 'I was looking out of the window to make sure Ruby wouldn't step on my lawn. I remember there was a car gunning out of the Haney's driveway. Around 5 p.m. Just before we discovered Joyce was missing.'

Mick stares at her. 'And you think it was Jimmy?'

'Well, I didn't see the driver's face. But the car was silver and had black fenders. And something green at the rear. Do you . . . do you think that sort of information would get him arrested?'

Mick swallows. 'Let's say it was Jimmy. Why would he harm Joyce?'

'She told me he didn't take the rejection too well.'

A vision rises before Mick's inner eye. Joyce in the kitchen, tidying up after lunch. The silhouette of a man in the terrace doors. *I cannot stay away from you.* Or, maybe: *How dare you say 'no' to me?* And her reply: *Jimmy, I could never leave Frank.* Words turn to blows. She falls and hits her head. Or, perhaps, she confronts him. *I am pregnant, Jimmy.* He threatens her. Or drags her into the car to—

No, somebody would have heard her scream.

What if she came willingly at first? *Let's talk in the car, Joyce.* And then he knocks her out and drives off. But what about the blood?

'Sounds like a movie,' he says. 'Two men desire the same woman.'

'It happens.' Mrs Ingram's voice is dry. 'A love triangle. To outsiders, it's a flip, but to those inside . . .'

'You wouldn't know this fellow's surname? And do you have a description?'

'McCarthy,' she says. 'Jimmy McCarthy.'

A firework explodes in Mick's brain. He has to phone the station, right now. Get some officers burning up the lines.

'I really do hope you'll find him,' Mrs Ingram continues. 'Please, let me know if . . . well, if I win the money.'

Mick's mind drifts back to a conversation he had with Ruby, back in her kitchen. How she'd insisted she wasn't in it for the reward, and *really* wanted to help Joyce. But surely Mrs Ingram too is first and foremost interested in the welfare of her friend.

The friend whose husband she sleeps with.

Mick dismisses the thought. Eyes on the prize. Jimmy McCarthy, bingo.

He smiles at Mrs Ingram. 'I'll let you know for sure,' he says. 'Can I get you another drink? And then, would you kindly show me where the phone is?'

He calls the station. Someone picks up on the third attempt, a young man named Barnes, who, Mick figures, is the Sunday substitute for Jackie. Barnes notes down Jimmy's surname and the car's description, and promises to get to work.

When Mick returns to the exhibition, Genevieve Crane is giving a speech, thanking the mayor of Sunnylakes and the library staff and the many artists who have worked so hard for this. 'Including,' she says, 'Joyce Haney, such a talented and wonderful young woman, a close friend whose disappearance has shaken us all to the core. And, of course, Deena Klintz, who sadly cannot be here today.'

Mick glances at Nancy Ingram, whose smile does not quite reach her eyes. The other women look stony. One thing is for certain. Deena Klintz will *not* be sadly missed.

Gloved hands clap together and glasses clink.

After, Mrs Crane extricates herself from a gaggle of women and sweeps toward him. She smiles her enigmatic smile and sets her drink down on a nearby table.

'What do you think, Detective?'

'Well.' He's definitely sweating now. 'Some great realism. And the color combination of this one' – he points at a vase of sunflowers – 'almost like Whatshisname . . . you know, the one with the ear.'

'Van Gogh,' says Mrs Crane. 'And if that's like a Van Gogh, I am Marilyn Monroe.'

'I beg your pardon?'

She lowers her voice. 'Come on, Detective. This is amateur art. Nothing to write home about. Except, of course, for Joyce's work.'

They both turn to the picture of the pool. Two older ladies, whose lips have never tasted Appetrol lunch substitutes, are blocking it from view with their substantial rears.

'Joyce would have loved Amblioni,' Mrs Crane says.

'The exhibition in LA? Are you going?'

'It sold out months ago. I tried to get tickets for us, but . . .'

Mick nods. 'I'm sorry. Well, I . . . I've got to beat feet. Adieu.'

'Detective, wait.'

'Yes?'

Her voice, when she speaks, is so subdued he can hardly

make out her words. 'To leave the child in the flowerpot. Such a horrible secret. Why do you think she did it?'

He swallows. 'To keep it close, perhaps? To ensure it always had a lovely place to rest?'

She moves her head this way and that. 'I think it was something else. To have it so prominent, always in view and adorned with red flowers . . . I believe part of her wanted it to be seen. As an accusation.'

'To whom?'

'Maybe to herself. Maybe to the world. Her beautiful house, her beautiful children, her loving marriage – and in the middle of it all, this terrible secret. She was screaming it out to the world. Here is my dead baby. See what you have done.'

'But no one really knew.'

'That,' Mrs Crane replies, 'is the point of secrets.'

Chapter Twenty-Eight

Mick

At the station, Mick finds Barnes at the front desk. Barnes is a young fellow, barely out of school, with freckles and a distinctly rattish look.

'Detective, sir.' The boy looks up as soon as Mick draws near. 'I have some phone records for you. From a Deena Klintz. Jackie had them couriered over.'

Mick takes the papers. Jackie, who deserves a bouquet of medals, has highlighted the relevant sections. Deena does not make many calls, but on Monday afternoon she was burning up the lines. She called Joyce's house several times, and Nancy's number, too, three times between 3 p.m. and 4 p.m.

'Good stuff,' he mutters. 'Any luck on Jimmy McCarthy? You phoned the hotels?'

'Yeah. No luck at first, but then I called the gas stations, too. A silver Crestliner showed up at Crankton Gas 'n Oil Friday noon. Pennsylvania license plate. Gent who drove it demanded a full wash and polish on the fenders. The attendant couldn't recall too many details, but it was a dark-haired fellow. Said he was down on some business and staying in Florendale, LA.'

Mick tenses. 'And?'

'So I phoned round the hotels and bunkhouses and, bingo. A Jimmy McCarthy's got a room at Geraldino's Guesthouse on Witterman Street.'

'Good work, man. Let's go get him.'

'Should I call the chief?'

'Screw him.' He enjoys the uncertainty on Barnes' rat face. 'We've got no time to lose. Round up the boys.'

'The . . . pardon, sir?'

Mick peers into the main office, where the rank 'n file scrape a living from speeding tickets and stolen purses. Two rookie cops are sitting at the desk closest to the coffee machine, bent over the Sunday crossword.

He turns back to the front desk. 'That's it? That's all there is? We have a baddie to arrest. I need manpower. Gunslingers. Big boys who can kick down a door.'

Barnes gets up from his chair. He's thinner than the table legs. 'I go to the gym three times a week, sir.'

Mick groans. 'All right, Charles Atlas. Here's what you're going to do. Go tell those fart butts in the kitchen to put on some plain clothes. Meet me at my car.'

'But Moggs likes to finish the crossword. He says it sharpens the brain.'

'Well then, Barnes, you tell dear Moggsie that if he's not

in my car in five minutes, armed and dangerous, I will personally whittle his brain to a point, using my locker key.'

Barnes swallows so hard his Adam's apple jumps. 'Yes, sir.'

Geraldino's Guesthouse is half bunkhouse, half hotel, and one hundred percent cheap carpet and splintered plaster. Detective Mick Blanke and his squad of hard-nail lawmen – namely officers Barnes, Souza and Moggs, whose crossword puzzle now lies shredded on the station floor – arrive with screeching tires and the sunset in their wake. When they enter the lobby, Mick utters a silent prayer to the God of rookies that Jimmy will come quietly.

He takes out his badge and shoves it into the wide-eyed face of the receptionist. 'Santa Monica PD, we're here to see one of your guests. A Jimmy McCarthy.'

'McCarthy?' She makes an o-shape with lips that beg for a reapplication of lipstick.

'Yes, Jimmy McCarthy. Where is he?'

The receptionist takes out a tattered cigarette box filled with index cards and begins to flip through them. The cards are dog-eared and some are stuck together. She drops a few and apologizes, then starts afresh.

A fuse bursts in Mick's head. He grabs the whole box from her and tips it out. A quick rummage reveals that McCarthy is staying in room 17. His check-in day, the date next to the name, is the Saturday gone. Two days before Joyce went missing.

He pockets the card for evidence. 'Room 17. Come on, lady, where is that?'

'Third floor,' the receptionist says.

Mick gathers his squad. 'Barnes and Souza, you're coming with me. Moggs, you go round the back. There's sure to be a fire exit. You watch that as if it's your sister's virginity, and this time you make a better job of it than you did with the real thing, right?'

'Yes, Chief,' says Moggs, then gulps. 'Detective.'

'Go, man.'

Moggs disappears through the front doors. Mick waves at Barnes and Souza to follow him. They creep up the stairs to the third floor.

The windows in the corridor let in a little streetlight, but the hideous green carpet swallows most of it up. The door to room 17 is closed. Mick leans against the wall, pulls out his gun and holds it up. Barnes does the same. Mick waves at him, the dummy rat, to stick his heat back where it belongs. Someone's got to pin the suspect down, hold him tight and scan the room for others. Don't they go through this in training anymore?

Somebody coughs inside the room. Souza also pulls his weapon and cocks it, then meets Mick's eye and quickly de-cocks it again. The two snaps of metal pierce the silence, as deafening to the trained ear as the double-bang of supersonic speed. A heartbeat follows during which the world is absolutely still.

Then a chair falls over in the room, followed by the crackle of curtains being ripped aside. Mick curses and throws himself against the door, which does not budge. He yells for Barnes, who puts his weight to it with all his gym-honed strength. From inside the room comes another thunk and the rattle of a window opening.

Mick grabs Barnes and shouts into his face: 'Together, you moron. One, two—'

They crash into the door at three and crack the lock. Barnes yelps. Mick takes the door out with his foot and bursts into the room. The first thing that meets his eyes is the sight of McCarthy's slacks disappearing through the window.

He stumbles forward. Jimmy McCarthy is already on the fire escape and descending rapidly into the dark, shirt-tails flying.

'Souza,' Mick yells. 'Back down, back down. Suspect on the run.'

'What?'

'Run, man. Get to Moggs.'

Souza darts away like a rabbit. Mick jumps through the window and onto the fire escape. Behind him, Barnes pipes up: 'I think I hurt my—'

But Mick doesn't even catch the rest. This is the real thing. This is what he's good at. The hunt. Nothing matters now but the man flying down the stairs a floor below him. Not the gutters and alleys and the evening wind. Not the smell of trash and hot bricks. The world is reduced to the clank-clank of his feet on rickety metal and the shape of the bad guy he must pursue and catch.

Jimmy McCarthy hits the alleyway at the bottom of the fire stairs. He turns around and their eyes meet, two whites in the dark, the hunter and the hunted, predator and prey.

'Police,' Mick yells. 'Freeze.'

McCarthy rushes toward the street. Like a shit Phantom Stranger, Moggs appears and blocks his way. He draws his gun and goes into textbook style stance, his knees bent and his arms straight as a musket.

'Stop, or I'll shoo— arrest you,' he shouts.

McCarthy backs away. His eyes swivel to Mick, who is on the last flight of stairs. Exhilaration explodes in Mick's chest. *You're in the bag, buddy. It's all over.*

McCarthy's hands fly to his belt, where something silver gleams. A gun.

Oh, no.

The world goes slow-motion. Mick's feet don't seem to connect with the stairs anymore. He spends an eternity asking the universe what to do. Shoot or keep on running? Fight or freeze?

And there is Ruby's voice, from the deepest part of his soul. *I don't think I could kill anyone, ever.*

And so, he runs.

In the alleyway, McCarthy aims at Moggs. The glint of his gun is sharp like a snake bite, and just as deadly.

'You got nothing on me,' McCarthy shouts. 'Get out of my way or I'll spike your bacon with some lead.'

'I am the police,' Moggs says. His hands are shaking. 'Put your weapon down.'

Stop that, Moggs. The words race through Mick's head at light speed, too fast for his mouth to catch up. *Stop that. Give in. It's not worth it. It's—*

'Fuck you,' McCarthy yells, and moves his finger.

The shot lights up the alleyway. For one split second the world is sketched out like a drawing. McCarthy's face, white with rage. The supernova in Moggs's eyes. Souza appearing behind him, frozen mid-run. An overturned trash can, vomiting banana peels and styrofoam trays. A distant traffic light.

Then Moggs falls over. The universe answers. *You should've taken that shot, Blanke. You failed again, you coward. Again.*

And time speeds up.

Mick jumps the final railing, yelps at the pain shooting up his leg and throws himself onto McCarthy. With one punch he knocks the gun from his hand and then it's man on man. McCarthy grunts and falls backwards. They go down together. Mick's punch flattens McCarthy's nose against his cheek. In turn, he gets an elbow to his stomach and a knee in the groin. McCarthy fights dirty, battle-scarred. Like a soldier when the bullets are spent and all that's left is the deep, red, grandiose fear.

McCarthy's next blow lands on Mick's arm. Before Mick

knows it, his gun changes hands. He's flipped over and thrown on his back. The barrel of his own weapon rises before his eyes.

'Fuck you, too,' McCarthy grunts.

Time stops once more. Mick stares into the barrel and waits for the light of death at the end of the tunnel. And he thinks of Fran. There is a really soft and kissable bit of her, where her shoulders run into her neck. He hasn't kissed it for a while and he regrets that now, more than anything else . . .

McCarthy flies sideways and lands on the sidewalk. A fist hovers in the dark, clutching a gun by the barrel. Its handle has just connected with McCarthy's skull. It's Barnes, his eyes as large as saucers.

'I couldn't shoot,' he says. 'My shoulder . . . I-I'm sorry.'

'Shit happens.' Mick scrambles to his feet, picks up his own gun and points it the way it should be, right between McCarthy's shoulders. 'Jimmy McCarthy, you are under arrest for the murder of Deena Klintz. You have the right to remain silent.'

On the ground, McCarthy scrapes his legs against the dirt. Mick handcuffs him and kicks him down. McCarthy's head hits the flagstones with a thunk. Not standard protocol, of course, but what happens in dark alleyways stays in dark alleyways. The kick is a temporary, one-second relief from what he needs to do next. Which is to turn around and look at Moggs.

Less than a year ago, Mick's career was nearly ended by

a bad decision. Bad decisions turn reality into a series of slides. And here is Officer Moggs, sprawled out on the sidewalk. Mick looks and knows with sinking certainty that this slide will stay with him forever. The projector will be stuck here, *click*, through the suspension and the public apology to Moggs's grieving parents, *click*, *click*, through the court case and the divorce, *click*, and always back to Moggs, lying motionless on the sidewalk, his eyes staring up into the night . . .

Then Moggs groans and turns over.

The relief is a vortex that sucks Mick down. His knees buckle and he falls. Billy Benson appears in his mind's eye, staring down at him. *You nearly fucked it up, Blanke. Don't ever do that again.*

'Detective, sir?'

Billy vanishes and Barnes reappears. Mick scrambles to his feet and brushes away any doubt. It's all good. They got McCarthy. And Moggs is alive.

Moggs seems to struggle to believe it himself. 'Bullet must have missed me,' he says. 'Gone right past me. I heard the whistle in my ear, man. Shhhit.'

'Souza, take your buddy's gun.' Mick yanks McCarthy to his feet. 'Moggs, your hands are shaking. Butch up. You're a cop. This sort of shit is your breakfast.'

He bundles McCarthy into the car. The man isn't bleeding, which is good, but the hair on the side of his head is matted and the skin underneath is swollen and discolored. Mick pulls at McCarthy's arms to look at his hands. Two fingers on his right hand are shortened, with big, knobbled ends where the fingertips should be. Just like the fingerprints on that bottle.

He laughs, louder than he wants. *Jackpot.*

Barnes, who is still clutching his shoulder, gets to sit on the passenger seat. Moggs and Souza take their places on either side of the suspect.

McCarthy groans and lifts his head. 'Lemme out,' he mutters. 'I done nothing.'

'You are under arrest for the murders of Joyce Haney and Deena Klintz. Your car was spotted at the scene.' Mick sets the blinker.

'My car's in a garage. I didn't . . .'

McCarthy's head lolls back. His eyes half-close, the whites still glowing under heavy lids. He sinks forward and Souza reaches out just in time to stop him falling. Mick swerves onto Witterman Street and takes a sharp left. Just then, there comes a cough and a splatter from the back seat. The stench of vomit fills the car, sour and terribly human.

Mick rolls his eyes. Fran is going to lynch him. She just bought new foot mats.

Chapter Twenty-Nine

Ruby

Ruby pushes her torso out of the window and cranes her head to check the street. It's that time of the day when the working folk are heading home and the boys are coming out. There's boys everywhere. Darting across Trebeck Row, dodging cars and hollering at friends. Boys with scowls, at odds with the world. Boys who grin slyly at the sight of a pretty girl.

She can sense trouble in the air. These boys are taut like bow strings. Last night, Pa told her why. There's rumors that the governor canceled the freeway through Beverly Hills. Now they're gonna build it on Eastside. The evictions keep on coming. And the Latino folks who live there are gonna be told to settle in South Central, where the rents are already sky-high and the jobs are scarce.

She tears herself away from the window and rubs her arms where the frame has left indents. All those things are happening out there, and she's got her own world of trouble, right within these walls. Pa's silence and

Mimi's nagging and the endless worrying about money, always money. And Joseph, of course. Joseph, who hasn't called.

The yearning hits her like a slow-motion car crash. She's got to see him and figure things out. She needs to escape the apartment, even if the air outside is twanging with aggression.

She chooses her outfit carefully. A white blouse, tucked into her pants. The green sandals. A big, green bangle that she's been fighting over with Mimi for so long they've forgotten who owned it first. A dab of Vaseline on her bangs and a quick rub-down along her ankles.

Feeling better, she walks down Compton toward Geddit Fixed. It's Sunday, but part of the reason Old Man Toby hires only Blacks is that they don't have a union to back them up and will work any day. Joseph oughta be on shift. She'll swing by, pretending she's on an errand for Pa. Just to see what's up.

A big delivery truck stands out front, its hood and trunk wide open and the tires taken off. Behind it, Leroy is leaning against the wall, blowing smoke rings, while Old Man Toby is polishing the fenders.

Joseph pulls his head out from underneath the hood and mops his brow. He shouts something to Leroy, the end of which sounds like 'police'.

Leroy flicks away his cigarette and answers: 'Eastside, loads of them. They're gonna tear the place apart. They're not gonna lay low no more, brother.'

Ruby glances at Joseph, who has his shirt unbuttoned and looks fit to bite. He hasn't noticed her. No one has. Gingerly, she takes the watch off her wrist and slips it into her pocket.

Leroy sees her first. 'Hey, sugar,' he hollers across the street. 'What's kicking?'

She saunters over, slowly. Joseph turns toward her and she looks past him for a second or so, before letting their eyes meet. 'Oh, hi.'

His face. The energy in his angry eyes. It makes her chest feel as if a whole galaxy is swirling around inside. Damn this. She was gonna be cool, and now she's gonna melt into a puddle on the asphalt.

'I hear you got yourself some special friends,' Leroy says and grins. 'The pigs. Got yourself right and tight with the cream of high society.'

'I got arrested.' Ruby tries not to look at Joseph. He's told on her. *How dare he?* 'I got slammed up for one night, in case you didn't know.'

'Yeah, but now you've got an admirer driving up to your house. Or you go and meet him, huh? On Skid Row? Say, Joseph's not good enough for you?'

'Leave her alone,' Joseph mutters. 'None of your business.'

Leroy scoffs. 'Beg your pardon, sir. It's everyone's business. Can't trust a snitch. Good you two ain't hanging out no more.'

'I'm not snitching to no one.' Ruby glares at Leroy, but

the look in his eyes shrivels her anger into flakes of dust. 'I'm just . . . Ain't my fault my boss got abducted.'

'Yeah.' Leroy grins. 'Nothing's ever anybody's fault, little girl, until it suddenly is. Ah well, if you're too good for Joseph, there's enough sisters in his neighborhood to do a man like him proud.'

Tamona. Heat rises under Ruby's shirt. Who knows how often she's been rocking past the garage? Often enough to catch Joseph's eye for sure. And she goes to the committee. Leroy'd love that. With Tamona, he's gonna get Joseph completely under his spell.

Leroy wipes his forehead with his sleeve and nods toward the garage. 'Phew, it's hot today. Go get a soda, Rubes. There's a good girl.'

She turns to Joseph, but he just grins.

The need to scream at Leroy rampages through her chest. But the words won't come. She oughta tell Leroy to suck on it, but she can't. He's so self-assured, so powerful. He always takes command, and he ain't leaving space for backtalk. It's like getting on the bus to Sunnylakes. Only there they call her Negro, and here they call her sugar.

A hissing noise cuts into her thoughts. She spins around. In one corner of the dark garage, a man is spray-painting the chassis of a formerly silver-black Crestliner. Red varnish has spattered all over his boiler suit. In the dim light, it looks as if he is covered in blood. He grins as she walks past.

'Nice, baby,' he yells over the hissing of the spray gun.

Ruby nods politely. 'It's a lovely car.'

'Oh, baby. I'm talking 'bout you. How 'bout you get over here and check out my tool?'

His screeching laughter chases her away. She beelines for Old Man Toby's little office at the back, which houses the paperwork and, most importantly, the refrigerator. While she roots around for a soda, her mind flicks back to the car. A green rear fender and that dented, silver roof. She's seen it before. On Monday afternoon.

Carefully, she peers past the pinups plastered on the window that provides Old Man Toby with an overview of his business. The Crestliner stares at her with empty eyes, half-submerged in gloom. Its right fender and door are now a dusky red. The color looks familiar. A rich and juicy crimson. Just like . . .

Just like blood.

She scans the garage. Joseph and Leroy are still outside, shadows moving slowly in the bright sunlight. The man with the spray gun has receded behind the Crestliner, working on the trunk. There is no one else around.

Her stomach buzzing, she opens the drawers in Old Man Toby's battered desk. There is a registration book up top, its cover frayed and greasy. She pulls it onto her lap and flicks through the jobs covering the past two weeks. There is nothing in here about a silver Crestliner. But you gotta know Old Man Toby. If this is a cash job, he won't have it in here, in his regular orders. Joseph told her once that there's a second book, the one the tax man doesn't get to see.

Two drawers down she hits gold. A diary, the name Melanie scrawled across the cover, hides between some broken screwdrivers and a couple of yellowed petty cash slips. On Friday, Old Man Toby made a note. *12 noon Crelin. Aliz, specifics. CMJ.*

Old Man Toby ain't very smart. He's got his own system of making notes, and once you've read Dr Futterer, it's easy to crack. Crelin, that's a Crestliner. Aliz, specifics, that's gotta be some sort of clue to what the job entails. But CMJ? That could mean anything.

She slips the book back into its drawer.

An idea pops into her head. She grabs a second bottle of soda and leaves the office. This time, she sways her hips a little as she walks back. The eyes of the spray man latch on to her with unnerving inevitability.

'Baby girl,' he shouts. 'Changed your mind about my tool?'

'Looks like thirsty work.' She approaches cautiously, the sodas clinking between her fingers. 'What's it you're doing?'

'Just a little beauty job. This baby needs one. Unlike you.'

Ruby ignores his leer. 'What's that color? I like it. It's so pretty.'

The spray man pulls at his goggles and moves closer. 'Hot red,' he says. 'Like your lips, sugar.'

He lowers the spray gun. The can of color attached to it comes into view. Written on the label are the words: Alizarin Crimson.

Aliz. Alizarin. *Old Man Toby, you really ain't very smart at all.* Ruby bites her lips to kill the grin spreading on her face. She puts the soda on the silver hood and slinks away, quickly, before the spray man's fingers can make contact with her skin.

Outside, Leroy cracks open the bottle and takes a long draft. When he is done, he throws the bottle onto the sidewalk, where it splinters into a thousand diamonds. Old Man Toby looks up from his polishing, seems to want to say something but then leaves it.

'You should come with us,' Leroy says. 'Our committee. We're starting a ladies' night.'

'She ain't going,' says Joseph. 'She don't care about the movement.'

'Come on.' Leroy winks at her. 'Tamona will be there. You'll love it. Might even learn something.'

Joseph puts down his screwdriver. 'I said no.'

Ruby spins around. 'You talking about me?'

'Ain't like you ever listen,' Joseph replies. 'But Leroy, she don't wanna go.'

'Speak for yourself. I sure got something to talk about, considering—'

Leroy laughs. But it's a dark laugh. His eyes remain hard and piercing, like those of all the boys on the street. 'The time for talk is over, sugar.'

'Go home,' says Joseph.

'But I thought we could . . . I was gonna—'

'It's too late, Ruby.' He doesn't even look at her. 'Go. Check on your pa.'

Leroy laughs. 'Yeah, run home, baby girl. To your papa and your cop-man. He'll sort you out, no problem. What did you do so he'd let you go, huh? You let him taste a bit of that sugar?'

'Hey, man—' Joseph begins.

Ruby cuts him short. 'Shut up, Leroy. You think you're so clever with your committee and your big talk, but you understand nothing.'

'Ooh, I love it when you're angry.' Leroy grins, and the grin makes her shiver. 'Why not put your money where your mouth is? Ah, here's Tamona.'

A cab draws up to the curbside. The door cracks open and Tamona emerges. Her endless legs unwind like she's a ballerina and the asphalt her stage. She is wearing a blouse with a swirly pattern of reds and greens and browns. The supple, shiny material accentuates her curves. She's stopped using relaxer. Her hair poofs out from her head in a perfect black halo. She looks powerful and real. Better than Ruby ever will, no matter how many orange hair clips she sticks onto her head.

Joseph gapes at her as if she's made of ice cream. It's too much to bear. Ruby pushes past Leroy, away into the street. But Tamona is faster. She intercepts her and gives her a once-over with her large, kohl-rimmed eyes.

'Hey, Ruby, fancy seeing you out and about. Shouldn't you be working?'

'At least I *got* work,' Ruby mutters.

'Joseph told me all about your arrest.' Tamona smirks. 'But you done all right, from what I hear. Got yourself a swanky little job up in them hills. I can just about picture it.' Her voice turns higher. 'Yes, ma'am, yes, ma'am. Always at your service.'

Ruby balls her fists. 'You don't know nothing.' She spins around to Joseph. 'And you? Got anything to say to my face, rather than talking about me behind my back?'

Joseph shrugs.

'All right.'

She hastens down the street, back toward Trebeck, each heartbeat a thunderclap. Waiting for the lights to change, she catches her reflection in the storefront of Wheeler's Radio Service. Her hair looks silly. She's tried to straighten it, but the kink has returned to her parting, making it messy and dull. Her face, warped by the glass, is puffy with tears. Joseph's watch is weighing down her pocket, heavy as a brick.

Chapter Thirty

Joyce

By the time I hear the roar of a car coming up the road, my face is fixed and my hair laid. Barbara is playing nicely in her frilly blouse. Lily is still sleeping, which is perfect. I will dress her once she wakes. The last thing I need at this moment is a cranky toddler.

The engine revs and throttles. I rush to the door and fling it open. I wish he wouldn't roar his engine so – the neighbors might hear. But old habits die hard.

And how hard they die. I am in his arms before the door has fallen shut. I match myself against him. His scent, the mold of his back, the pressure of his arms. My chest roars with anguish and joy. Jimmy. He has come for me.

'Let's go,' I say.

He untangles himself from my embrace and laughs. 'Baby, you're insatiable. I thought you'd cooled off. But seems the old bastard isn't doing it for you, huh?'

I ignore his words and take his hands. He laughs harder and pulls me toward the bedroom. He has misunderstood.

'Los Angeles,' I say.

Jimmy stops. 'What?'

'I want to get away. Please. Please take me.'

'Oh, don't worry, baby. I will take you, all right. Come here.'

'No.' I let go of his hands. 'Not now. Not like this anymore, in secret. Take me away from here.'

'You mean . . .' The realization dawns on his face. 'You want to run away with me?'

'Yes.'

I expected elation. I had it all planned out. We would race away from Sunnylakes and find a motel for the first few nights. We would picnic on the beach and make love to each other every night, until we found a small house to rent. I would paint again and begin selling, and perhaps exhibit in New York and then in Paris and—

There is something guarded in his eyes. Not like I had imagined. Not at all.

'I am ready,' I proclaim. 'I don't want this anymore. I want—'

You, I should say. But suddenly the clouds part from my soul and I see it. See it clearly. My art and New York and Paris.

'Freedom,' I whisper. 'I want to be free.'

A thin wail emerges from the nursery. Jimmy stares at me. And then he scoffs. 'Honey, it's not that easy.'

'Yes, it is,' I say. 'We'll stage it. We will pour a bit of blood in the kitchen and leave the front door open. They'll never know I went with you.'

'And have you packed anything?' His words don't quite reach my brain. 'Have you got any money?'

'No money. That would be suspicious. I want to make it look like an abduction.'

'No way. You're crazy.'

It is as if my head is wrapped in a scarf. I cannot quite comprehend. But he looks angry now. Worryingly so.

'No way,' he says again. 'Frankie-boy'll see right through your stupid plan. He'll get the police on my ass before you can snap your fingers. We'll be . . . And what about the kids?'

'They'll stay with Frank. They are better off with him.' It's true. I am a terrible mother. Dangerous to her children.

'Darling.' Jimmy wraps his arms around me, while Lily's screams reach fever pitch. 'This is not the time. Come on, we— Oh, for Christ's sake, will you shut up that little pest? She's rubbing me raw with her screeching.'

I step away from him. My mind is swept blank. I want to speak up. But still, I can't.

'Honestly.' He shakes his head. 'Thank God I don't have kids.'

Something inside me cracks. *You do.* I want to scream it in his face. *He was our boy. Our son. He died, because you left us all alone.*

He looks at me softly, smiles at my anger. 'Come on, baby, what's with the sour face? Be a good girl.'

'No,' I reply.

And therein lies my revolution.

'No,' I say again. 'I . . . I don't want to.'

Jimmy's face goes cold. 'What's that? Look, we only have an hour or so. Goddammit, Joyce.'

'Goddamn you,' I whisper. 'Goddamn you, for what you did.'

He swallows. His skin is very white. There is nothing recognizable in his face. But I don't care. I am cold inside, and dead. Where there once was life, there is nothing but a gaping, aching hole.

'I had your boy,' I say. 'We had a child. But you were not there. You left me alone. All of you. I – I can't . . .'

I turn and run. Past the nursery door, which is open, and where I spy Barbara's big eyes. I run to the bedroom. Bring out the painting. Press it to my womb as if I could return him there. I grab the little sleepsuit and hide my face in the flannel. *I wish you had lived.* I stifle a sob. *Oh, how I wish you had lived.*

Jimmy has gone to the kitchen. I follow. 'There,' I say, and hold the painting up so he can see. So he *will* see. 'Your son.'

He stares at the painting. His mouth opens and closes. His fingers twitch. Inside me, a little flame begins to spark. I am enjoying this. I have never made a man feel bad in my entire life. I have always striven to please. No more. *It's over.*

'Where . . . where is he?' says Jimmy.

I curl my lips around the word. 'Dead.' I mouth it more than I say it. It cannot be spoken out loud.

He strikes so fast I hardly know it happens. I am lifted off my feet by the blow, the painting slips from my fingers. I fly backwards and my head slams into the kitchen sink. I fall like a sack of flour. The light dims and I see the strong shape of his back recede.

Chapter Thirty-One

Ruby

Detective Blanke phones on Sunday night to say that a suspect, the same man who broke into the Haney house, has been apprehended. Ruby lets his words ripple through her mind. Apprehended. Boy, that feels good.

Also, Mr Haney has been released on bail. Which means that, on Monday morning, she's back on the bus to Sunnylakes, ready to clean up for the mother of all dragons.

While she mops the kitchen floor, voices start drifting from the living room. Mr Haney is on the phone, talking loud enough for his words to carry. 'The police treated me like a killer. It's defamation . . . locked up for two nights. Come on, Marv, what are our options? I want to sue.' A pause. And then, 'No, I'm not a suspect. A person of interest. Of course I am – it's a dead baby. But it's got nothing to do with me.'

The kitchen grows very hot. Ruby leans against the mop, which has gone slippery in her hands. Mr Haney didn't say anything to her when she arrived. He cannot know the truth about who broke the pot and let the big secret come tumbling out. But still, her heart thumps in her chest.

She pushes the mop over the same three tiles again and again. Mr Haney's conversation switches to the police.

'Blanke,' he says. 'B-l-a-n-k-e. Dunno. Yankee fellow. Sounds foreign, right? Maybe a Jew. Ah, well. You let me know.'

He hangs up and silence returns to the house.

Ruby wipes her forehead. The air is humid and the water won't dry. She opens the front door to let a little breeze run through the house.

And then she sees Barbara walking down the driveway all by herself. The sunlight plays on her hair and the frills on her white socks shine like angel wings.

Ruby drops the mop and runs outside. She catches up with Barbara halfway to Mrs Ingram's house. 'Barbie,' she shouts. 'Where are you going?'

Barbara steps behind a tree, then peers around it, beaming. 'I'm waiting for Mommy,' she says.

Ruby's chest grows tight. 'Mommy is out. She's not coming home just yet.'

'She's gone to live in a different place. With him.'

A bolt of lightning freezes Ruby into place. *Dr Futterer. Help me out here.*

She kneels down to make herself less threatening and evens out her voice as if she were asking the girl to tidy her dolls. 'Barbie-baby,' she says, 'who are you talking about?'

Barbara falls into sing-song. 'Mommy's in a different place, a different place, a different place.'

'Where?'

And Barbara points at Mrs Ingram's house.

Ruby shakes her head. 'Barbara, that's where Auntie Nancy lives. She's not your mommy.'

Barbara scrapes at the tree bark with her fingernails. 'But she's looking after us.'

'Baby-girl, don't listen to her. Come on inside. I'll give you a cookie.'

Barbara squirms. 'Is the man still there? The one who came when I banged my head?'

Ruby's heart skips. 'Nah, he's gone for good.'

Barbara falls silent. Ruby joins her in scraping at the tree bark. Now there are two grayish lines on the trunk, and they both have dirt under their fingernails.

She's burning to know if Barbara saw Jimmy McCarthy here on the day Joyce Haney disappeared. But she's not allowed to ask straight up. Dr Futterer says that's planting ideas in a child's head.

She waits a little until Barbara gets tired of scraping. 'Last time the man came to your house, what did he do?'

Barbara investigates the tree bark under the tiny half-moon of her fingernail. 'He slammed the door and Mommy said I have to be good and go to Joanie. He said Lily is a pest and Mommy said, "you left me all alone".'

'Mhm.'

Barbara picks at the dirt. Ruby reaches out and lets her fingers run over the girl's arm.

'I promised Mommy to be good,' Barbara says quietly.

'You are being very good. You are a wonderful, brave little girl.'

'But Daddy didn't get me a present from the counter fence.'

'The conference. That's because he had to come back in a hurry. Because Mommy went away.'

Barbara smiles. 'I never tell a secret, Whoobie. I didn't tell Daddy about my head.'

Dammit, girl. You're too good.

'I have an idea, Barbara,' Ruby says. 'If you tell me about the man, I will tell you what happened to him. I'll trade you a secret for a secret. OK?'

Barbara's tiny lips purse to a point. For a moment, she looks like her grandma. A sad sight. It'll only be a few years until the dog-poop face will become part of her repertoire.

'Is it like a spell?' she asks.

'It's a magic promise.'

'And you're going to give me a cookie?'

'Sure.'

Barbara flinches. 'He put a spell on mommy.'

'He did?'

'He's a wizard. He came to the house and I promised Mommy not to tell. He put a spell on her and she fell to the floor and then she went out.'

'Where to?'

'She said they wouldn't be long.'

'Where did she go?'

Barbara smiles. She gets up and twirls around, twice, thrice, light and shadow dancing on her dress. 'Third star from the left,' she says, 'over the hills and far away.'

'Stop that.' Ruby grabs Barbara's arm and brings her to a halt. 'Come on, baby. You have to tell me. Where did she go?'

Instead of an answer, Barbara freezes. She points a finger over Ruby's shoulder and beams. 'Oh, look. There's Mommy now.'

Up the driveway walks Mrs Ingram, in her yellow dress and the matching hat. She holds Lily by the hand, the two of them strolling in unison, Mrs Ingram bending a little at the hip to reach all the way down to the bulb of Lily's fist.

Barbara tears herself away from the tree and runs down the path. 'Mommy,' she yells. 'Mommy.'

Mrs Ingram lets go of Lily and opens her arms. Barbara throws herself in and is lifted high into the sky.

'Oh, darling,' says Mrs Ingram and plants a kiss on the girl's hair. 'You are getting heavy.'

Then her eyes meet Ruby's and she breaks into a smile. 'Ruby, perfect timing. Could you take these two? I've got to go to work.'

Ruby cannot move. The spell is not quite broken. It could have been Joyce on the path. Joyce, in the afternoon light, laughing and playing with her kids.

'You look spooked,' Mrs Ingram says. 'Any more men stalking the woods?'

'It's Barbara,' Ruby replies and takes Lily's hand. 'She called you "mommy".'

'I know. It's not the first time.' Mrs Ingram's face grows serious and she lowers her voice. 'I told Frank the girls should see a doctor. It is too much stress for their little heads. Oh, Lucille. Yoohoo, we're home.'

Mrs Haney senior peers out of the door. 'Ruby, you have work to do.'

'I was just running after Barbara,' Ruby replies. 'She was outside, and—'

'You let go of that child.' Mrs Haney senior yanks Lily away from Ruby and shouts back over her shoulder: 'Frank, I wish her not to touch the children.'

Ruby slips back into the kitchen, where the floor has dried. She leans against the sink and breathes, twice, thrice, until her heartbeat slows down to a level where she ain't gonna keel over and drop dead.

Outside, Lily starts wailing. There is a commotion in the hallway and soon Mrs Haney senior raises her voice from the living room. 'The children need a proper home. I have said before, I don't *mind* taking them back to Pennsylvania, out of this infernal heat.'

Mr Haney's answer is inaudible, but his mother replies: 'It's too much to put on poor Nancy. And I've raised children all my life.'

The rest of the conversation is drowned out by Lily's

screams. Soon after, Mrs Haney senior pops her head into the kitchen, wailing Lily on her arm and Barbara, her face all closed up, by her side.

'I am going out with the children,' she says. 'I want you to leave now. Frank is in no state to supervise your work.'

'Yes, ma'am.' Ruby looks at Mrs Haney senior's feet. 'Of course. It's been an hour and—'

'You've done hardly any work at all. I don't see why you should get paid.'

And with that, she sweeps out of the house and slams the door. A few seconds later, a car engine roars and fades out.

Ruby takes off her apron and hangs it away. She empties out the bucket and puts it under the sink. Then she steps onto the terrace and slides the kitchen door shut. Now the geraniums are gone, the garden has lost its color. All that remains are a few dried-up, paper-thin petals, huddling in the corners.

She walks around the house. The stillness is making her nervous. When she reaches the living room windows, she hears Mrs Ingram's voice. 'Don't worry about it.' There is something treacly in the quietness of her voice. 'It calms the children down. And that would help you, wouldn't it? Frank, darling, I—'

'Hush, Ruby is still here.'

'No, your mother sent her home.'

Ruby presses herself against the wall. If she walks on now, she'll have to go past the window. They'll see her.

And a pulsing nausea in her guts tells her that would be very, very bad.

'It's not right, Nancy,' Mr Haney responds. 'I don't want them to forget their mother. Please. Next time they call you "Mommy", you tell them not to.'

Mrs Ingram sighs. 'But I am tired of being Auntie Nancy. I want more, Frank. You know that I would be a wonderful mother.'

'They have a mother.'

A sharp, little laugh. 'Yes, one who is pumped full of chemicals. Who lets the help run the house and dumps her own children with the neighbor at every opportunity. You know how much I've been taking care of these kids, Frank. Come on, let me take care of you . . .'

'Get off me.'

Something clatters in the lounge. Mrs Ingram's voice, when she next speaks, is whiny, almost pleading. 'What's wrong with you, darling?'

'This can't go on. This . . . You coming over here. Joyce is missing.'

'Darling. You're so tense. You—'

'Of course I am damn tense. It's been a week.'

'Yes. A week, Frank. Now think about how I've felt, for more than a year. All that waiting and hoping and running for the phone and not leaving the house, just in case you—'

'Come on, it's not like I forced you into it.'

'But I didn't think you'd drag it out for so long.' Mrs

Ingram's voice somersaults. 'You're insane to wait for that frigid, uptight bitch.'

There is a pause. Ruby digs her nails into her thighs. The memory of Mrs Ingram's sheets floats into her mind, the look she gave her. Now she understands. Mrs Ingram really was showing off. Marking her territory. The sheer primitiveness of that makes her skin crawl.

'She's my wife,' Mr Haney says, his voice deep and vile. 'You knew that from the start.'

Mrs Ingram laughs. 'Ha. Tell me, darling, what do you see in her?'

'She's the mother of my kids. That's what I see in her.' Mr Haney seems to hesitate. 'The good life.'

Mrs Ingram scoffs. 'The good life. And here you are, mocking me for wanting just the same. A house and a husband and two beautiful girls to love me.'

'Nancy, you're mad.'

Another little laugh, like the clink of glasses. 'I know you're not the perfect husband. Darling, did you do it? Did you tidy that lovely, crazy wife of yours right out of your life?'

'Shut up.'

'No, I won't. I know you weren't in Palmdale. Where the hell were you, Frank? Hiding? Waiting? Burying a body?'

'Nancy, darling, I would never—' Mr Haney makes a sound that's almost a sob. 'Oh, God. Please, not you, too. I'm innocent.'

'I drove to Palmdale on Sunday night. I wanted to

surprise you.' Mrs Ingram sighs. 'I even took Monday off. All morning I waited for you in that motel. But you didn't show up. And when I finally went to the convention center . . . well, they didn't let me in. But I saw your day badge on the table. Frank, you didn't go to the conference. You weren't there.'

'I . . .' A groan. 'I was just driving. Clearing my head . . . I needed to get away from the house . . . Nancy, you must never, ever tell anyone about this.'

'Of course not. Same as I won't tell anyone about you forgetting that you gave me your gun on Friday.'

Mr Haney groans. 'God, Nancy, please. I feel like everyone is after me. Promise you believe me. I did not hurt Joyce.'

There is a pause, filled only by the sound of shuffling. Then Mrs Ingram's voice again, soft and light, like Marilyn Monroe's.

'I promise, darling, if you promise you'll marry me when all this is over.'

'Nancy, I—'

'Hush. I know what you need, darling. I know best.' More sounds of shuffling, and then a quiet little moan.

Enough. Ruby sneaks along the wall, back toward the terrace. She walks up to the garden shed, flexes her toes and jumps. Her fingers grab the ledge and strain under her weight. Lord, she's not a child no more, but a woman with the weight to prove it. She scrambles against the wall, sets her toes right and heaves herself up.

The tar on the roof is soft with sunlight. Her shoes leave little indents as she tiptoes across. At the far end, she counts to three and jumps.

She lands with a thud and rolls into the trees, where she listens for noise from the Haney house. But nothing stirs behind the fence.

All right. She struggles to her feet, shakes out her blouse and wipes her tarry palms on some moss. The lake is just a few yards away and she sits down at the bank.

The water lies serene and the houses are quiet. Candy houses in a magic forest, where women disappear and witches guard their palaces and their enchanted men.

She can't make sense of what she's heard. Mr Haney wasn't at his convention. He insists he doesn't remember giving the gun to Mrs Ingram. Her. How she appeared, in that dress, and Barbara running toward her . . .

A peal of laughter echoes from the forest. Ruby spins around, but there is no one there to see. The noise dies down before she can locate it, and the stillness returns. The only sound remaining is in her head, where her thoughts are whirring at light speed.

Chapter Thirty-Two

Mick

On Sunday night, Mick finds a Moses basket on his doorstep. He picks it up, but then he sees that the baby is a skeleton. It's Sandy. Something's gone terribly wrong. He tries to hide her so Fran won't find out. But she does anyway and backs him into a corner. Mick turns around, his heart pumping, the weightless baby in his arms, and it's not Fran but Joyce, in a yellow dress and immaculate lipstick. She holds a knife in her hand and he realizes then, with debilitating horror, that it was his own blood on the kitchen floor all along.

He wakes up. His mouth tastes like vomit and his sheets are drenched with sweat. Carefully, he turns to check if he's woken Fran. Nope, she's still piling up the Z's in blissful innocence. Her naked shoulder peers from the sheets, and the sight of it sends a little swirl of warmth into his guts.

He'd expected a row. After McCarthy's arrest, he missed dinner over the paperwork and came home late, his ear still hot from his calls to Ruby and Florence Delawney and Sergeant Major David Potter from the US Armed Forces base in Philadelphia, who confirmed everything Mick already suspected about Jimmy McCarthy.

But Fran didn't sulk. Instead, she poured some whiskey and they sat down in the kitchen and talked. Really, properly talked. She listened patiently to his sweaty, sweary account of Jimmy's arrest. He apologized for working so hard. She flashed him a smile, and he remembered the gun barrel in his face and took the opportunity to kiss that soft spot on her shoulder.

The station is busy with Monday cases – wife-beaters, drunk drivers and the occasional loose woman recovering from a long weekend. Mick makes some strong coffee and airs his office. The sky is blue like a Sanforized sleepsuit and the sea breeze smells of salt and gasoline.

His mind drifts to the case of Deena Klintz. Deena – born with brains and enough moxie to want something better from life. She knew about Joyce and Jimmy. After Joyce's disappearance, she might well have put that knowledge to use. A bit of blackmail here, a bit of hush money there. Until Jimmy put an end to her games.

Someone crosses the hallway. Moments later, a voice like a foghorn shatters the silence. 'Fuck me, what kind of hellish brew is that?'

'Yankee blood, Murphy,' Mick yells. 'Proper good stuff. Choke on it.'

The door bursts open. Murphy enters, looks around for

a chair and frowns. 'Blanke, you troglodyte, the polite thing is to offer the chief a seat.'

'I made a request two weeks ago.' Mick grins and sips his coffee. It is strong and dark and dreadful. 'Seems my boss hasn't processed the forms.'

Murphy gives him a dark look. 'You better fill me in. Who's this McCarthy and what do we have against him?'

'Quite the pile. He was Joyce's lover before she met Frank. Went to Korea with the last shipment and couldn't forget her. After he returned, he asked her to leave Frank. She refused. They lost contact after the Haneys moved down here, but a few weeks ago he showed up again. On Saturday he broke into the house. He simply walked through the back door and said he was looking for some paintings.'

'And that's all?'

'He owns a gun. It's in the lab for ballistics tests. And then there's the fingerprints on the beer bottles in Deena's trailer.'

'What about them?'

'Two fingers missing, same as the ones on the bottle found in the Haney house. I spoke to McCarthy's sergeant major. McCarthy was a Korean prisoner of war. He lost them under torture. Plus, a silver car, just like what he drives, was seen at both crime scenes. Mrs Ingram, Joyce's neighbor, saw it the afternoon Joyce disappeared. And Deena Klintz's neighbor said she saw a silver car drive away shortly after she heard the exhaust bang. But I think it was the shot.'

'Why would this fellow kill Deena?'

'Joyce and McCarthy used to meet at Deena's house, so she knew of their affair. Joyce spoke to Deena that afternoon. She might have told her McCarthy was coming over. When Joyce disappeared, Deena might have tried to blackmail him. I saw her on the day after Joyce Haney vanished. She was coming from the house, putting something into her purse.'

'How the hell did she . . . ?' Murphy moans. 'Hodge.'

'Yep. We found one of Joyce's paintings in her trailer. Perhaps there were others that would have given Jimmy away. But Jimmy McCarthy wasn't going to bow. He's a violent man, and Korea made him worse. The army gave him a dishonorable discharge because of his rages. I wouldn't be surprised if—'

'OK, let's say he killed Deena. But Joyce?'

'She didn't want him. So, if she didn't want to come willingly . . .'

'God, Blanke.' Murphy's eyes widen. 'Do you think he kidnapped her? Maybe she's still alive.'

A gentle wave of nausea sweeps along Mick's throat. 'I don't think so. Kidnapping takes planning and cool. This was a crime of passion. Things gone wrong between lovers.'

'I thought she was frigid.'

'With Frank, anyway.'

'What kind of woman closes up against her husband but lets another guy taste the clam?'

Mick shrugs. 'Let's assume Joyce and Jimmy were in

love. Or at least they had an affair. He wants her to come away with him. Joyce sends her daughter outside so Barbara won't see the strange man in Mommy's bedroom. But then she changes her mind. They fight. He runs off. Joyce phones Deena and tells her about it. Deena called several times that afternoon. But then Jimmy returns. He injures Joyce, or maybe even kills her. He gets rid of the body and leaves the area to lie low, until Deena contacts him. She wants money to keep quiet. He goes to her place and shoots her. And that's that.'

'All right. Say, who's the lady who witnessed the car? Is she trustworthy?'

'Mrs Ingram. A family friend. Lived in the area for a while. She'd notice a strange car.'

'That's good.' Murphy shifts his weight. 'In fact, that could be the deciding clue. If she is willing to testify. Tell her she'll get half the money now, and half after the court case. And you need to talk to Frank Haney. Give him a little pressure. He's not entirely off the hook. We still need an explanation for the dead baby.'

'Will do, boss.'

Mick waits for Murphy to leave and calls Mrs Ingram. She repeats what she said at the exhibition and swears she didn't know Jimmy was back in town until Ruby pounded on her door. Yes, she's prepared to go to court and testify about seeing Jimmy's car drive away just before Joyce was found missing.

He didn't mention the break-in on Friday to Murphy.

A tiny part of him worries about that. It's the wonky puzzle piece, the bastard cousin in this case. Why did Jimmy McCarthy want the paintings? He should have run, should have driven north and never looked back. Why did he stick around? Why did he book a room under his own name?

He wipes the doubt away. Who knows why scumbags like Jimmy McCarthy do what they do?

Once again, traffic stalls around the Harbor Bridge construction site. Ahead of Mick, cars snake over the dusty hills. The Buick's engine hisses and splutters from the constant stop-start.

He recalls a time when a passing car was enough to bring the kids out running from the backyards of Troy. For little Mickey Blanke, a ride in the car was the neato-keano. It meant you were either going to a wedding or to the hospital. He remembers vividly how it made you feel like John Carter in a rocket ship to Mars. Now, he is the proud owner of his very own car, and mostly he just rolls along at walking speed, cursing and groaning and sweating through his shirt.

It takes him half an hour to find a parking space near the Griffin Corps headquarters, and he still has to walk three never-ending LA blocks. But at least the receptionist, pretty in a cellophane-wrapped sort of way, is courteous and friendly. She calls Frank Haney and asks him to come down. Five minutes later they are sitting in the deli across the road, mugs of weak coffee steaming between their palms.

Haney is looking tired. The strain has carved deep lines around his mouth. His eyes lie in shadow and his skin is porous and sallow. Mick tries to be cordial, to make this a chat among men, a sympathetic attempt at the truth.

'Yes, I know of Jimmy, of course.' Frank bites his lip. 'Nasty piece of work. Joyce dated him before . . . well, before he joined up.'

'You've never met him?'

Frank snorts. 'Of course not. I would have booted his sorry ass all the way back to Korea.'

'Did you know he was in the area?'

'If I had, I would never have left Joyce alone.'

'Deena said Jimmy and Joyce were going to run off.'

'Deena was a two-tongued snake. I wouldn't trust a word from her mouth.' Frank Haney's guard goes up almost as quickly as it came down. 'Well, I didn't mean to . . . She was not a particularly pleasant woman.'

'Yet Joyce and her were friends.'

'I guess. Maybe Joyce felt sorry for her.'

'Why do you think Deena would tell me the relationship between your wife and Jimmy was serious?'

'I told you, there was no relationship.'

'We're still investigating that.'

'Look, Joyce told me about Jimmy after we got engaged. She didn't want me to be surprised when, during the wedding night . . . you know.'

Mick doesn't. Him and Fran shared many a prenuptial afternoon in his tiny apartment, scuffling under sheets. They'd made sure that their own wedding night would hold no surprise.

He swallows his coffee too hot, burns his tongue and forces his thoughts back to the conversation. 'So, Joyce and Jimmy had a physical relationship before your marriage?'

Haney winces. 'He . . . forced himself onto her. Or, at least, he initiated it. She told me it was a big mistake. She didn't repeat it with me. We held out for marriage. I was always proper with her.'

Aha. Poor Frank Haney wasn't getting any even before he got married. That should have been a clue for him. But, Mick thinks, men like Haney don't pick up on clues.

Haney seems to feel a need to fill the silence with a sigh. 'Women don't ever know what they want. I'm sure you've had your fair share of trouble with them in your line of work. Your colleagues told me a thing or two . . .'

Mick's inner alarm begins to shrill. He flattens his palms on his legs and keeps his face as smooth as possible. 'If this is about my transfer, the lady in question knew full well what she wanted.' Out of O'Leary's gang and into witness protection. And she'd found just the right dumbo detective to fall for her lies. 'She was a mobster moll,' he says. 'I was going to use her to get to her boss, but then I guess I got used instead. I . . . I got no one to blame but myself.'

Haney grins, but it is a weak effort. 'That's our goddamned weakness. Women. We're just too nice to them. And then they take us for all we're worth.'

'You just said they never know what they want.'

'They don't.'

'Are you talking about your wife?'

Haney picks up his coffee. 'First, Joyce wanted me. But suddenly I wasn't . . .' He pauses and runs his fingers through his hair. 'Who knows . . .? Detective, if it's worth it, I think Jimmy did it. He had unquenchable desires for my wife. I think he killed her.' His voice snags. 'There was the baby.'

Inside Mick's brain, the puzzle pieces fall in place with silent finality. The baby. Jimmy's baby. Pride spreads in his chest. Joyce's murderer is already under arrest. And once his little headache is cured, McCarthy'll go to court and then dangle. Mick Blanke saved the day. Screw the Murphys of this world. His methods work just fine.

'Listen,' says Haney, and his expression confirms it all. 'Please. You have to promise not to tell Mother. She still thinks it was mine.' He pulls at his hair. 'I thought we were so happy. I laid my heart at Joyce's feet. And then . . . and then . . . this.'

'She cheated on you?'

'After everything I did for her. I thought it was just the birth of Barbara that had made her so . . . reluctant. But then I found out that wasn't the reason . . . I went back to my mother. To clear my head.'

'You upped and left while she was pregnant.'

'You don't understand.' Haney wrings his hands. 'She was crazy. Said she didn't want me, didn't love me. She called me a moron and a dumbass, said I'd ruined her life . . . things no normal wife would say to her husband. I had to get the doctors involved. They gave her medication. Strong medication. I thought it would be best for Barbara not to see all that.' He hides his face behind the palms of his hand. 'She pushed me away when she needed me most.'

'She was pregnant.' He cannot let this go. 'She was having a breakdown. She wasn't in a good place, and you just left her alone.'

'I wasn't in a good place, either. It was hell. I beat myself up for it now, Detective. Trust me.'

The image of Haney screaming at the station comes to his mind, the way he crumbled to the floor.

'Hm.' Mick sets his coffee down. 'Well, I better let you get back to work.'

Frank Haney nods, but his eyes have glazed over. When Mick pays up and leaves, he is still sitting at the table, his head propped up on his hands, staring at the coffee grounds in his mug as if he's trying to read a future that never came to pass.

Chapter Thirty-Three

Ruby

'For the last time, Ruby, I'm not signing nothing.' Pa pushes the application form across the table and folds his arms. 'It's not gonna happen. Period. Why do you even have this thing?'

'Because I want to go.' Ruby clasps the form, then slides it back to him. 'I thought . . . I mean, I was expecting . . .'

'We were all expecting.' Pa's eyes grow dark as tar. 'But that's how it goes. God rest your momma's soul. The city ain't giving nothing. So you gotta put your ideas out of your head.'

Ruby jumps up and grabs a glass, but the water faucets have been dead all afternoon. Thirst claws at her throat and turns into anger. 'Let Mimi pull her weight a bit more.'

Pa scoffs. 'Yeah, let's take Mimi out of school and send her to work at Fine 49. That something you want?'

'No.' She clutches her chest where something burns bright and searing. 'I'll earn it myself, then. I'm getting there with the Haneys.'

'Well, how much do you have?'

'Nearly a hundred dollars.' Ruby's eyes well up. 'That's . . . that's . . .'

Pa smiles a sad smile. 'That's good, girl. That's mighty fine. But it's so far from enough. You should get real.'

'I—'

A knock on the door cuts off Ruby's reply. It's Mrs Estrada, in a shapeless red dress, her eyes rimmed with red.

'I'm going out,' she says by way of greeting. 'My sister's got the eviction notice.'

'The freeway?'

Mrs Estrada nods. 'The governor been sending letters out today. Them folks in University, they've cut off their water already. They're gonna bulldoze it all to dust.'

'Shit.' Ruby swallows. 'We have no water. Is that why—?'

'That's what they do.' Mrs Estrada sniffs. 'Cutting us off and cutting us up. Anyway, a Mrs Haney called. You're fired. She don't want you nosing around no more.'

'But I—'

Mrs Estrada turns away and lumbers down the stairs.

Ruby watches her leave. She cannot move. Her entire body has gone numb. Her lungs contract, each breath sending needle pricks of pain into her ribcage.

'I'm gonna head out for a bit,' she says into Pa's general direction. 'See ya.'

When she steps into Trebeck Row, it's nearly empty. Only a few people hurry to their homes or to work. Fine 49 is shut up. In the distance, Mrs Estrada is making her way to the bus stop, her dress aflame with evening light.

Ruby walks. Her feet don't seem to reach the ground. Out of work again. Why does everything always—

A car comes up behind her, dawdles, then honks. She doesn't turn around. Must be a peeper wanting to get a feel, or a gaggle of boys drunk on the roar of an engine. She walks closer to the wall, away from the reach of an arm.

But the car doesn't drive off. From inside, a man shouts: 'Hey, wait up.'

Fear flares and turns into anger. She spins around and hollers: 'You wanna see ass, go back to your mother.'

Detective Blanke's jaw drops onto the steering wheel of his Buick. Then he blushes. 'I . . . I wasn't . . .'

'Oh.' She quickly wipes her eyes. 'I didn't know it was you.'

'Can we talk?'

She opens the passenger door and gets in. The detective signals correctly and looks carefully over his shoulder before he rolls into traffic. 'You OK?'

'Yeah, fine.'

'I just wanted to let you know we're building our case against Jimmy McCarthy, the man from the break-in. We're pretty sure he murdered Deena on Friday afternoon. She may have tried to blackmail him. She was killed with a small caliber gun, just like the one he owns.'

'Hm.' Of course, Mr Haney also had a gun. And then

he gave it to Mrs Ingram and, conveniently, forgot all about it.

The detective slows down at a yellow light and stops right at the marked line. 'You're not convinced?'

Ruby considers what she's overheard this morning. Thinks again of the beer bottle. Of Mr Haney's false alibi. And then, like God's light shining upon the sinner, she discovers the trump card that's been hiding in Old Man Toby's garage all along. Jimmy McCarthy, CMJ in reverse.

'I can prove it wasn't that Jimmy fellow who killed Deena,' she says. 'I found his car.'

'What are you talking about?'

'I saw him drive away from Mrs Haney's house on the day Joyce disappeared, just before I found the blood in the kitchen. A silver Crestliner with a green rear fender. It was brought to Geddit Fixed Garage. They're changing the coat.'

The detective accelerates and turns onto the Harbor Freeway. His lips are set tightly and he stares straight ahead. 'Mrs Ingram mentioned that car. Why haven't you told me that before?'

'Because I . . .' Because she wasn't going to give it all up at once. Never a smart move. But he doesn't need to know.

'It's an alibi for Jimmy,' she says. 'Mrs Ingram told me she saw nothing after Jimmy broke into the house. He brought his car to the garage on Friday at noon. Must have been right after the break-in. He couldn't have gone to Deena's.'

'Are you saying Mrs Ingram is lying?'

'Perhaps. Ask Old Man Toby. You'll have to look at Melanie's diary, though, 'coz Old Man Toby's keeping the cash jobs separate.'

The detective is silent for a while. 'You say that man who runs the garage cooks his books?'

She nods. 'Old Man Toby doesn't like the tax man.'

'Then the timings are probably false.'

'Nah, he keeps things in order.'

'I don't think a jury would buy that.'

'But what if it wasn't Jimmy? What if . . . ?'

'Yes?'

She takes a breath. 'I think it was Mr Haney,' she says carefully.

The detective frowns. 'Why do you think that?'

'His alibi is a fake. Mrs Ingram said he wasn't in Palmdale. I overheard them talking. Did you ever ask around at the conference he was at? Did anyone see him?'

'He showed us all the bills. He stayed in the motel. And he wrote a report for his boss, which we've also seen. It all checks out.'

'How long is the drive from Sunnylakes to Palmdale?'

'About three hours.' The detective sighs. 'Ruby, you've got to look at the evidence and then build up the case. You don't make up a story and then fit the facts around it.'

'But I'm not making it up. I'm looking at the evidence, just like Dr Futterer says. The beer bottle, for example – it doesn't make sense that it was there.'

The detective takes his eyes off the road for a moment. 'How do you know who Dr Futterer is?'

'I got a book on . . . Look, I'm just saying. The bottle—'

'The prints on it were McCarthy's.'

'Yeah, maybe. But what if someone's trying to frame Jimmy? Perhaps Mr Haney wants to get rid of his rival.'

The detective accelerates. 'That sounds preposterous. The district attorney won't buy it. Especially not from a . . .'

He stops just in time and clears his throat. But Ruby's mind fills in the pause regardless. And once that word has been put in place, it can never be erased.

'Well, someone like you,' he continues lamely. 'Plus, you just said you saw McCarthy's car driving away from the Haney property on the Monday Joyce disappeared. That's evidence against him, not exonerating him.'

'I did, but . . .' She sighs. Yes, she saw his car. And Jimmy may be a bad apple. But why would he kill the woman he loved?

'Anyway,' the detective says, 'I just wanted to say thank you. And, if it was up to me, you deserved the money.'

She inhales. So that means . . .

College. Oh, no.

Oh, well. It was dirty money anyway. She never really wanted it, not for the price of Joyce's blood. But now that it's not coming her way, it just twists the knife that little bit more.

'Who . . . who got it?' she asks.

'Mrs Ingram. She's a sharp one.'

'But,' she says, and her voice wobbles. 'But it's wrong. It's all wrong. Mr Haney . . .' Warmth rises in Ruby's throat. The watery heat of tears. *Oh, Lord. Why do You always do this? Why can't I ever win, for once?*

Cars idle three deep where traffic has been diverted from University. They stop and go and stop and go. The warmth in Ruby's throat contracts into anger. She needs to get out of here. Right now.

'I guess that's goodbye then.' She grabs the door handle and pulls while they're accelerating.

The detective slams on the brakes. 'Ruby, wait. It's not like—'

'I gotta go. And it's Miss Wright to you.'

She jumps out and runs into an alleyway where he can't follow. Tears drown out the yowl of sirens from the street. She presses her hands to her chest where everything hurts. Her heart pumps like an engine, and every breath wracks her with pain. Because she's failed. Even though she read Dr Futterer back to back, and used non-leading questions and did everything right.

Joseph spoke true. She should never have trusted the detective. He's a cop, after all. He's white. He almost called her *that* word. He listens to goddamn Pat Boone. He was never, ever on her side.

She walks without seeing. The block is very quiet. There are no cars on the street, only litter. A movement catches her attention. In the distance, where the road curves toward the freeway, a wall is moving. She blinks to clear her vision. Now it looks more like a centipede, with many legs and shields that glint.

Police. Hundreds of them. Marching toward her.

Something hurls over her head and smashes into a store window. Glass explodes. She jumps and turns. There are boys running down the road. Angry boys, wild boys. Their shirts are torn and bloodied. Some have scarves wrapped around their face. They scream and howl like devils. One boy at the front carries something burning. He throws it high, and it flies like a comet trailing fire before crashing onto the asphalt, setting it aflame.

Ruby stares. *Them folks in University, they've already cut off their water.*

And then she runs. Away from the police and through the streets full of boys. Two buildings are burning. Smoke billows down the street. It sticks in her eyes and makes her retch. The air tastes of plastic. A man runs past her, grinning, a baseball bat dangling from his fist.

Ruby darts toward where there are cars and people, where there's life in the streets. But she's lost among the smoke and the shouting and the shapes. Glass crunches under her feet. Something sharp slips into her shoe and stings her ankle. Finally, she sees the traffic along the freeway. And then two men step out of the shadows and cut her off.

Their faces are covered. Their eyes, very white and also terribly dark, pin her like prey.

She staggers back and runs. They come after her. She takes an alleyway and another, toward the road, toward the cars. Taillights wink, hundreds of them, like a chain of Christmas lights. She dives between them. Tires screech and horns honk. Behind her, the footsteps come closer.

'Wait up, baby,' shouts a man. 'Tonight's a free-for-all.'

She turns and screams. The men laugh. One of them lunges forward. An arm shoots out from nowhere and grabs her. She thrashes about as the world turns red. It doesn't help. Someone drags her back and pulls her into a car.

'Jesus Christ, Ruby, it's a fucking riot down there.'

The detective steps on the gas and swerves into the middle lane. He zooms down the highway toward Beverly Hills. 'What the hell were you thinking? Don't you listen to the radio? You're damn lucky I was still stuck in this jam.'

Ruby doesn't answer. She has no answers left.

The detective makes a U-turn and sighs. 'Look,' he says. 'I'm really sorry. I know the reward would have made a real difference.'

He knows nothing. His neighborhood's not burning. His daughter is in college. He's never been evicted for a fucking freeway.

Ruby sinks back into the seat. 'You know what?' she says after her heartbeat has steadied and her hands have stopped shaking so much. 'I still think it's Mr Haney and you're wrong. And if you're hanging the wrong guy, Joyce will never see justice. Her daughters will be raised by her killer. It's . . . it's not fair.'

The detective's voice is strained. 'I know how you feel, but—'

'You don't. Mrs Haney senior fired my ass. I lost my job for this. I'm not speaking to Joseph no more, because of this case. I just don't . . .'

I don't want it to be over like this.

'I'm sorry,' the detective replies.

They are silent until they glide into Trebeck Row. The detective pulls up in front of Fine 49 and turns the engine off.

'Listen,' he says. 'Call me if there's anything. Really, anything. Just give old Blanke a buzz.'

'Yeah,' she replies and cracks open the door. 'See ya.'

'Honestly, you got my number.'

She doesn't answer. She won't call. That bridge is burned forever.

Chapter Thirty-Four

Mick

The nurse guides Mick to a four-bed ward that's been cleared of all other patients. The beds are made perfectly and the brave soldiers of medical care – drips and wheelchairs and oversized floor lamps – are standing to attention. The room is pleasantly air-conditioned. Since it's always good to put a fink like McCarthy at ease, Mick takes off his coat to look less official and lets the breeze scatter goosebumps over his back.

McCarthy is lying in bed. His eyes are closed. A bandage is wrapped thickly around his head, turning him into a giant marshmallow ready for the toasting.

Mick draws up a chair and pulls out his notebook. Jimmy McCarthy flutters his eyelids like the blond lead in a monster movie. But the voice that gurgles from his throat is anything but helpless.

'Fuck off. I got nothing to tell you.'

Mick smiles. 'Then you've got nothing to hide, either. That gun of yours, is it licensed?'

'Registration's in the post.'

'I see.' Mick doodles a gun into his notebook. 'Your sergeant major told us you moved down here about two months ago. What brings you to sunny California?'

'Business.'

'What kind?'

'Looking for work.'

'You didn't come to see someone?'

'Nope.'

'No old flame of yours?'

'Dunno what you're talking about.'

'Jimmy, come on. What's her name? I want it from your mouth.'

'That's what your wife said last night.' Jimmy cackles, then smooths his face.

Mick lets him have it. There won't be many more laughs in this fellow's life. 'We have witnesses,' he says. 'You've been visiting Joyce Haney, haven't you? Now, come on. I'm trying to protect you. You know that Joyce is missing, right?'

'Got nothing to do with me.'

'Then we have to eliminate you from our inquiries. But we can only do that if you cooperate, you hear me? We need to know the exact details of when you last saw her.'

A moment of hesitation, as if he's trying to do the math. One, two, three . . . 'Friday. Last Friday, I mean. Friday a week ago.'

Three days before her disappearance, of course. Mick sighs. 'What were you doing?'

'Just catching up, like old friends.'

'Sure you didn't quarrel?'

'About what? I was just stopping by to say hi. Been a long time.'

'And did you meet up with her before Friday?'

Again, that calculating look. 'A couple of times since I came down here. She's a good pal. Invited me to meet her kids.'

'But not her husband.'

McCarthy scowls. 'Frank would have made a big deal out of it. In fact, maybe he did make a big deal out of it. Have you asked him where his wife is?'

'His alibi is watertight. But yours isn't.'

McCarthy's eyes ignite. He grips the side of the bed. 'I didn't harm a hair on her head. You're not going to collar me for this, Officer.'

'It's detective, actually. If you weren't going to harm her, why did you bring a gun?'

'I know what's going on here,' McCarthy splutters. 'That bastard. That rich, fucking, Mr Shiny-Car Frank fucking Haney. He set this up, didn't he? He told you it's me that's done it, but he's wrong. He's a liar and a cheat and a fucking killer, I swear it on my mother's honor.'

'Give me one good reason why Haney would kidnap his wife.'

'She's not kidnapped, Officer.' McCarthy sneers. 'He killed her. Because he found out.'

'About what?'

'About me, of course. Maybe Joyce couldn't shut her cute little pie hole. Or he probably beat it out of her. He knew she loved me. She always did. So he took her away from me just like he did in fucking '54.' He groans.

'In '54?'

'While I was kneeling in the mud in fucking Kaesong. I sweated for her, I killed for her. I licked every boot that kicked me in that dank fucking forest. And then I come back and what do I find? He took her. Like that. Snap.' He tries to click his fingers but they don't make a sound. 'Just like that.'

Mick nods. 'Tell me from the start. You met Joyce when she was in college?'

'Yep. We started dating. Her mom – her stepmother – told her I wasn't a catch. I had no money, no education. No career. I couldn't marry her. So I took the best option I had. I joined up. And they sent me to Korea.'

'In 1952.'

'Yep.'

'And you got back the next year.'

'Get your facts straight, Officer. I got back in 1956.'

'It's detective. And the war was over then.'

'Huh.' A sharp laugh, like a gunshot. 'You go on thinking that. But I tell you how I see it. Eisenhower may have said on the damned news that the war was done, but the operations continued. Operation Glory, man. Exchanging bodies, all day long. Bag after bag after fucking, stinking bag. Some of them, they came apart in our hands.'

'You received a dishonorable discharge?'

'You've done your research, mister. But not before I spent a year down the rat hole. Might have been a little too keen to punch something that wasn't already dead. The fucking chinkos arrested me. Threw me in the hole. No food, no water, shit running down your leg. Scurvy. And they know how to make a man suffer. You don't even know the shit I've seen.' His hands crunch the bedsheets. The two stubby fingers on the right barely curl.

'Careful now.' Mick can't let that one go. 'I'm a veteran myself. Pacific theater, '45. You don't know the shit *I've* seen.'

'Ha.' Jimmy's eyes darken. 'At least you had the bomb to put an end to those vermin. You were the brave ones. We . . . we were forgotten.'

The brave ones. Mick presses a hand against his gut. 'You were court-martialed, right?'

'When I got out, the sergeant put me down for treason. Gave me another year in lock-up, just for good measure. You serve your country and that's what you get. Dysentery and discharge, and nothing to show your gal.'

McCarthy falls silent. Mick lets him stew. But just as he takes a breath to ask the next question, McCarthy speaks again. His voice is softer now, and cracking at the edges.

'All that kept me going was her. And our future. The two of us, together.'

'What did you do when you got back?'

'I could tell she still loved me. I could not stay away. She . . .' A flicker of a smile crosses his face. 'She liked having a good time. With me. We hooked up again, in early '57. But Frank found out. By spring, he was on to us. I broke off all contact with her. No way I was going to go up against that guy and his lawyers. I left her in the nest she made herself.'

Mick shivers. The room seems cramped. The empty beds, the dead machinery, they clutter up the place and take all the light away. He thinks of the baby in the flower-pot, the tiny, wispy bones.

Jimmy McCarthy doesn't notice. He chuckles as if he's told himself a joke. 'Next thing you know, she called.'

'She called?'

'Yep, Officer. Called my old man 'bout two months ago. Got my number. Asked me to come down here. I didn't even know they'd moved. But I thought I'd better stop by. See what's up.'

'You met at Deena's place?'

He grins. 'There's a filthy whore if you ever saw one.'

'You slept with her.'

'Beggars can't be choosers. I went there with all sorts of hope, but Joyce got skittish and left. I hung around for a couple of drinks. And when the woman of your dreams gives you the cold shoulder, you've got to warm your balls where you can.'

Mick folds his arms across his chest. 'Did you see Joyce on the day she went missing?'

Jimmy closes his eyes. For a moment, he seems to fight himself. Then he sighs and talks. 'Yep, Officer. Went to Frank's lair in the afternoon.'

'You wanted to run off with her?'

'She wanted to run off with me.'

Mick leans back. 'Really?'

'Really. She was behaving weird. High, or something. I said I couldn't do it. Frank would skin me alive. She wouldn't listen.' McCarthy smirks. 'Then she said she'd made something for me. And you know what it was?'

'What?'

'A painting of a kid.'

Mick jerks his head up. 'A baby?'

'Toddler, or something. She wanted me to have it.'

'And did that mean anything to you?'

His eyes flick away. 'Nah. Like I said, she seemed kinda high.'

Mick inhales. Somehow, a truth has just been revealed. He spools back their conversation in his mind, but it remains hidden just under the surface, like the carps he used to fish with Gramps on the old Troy reservoir.

'I freaked out,' McCarthy continues. 'I left. Next thing I hear, she's gone. Frank did it. It was his revenge, you see? He couldn't get me, so he got her.' A shudder runs through his body, from the shoulders to the toes. 'He got her after all. She'll always be his now. Forever.'

Mick swallows. A hot whiskey would be good, double, please. Something to melt the ice cube in his stomach.

'Mr McCarthy, where were you on Friday, two days ago, around 2 p.m.?'

'Took my car to a garage. What's your problem with that?'

'The fellow who runs it is a dodgy dealer. How much did you pay him to make the right note in his files?'

'I gave him nothing. He wrote it all down. It's pay on collect.'

'Don't waste my time with that nonsense.' A belated dose of adrenaline shoots through Mick's veins. 'You broke into the Haney house on Friday. You were looking for something, right? We have a witness.'

McCarthy's eyes darken. Something feral grows in them. Mick thinks that, if he were a woman, this would be the moment he'd scream for help.

'That bitch.' McCarthy hisses the word.

'Do you admit to breaking and entering at 47 Roseview Drive?'

'She set me up. That bitch is in it with Frank. He's probably humping her on the sly.'

'Let me repeat that. What did you do on Friday afternoon?'

'I drove to the garage, because I saw her looking out the window while I was driving out of Sunnylakes, and I knew she might recognize my car. So I went to get a paint job, near my hotel. I spent the weekend lying low. Until you kicked my door in.'

'Did you kill Deena Klintz?'

McCarthy's eyes widen. 'She's dead?'

'I ask you again, did you kill Deena Klintz?'

'I know nothing.' He grips the metal railing fixed to the bed. 'I wasn't even there for long. I got nothing to do with that.'

'Deena blackmailed you, right? She knew about your affair with Joyce. She knew you had a motive. And so she had to die.'

'You think I give a damn about some diner hussy? I could have bought her off with two beers. And anyway, she didn't blackmail me. She had no proof.'

The carps surface and somersault in the morning air. It was Deena who had insisted that Genevieve Crane drive her to the search. The Haney house was a crime scene, but Hodge was out back, drinking soda. Not difficult for someone as unnoticeable as Deena to slip into the house unseen and steal a painting. When he'd encountered her among the trees, on his way to meet the search party, she had just slipped a few reams of paper into her bag.

'She had proof,' Mick says. 'Joyce and Deena spoke that afternoon. Joyce must have told her you were there. When she turned up missing, Deena put two and two together. She stole the painting of your child and confronted you with it. She also saw a bottle of the same beer you like to drink in Joyce's kitchen. You had to kill her. What did you do with the painting? Burn it? Throw it in the trash?'

'You're trying to set me up. I did nothing. It had already happened.'

Mick's veins buzz with so much electricity it's a miracle the chair doesn't start sparking. '*What* had already happened?'

McCarthy presses his lips together. A tiny sound bubbles from his thorax, like a tiny sob.

'It's true,' he says. 'We fought. I . . . I might have struck her. But not, like, hard. She was fine when I left. I swear. Once I cooled off, I came back. I wanted to make up, before Frank came home. I went in through the back door. And there was . . . blood. In the kitchen. And no sign of her.' He sighs. 'I hightailed it out of there.'

That would explain the car Ruby saw. But it's too convenient. Too easy.

'I knew Frank had done it,' McCarthy continues. 'He was never going to let her get away.'

Silence. And in McCarthy's eyes, terror.

Mick doodles again on his notepad. Thinks it over. It's not perfect. But it's good enough.

He pushes himself off the chair. 'Mr McCarthy, I am arresting you for the murder of Deena Klintz and Joyce Haney. You will remain in hospital until a doctor certifies you ready for release, after which the SMPD will transfer you to a holding cell. Any information as to the whereabouts of Joyce Haney or her remains will count in your favor during an upcoming—'

Jimmy McCarthy grins. It's a malicious, terrified grin that splits his marshmallow head apart. 'You got the wrong guy, Officer,' he says. 'You got the wrong guy.'

Mick calls Jackie and instructs her to send some underlings to Geddit Fixed. When he arrives, the whole glorious operation is already in full swing. The owner is being questioned on the sidewalk while two officers siphon through the paperwork. In the back, Officer Souza scrapes at the paintwork of a blood-red Crestliner with a screwdriver.

It hits Mick while he crosses the road. That paint job. McCarthy said it was because someone saw his car at the Haney house. No, not someone. *She*. She saw the car. *That bitch is in it with Frank. He's probably humping her on the sly.*

Doubt starts clawing at his chest. Mrs Ingram told Ruby she saw nothing on the day Jimmy broke into the house. And on Monday, when McCarthy roared away from the crime scene, she was at home, concealed by the curtains. He might be talking about Ruby, who definitely saw his car. Not on the day of the break-in, but the day Joyce disappeared.

Ah, well. McCarthy's head got bumped. It doesn't matter. He's got this solved. He'll prove to Murphy and the whole station that he's still got it.

Souza looks up and his face brightens. He points at the green stripes revealed under the red of the fender.

'Nice work,' Mick says and lays a hand on the metal. 'Souza, we've got our man.'

Chapter Thirty-Five

Ruby

That night, South Central doesn't rest. Ruby kneels on her bed and watches the fires glow against the sky. When the detective dropped her off, Pa almost squeezed her to death. He'd been listening to it all on the radio. When was the last time they'd hugged like that? Not even at Momma's funeral, that's for sure.

The fires conceal the coming dawn. It's not until the neon sign of Fine 49 switches off with a clack that she realizes it's daylight outside. In the kitchen, Pa is staring at day-old bread.

'Did they say anything on the radio?' Ruby asks as she enters.

'It turned into a war. Lots of injuries. Two dead. Our boys, of course. None of *them* got hurt.'

'Yeah.' Ruby's mouth has gone dry. 'Any . . . Did they say . . . ?'

But she cannot say her deepest fears out loud. Where is Joseph? Is he OK?

Pa reads her mind. 'You heard from your fella?'

'Mrs Estrada's gone to her sister so I got no telephone. Lord, I hope she wasn't caught up in it.'

'She'd knock 'em out.' Pa smiles sadly. 'Joseph can look after himself. I was more worried about you. I . . . You better get a shower before the hot water runs out.'

With that, he disappears into his bedroom.

Ruby walks into the bathroom and shuts the door. The air is stuffy and she opens the window. A breeze wafts in, and with it the smell of smoke. She slips out of her nightshirt and gingerly pulls the shower curtain shut. The rail is prone to falling off the wall.

The hot water is a blessing from the Lord. Of course, technically it's delivered by LA Water and Power, but she still utters a quick prayer in thanks. She lathers her skin with soap. The room steams up and the orange scent drives away the smoke stench.

Against her will she thinks of Jimmy McCarthy. Two murders. They will hang him.

Thing is, though, it's not right. He brought his car to Geddit Fixed while Deena was killed. He came gunning out of the Haney's driveway, but Joyce was already gone by then. And Frank Haney lied about being at the conference . . .

They're gonna hang the wrong guy. But what's she gonna do about it? Nothing, that's what. Why should she go wreck her ass for a scamp like McCarthy? Hell, he'd never lose a minute of sleep if she were left dangling in the breeze in some godforsaken prison yard.

But Joyce and her baby . . .

Something crashes in the apartment. Pa shouts. Another crash, followed by a high-pitched scream. Mimi.

The cops. The image zings through her like lightning. McCarthy's told them about her hitting Barbara. She'll see that prison yard soon enough.

Her bones freeze. The water burns her skin but she cannot move. *They're coming. They're coming for me. They're here.*

Someone bangs on the door. The sound breaks the spell. She yanks the shower curtain open and the curtain rail clatters to the floor. She grabs the dirty plastic and wraps it around her shoulders like a toga, just in time.

'She's in there,' says Pa. 'Ruby, open up.'

The bathroom lock ain't trustworthy at the best of times. With one bang, it flies off and skitters on the tiles. The door bursts open and Joseph appears.

Ruby stares, uncomprehending. His hair is matted with dust, his shirt torn and bloody. His eyes are wild. They range over her body, up and down, and finally lock with hers.

'What?' he asks. 'What are you staring at?'

Ruby licks her lips, which are dry as sand. 'I thought—'

He won't let her finish. 'They set everything on fire.' His hands begin to fly. 'It wasn't supposed to . . . All the cars were burning. The boys wouldn't listen once the police showed up. Leroy's in hospital. They beat him till he was bleeding. He might not—'

'I thought you were the police.'

He frowns. Silence hangs between them, heavier than smoke. Then she sees it. A rim of water on his eyelids. A telltale shiver across the soft part where his neck meets his chest bone.

She opens her arms. The shower curtain drops to the floor, but it doesn't matter. Joseph flies toward her. She wraps him in her embrace and holds him tight. She's not gonna let him go. Not again. Not ever.

'I'm sorry,' she says. 'Sorry it all went wrong.'

It is only when he pushes her back and looks at her with increasing alarm that she realizes she's crying as well. He pats her hair, which is still slippery with conditioner, then wipes his hand on his shirt. A bubble of laughter rises in her throat, despite the tears. She lets it out, but it is defeated by sobs.

His face falls at the sight of her tears. 'Now, why are you crying?'

'Because.'

Because we always wanna change things and we can't. Because I don't know if it's a sin like murder if you let someone go hang even though you could have stopped it. Because they found a dead baby on my kitchen floor. Because Joyce'll never get justice and I can't do anything about anything.

Joseph wraps her up in his arms and she cries some more against his chest, like the white girls in the movies when the swamp monster is dead. Somehow, sometime later, the crying stops. Joseph hands her a towel and says: 'You wanna rinse your hair? And when you're done, mind if I take a shower, too?'

The curtain rail won't stay up no more. He holds the shower curtain for her, and then she tries to do the same for him, but she's too small. He keeps ducking and diving to escape her gaze, and it turns into the funniest thing she's seen for too long a time. Her insides go all fuzzy at the sight of his grin. She even contemplates dropping the stupid curtain and getting right in there with him. But the bathroom lock is busted, and soon Pa knocks with fresh clothes for Joseph and hints at coffee.

'I saw what happened last night,' she says, once they're all in the kitchen. 'I went for a drive with Detective Blanke to talk about the case. When I got out . . . I didn't know I was so close to University. It was bad.'

Joseph's eyebrows contract. 'So, you're still partners in crime?'

'Don't think so. The case is solved.'

Pa looks up from his coffee. 'Atta girl. That might help the college fund.'

'Yeah.' She takes a sip of coffee. 'Would be great if I got the reward, huh?'

'Greatsville.' Joseph laughs. 'Say it like a white girl. Gee, Big Daddy, that's totally primo.'

'Absolutely golden, papaw, sir.' Ruby chuckles. But the laughter in her belly is hollow. 'Joseph,' she says. 'Let's go get some breakfast.'

'I dunno.' Joseph eyes the window. 'The police might still be—'

'Please. I want to . . . I want to talk to you.'

One corner of his mouth curls into a smile. It's a wonderful sight. 'Sure,' he says. 'Mr Wright, can I borrow your daughter?'

They hit the street just as the ocean breeze gives way to summer heat. The stench of burnt rubber lingers; it tickles the back of Ruby's neck. Not sure what to say, she brings the conversation home to the obvious.

'Why did things turn so bad last night?'

Joseph flinches. 'We had it all planned out. We were gonna do the peaceful thing. Demonstrate against the demolitions. Folks were meant to stay together. But then the police showed up and started beating everyone. The old ladies. The kids. Our boys wanted retaliation.'

Ruby swallows. 'That ain't right.'

'The hell it ain't. But we're angry, Ruby. We're all—'

'I mean what the police did.'

'Yeah.' He sighs. 'It ain't right.'

They walk toward South Park. The streets are full of litter and only the straight folks with jobs are about. They're scuttling for their buses, heads pulled down low.

'They wanted it to happen,' Joseph says to the morning sun. ''Coz now they can make us look like . . . like rebels without a cause. Which we're not. We got a cause.'

She takes his hand and presses it. 'Yeah, we do.'

'They're gonna build that highway and people are gonna lose their houses and all we did was for nothing. All our committee work. All our debates on fighting without fighting. It's just hopeless, ain't it so?'

'No, at least you did something. I mean, we have to keep at it. It's too easy to stand by and see injustice, and not to do anything about it.'

Her words hang suspended in the air. Thoughts intrude and march in rhythm with her steps. When there are so many problems in this world, where do you even start?

'Joseph,' she says, 'I've got to ask you something.'

'Like what?'

'If you could save a white man's life, would you do it?'

He shrugs. 'I dunno. What kind of white man?'

'A bad one. But would you do what's right? For a mother?'

'You talking about the Haney woman?'

'Thing is, the detective has found his man. But he's the wrong guy, I know it. That man's going to hang if I don't speak up. But . . .'

'But?'

'Well, the problem is the man who really did it is probably gonna come after me.'

'And who's that?'

'Mr Haney.'

'Damn.' Joseph swallows. 'Your boss? Mr Rich?'

'Yeah. I think he's framed the other guy. I think Frank Haney and Mrs Ingram are working together to put that man away. They've been cheating together, you know?'

'Shit. Ruby, don't say anything. I told you before, don't get involved.'

'But if I could prove it was Mr Haney who killed Joyce, it would make things right. And I'd save McCarthy from the rope.'

'Is he worth saving?'

McCarthy's grin jolts her memory. The way he swung open the bedroom door. Barbara's fingers clawing at her neck.

'No,' she says. 'No, he ain't. But look.' She searches for words that will explain the rift in her belly. 'Joyce was the only one in Sunnylakes who treated me like a person. I know you keep saying we weren't real friends, but . . . she saw me as a friend. Maybe the only one she had there. And now she's dead, and so is her baby. Remember him? Remember how tiny his fingers were? If they hang the wrong guy, then—'

Joseph picks up her thoughts. 'Then the real killer will never be found. It's an injustice.'

'And, like I said, it's too easy to see injustice and not do anything about it.'

'Truth, justice and the American way.'

'Joseph. You don't get me.'

'I do. But are you sure about this? After all, it's nice to see a white guy getting done in, for once.'

'I guess.'

'So, what do you wanna do? Call the detective and tell him it's Mr Haney?'

'I tried to tell him already, but he doesn't believe me.'

'Figures.'

'So I need to prove it. But I don't know how.'

'What's your evidence so far?'

She sighs. 'Mr Haney gave Mrs Ingram his gun right after Miss Klintz was killed. And I know he wasn't at the conference when he said he was. So I gotta find proof for that. Have a little rummage, you know?'

'Why don't you?'

She turns to him. 'First of all, his mother fired me. Second, because I'm scared. That house is freaky. Mr Haney and Mrs Ingram and his mother, they're all, like—'

'Plastic,' Joseph says. 'Like storefront dummies. Make-believe.'

'That's right. I don't like going there anymore.'

'Did you ever like it?'

She shrugs. 'The kids are sweet. And I like the way the lake brings up a cool breeze.'

Joseph laughs. 'Sounds romantic. The hum of the refrigerator, the scent of bleach on a shitty toilet bowl . . .'

'Stop mocking me. At least I'm making—'

He puts an arm around her. 'Just teasing, honey. Don't worry.'

Honey. Ruby blushes all the way down her neckline.

'So,' Joseph says. 'How 'bout you take me along next time? I'd sure like to see the wonders of Funnylakes.'

'What? Are you mad? Mr Haney's mother—'

'She doesn't need to know. You said there's trees. I can

hide out. Keep an eye on you. Then you do your rummaging, we get the proof and take it right to your detective.'

'Yeah. But I got fired. Mrs Estrada told me yesterday.'

'So what? Pretend you didn't get the message. Ring Mr Haney up tonight and ask if you're supposed to come in tomorrow. For forty cents an hour. Cheaper than anything. He won't say no.'

'You think that's gonna work?'

'Like piston grease on roller-skates. You'll get some college money and save a white man from dangling, and therefore you won't be guilty of . . . what'd you call that? Inverted lynching?'

Ruby elbows him in the side. 'Don't even joke about that.'

'If you can't laugh, you gonna cry. So you better laugh.'

'That's what Momma used to say.'

'No wonder she got a daughter like you.' He squeezes her. 'Come on. Let's get your sister some breakfast.'

Chapter Thirty-Six

Mick

On TV, when a case is closed, there's this moment of elation. Perry Mason grins in triumph as the guilty man is led away. When it all clicks into place, the chief will shake Joe Friday's hands and he'll be thanked by a lady with a tremble on her crimson lips. The officers will crowd to cheer, and the youngest, the one with freckles and shiny eyes, will say: 'Gee, Mr Detective, I sure wish to be as good as you some day.'

Reality isn't quite like that.

Santa Monica station is humming the tune of a Thursday morning. Just as Mick weaves past the officers, Jackie raises a hand to stop him. 'Murphy's considering a deal. If McCarthy gives up Joyce's remains, maybe he'll dodge the rope.'

'All right,' Mick says. 'Sounds about fair.'

'Wait. You're forgetting the tickets.' She hands him an envelope.

'How'd you do that?' He thinks of Genevieve Crane. 'I thought they were sold out.'

'I told them I'm from the police.' She winks. 'Although I'm not sure you can claim for them anymore. Now that it's over.'

Now that it's over. That's about as much cheering as he is going to get.

He pockets the Amblioni exhibition tickets and surveys his office. The crime scene photographs are buried under soda bottles. He pushes them aside and picks up the picture of the kitchen. It's a good photograph. You can almost feel the warm rays of the sun filtering through the curtains.

If only it weren't for the bloodstains. That's the thing about crime. Twenty years a cop, and he never gets used to the loss. Jimmy might reveal the location of Joyce's body. They'll dig her out and bury her properly. But a murder cannot be undone. No matter how much policing he does, the blood stain will never disappear.

He should tidy up in here. Get ready for the next tragedy. And the one after that. Maybe, in ten years, they'll give him a golden lapel pin.

Ah, forget about it. He grabs the car radio, just in case, and his notebook. Maybe a final chat with Haney will cheer him up.

At Griffin Corps, Mick is ushered into a climatized meeting room with views of Beverly Hills. Somewhere in the haze beyond lies Sunnylakes, where hundreds of wives stand in hundreds of kitchens and wait for their husbands to escape from meeting rooms just like this one.

He's just taken a seat on a leather couch when Haney enters. The man has made it past wrecked and is now merely broken. His hair is freshly cut and his tie a tasteful match to his blue shirt. Only the bags under his eyes speak of too many sleepless nights, and many more to come.

'Detective,' he says. 'I ought to thank you. For everything you've done. I . . . I should feel relieved, right? But I just keep thinking I'd love to twist that bastard's head right off.'

Mick shakes the proffered hand. It is slippery and cold. 'That's entirely normal,' he says. 'Just don't actually do it. I've come to tell you that we've even offered him a deal. If he gives up the body, he might not swing.'

'It will go to trial, though, right?'

'The evidence is overwhelming,' Mick replies. *And a jury of Frank Haney's peers will do the rest.*

Haney nods. 'My lawyers will need to know about any holes in the case.'

'No holes.' Mick forces a grin on his face. 'Well, some witnesses have told us different things, but that's entirely normal in—'

'What? Who?' Haney's face pales. 'You just said the evidence is overwhelming.'

'It's just . . . it's not quite clear yet where McCarthy was during the time Deena Klintz was shot. He handed in his car at a garage that day. We found it. I mean, Miss Wright found it, actually.'

'The help?'

'Just by coincidence. Her steady works in the garage where McCarthy handed in the car. The papers show he did so at the time of Deena's murder. But the fellow running the place is cooking his books. It's not going to be a problem.'

'But what's she got to do with you? Why'd you talk to her?'

'She was a witness, remember? Which reminds me, we need to speak to your boss again to confirm your whereabouts on the day. There seems to be some doubt about how long you spent at the conference, and—'

'That also something Ruby told you? What's going on here?'

'Nothing.' Something pings in Mick's stomach. 'Mrs Ingram is our star witness. With her help, it's a watertight case.'

Haney's handshake is firm this time. Mick lets himself be guided down the corridor and to the lifts.

'Send it back up, will you?' Haney tries a tired smile. 'I'll do a half-day today. I want to be with my kids.'

'Of course.'

Mick keeps his face tight until the doors click shut. Then he bites his knuckles and curses. *You and your big, fucking trap. If Ruby wasn't already fired, that would have cost her her job.*

He pats his coat pocket, where the Amblioni tickets sit

crisp and tight. The Buick won't start, but he bangs his fists on the dashboard until the engine comes on with a whine. Five minutes later, he's on the road to Sunnylakes.

Mrs Crane's lounge is a haven of sophisticated tranquility. On his way here, Mick thought long and hard over which excuse he could use to see her again. Closing the case, however, is as good a reason as any. He called Jackie to tell her he'd be out all day tying up loose ends with the witnesses, and now he finds himself back on the comfortable couch, a lemonade in hand. Mrs Crane is grief-stricken, but composed.

'How sad that it must end like this,' she says. 'I had really hoped . . . I mean, it sounds silly, but she is not alive anymore, right?'

Mick lowers his head with a suitable amount of gravity. 'I'm afraid it's unlikely.'

'I knew it. I knew it the first day.' She sighs. 'When Deena and I drove to the house on Tuesday afternoon, I had this feeling that something horrible had happened.'

'Well, it was a crime scene.'

'But you couldn't tell from the outside. I mean, the police and the neighbors were all out searching. The house wasn't locked up. We had no idea it was something this bad. Deena even went inside. She had something she wanted to return to Joyce, so she just popped in to leave it in the house while I walked around to find Laura Kettering. The whole search operation was organized from her backyard. When Deena returned, she was shaking. She told me she'd seen blood all over the kitchen.'

In Mick's head, a billion particles compress into a star. Deena stole the paintings. But she did more. The beer bottle. Now you see it, now you don't. It wasn't there in the morning, and then it appeared in the afternoon. What had Ruby said? *It was weird-looking.*

Damn that Hodge and that ugly lawn chair. What good is crime scene tape if you snooze in the garden and don't lock the goddamned front door?

'She planted that goddamned beer bottle,' he mutters. 'I can't believe we've been so stupid.'

'Pardon?'

'I'm sorry.' He shakes his head. 'The crime scene photos taken the afternoon after Joyce disappeared, they show a big-ass bottle of Blue Ribbon on the kitchen counter. Right by the sink. But when I visited the scene earlier that same morning, it wasn't there. I thought I'd just missed it.'

'You think Deena . . . ?'

'She drank with Jimmy McCarthy. We found more bottles at her house.'

She stares at him. 'Detective, I'm not sure if I should ask this, but do you want a drink?'

The whiskey is excellent. Not that blended shit, but real, single malt. Mick listens to his intestines twang and allows himself a smile. He always had Genevieve Crane down as a whiskey girl.

She inhales the vapors from her glass before she sips. 'Why did she do it, do you think?'

'Leave the bottle?'

'Yes.'

'To blackmail Jimmy. To make really, really sure she could nail him down. They were intimate, did you know?'

Mrs Crane looks up sharply. Her lips compress, which makes her look too much like a schoolmistress for Mick's liking.

'I didn't know. Oh, my. Who told you this?'

'Nancy Ingram.'

Mrs Crane sighs. 'Of course. I should have known.'

'Known what?'

'Deena had only one ally in that committee and that was Joyce. No matter what I tried, the other women could not see past her . . . origins. With Joyce gone, Deena was fair game.'

'Maybe she ought to have behaved better around her best friend's lover.'

She pinches the bridge of her nose. 'It is more complex than that. A woman like Deena cannot win. Society tells her that she needs a man to be complete. And if she does not find one, she is branded a failure. I know that, despite their friendship, Deena was jealous of Joyce, of all she had achieved through her marriage. Perhaps she thought that Jimmy might do for her what Frank did for her friend. Give her a kind of stability. A feeling of worth.'

Mick nods carefully. 'But she also tried to blackmail him.'

'To coerce him. From the moment she was born, Deena was told that she was worthless. Perhaps she simply couldn't imagine that a man would stand by her just for her sake. She wanted to make sure he wouldn't up and leave, like all the others.'

'Not quite the lesson you wanted to teach, I guess.'

'Sometimes I despair.' She nips at her whiskey. 'Nancy Ingram is just the same. Her husband was in Korea. And just like Jimmy, he came back wrong. She left him after years of hell. But instead of looking for a partner who'd respect her, she grew jealous of Joyce and her children.' She sighs again. 'It's always about the men. The men rule their lives. And they do not learn. They pick themselves up and redraw that lipstick and set out for the next one. Until one of them ruins them.'

'Ruins them?'

Genevieve Crane gives him a look. He refills his whiskey glass and leaves the silence hanging. There are things he does not want to think of. Things Genevieve is right about, and she really, really shouldn't be.

Mrs Crane lowers her glance. A shiver shakes her shoulders. The first sob hits him with terrible certainty.

He sets down the whiskey glass. 'Genevieve,' he says. 'Please. I know how you feel.'

'How could you?' She moves away from him. 'You don't see the misery I see. The violence. The hiding. The pretending. All that darkness.'

'I do.'

The images run past him. The wives who cannot hide their relief when their beloved husband is finally found drowned in the canal. Mothers calling the cops about their daughters' broken arms, and when the cops show up at the hospital, there's the little boyfriend with roses and his tail between his legs. And the broken arm was from a fall. Honestly, sir. Just a fall.

Joyce. She must have been utterly, utterly alone. The thought sickens him. No, it's not that. He is sickened from the things he refused to see.

Genevieve turns around to face him. She reaches for her glass and empties it. 'Sometimes . . . sometimes I feel I only make things worse. When I talk to these women and encourage them to leave, to run as fast as they can, am I really helping them? Or am I just tormenting them, because they know they'll never run fast enough?'

'You're not hurting anyone.'

'Well, look at what happened to Deena. I told her to make her own luck and find a man who would do right by her. And off she goes to seduce her best friend's lover. Perhaps she thought that silly plan with the beer bottle would keep him on her side. And now she's dead.'

'That's not your fault.'

'And Joyce? I supported her art. Maybe I encouraged it too much. She was like a caged bird waiting to be freed . . . Oh, that's a silly metaphor. I just didn't want her to wake up one day and find that her life had passed without meaning. What if . . . what if that drove her to her death?'

'How would a little painting kill her?'

'I don't know.'

'Then it cannot be your fault.'

She turns toward him fully. Something passes between them, and if she were a man he might have called it brotherhood. Or is it more?

Snap out of it. He pinches himself so hard he has to suppress a wince. This was how it got started with Beverly. The feeling that he was the big protector, the grand detective who'll take care of things when the little ladies reach their wit's end. It hits him like a brick. That's why he got the tickets for Amblioni. To show her he cared. Just like he bought bracelets and hot dinners for Beverly Gallagher, that poor, poor girl so badly in need of help.

But this is different, isn't it? Genevieve Crane is a classy lady, and there's nothing wrong with brightening her day.

'By the way.' He hates himself and yet he cannot stop. 'I've got these tickets to Amblioni . . .'

He nestles them out of his breast pocket. Mrs Crane stares at them, and then at him. A smile blossoms on her lips. But it is the wrong sort of smile. Sad, and almost mocking. It doesn't break his heart. It seals it right up.

'You are a lucky man,' says Mrs Crane. 'The exhibition is sold out. Your wife will be delighted.'

She will be. That's the thing. The realization washes over him in one warm wave. Fran will love to go to this thing.

They've been here months now, and he's never taken her to LA.

They could make a day of it, head to Calcotti's for lunch, see the exhibition, and, in the evening, stop by O'Toole's for a whiskey. If they're lucky, they'll get to sit right by the beach. They'll watch the sunset and, when the words run out, they'll just listen to the surf like they used to on Coney Island, before the girls came along.

Better that way. Better than any Beverlys and Genevieves. Better than that look Fran gave him after it all came out and he saw her trust breaking in a way that might never be fixed. In that moment he had thought that maybe letting Billy die had not been the worst thing he'd done in his life.

He puts the tickets away and nods. 'It's going to be a surprise,' he says.

Chapter Thirty-Seven

Ruby

As they get off the bus, the driver looks at them strangely. Ruby's stomach rolls. She can feel his suspicion settle on her skin. He drives on, but slowly, idling so as to miss the traffic light, watching what they're up to in a town like this.

Joseph appears completely unperturbed. He starts whistling a song and saunters up Roseview Drive as if he's just nipped out to Safeway to get some patties.

'Stop whistling,' Ruby hisses. 'Someone's gonna hear you.'

'Even better. 'Cause I'm a humble gardener, here to pick your flowers, sir. Ain't got no care in the world.'

Ruby has to bite her lip to stop herself from laughing. Joseph's got a talent for acting. He's put on some work pants from the garage and a light-blue shirt. A metal bucket dangles from his hand. Ruby asked him what a gardener needs a bucket for but Joseph just shrugged off the question. 'People be seeing what they wanna be seeing.'

But no one's seeing anything. There is not a soul out and about. The only sound is the *tss-tss* from the sprinklers working hard to keep the back lawns juicy.

Joseph lowers his voice. 'It's like the aliens have landed and teleported everyone up to Mars.'

'It's always this quiet in the afternoons. The husbands are at work and the wives are cleaning or making waffles for the children. And the children are watching TV.'

'You think everyone here has a TV?'

'For sure. And when one of them gets a bigger one, the neighbors run off to the mall to buy the same. On Sundays they all do barbecues in the yard.'

'I'd fancy some barbecue.'

'Not this one. They never marinate the meat. And the wives put salad in a Jell-O.'

'What?' Joseph stops dead. 'That's awful.'

'Shh, we're here.'

They've reached the end of Roseview Drive. Number 47 stands guarded by a row of trees, the white fence glowing against the dark underbrush.

'Through there.' Ruby turns Joseph toward the patch of trees where Barbara stood that afternoon, waiting for her mother who never came back. 'Go round the fence and wait. I'll scream if anything happens.'

'Sure.' He steps into the shadows. 'You take care, honey.'

Mrs Haney opens the door. She is dressed in a weird, billowing dress that looks like a kid's party tent. But her face is hewn in stone.

'I can't believe you went over my head like this, Frank,' she says by way of greeting.

'Mother.' Mr Haney's on the terrace, sharpening a pair of gardening shears. 'You never asked me in the first place. Ruby is back and that's that. No more discussion, please. Didn't you want to go out? That's why I left the office early.'

'I said no such thing.' Mrs Haney senior turns away. 'Oh, this heat. I need a rest.'

Ruby dons her apron and grabs the vacuum cleaner. She heads for the bedroom and opens both windows. The white fence blocks her view of the trees, but she's sure Joseph would vault it in a second if she started to scream.

She vacuums with fervor. After five minutes, she pauses to take a look around.

Her heart pulses in her throat as she slides open the drawers in the bedside tables. Mr Haney has a Tijuana bible in his and uses a photo of Barbara as a bookmark. But there is no sign of anything useful.

An organized man would leave any important papers with his secretary. Only, Mr Haney doesn't strike Ruby as an organized man. Not after what happened to his wife. He's been frazzled like a cat on the interstate these past two weeks.

She spots a suitcase on top of the closet. The sleeve of a shirt is protruding from the zipper and one of the clasps is unfastened. It's been stuffed there, for someone else to deal with.

Ruby switches the vacuum cleaner back on to mask the

noise and, gingerly, pushes Mrs Haney's dressing chair up to the closet. She slips out of her shoes and climbs onto the seat. The suitcase is not big. She clicks open the remaining clasp. The smell of worn clothing with hints of aftershave rushes out. She has to rummage through underwear and a swarm of single, smelly socks before she finds his pants. Their pockets yield a piece of paper, flimsy and crumpled. She unfolds it and covers her mouth with her hand.

It's a check. For lunch at a motel called Family Inn. The address stamp at the top says it's in Santa Clarita. The waitress has put the date on: Monday, August 23. And it was lunchtime service. Between 12 noon and 3 p.m.

The room grows very hot. So Mr Haney wasn't in Palmdale on the day Joyce went missing. At lunch, he was halfway home.

Ruby stuffs the paper down the front of her blouse. She puts the chair back and jerks the vacuum cleaner across the carpet. All of a sudden, it goes out with a moan.

She spins around. Mrs Haney senior is standing in the doorway, grim like the archangel Azrael come to claim his own. But instead of a scythe, she holds the power plug in her hand. Her gaze snakes along the cable toward Ruby's feet.

'Where are your shoes?'

'Sorry, ma'am.' Her slippers are still parked up by the closet. 'Mrs Haney never liked me to wear them in the bedroom.'

Mrs Haney senior sighs. 'Nancy just stopped by on her

way to work. She's asking you to deal with her kitchen. There's a dollar in it for you.'

She holds up a house key and a crisp dollar bill.

Ruby puts on her daft voice and says: 'Why, thank you, Mrs Haney. I'm a lucky girl today, me.'

Mrs Haney senior mutters something under her breath and leaves the room.

In the kitchen, Ruby fills the mop bucket. The paper in her blouse rustles with every move she makes. She opens the terrace doors and sings, a little louder than usual, to make herself heard over the snip-snap of Mr Haney's shears. Just so Joseph knows she's OK.

Predictably, the mother of all dragons reappears and tells her to shut up. Ruby mops in silence, puts the bucket away and leaves by the front door, quiet as a mouse.

Joseph catches her up between the trees, a mischievous smile on his face.

'You look like Robin Goodfellow,' Ruby says.

'Who's that?'

'Some guy from England. Guess what, we're stopping by at Nancy Ingram's. She's gone to work and left the key with the Haneys.'

'We can turn the whole place upside down. Nice going.'

'No way. You wait outside. Round the back. If anyone sees you—'

'Who's gonna care?'

'Everyone. They're crazy here. Imagine if Mrs Ingram came back. We'd—'

Joseph waves a hand. 'All right. I'll hang back. Gonna sit on my bucket.'

Mrs Ingram's house is the usual scene of chaos. The living room is covered in dresses, discarded like the skins of a rainbow snake. In the kitchen, someone has attempted to cook and given up halfway through. Bowls filled with mashed peas and Jell-O are stacked up by the sink. The oven smells.

There really ain't no point in even starting. Ruby's got a dollar in her pocket already, and once she's called the detective and shown him the proof, she won't ever be working for these people again.

Upstairs, the bedroom curtains are drawn shut. She parts them a little and glimpses Joseph among the shrubs near the lake, sitting on his bucket as promised, his head turned toward the house. When she opens the closet, dresses tumble out, some still wrapped in plastic and with dry-cleaning tags. She cannot find the yellow dress, the one Mrs Ingram was wearing the other day. But there is another one, made from the same daisy-patterned fabric Mrs Haney found at the sale. Maybe Mrs Ingram got lucky, too.

No, she didn't. Ruby's heart beats faster. This is the same dress. Exactly the same. These are Joyce's clothes.

Ruby throws the dress onto the bed and stares at it. Something that Barbara said, so long ago, creeps into her mind. *I found Mommy's dress.* She thought it was a dream, but perhaps she had really seen it. In Mrs Ingram's house.

A possibility opens up, silent and wide like the space between stars. Mrs Ingram. She's trying to make the illusion perfect.

She tears her eyes away from the dress and burrows deeper into the closet. Her fingers are sweaty. They hit something hard. She pulls aside coats and skirts to reveal a piece of stiff paper.

A painting. She pulls at it. It slips out, reluctantly, as if something holds it back. She unfolds it and lays it onto the bed. And the world flips over.

The painting is not big, but it holds all the answers. It shows a pool, fringed by potted geraniums. The water is crystal blue and clear, soaking up the sky above. The geraniums jump off the paper in vivid reds, almost purple where the reflection of the water catches the bottom of the petals. In the middle, smiling shyly, stands a little boy.

He has Joyce's eyes. He is Joyce's child. But he's not Frank's. The face betrays the secret. Ruby knows his father. He has tousled black hair and a lean walk like a panther's. Right now he's sitting in a cell, waiting for his conviction.

Behind her, a man clears his throat. 'So, Nancy was right.'

Ruby spins around and stares into Mr Haney's face. A scream dies in her stomach. Mr Haney's face is weary but his eyes are blazing with something that is deeply frightening.

'I-I'm just . . .'

He shrugs. 'I thought you were the one person in all this who did not give a damn.'

'But I do.' Ruby backs away. 'I give a damn about Joyce. About what happened to her.'

Mr Haney laughs. 'The killer is in custody. A violent man. I promise you, Ruby, my witness statement in the stand will incriminate him most severely.'

'You're sending an innocent man to death.'

Mr Haney's laugh turns into a roar. 'Innocent? He's a criminal and a drifter. A home wrecker. Men like him are the cancer in America's belly. The fewer of them around to menace our families, the better.' His eyes narrow. 'But now to you. You've been at my things. Give me what you found.'

He moves closer, and Ruby shrinks back. 'No, I won't. It's proof. For the detective.'

'Yes, he told me you've been meddling. I've come to make sure you won't wreck the case. Now, come on. Give me what you found.'

Ruby edges toward the wall. Joseph needs to be here, right now. Where is he? Where—?

Finally, her lungs comply. She takes a breath to scream, scream like Momma, who could holler a street to pieces.

But Mr Haney is too fast. He grabs her and slams her into the wall. Her breath cuts off as his hand locks onto her face. He presses down on her mouth and nose. The scream dies on her tongue. His other hand curls around her throat.

'You little bitch,' Mr Haney says. 'I wish you'd never set foot in my house.'

She tries to fight but she's got no fight left. Her chest roars for air that will not come. His fingers dig into her windpipe until her lungs reach bursting point. The world turns hazy. Her muscles give out. His eyes are blazing galaxies in the encroaching darkness. At the center of each galaxy lies a black hole.

Chapter Thirty-Eight

Ruby

Reality shatters with a bang. Mr Haney's eyes grow wide. He slips out of Ruby's vision, revealing Joseph, standing tall. He drops the bucket and pulls her up. His voice sounds muffled in her head. 'Ruby, Ruby. Please, Ruby.'

The room is oddly skewed. She coughs. Air streams into her lungs. Precious, beautiful air. She retches – and the pain sets in, heavy and throbbing. She puts her hands around her throat, just like Mr Haney did, searching for the dents and valleys his fingers must have left.

'Ruby. Jesus Lord, are you OK?'

She nods, uncomprehending. Mr Haney groans and moves one arm. Joseph vaults toward him and squats on his back, one knee pressing between his shoulder blades.

'Get me something to tie him up.'

But Ruby can only stare and endure the pain. Red stars pop before her eyes. And the stabbing in her lungs is so excruciating it leaves room for nothing else.

Joseph pulls his shoelaces out, ties them together and wraps them around Mr Haney's hands. He ties a stocking around his legs and stuffs the sleeve of one of Mrs Ingram's silk blouses into his mouth.

He tried to kill her. *Frank Haney nearly killed her.* It's only now that Ruby begins to understand what has just happened. And what Joseph has done.

'Thank you,' she says. 'You saved me.'

He grins. 'Like I promised. Truth, justice and the American way.'

Ruby picks up the painting. She opens the curtains and holds it up. The sunlight sets the geraniums on fire and throws sparkles over the pool. The boy's face glows with life.

'Neat,' says Joseph. 'Who is that?'

'I think it's Joyce's baby. The one we found in the flowerpot. What he would have looked like now.'

'Lord have mercy on his soul.'

'It's not Mr Haney's child. Jimmy is the father. Joyce's boyfriend.'

At her feet, Mr Haney grunts.

'But why was the baby in the flowerpot?' Joseph wrinkles his nose. 'That's just . . . weird.'

'She kept it.' Ruby looks at the painting. 'Can you imagine, all these years? Pouring water in there and watching the geraniums grow and maybe hoping against all hopes that one day her little baby will pop its head out and say: "Mommy, I'm fine".'

'That's messed up.'

'No, it's sad.' Ruby lays the painting next to the dress. 'She must have missed him. She must have missed that baby something fierce.'

Joseph stares past her. His face grows pale.

'You OK?' she asks. 'Joseph, what—'

Joseph raises both his hands.

Ruby's feet turn to lead. She wants to turn around, to see what Joseph is seeing, but it is impossible.

'Hands up,' says Mrs Ingram.

Ruby lifts her arms over her head. When she turns, it's like fighting a storm. Mrs Ingram is standing in the door with a gun gleaming in her outstretched hands. Her eyes sparkle with joy.

Mrs Ingram's eyes snag on Joseph. 'Who are you?' She chuckles. 'Oh, Ruby. What is this? Bring your date to work day? For a little bit of daylight robbery?'

'This ain't want you think,' Ruby says, but it only makes Mrs Ingram laugh louder. Her whole body is shaking. She laughs and laughs, but the gun remains trained on both of them.

'No, Ruby,' she says. 'You got it all wrong, honey. This is not what *you* think. I should have gotten rid of you much sooner. As soon as you saw me in her dress. You knew then, didn't you?'

The ground trembles. Or maybe it's Ruby's knees, giving way like rotten wood. She stumbles backwards against Joseph.

'I know nothing,' she croaks. 'Please. Just let us go.'

Next to Ruby, Joseph shifts. The fabric of the green dress rustles. With two steps, Mrs Ingram is beside him and snatching the dress to her chest. 'Don't touch that.' She holds it up with one hand and shakes it out. Then she twirls side-to-side, slowly, always keeping the gun aimed true. 'How is this? Does it look good?'

'It's Joyce's.' Ruby's arms are beginning to get heavy. 'Why did you take it?'

'It was meant to be a surprise for Frank.' Mrs Ingram's expression is almost gentle now. 'And for the children. They loved their mother so much, poor things. I thought they might like to see me in her clothes.'

'You're trying to be like her.'

'No, darling. I'm trying to be better than her. Look at that.' Mrs Ingram picks up the painting. 'Joyce Haney. With the perfect hair and the lovely home and the muffins on a tray . . . and all the while she was a killer. A reckless, heartless killer. She threw a life away. A precious, lovely little boy.'

Mr Haney twitches. Mrs Ingram's glance flies toward him, just for a moment, but her attention never leaves the gun. 'Oh, come on, Frank. I know you are mourning her. But she had it coming. A lovely, little baby . . . Joyce can never be forgiven for what she did. I will never forgive her.'

Her eyes sparkle as she speaks. Ruby shudders. Mrs Ingram has completely, utterly blown her fuse.

Ruby swallows. Her thoughts run like a steam train – slow and sluggish, shrouded in smoke. She fights the truth, but it rolls over her regardless. Barbara's words. *She* left the house. *She* said they wouldn't be long. Barbara didn't mean her mom, she meant Mrs Ingram. *She* did it. Mrs Ingram killed Joyce. Because she hated her and her beautiful life.

'Now,' says Mrs Ingram. 'I have a wonderful idea. Ruby, come here for a minute.'

Ruby's chest burns up in panic.

'Just over here.' Mrs Ingram pulls her away by her arm. Her grasp is strong as steel. She grabs a silk scarf from the pile in front of the closet, makes Ruby kneel and ties her hands to Mr Haney's. The knots are tight; they squeeze the blood from Ruby's hands.

'Good,' says Mrs Ingram. 'Now, Frank. Don't worry about me or the children. Your mother has taken them to the mall.' She bends down and kisses him on the forehead. 'You'll have to stay here a little while longer. You understand, it needs to look right. Don't say anything, I'll fix up a story.' She nods at Ruby. 'Once I've been rescued, I'll tell the police to come here. I'll say I've managed to overwhelm one of them, but then was kidnapped by the other. Now, come on.'

She pulls Joseph up from the bed and puts the gun to his head. He goes limp. The sight drives a knife through Ruby's heart. He's so strong and tall, bigger than Mrs Ingram by any measure. And yet she's got all the power.

They always have all the power.

Joseph throws Ruby a look that sets the room on fire. Mrs Ingram pulls him away, and the last thing she sees is the desperation in his eyes. The front door falls shut behind them. Moments later, the roar of an engine cuts the golden air. Then, all is quiet.

Ruby breathes – three, four, five. She cannot think. Her heart pounds so hard it drowns out Mr Haney's muffled breathing. She tries to move her fingers, which have begun to tingle. But the knots are holding tight. Ain't no jigging these free.

She's got to get out of here. Joseph. If the police find him in the car with a white lady and a gun, he's done for. *That clever bitch. That vampire.*

Mr Haney turns to look at her. He has the expression of a man who's been thrown off a rocket ship. Adrift and utterly alone.

Ruby tugs at her hands some more. She's got to work that damn knot loose. But she's got no knife, and anyway, she—

The hair clip. She bends her head low and pushes against the scarf. The green clip is wedged tight in her curls. It's sturdy, powerful enough to keep the kink down. The silk soon snags on it. Ruby shakes her head, slowly, and eventually hears the satisfying tear of threads. Mr Haney's hands move as he strains against Joseph's shoelaces. She pulls away, the scarf rips apart and she is free.

She sits back and rubs her wrists. Her fingers don't want to move for a long time. She cries a little, just because it helps. Mr Haney makes a moaning sound, but she ignores him. Not his damn time now.

Joseph and the vampire. There's only one man who could stop them. The detective. He'd know what to do. He's gotta get here, and fast.

She runs downstairs, where the telephone gleams like a beacon. She tries the front door, but of course it's locked. She'd have to climb out a window to get away from here, but then the neighbors might see and—

Ain't no time to waste. She presses the receiver to her ear, fumbles the detective's card from her purse and dials. A woman picks up. She sounds annoyed.

'Santa Monica PD, Jackie speaking, how can I help?'

'Please.' Ruby swallows a sob. 'I need to speak to Detective Blanke. Please.'

'May I ask who's calling?'

'Can you put me through, miss? Please. It's really important.'

'I'm sorry,' the woman says. 'But the detective is not here.'

Chapter Thirty-Nine

Joyce

Jimmy's car roars away, bearing him out of my life again, and this time, it is forever. I try to hoist myself up, but the room is spinning. My head pulses, and there is blood on the tiles. From my heart. My heart is bleeding out. He has left me. Like he always does.

I need to speak to someone. Deena. She will understand. I dial with shaky fingers. Bless her, she picks up.

'Deena,' I say. 'I wanted to run away with him.'

Deena's voice is tense. 'Joyce? Is Jimmy with you? Do you need help?'

A silver car approaches. For a moment I think it is him. But then Nancy emerges, back from her job.

'It's fine,' I murmur into the receiver. 'Nancy is here. Nancy will take care of me.'

'Joyce, wait—'

I hang up. Nancy sees me and her jaw drops. She comes running toward me as fast as her heels will allow.

'Joyce, darling, what happened?' She holds my shoulders and turns me around. 'My God, you are bleeding. Did you fall?'

'He hit me,' I croak. 'I want to go to Los Angeles. I want to see Amblioni. He did not want me. He left me alone, again.'

'Frank?'

'No, Jimmy.'

Her face twists. She drags me into the kitchen and presses some paper towel to my head. The phone rings, but we both ignore it.

'Who is Jimmy?'

'He . . . Jimmy McCarthy,' I explain. It sounds so silly, but the fog in my head does not allow me to be sensible. 'I love him. Don't tell my mother.'

Nancy nods. Her movements are oddly slowed. I don't feel pain in my head even though I can see blood all over the kitchen floor. The painting lies there, too. My baby boy. He squirmed and opened his eyes. He was so beautiful.

I tear myself away from Nancy's grasp and pick up the painting.

'What's that?' Nancy reaches out, but I pull away. 'Did you paint that?'

I want to tell her. The whole world needs to know. 'We had a baby,' I say. 'Me and Jimmy. Three years ago.'

Nancy gasps. 'You . . . Does Frank know?'

'He did not want to know. Nancy, neither of them wanted to know. Jimmy and Frank, shimmy and crank. I swam and I sank.'

She looks at me with eyes that are uncomprehending. 'You need to sit down,' she says. 'You are not well.'

'He died.' It wants out. The secret wants out. 'My boy. I had him in Philly on the kitchen floor. Frank did not come, and neither did Jimmy. I was so alone, Nancy. So terribly alone. He squirmed and opened his eyes. He was beautiful. Pearly and blue. I think I meant to wash him. It's all a blur. There was so much blood. I took him to the pool. I meant to wash him so he would be lovely. For them. But they did not come. Not Frank, not Jimmy. And when I woke up . . .'

I need a pill. I am getting worked up again. I'm sure my hair is a mess.

'What then?' Nancy looks at me earnestly. 'What happened?'

'He was floating in the pool. He wasn't squirming anymore.'

I look outside where the geraniums are letting their heads hang low. They need water. I need to go water them, but somehow something is wrong and I cannot quite remember what.

'I think I killed him,' I whisper. 'I am so sorry.'

Nancy says nothing. She looks at the pot for the longest time, and then at the painting, and then at me.

'You do not deserve all this,' she says.

She is right. I do not deserve to suffer so. And neither did my boy. I feel a hint of something in my chest. Anger. At them. All of them, who left us alone in our greatest need.

'You are right,' I say. 'I did not deserve any of it. That's why I want to go to Los Angeles. To see Amblioni.'

Nancy's eyes dart here and there. Suddenly, she plops me down on the floor. 'I will take you to the exhibition,' she says. 'But first, let's prepare a little bit.'

She runs into the bedroom and returns with something, clutching her purse tightly. She grabs my own purse, opens it and pulls out the pill jar. She pours out three Miltowns and shoves them into my mouth. I retch, and she hands me a glass of water. It's too many, I think, but I don't really care.

Barbara pokes her head in. 'Mommy,' she says. 'Where is the man? Mommy, everything is a mess.'

Barbara is right. The kitchen looks dastardly. I grab a cloth and begin dabbing at my own blood. Too late I realize that I am using the sleepsuit.

'Tell her to go outside,' Nancy mumbles. 'She doesn't need to see this.'

I shoo Barbara away. 'Go play in the trees, darling. I will send Joanie's mom, all right? Auntie Nancy and I, we'll be back soon.'

'But Mommy—'

'Be good. Promise me, darling. Don't tell anyone. Be a good girl.'

Barbara goes away.

'I'm bleeding,' I say to Nancy. 'Help me.'

'Don't worry, darling,' she coos. 'You think this is bad? You haven't met my husband. He wasn't like your Frank. Or like Jimmy. Zac would have truly shown you hell.' She giggles wildly. 'No one ever saw a thing. I was in agony. I lost two babies under his kicks. I will never have a child. And you threw yours away.'

She hoists me up. My legs are soft. I cannot quite remember why I sat down. But I do know one thing. I need to see art. Colors. Red and yellow and blue, like the pool.

'Let me swim,' I whisper. 'Where is Frank?'

'You stupid cow,' Nancy hisses. 'These pills are really kicking in, huh?'

Then she helps me up, grabs the painting and my art materials, and walks me to the car.

I slip inside. The span of the road. Freedom and laughter.

'Amblioni,' I murmur, but the syllables do not come out right.

I dream. In my dream I fly high over Sunnylakes. I am warm and light. I am the glint in a bird's eye and the sparkle on the ocean. I am poolside blue and ice cream pink. I am life. I am love.

I am so very tired.

We reach the beach, but it is not the beach, although there is a lot of sand. Nancy rips open the car door and pulls me out. She drags me up a concrete ramp and we stand in space. Beautiful, terrible space. The sky is endless up here, but it is not Los Angeles, and that's where I wanted to go.

'Do you even know we're fucking behind your back?' Nancy's voice is strangely low. One fist is plunged into her purse. 'Frank loves it with me. He can't get enough. I know how to please him like you never could. He told me you were always cold. Cold-hearted. Now I know why. Because you are a killer.'

I do not understand. 'Frank?' I say, and the name draws a blank.

'See? You don't even care about that. Your own husband fucking your best friend, and you don't give a damn. You do not deserve what you've got. But I do.'

Nancy withdraws her fist. She is holding something silver. *Silver-blue, me and you.* I am wobbling. I'd like to sit down. I'd like to drive through Los Angeles with the wind in my hair and with my bare feet on the pedals. Floor the gas and fly away.

'It is my turn now,' Nancy says.

'No,' I reply. 'It is mine. Finally.'

'You never made him happy.'

'I am happy.'

'They'll never find you under the rubble.'

'That's fine,' I reply, and laughter gurgles in my throat. 'Because I won't be there.'

I won't be there. I will be summer light on a pool, and the laughter of a baby boy. I will be cadmium yellow and sap green. I will be the water soaking into paper and the air stream on a freeway. I will be me, at last.

The pain in my womb explodes with a bang. I spin and tumble. The sky engulfs me and wraps me up. Blue, so blue. False and true.

Me and you.

Chapter Forty

Mick

Genevieve returns with the drinks. 'Now, Detective,' she says. 'Here's to Joyce.'

Mick lifts his glass – and the ring of the telephone cuts him short.

Genevieve puts her glass down with a clink. 'Just a moment.'

Goddammit. If this is some old gal from the women's committee chin-wagging about the milkman, he's going to find out where she lives and water her roses with gasoline.

Genevieve says things like 'u-huh' and 'of course' and 'right away'. She hangs up and comes back into the lounge. The look on her face makes Mick's stomach sink.

'It was your secretary, Jackie,' she says. 'Ruby called your office. She said it's an emergency and asked that you come to Nancy Ingram's house as soon as possible.'

'Mrs Ingram's house?'

'Yes. Jackie said there's been some sort of altercation between Ruby and Mr Haney. He's injured. A patrol car is on its way.'

Mick's brain switches into overdrive. A patrol car in Sunnylakes. Frank Haney hurt and Ruby at the scene. That's—

That's not going to end well.

'I have to go.' He grabs his coat and pushes past Genevieve into the hallway. 'Sorry.'

On the driveway, he breaks into a run. He digs for his car keys, drops them, curses and jams them into the lock. Heat slaps him in the face as he sits down, but he doesn't care. The Santa Monica Freeway will be clogged with rush-hour traffic. There's just the sliver of a chance he'll get there before the boys.

He turns the key. The car yawls and coughs. He smacks the steering wheel and turns the key again. Another yawl, followed by the soothing purr of the engine. He cranks the car into reverse, pins the pedal and hurls out of the driveway.

He almost makes it onto the street before a nasty splutter emerges from the hood. The Buick grinds to a halt in silence. Terrible, ominous silence, broken only by a faint ticking from somewhere in the car's bowels.

'Fucking piece of crap.'

He twists the key again, twice, thrice. Nothing.

'Mr Blanke, what's happening?'

In the rearview mirror, he sees Genevieve running toward him. She's put on a little hat and clutches a purse to her chest. He opens the door and gets out.

'The fucking car. That old bastard pile of fucking trash.'

He kicks the fender and misjudges the force. Pain shoots up his legs. 'Dammit!'

'We'll take mine.' Genevieve grabs his arm and pulls him away. 'Come on, we've got no time to lose.'

At least he remembers to grab the radio from the glove box. They head to the Pontiac. Genevieve pumps the pedal before he's even closed the passenger door. They fly down the driveway and onto the road.

'What do you think has happened?' Genevieve asks.

'No idea.' He mops his brow. 'What worries me more is what's going to happen if the boys arrive before us.'

'Oh. Oh, yes, I see.'

Genevieve drives like a racer, fast and sleek and confident. The car flies past the shops and the library, past a thousand lawns and rock-fronted houses until, with a swerve that knocks his head, they turn into Roseview Drive.

All the muscles in Mick's body tense up when he sees the patrol car parked in front of Nancy Ingram's pink house. It stands out like a commie in a kindergarten. Genevieve clunks the Pontiac over the sidewalk. Mick jumps out and starts running.

The door to Mrs Ingram's house has been kicked open; the frame is splintered where the lock gave way. He dashes into the lounge and hollers, 'Ruby!'

The response is loud and clear. A man's voice, coming from upstairs. 'You're under arrest.'

He takes the stairs two at a time. They're in the bedroom. Ruby is lying on her stomach on the floor.

Hodge is twisting her arms over her head, while another officer kneels on her back, holding her legs. Her face, pressed into the carpet, is purple and puffy with tears.

'Stop,' Mick yells. 'Let her go.'

He tries to pull at the unnamed officer. But the man knocks him away. Mick reaches for his gun, which is lying safe and sound in the Buick. *Bloody shits.*

'She's a burglar,' Hodge pants. 'We got to subdue her, sir.'

'Jesus Christ. Don't you think you've done the job?'

Finally, he manages to wrestle them off Ruby's body. She gasps. Her forehead is bleeding and there is blood on the bed frame. She whimpers and tries to push herself up. Hodge draws his gun.

'For fuck's sake, I'm a superior officer.' Mick pushes Hodge's arm away. 'You two stand down.'

It's only now that he spots Frank Haney under the window. He is tied up and inexpertly gagged. His expression could not be more elated if the holy trinity had manifested on this carpet.

'You – what's your name?'

'Cooper,' says the other officer.

'Cut that man loose, Cooper.'

He helps Ruby up. She pulls away from him. Her eyes are wild. Blood is trickling down her forehead and along the sweep of her nose.

'She took him.' She presses herself into the corner between the bed and the closet, as far away from Haney as she can get. She gestures at him. 'He tried to kill me. I-I gotta get out.'

'Just tell me what happened first. Ruby . . . Miss Wright, please.'

One of the officers takes the gag off Haney, who gasps for breath. 'Arrest her,' he snarls. 'She's lying.'

Ruby starts breathing rapidly. Her eyes are bloodshot and her throat is marked with purple splotches.

Mick grabs Hodge's handcuffs, clicks them around Haney's wrists and uses his pocketknife to cut the bindings around his ankles. Then he takes the blouse Cooper just extracted from Haney's mouth and stuffs it right back where it belongs.

'Get that man into the patrol car. Now. And don't you dare unlock those cuffs.'

The officers help Haney to his feet and escort him out of the room. Mick backs away from Ruby and raises his hands.

'He's gone, OK? You all right?'

She shivers. 'She's gonna kill him. She's gonna make them shoot him.'

'Shoot who, Ruby?'

'Joseph.'

Her tears spill over. Mick recalls a tall, sullen-looking man in a South Central kitchen. A picture pieces itself together.

'You brought Joseph with you, because you were afraid. And rightly so, by the looks of it. Did he tie up Mr Haney?'

Ruby nods. 'Detective, we were wrong all the time. It wasn't Mr Haney. *She* did it. She took Joyce's dresses and her painting and her husband. She wanted everything Joyce had for herself.'

'Who, Ruby?'

'Mrs Ingram.'

The name thunders in Mick's head. For a moment he can think of nothing. And then the pieces fall into place with silent finality.

'She did it,' Ruby pants. 'It all fits. I thought she stayed late at work that Monday, but she told Mr Haney she took a day off. She stole his gun and then told him he'd forgotten about giving it to her. She went and shot Deena and placed all the blame on Jimmy. And now she has Joseph.'

Mick gasps for air. He always knew there'd be a reckoning and here it is. He should have checked and double-checked, followed procedure, brainstormed with Murphy. Hell, he should even have listened to Fran. But once again, like the coward that he is, he stepped back from it all.

He leans against the wall. 'Nancy Ingram told me she'd seen Jimmy's car,' he breathes. 'She gave me his name. She mentioned he'd slept with Deena and . . .'

The world swirls. From far off comes Ruby's voice. 'She's lied to us. I know she did, but we ain't got time.' She yanks him toward the door. 'You gotta find them. *We* gotta find them and get Joseph and send that bitch to hell for what she's done.'

He stares at her. 'I . . . I let everyone down,' he says quietly. 'I was wrong.'

She cannot possibly know that he means Moggs and Joyce and Fran and Deena, all those whose lives he wrecked, or nearly did, because of his goddamned need to prove himself. She cannot know that this is the reckoning that has awaited him, ever since the moment he watched Billy go down and did nothing. The moment he was cursed to spend his life convincing himself of his bravery, his worth, from the outside in.

Ruby doesn't know any of this. But when she looks at him, her eyes are dark with determination. 'Now's your chance to make it right.'

Outside, Mick darts past a bewildered-looking Genevieve and pulls the transmitter from the dashboard. The radio crackles into life. He squeezes the PTT. 'Need assistance. Find me the license plate of one Nancy Ingram, 45 Roseview Drive, Sunnylakes. We have a kidnapping. Looking for a—'

Another message cuts in. 'Patrol 197 on Santa Monica, southbound. Got sight of the suspect, silver Ford passing Crankton, heading toward LA.'

'I need to trace the license plate of a Mrs Ingram,' Mick shouts. 'This is urgent. Mrs Nancy Ingram, 45 Roseview . . .'

Only then does he connect the dots. She's turned the tables. *Mick, you stupid, stupid bastard!*

'Sighted and confirmed,' the voice on the radio says. 'Victim is a Caucasian female, blonde hair. Suspect on passenger seat is a male Negro. Caution, he's armed and dangerous.'

'No,' Mick shouts.

The radio crackles again and Murphy's voice bellows through the ether. 'Blanke, get the hell off the frequency. We have a kidnapping on our hands.'

Mick grasps the radio until the plastic creaks and shouts: 'It's not the boy. It's her. Mrs Ingram. She's the kidnapper. She—'

'Shut the fuck up, Blanke.'

A voice interrupts. 'Patrol 197 here. Managed to block them. Car's turned off Santa Monica toward the Harbor Bridge construction site. Following with blue light. All nearby squads assemble. Ready your guns.'

'For God's sake,' Mick shouts. 'Don't shoot that boy. Don't do anything. I'm coming.'

He slams down the transmitter. Ruby and Genevieve stare at him. Hodge is lighting a cigarette, his hand curled around a flame that just won't spring into life. Frank Haney sits in the patrol car, eyes shut tight.

Mick pulls off his tie. 'We've got to move,' he shouts. 'Hodge, Cooper, you follow me. Ruby, Genevieve, get in the car.'

Genevieve asks neither why nor where to. She helps Ruby onto the passenger seat and then hands Mick the keys. 'Drive,' she says, and slips into the back seat.

And drive he does. The Pontiac is a heavy beast, but once it's at speed it reacts to every gentle touch. He steps on the gas and is careening past the bus stop before Hodge has even revved the engine. They race down President Avenue and toward the freeway.

The radio comes alive once more. 'Patrol 197. Ford has stopped by the bridge. Suspect and female still inside. She has a gun to her head. Permission to use force?'

Ruby makes a sound as if she's swallowed a canary. Before Mick can stop her, she grabs the transmitter and yells, 'You gonna do nothing to my baby or I'll come over there and beat your sorry asses till they ring like church bells.'

There is a second of silence. Then Murphy screams: 'Who the hell was that?'

Mick grabs the transmitter. The Pontiac swerves but settles again smoothly. 'Ruby Wright,' he bellows. 'And you better do as she says.'

They hurl down the Santa Monica Freeway, trailed by honking and the sound of screeching brakes. The radio emits only static and the distant sound of voices. The cops in Patrol 197 have left the car. Any minute now a shot is going to fall.

'I'm sorry,' Mick says to Ruby. 'About McCarthy. I'm sorry I didn't believe you.'

'I thought it was Frank.' She sighs. 'She's set everyone up, you know? Even him.'

The bridge comes into view. The construction site is marked with orange flags. Several tire tracks are carved into the sand. They disappear behind the desert dunes.

Mick pulls across, cuts off a semi, whose driver honks and swears. In the back seat, Genevieve flips him the finger.

The Pontiac coughs as the road turns from asphalt to rubble. Sand and dust fly up around them. They crest a hill and—

'There.'

Ruby points to the right. Against the dusty foliage of trees, a blue police siren flashes its lonely call.

They swoop down toward the bridge and the Pontiac screeches to a halt right next to Patrol 197. Two officers have taken cover behind the car doors. One of them is Souza. Both are pointing their guns.

Nancy Ingram's car is parked at the bottom of the half-finished bridge, which reaches out into the sky like a skeletal arm. Inside the shadowy car, Joseph has his head lowered. It's hard to make out what he's doing. Mrs Ingram's hair shines like gold threads in the afternoon sun. The light catches the glint of a gun, which is pointed at her head.

A dust devil dances across the empty space between the bridge and the police cars. It twirls in a frenzy, then dissipates among a pile of shovels.

Next to Mick, Ruby lets out a single sob.

Chapter Forty-One

Ruby

Ruby's heartbeats come in slow explosions. Blood rushes through her capillaries, swirls around her body. But her mind is frozen. She can't do nothing but stare at the sight beyond the windscreen.

By the bridge, Joseph sits slumped over inside a car filled with shadows. The sun glares off the silver roof, obscuring any detail within. But the gun stands out. It is pointed at Mrs Ingram's head.

The world speeds up. Her hands, which have been slippery and unreliable, grow steady. She unlocks the car door and, before the detective can stop her, steps out and stands up straight.

The cops shout something. One of them trains his gun on her. In the car by the bridge, Mrs Ingram leans forward. A flinch crosses her face. Anger and surprise. Then she play-acts again. Her lips are trembling and her eyes are wide with terror.

Ruby stares at Mrs Ingram as if she could pull the truth

from her by sheer force of will. 'Let him go,' she shouts. The breeze carries her voice. 'Let him go or I'll tear you apart.'

One of the cops cocks his gun. Detective Blanke hisses something and the gun goes down.

'Help,' Mrs Ingram screams. 'Shoot him, officers. He's going to kill me.'

'Detective,' hisses one of the cops. 'I've got a clear line on the fellow.'

Ruby takes one step away from the Pontiac and rolls her shoulders back. 'You're holding the gun against your own head,' she says. 'You're only pretending. I can see it from here.'

The roar of a car echoes across the construction site. Ruby does not turn to look. She keeps Joseph in her sight, and she will do so forever. As long as she's got him in her gaze, he'll be safe from harm. *Lord Almighty. Hold Your hand over me and my man.*

The car comes to a stop and doors slam shut.

'Chief,' says the detective. 'You—'

'What the fuck? Blanke, what sort of set-up is this?' Whoever is yelling is a white man. She can tell by the bluster in his voice and the immediate assumption of authority. 'Is that Ruby Wright? What's she doing here? Is she his accomplice?'

'They're sweethearts.'

'Arrest her. Blanke, for fuck's sake.'

There is a bit of hurried conversation.

'Help,' Mrs Ingram shouts again. 'Help me, please.'

Ruby inhales. 'The cops have Mr Haney,' she calls across the space. 'I know what you did to Joyce. That bridge is gonna span all the way to Mexico before you see him again.'

Another car approaches. The patrol car from Mrs Ingram's house. Just in time. Perhaps. *Lord, please protect us. Lord, please have mercy.*

'You shoulda killed me earlier, Mrs Ingram,' Ruby shouts. 'But you didn't want to, huh? Not in front of Frank. Because then he would've known you're a murderer. And maybe, a few years down the line, when you settled down and Barbie's all yours and Lily ain't even remembering her mother no more, then he would've started to wonder about it all. Wonder why you didn't untie him up in that room. And where you were, on that afternoon, when Joyce lay bleeding in her kitchen.'

Everyone is listening to her. She can sense their eyes on her skin like physical touch.

'Look,' she continues. 'I'm the one who knows everything. So, you could shoot Joseph but you really gotta shoot me. Otherwise the game is up.'

The detective winces. Behind Ruby, there are scuffles as if someone is being dragged from a car against his will. Mrs Ingram's eyes widen and her mouth opens into a little heart-shaped O.

'Frank,' she calls out. 'My God.'

The detective steps forward, grim determination written

on his face. He raises both hands. 'Nancy, come on. It's over. Let that boy go.'

Mrs Ingram laughs. It's a high-pitched laugh, just short of a shriek.

The detective walks over to Frank Haney, who is wedged in between the cops like a convict sandwich. He smiles – and pulls out the left cop's gun. He has it against Mr Haney's head before anyone can say a word.

'Nancy,' says the detective. 'It seems we have a standoff. Let's swap and we'll let you go.'

Mrs Ingram's eyes narrow. Her face flips to calculating hatred. Slowly, the gun in the car turns against Joseph's head. He closes his eyes. His chest is palpitating like a rabbit's heart. The floor slithers under Ruby's feet.

'Oh, look,' says one of the cops. 'It was the lady holding the gun all along.'

The detective walks toward Mrs Ingram's car, his gun stuck firmly to Mr Haney's head. Ruby licks her lips; they are dry and salty. Mrs Ingram opens the door and unwinds her long legs, clad in turquoise pants and crowned with red heels. One of the cops whistles through his teeth.

Mrs Ingram nudges Joseph with the gun and he tumbles out of the car and into the dust. The detective shoves Frank Haney forward and grabs Joseph by the arm. He tries to pull him up, but he's not fast enough. Mrs Ingram kicks Joseph in the ribs and he tumbles against the detective, who stumbles.

Quick as a snake, Mrs Ingram trains the gun on him. 'Oops,' she hisses. 'It seems I am very distressed.'

The detective scoffs. 'You and me both, Nancy.' He could retreat, but he does not budge an inch.

Mrs Ingram turns to the car, the gun still pointed at the detective. She ushers Mr Haney into the passenger seat. 'Nancy,' he mutters. 'Come off it, now. This is crazy.'

Mrs Ingram looks straight at Ruby. Her red lips twist into a grin. Her teeth part. *Vampire woman.* There is so much darkness in that smile. She is the black hole at the center of the galaxy. The nothingness between the stars.

And Momma's voice sings in Ruby's head. *You hold your head up high, girl. Ain't no one gonna give you no bad eye.*

Ruby steps forward and walks right up to the car. 'You killed Joyce,' she says quietly, 'because you wanted her husband and her kids and her life.'

'Nancy,' Mr Haney says. 'Nancy, what—?'

'Oh, Frank, stop fretting.' Mrs Ingram's voice turns soft. 'Joyce wasn't worth it. You know what she did, your precious little wife? She killed that baby. Your perfect little boy. Perhaps you believed he just died, but she drowned him like a puppy. She deserved to—'

Out of the corner of her eye, Ruby sees Joseph inching toward her. He's almost by the car's fender. She raises a hand to stop him, but at the same time, Frank Haney also lifts his hands. His eyes are dead. His fingers clasp around Mrs Ingram's arm, the one that is holding the gun.

'You are lying,' he says.

'Darling.' Mrs Ingram's hands start shaking. 'It had to be done. She . . . I didn't lay a hand on her. Jimmy did it. He came over that afternoon. She wanted to go off with him and started a row. He punched her up right good.'

Mr Haney wheezes. 'I'll kill him.'

'I found her in the house,' Mrs Ingram continues, 'hysterical and bleeding. She asked me to help her run away. Said she wasn't the kind of wife you deserved. Well, she was right, there.' She flutters her eyelids. 'I am the wife you deserve. Frank, darling. Am I not everything you desire?'

Mr Haney's voice is dry as the dust. 'Nancy, what did you do?'

'"Be free, Joyce", I said. "Go away. Indulge in your silly little daydreams. Run off to Paris and be a famous artist. Move into a studio and sleep with useless men. Get a political opinion. Do everything Genevieve told you to do."'

'Did you hurt her?' Ruby asks.

Mrs Ingram's voice grows whiny like a child's. 'Frank, you understand why I had to do it, don't you? She would have come back to you, rueful like a dog, and you would have taken her in. Because she was that kind of woman. No matter how much she messed up, every man just wanted to make her life wonderful.'

Frank Haney says nothing. His eyes are two pinpricks in a sea of darkness. He has found the black hole, and it is sucking him in.

'No one ever wanted to make my life wonderful,' Mrs Ingram whispers.

'So,' Ruby says, and the truth weighs every word, 'you had to make sure she never came back.'

'I—' Mrs Ingram says, but she does not get any further. Mr Haney jumps up from his seat. He throws himself at her with all his weight. His eyes remain dead but his hands, still shackled tightly, close around her neck. He pushes her to the ground and strangles her with the same terrible hands that squeezed at Ruby's life until it was only a sliver.

'Where is she?' he snarls. 'Where is my wife?'

Mrs Ingram's eyes roll back. She drops the gun and makes a sound like paper tearing. A woman's scream flies across the dust – it's Mrs Crane, but in Ruby's head it's Joyce, screaming for her life. The life she missed out on, that is gone now forever, until the universe turns to dust.

Oh, hell, no.

Ruby hurls herself against Mr Haney and tears at his clothes. She scratches and claws and kicks, until the cops come and pull him off Mrs Ingram. The detective grabs Ruby's arm. She smells his aftershave and sees the stubble on his chin with perfect clarity before he lets her go.

'That's enough. Nancy Ingram, I am placing you under arrest for—'

Mrs Ingram sputters and gets on her unsteady feet. She looks up at Frank Haney, her eyes speckled with red, and clasps her hands against her chest.

'She's here, Frank. Right here. She asked me to give her

a ride. She thought we would go to LA to see the exhibition, but I decided she had reached the . . . the end of the road.'

'The bridge,' Ruby says.

Mrs Ingram laughs her shrill laughter. 'I shot her with your own gun, Frank. I stole it from your room. It was easy as pie. She fell into the pit. I didn't even have to cover her up much. The sand trucks were already on their way.'

'What about Deena?' the detective asks.

'That pissed-up little whore. After Jimmy left, Deena called and Joyce told her I was coming over. Well, Deena put two and two together. She wanted money. Stupid cow. I put it in her head that we'd do something better. We'd be best friends. We'd work together on getting a suspect apprehended, and we'd share the reward. She did a good job leaving that bottle.' She grins, but the smile has a crack in it. 'She also stole the rest of the paintings. But I already had what I needed. She was stupid. And a hussy. Just like Joyce.'

A shudder runs through Frank Haney's body. The cops try to keep him upright but he is too heavy. He sinks down onto his knees, heaving. *Mourning*. Ruby's heart clamps up. Despite what he did to her, what he is, he is mourning his wife. And, perhaps, the baby too.

'Frank?' Mrs Ingram leans forward. 'Frank, darling. What's wrong?'

'Get away from me,' says Mr Haney.

'But, honey. This is all just a misunderstanding. We will

tell them that Joyce was a mental case. We'll tell them about her addiction. The judge will understand. It will only be a few years. Lily will wait for me. You will tell her to think of her mommy, won't you? I'll be with you soon. The children—'

'I wish the children never laid eyes on you.'

'Frank, what are you saying?' Mrs Ingram's chin trembles. 'I love them. I love you.' She stretches a hand toward him, red fingernails flashing.

'Get away from me!' Mr Haney scrambles in the dust, backwards, as if she is a demon come to eat his soul. 'Go away. I never want to see you again.'

'You can't mean it.' Under her makeup, Mrs Ingram goes whiter than she already is. 'Frank?'

He shakes his head.

'Frank. Frank, please. Darling?'

'Never. Go away.'

'Show's over,' says the detective. 'Ma'am, I am placing you under arrest for—'

Inside Mrs Ingram's eyes, something collapses. Her cheeks twitch. A little tremor shakes the corners of her mouth.

'No . . .' is all she says before she starts running. She is halfway up the bridge before the cops even break into a jog. A huge expanse of blue frames her slender body as she races toward the abyss, her hair trailing in a halo of gold.

Chapter Forty-Two

Ruby

Mrs Crane screams and the detective shouts something that is lost in the wind. His voice shakes something loose and Ruby starts to run.

So does Joseph. He is fast, faster than the detective and the cops. And Mrs Ingram is slow in her heels. Joseph overtakes Ruby, swoops onto the bridge and reaches out for Mrs Ingram just as she tenses for the final leap. They tumble down onto the concrete in a pile of limbs and golden hair.

Ruby darts up the bridge and stops, hands on her thighs, laboring for precious, wonderful breath. Joseph has his arms around Mrs Ingram, who screams and wrangles, but cannot get out of his grip.

The detective arrives next, and then Mrs Crane, who has lost a shoe. The chief is the slowest, but he's the first to find his words.

'You idiots,' he shouts at no one and everyone. 'She almost got away. Almost.'

Mrs Ingram writhes on the floor still, wedged tight in Joseph's arms. 'Let me go,' she screams.

'You're a crazy bitch,' Joseph pants. 'But you ain't gonna die today.'

'Nancy.' Mrs Crane's voice is cut up with gasps. 'Nancy, how . . . how could you? After everything we talked about?'

'Shut up,' Mrs Ingram snarls. 'You think it's so easy. You think all a woman ought to want is freedom. But freedom is damned hard, Genevieve. It's . . . it's so damned hard.'

'Well, you're lucky there,' says the detective. 'You won't have to bother with it now for a long, long time.'

The chief clasps Mrs Ingram's wrist with handcuffs. Two cops arrive and one of them grabs her collar like she is a cartoon criminal. They walk her back to the car.

The detective helps Joseph to his feet. 'You should have let her jump,' he says. 'Would have saved me a trial.'

'Yeah, but she's gotta face the music.' Joseph smiles. 'Enough now with all the dying.'

Ruby takes his arm. He is so warm and steady. She leans into him and, slowly, reality adjusts. 'Too right,' she says. 'I kinda fancy just living for a bit.'

And then she thinks of Joyce, dead down there, under the sand and rubble. It chokes off her voice. Joseph notices it and hugs her tight.

The detective looks away, almost as if he is embarrassed. 'They'll come and get her today,' he says quietly. 'She won't have to . . . Perhaps you could come to the funeral.'

Ruby considers it, then shakes her head. Maybe it's

wrong, but she'd rather remember her alive. Joyful Joyce, whose smile was real, the most real thing in Sunnylakes, even if everything else about her was a lie. She will preserve her that way. Happy, underneath it all.

'I still don't understand,' says the detective. 'Why didn't Nancy simply tell Frank what his wife got up to and wait till he divorced Joyce?'

'Because he wouldn't have.' Genevieve Crane sighs. 'I don't think he ever loved Nancy as much as she believed he did. I just . . .' Her eyes grow teary. 'She is wrong. It's not that hard. Maybe she could have understood that there is more to life than men. I failed her. I couldn't show her what's possible.'

The detective puts a hand on her shoulder, briefly, then pulls away. 'Stop that. Who knows, she might have killed you, too.'

Mrs Crane smirks. It is clear she's not entirely convinced. 'Anyway . . .' She turns to Ruby and Joseph. 'Do you kids need a ride?'

Joseph sends Ruby a glance. 'It's South Central, ma'am,' Ruby replies. 'Trebeck Row. Not your kind of place, I think.'

'Oh, I don't mind at all.' Mrs Crane smiles. 'I'm sure it's not as bad as they always make it out to be.'

'And me?' says Mick. 'My car packed in this morning.'

'We can sort that out,' says Joseph. 'Look us up – Geddit Fixed. You give us a call and let us know the address. We'll be there tomorrow, with the tow truck.'

In the distance, Hodge and Cooper jostle Frank Haney into a police car. The two other cops lock Mrs Ingram in their car. Her eyes seek Frank Haney's, but he keeps his head down as he is driven away, hunkered in his own private hell.

The chief shrugs. 'That's that then,' he grunts. 'Anything else, Blanke?'

'Yes,' says the detective cheerfully. 'Chief Murphy, may I introduce you to Ruby Wright, a witness on this case. She figured all of this out. She alone uncovered Mrs Ingram's deception. I think she deserves the full reward.'

She does? A finger pokes into Ruby's heart. Because, the thing is, she didn't figure it out at all. Not until she found the painting and the dress. She—

'Miss Wright provided vital clues,' the detective continues with a smile. 'She told me about the affair between Mr Haney and Mrs Ingram. She also found the stolen painting. And she assisted me with information that will fully exonerate Jimmy McCarthy in the death of Deena Klintz.'

'But I didn't,' Ruby says. 'I mean, not straight away. I—'

One look from the detective shuts her up. And then Momma whispers in her ear: *You got a winning streak, girl, and you gonna pull the handbrake? Hell, no. You take what you earned. You done good.*

'All right,' says the chief. 'Miss Wright, please come to our station on Monday. We'll write you a check for a thousand dollars.'

'Yes, sir.'

The wind picks up again. The breeze tastes salty, and in the distance, the coast gives way to shimmering water. For a moment, nobody speaks. Ruby holds on to Joseph's arm for dear life. If she lets go for one moment, the sheer amount of happiness in the air will wash her away.

A thousand dollars. *I will go to college. It is really, truly happening.*

She can't wait to tell Pa. And Mrs Cannon. There'll even be money to spare. They'll take a family trip to the beach, all three of them. No, four, Joseph included.

'Good work, everyone.' The detective turns to Ruby. 'Especially you. You've got the stuff to be a proper . . .'

He halts. The truth dawns in his eyes and the barriers rise up. There is an awkward silence, filled with so many things that are not yet ripe to be said out loud.

But she says it anyway. 'A cop, you mean? Thanks, mister. Maybe someday.'

'A lady cop,' the detective says. 'If anything.'

The chief scoffs. 'A lady cop? Blanke, you've blown your—'

But Ruby cuts him off. 'Some day,' she says, and her voice does not wobble one bit. 'Someday soon.'

'Your word in God's ear,' says Mrs Crane.

They look out over the construction site and the hills beyond. Soon, there will be a road here, a road that connects up to other roads, leading to other cities and other states, and who knows where else?

Ruby wipes her eyes. Everything inside her is aglow.

And maybe it's that glow or the sunshine prickling on her skin, or even the possibility that the future may contain lady cops. But as the detective turns to go, she extends a hand toward him.

He looks at her, perplexed, then shakes it. His grasp is warm and self-assured. A busy man's hand, just like Pa's.

'Well done, Detective Blanke,' she says. 'Nice working with you.'

Acknowledgements

Now that it's time to say thank you to all those who helped bring *The Long, Long Afternoon* to life, I find myself facing the same problem as Mick Blanke. There are so many people with a stake in this story. Who carries the blame?

I'll start in the here and now. There's you, the reader. Thank you for choosing this book and making it to the end. I do so hope you've had as much fun reading as I had writing it.

Let's look at our line-up. Humongous thanks go to my wonderful agent Giles Milburn and the staff at the Madeleine Milburn Agency. If Giles hadn't pulled me out of the slush pile and put his endless faith and professional diligence into me and my book . . . well, you would not be reading this today.

Oodles of thanks and appreciation go to the team at Manilla Press, especially my editor Sophie Orme and her assistant Katie Lumsden, who took one look at this rough gem and handed me a polishing cloth and a bucketload of advice. Their vision and amazing insight have made *The Long, Long Afternoon* what it is today.

Sophie McDonnell, Felice McKeown and Matthew Laznicka poured their hearts into this book's design, look and feel. Francesca Russell and Karen Stretch made it their dedicated task to tell the world about *The Long, Long Afternoon*. They all deserve my most heartfelt thanks.

Extra special thank-yous go to Janina Lawrence, my sensitivity reader, Laura Lavington, my copyeditor, and Natalie Braine, my proofreader. Their wisdom and eagle eyes are much appreciated.

While these are the prime suspects, let's move on to other persons of interest. First of all, thanks to my partners in crime, the West London Writers, especially Caroline, Catherine, Pav, Steph and Zoltan. Their companionship was the fuel that powered this book to the end.

Thank you, Helma, for being my first fan and sharpest critic. Without your encouragement and diligent beta-reading, I would never have been brave enough to query this book.

Mum and Dad, thank you so much for reading to me and letting me read, and showering me with books all through my life. You've opened a world of wonders and imagination for me, and I still draw from its lessons. Thank you Anni, Mathies and Julian for the hikes and high jinks. A large part of this book was edited at 7 a.m. at your dining table.

Thank you also to that special person who said he believed in me and meant it when no one else even knew.

And the most generous and heartfelt thanks to Birgit, and the Arkaden Bookshop in Bargteheide. You provided all the books, all the confidence, all the love. 'School of life' does not even begin to capture it, hence the dedication.

Author's Note

When I was a teen in '90s Germany, our English teacher put a picture on the overhead projector that, he said, represented the American Dream. It was a family in a suburban home at Thanksgiving. Dad and two apple-cheeked children (the first-born a son, of course) smiled ecstatically as Mom served the steaming turkey. This, our teacher said, was perfection. The life we should all strive towards.

I raised my hand and said I found it creepy.

My teacher told me off for making an unsubstantiated argument. Years later, I wonder what it was that unsettled me so, and that fifteen-year-old me could not quite put into words. I think it was the way the woman's face was almost invisible, because she was looking down. She was not smiling. She alone was unable to share the moment. While her family was having a 'swell time', her own opinions, her identity and her personality were entirely obscured.

Diving into the prim and proper world of the 1950s

turned out to be an unsettling experience. While some things have changed – women can now work, enter politics and report abuse, all without needing the approval of man – other things have not. Women remain underpaid and under-represented, and their bodies are still subjected to violent assaults that all too often go unpunished.

When I started writing *The Long, Long Afternoon*, the #metoo movement was blooming around the world. Undertones of the rage I felt when reading the stories of countless women and their courageous battles have seeped into the book. So has my admiration for them, and my sense of indebtedness.

A word about Ruby. I am painfully aware that I, a white German-born Londoner, took a debatable step in writing her. But *not* writing her also seemed wrong. The Black Lives Matter movement and the daily stories of the abysmal, horrific violence faced by the Black community in the UK and US opened my eyes to Ruby's life. I am immensely grateful to have been given the chance to listen to her voice.

The Long, Long Afternoon is a book about feminism. Writing it, I was struck by the many battles faced by Joyce and Ruby that are still being fought today. It continues to unsettle me. But it also fills me with hope to see that we have made progress. And we have found allies, not least in the many, many men like Mick Blanke, who refuse to stand idly by.

The stories told in this book are deeply personal to the

characters, but they are happening against a backdrop of looming political and social change. I have often wondered when more change will come, so that I can play a role in it. Joyce, Ruby and Mick have taught me that there is no point in waiting. We can all start today. That, I hope, is the message of my book.

Hello!

Thank you for picking up *The Long, Long Afternoon*. I really hope you enjoyed the read.

This book is my debut novel, and therefore it holds a special place in my heart. It draws inspiration from so many different sources, but perhaps most importantly from my own nosiness. I love to hear stories about people's lives, struggles and triumphs – and I cannot resist a good secret.

Of all the characters, Ruby came to me first. I carried her in my brain and heart for months, ever aware that she had a story and it wanted out. But it wasn't until I came across a vintage Wards catalogue online, which praised the main benefit of mail-order shopping – *not* having to leave your house – that Joyce was born. The catalogue was illustrated with a woman peering through a curtain at the outside world. You could only see her nice housedress and slumped shoulders, but I immediately thought: there's Joyce!

Mick started out as a pastiche of pulp detective novels but became an homage. I'll let you in on a secret: trashy as these novels are, they contain some amazing pacing and writing and are a great training tool for budding crime writers.

And here's another secret, sometimes characters come out of nothing. Joseph holds a very special place in my heart because he was entirely unplanned – all I had on him when I started to write were four words at the bottom of Ruby's character sheet: she has a boyfriend. But when his turn came, he just jumped off the page and demanded to exist. So I let him be and the book is all the richer for it.

I could not have done this without the amazing support I've had from writers and readers like you, and would love to continue to share inspiration, excerpts and perhaps even a sneak preview of my next book. If you'd like to continue this journey with me or hear more about my books, you can visit **www.bit.ly/IngaVesper** where you can become part of the **Inga Vesper Readers' Club**. It only takes a few moments to sign up; there are no catches or costs.

Bonnier Books UK will keep your data private and confidential, and it will never be passed on to a third party. We won't spam you with loads of emails, just get in touch now and again with news about my books, and you can unsubscribe any time you want.

And if you would like to get involved in a wider conversation about my books, please do review *The Long, Long Afternoon* on Amazon, on GoodReads, on any other e-store, on your own blog and social media accounts, or talk about it with friends, family or reading groups! Sharing your thoughts helps other readers, and I always enjoy hearing about what people experience from my writing.

Thank you again for reading *The Long, Long Afternoon.*

All the best,
Inga Vesper

Reading Group Questions

1. How much of the mystery did you work out during the course of the novel?

2. What do you think of Sunnylakes as a place? How does the setting affect the story?

3. How does *The Long, Long Afternoon* explore racism and gender, and how do these things intersect within the novel?

4. What do you make of the friendship between Ruby and Joyce?

5. Who was your favourite character?

6. How do you think social pressures have affected Joyce Haney's life?

7. Mick is both of, and ahead of, his time. In what ways does he try to be better than those around him?

8. What makes Ruby and Mick a good team?

9. There is both a Women's Improvement Committee and a Black Man's Advancement Committee. In what ways does Ruby feel that, as a black woman, she falls through the cracks?

10. How do the characters in the novel rebel against the roles society has set them?

11. What did you make of Frank Haney? Do you think he really loved his wife?

12. What significance do art and painting play in the novel?

13. Mick, Joyce and Ruby all have family difficulties. Are any of their three families happy? Why, or why not?

14. What do you think the significance of the novel's title is?

15. Although *The Long, Long Afternoon* is a work of historical fiction, it shines a light on issues that are still relevant today. In what ways do you think the novel is commenting on today's society?

If you enjoyed *The Long, Long Afternoon*, don't miss Inga Vesper's second novel, ***This Wild, Wild Country . . .***

Coming spring 2022

Three women. A small, isolated town.
A decades old mystery.

1933. Cornelia Stover is not the kind of woman the menfolk of Boldville, New Mexico, expect her to be. A widow, she ought to be taking care of her house and her daughter. Instead, she's meddling with things that should not concern her.

1970. Joanna Riley, a former cop, packs up her car in the middle of the night and drives west, fleeing an abusive marriage and a life she can no longer bear. Eventually, her car runs out of gas and she finds herself in Boldville, a sleepy desert town in the foothills of the Gila Mountains.

Meanwhile, a young hippie, Glitter, is struggling to realise her plan for a commune. She thought a life of free love, away from the perils of consumerism, would bring her happiness. But things haven't quite turned out the way she had expected.

Soon, Joanna and Glitter will encounter a shocking modern-day crime and find themselves caught up in a decades-old mystery – the unexplained disappearance of Glitter's grandmother Cornelia . . .

A captivating, atmospheric new novel from the lauded author of *The Long, Long Afternoon, This Wild, Wild Country* simmers with secrets, lies and terrible betrayal, unravelling the lives of three women at the mercy of their times.